WAS ONCE A HERO

Book One of the Fenaday and Shasti Chronicles

EDWARD MCKEOWN

Ad Astra Books

Introduction

JANET MORRIS, AUTHOR AND EDITOR:

Edward McKeown intends to rock you and sock you with his new novel, "Was Once A Hero." Heroism and hardship begin on the very first page. Fast paced action abounds. Buckle your seatbelts for this epic of warships and aliens, love and death beyond the stars. As McKeown points out in this first novel of his ambitious Fenaday and Shasti Chronicles, "The peoples of the Confederacy are weary of the expense and disruption of war. They are demobilizing quickly, too quickly in a universe containing the Dua-Denlenn and the unknown. Your fleet and your people will not risk lives and treasure on the closed book of my race." Wrong decision. Wrong time. And there you have it: politics never intrude on this story, but they fuel it to a blazing conclusion.

Edward McKeown has a wonderful start on a series that plays to his strengths: young people of both sexes caught up in drama where individual heroism can make a difference. Buy it for the action, read it for McKeown's unique view of a far future that's all too likely.

-- Janet Morris May-2011

Janet Morris began writing in 1976 and has since published more than twenty novels. Her first novel, written as Janet E. Morris, was High Couch of Silistra, the first in a quartet of novels with a very strong female protagonist.

She has contributed short fiction to the shared universe fantasy series Thieves World, in which she created the Sacred Band of Stepsons, a mythical unit of ancient fighters modeled on the Sacred Band of Thebes.

She created, orchestrated, and edited the Bangsian fantasy series Heroes in Hell, writing stories for the series as well as co-writing the related novel, The Little Helliad, with Chris Morris.

Most of her fiction work has been in the fantasy and science fiction genres, although she has also written historical and other novels. Morris has written, contributed to, or edited several book-length works of non-fiction, as well as papers and articles on nonlethal weapons, developmental military technology, and other defense and national security topics.

Chapter One

Winter 2805 A.D.
Confed Forward Base Brendara

Robert Fenaday looked through rain-streaked windows at the field where the sleek shape of his wife's ship rested lay in its launch cradle and thought...*this can't be happening.* But it was. Ground crews were clearing the last connections holding *Blackbird* to Brendara base. The small scoutship was bound for war —a war that made no sense, against the Conchirri, a species out of a child's nightmare.

"Hey, spaceman," a voice called softly. He turned away from the concourse windows to see Lisa. She'd slipped up on him, her footsteps covered by the dull roar of the refugees and military filling the halls behind her. Her long auburn hair was tied back under a white naval cap that seemed too large for her delicate features.

Robert strode over and embraced her. Her face lay against his neck for a few seconds, and he felt a tremble run through her. Then she stepped back, all cool dignity again, for all that no one had paid them any mind.

"What's this?" she said. "Somebody might think you were afraid you wouldn't see me again."

"I love you, Lisa."

"I love you, too. Always will."

"Then let me use my influence——"

"No," she said, shaking her head. "I know you'd do anything to protect me, but not that. I'm *Blackbird's* captain and where she goes —I go. Darling, there are some things that can't be fixed with money, and even if they could, they shouldn't be."

"What good is my family's wealth if it can't protect you?" he said, twisting his hands. "I'd trade every credit if only it could."

Lisa's gray eyes were bright. "It's bought us more than most get. You've been able to meet me every time *Blackbird's* put in. Even if it meant diverting one of your family's freighters, something I shouldn't have let you do. Few others have had that luxury. The universe is on fire, darling, and I'm one of the firemen. My family has been Confed Navy since there's been one. I have to do this."

"This time I can't even follow you."

"No, not where I'm bound. You and your father have a shipping line to run. One that's vital to the Confederacy, and Robert, he's old now. So that's your post. Mine's with the fleet."

He looked at his wife and was filled with foreboding. "I wasn't much before we met, you know, a spoiled brat of a rich kid, partying like a fool."

She smiled through the tears in her eyes. "We've been good for each other, Robert. We will be again when this damn thing is over."

A claxon sounded overhead, and he jumped, fighting back a curse. A voice read out a string of numbers.

Lisa's smile faded into a grim line. "That's my ship's launch clearance."

Now that the moment was here, it seemed unreal. How could she be leaving? They stepped toward each other again and this time didn't care about military discipline or onlookers.

"Now," she said finally, "I want you to stay here. So that this will be my memory of you, until I see you again."

"When will that be?" he said, fighting down his anguish and trying to smile. *I can't make this harder on her.*

"I don't know, love, and I couldn't tell you if I did. But I think it will be a long time."

He kissed her again. "Return to me, Lisa. Return to *New Eire,* the house above the cliffs. It will all be waiting for you."

She touched his face. "I'm counting on it. Now, Robert, you have to let me go." She kissed him, then turned and walked quickly into the throng.

He watched her until her slender form in Navy dress whites could no longer be seen. "I'll never let you go, Lisa," he whispered. "Never. Not if all of time and space were arrayed against me. I swear it."

———

Eleven months later:

> To Robert Fenaday—*New Erie*
>
> *The Secretary of War wishes to express the Confederacy's sincerest condolences in the loss of the* C.S.S. Blackbird. *The vessel having been missing long past its life-support capacity, the crew must regretfully also be considered lost.*
>
> C.S.S. Blackbird *was operating alone in a classified operation far beyond the front and was last reported in the Fringe Star sector. We deeply regret...*

———

December 14, 2809
Enshar Star System

Telisan stretched his arm over his head, as he had every day since his release from the hospital ship. The injury had kept him from joining his fleet carrier on the final attack on the Conchirri homeworld.

"Gad, it makes me queasy just watching," said one of the human pilots draped over a chair in *Earhart's* ready room.

Telisan smiled, a gesture he'd learned from the humans. "I'm surprised you humans have only one joint in your arms, must have made it hard to swing from tree to tree."

"Hey Rico," another pilot called. "The commander knows your family." The humans began to shout good-natured abuse across the room.

Seeka, the only other Denlenn aboard, walked in. Like Telisan, he was tall and angular, with leathery skin, a lipless mouth, and golden eyes under a rough mane of thick hair.

"Greetings, young one," Telisan said in Denleni.

"Greetings, Mighty Warrior, Ace of Aces."

"Ah, knock it off," Telisan added, in Standard to his young friend's amusement.

"What word from the bridge?" Seeka asked.

Telisan shrugged. "We're still at defcon 4. There's been no signal, no sightings since we left jumpspace."

The young Denlenn's face looked grim. "Can it be? Can the freighter captain's wild story be true? Is Enshar destroyed?"

"I do not see how, with the Conchirri fighting in their home system," Telisan replied. "Pity the freighter didn't dare get closer to Enshar."

"Damn him," Seeka said. "He fled when he could not raise system control, even dumped his cargo."

"Perhaps it is best. Had he gone in, he too, might have been destroyed. As it is, we are here with a fleet."

"Fleet?" Seeka snorted. "A rust-bucket escort carrier and whatever else was handy in fleet resupply depot when the call came."

"Which included me," Telisan replied.

Seeka nodded. "That is the only reason we'd have a century ace like you on a CVE. Trust me; the Black Diamonds are glad to have you here."

"Now hear this," the speaker sounded over their heads, "all senior officers to the bridge."

"Now maybe we'll find out what's going on," Seeka said.

Telisan looked over at the rostrum where his XO, Lieutenant Bailey, stood. "Bailey, get the pilots down to the flight deck. I'm betting we sortie soon. We have time for once; I want everything double-checked."

"Aye, aye, Wing." He turned to the waiting room. "Black Diamonds, on your feet!"

Telisan nodded to Seeka and sped off, his long legs eating up *Earhart's* corridors until he arrived at the bridge. A Marine opened the hatchway for him, and he ducked to enter *Earhart's* bridge, with its multitude of holo screens and stations.

Officers filled *Earhart's* cramped bridge and stared at the multiple views of Enshar displayed on the ship's view-screens. Telisan, taller than most of the human crew, looked over their heads at the green and blue world they'd come to rescue.

"They're all dead," Captain Demidov said, passing a shaky hand through her gray-streaked hair.

"Gods," Telisan whispered, chills running through him. Billions of Enshari gone, along with thousands of other Confederate citizens, the scale of the catastrophe numbed the mind.

Demidov dropped into her chair, looking weary for the first time in Telisan's experience. She waved a hand at the expedition's chief scientist, a dark-skinned human male. "Fill them in, Doctor."

The scientist walked over to the screen. "Our probes show millions of corpses on the upper levels of their underground cities," he said, his voice grave. "We see trains wrecked and strewn off grav-rails. Thousands of ocean-going vessels are still afloat, but drifting or steaming to no purpose." He gestured at the one of the screens showing a metallic splatter in a field. "Destroyed aircraft litter the planet's surface. All movement we've detected is either robotic or animal in nature. All forms of intelligent life on Enshar are gone. We are assuming some sort of chemical or biological attack, though there is some evidence of direct-fire weapon being used."

Demidov nodded to the scientist who sat down at his station and stared at the deck.

"How can this be?" Telisan asked. "How could a Conchirri fleet strike here? Even at the height of their strength, an assault on Enshar's defenses would have been grueling. How could they manage it now, in the midst of defeat?"

"It makes no sense," Demidov said, staring at the screens as if she could will answers from them.

"Communications?" Demidov demanded. "Anything new?"

"No answer, sir," the officer replied. "I'm detecting some automated signals from Enshar...nothing else."

"Scan picked up clouds of metallic debris over Enshar," a tech added. "They're in the same orbit as Enshar's main space stations. The stations are gone."

"Any sign of debris from Conchirri vessels?" Demidov asked.

"None," he replied.

"Even if a Conchirri attack achieved total surprise," Telisan said, "Enshar's defense would have taken a heavy toll on any attacking force."

"Communications," Demidov ordered, "have the destroyer escort *Flamme*, move to the vanguard. She's handiest in atmosphere. Relay to the rest of the fleet that we are moving into orbit."

"Have you ever been to Enshar before, Commander?" Demidov asked, staring at the lights of the dead cities.

Telisan turned to look at the human. It still struck him as odd to be taking orders from a true female, even if of another species. His own people had three genders: male, demi female, and true female. A male or demi might command a warship, but never a true female. He'd served with her for only a few weeks, since leaving the hospital ship *Solace*, but Telisan respected her ability.

"No," the Denlenn replied. "It is too far from the Conchirri theatre of operations. Before the war, I attended university on Denla. I met an Enshari there, Professor Belwin Duna. He is my greatest friend, if he still lives."

"I never met one," Demidov said. "They withdrew from space travel as the war dragged on, hid out in the safety of their under-ground cities."

Telisan forbore to argue with her attitude. Humans measured everything in terms of the war effort.

Hours passed as more probes dropped into the atmosphere. They found no sign of radiation, chemical, or biological agents.

"We're not learning anything up here," Demidov finally announced. "I'm sending down a landing force. I want a complete chemical, biological ordinance protocol in effect. The assault group will go in three shuttles. Two will carry Marines and Air Space Assault troops; the third will carry a scientific and medical team. Commander Telisan, send half the fighters in with the shuttles; keep half with you as a combat aerospace patrol."

Telisan snapped a salute and left as launch alarms shrilled. Twenty seconds later, he reached *Earhart's* capacious hanger deck. His squadron had already manned their *Spacefires*. Telisan waved to Seeka, who grinned back and vaulted into his fighter. Armored doors dropped and the fighters spilled out. They hit their engines for a quick burn, moving the *Spacefires* through the formation to take station behind the winged shape of the destroyer escort *Flamme*.

"Black Diamond One to Casino," Telisan called, as his slender fingers raced over the controls. "We are taking position." He switched to the squadron frequency. "One to Six. Take sections Alpha and Beta. Stick close to the DE and the *Wolverines*. I'll fly high guard."

"Yes, mighty ace of aces."

Telisan smiled briefly at Seeka's informality. *One of these days I shall have to remind him to watch his manners with his elders.* He turned his attention to the world ahead. It filled his view—massive, dark, and enigmatic.

Three *Wolverine*-class attack shuttles launched from the *Earhart* and headed for the planet. They passed the lowest vessel, the destroyer escort *Flamme*, which had dropped to within one hundred thousand meters of the surface. Telisan and the rest of the fleet stacked between two hundred thousand and three hundred thousand meters.

"Fighter Computer," Telisan said, "display the landing force."

The *Wolverine* shuttles appeared on the fighter's small video screen. He watched as they cut through the upper atmosphere, heading for the city of Gigor, near the Confed naval base. The big, gray-green camouflaged ships landed far short of the base in a triangular formation.

Suddenly the picture on Telisan's screen changed. A cloud of dust sprang from nowhere, engulfing each shuttle. Then his screen derezzed and electronics on Telisan's *Spacefire* went mad with feedback and distortion. Sparks showered him as his electronics shorted. He cried out, snatching at his fire extinguisher. Telisan's helmet slammed against the canopy and he realized the fighter was tumbling. With one hand he fought his ship, using the other to trigger the extinguisher. With a fighter pilot's trained instinct, he climbed.

"All Black Diamonds form on me," Telisan called. Only a burst of static answered him. "Black Diamonds to me."

He dropped the extinguisher and switched frequencies. "Black Diamond One to Fleet, respond."

"This is the *Flamme*, enemy on board!" The voice cut out as Telisan heard a scream and a shot. His fighter's screen snapped back on, blurry and crackling. "Select DE *Flamme*," he ordered. The escort appeared on the screen. *Flamme* was tumbling end for end, plunging planetward.

"No!" Telisan cried as the ship exploded in the Northern Sea.

He frantically switched to the squadron channel. "Seeka, come in. Seeka!" He tapped the small fighter's AI screen. "Computer, progressively select all Black Diamond fighters." The scanner showed him what he feared. Only his section survived. All the others lay smashed into the world below, like the *Flamme*, or burned to cinders in uncontrolled reentry.

The captain's voice crackled in his headphones. "All ships, this is Demidov, general retreat. Climb, damn it—climb."

The surviving fleet units fought for control and altitude. No targets appeared for him to lock weapons onto. As he cleared five hundred thousand meters, his *Spacefire's* systems snapped back to normal. Telisan craned his head around to glare at Enshar, the deathworld that had reached out and claimed most of his squadron and the *Flamme*.

"We are not done," he swore to the looming world. "We are not done."

"All Black Diamonds," Telisan keyed his mike, "return to the carrier." The surviving four ships answered his call.

Chapter Two

Robert Fenaday sat alone in dark wood and leather of Luchow's Marsport bar, trying to get drunk. He wasn't much of a drinker, another of his father's several disappointments in him, but a man had to be somewhere. But tonight was the third anniversary of the day the young officer had come to his door bearing a flag and condolences that Lisa was missing, presumed dead along with her ship.

Here's to you, Dad, he thought. *Too bad you aren't here to share it with me.*

The bartender walked over to Fenaday's corner table. "You gonna nurse that all night, spaceman?" It was early, and the bar was far from full, but Fenaday had a prime table to himself.

Fenaday barely glanced up from the glass. "Put another one down," he muttered, rubbing his eyes.

"Sure," the bartender said, giving him a frankly curious look, as if he somehow sensed Fenaday was not the usual freighter officer.

Fenaday was used to the scrutiny. His uniform was not standard military, but the black leather jacket held a captain's bar. Like most things on his ship, the jacket was second hand, its name badge being newer than the jacket's old, worn leather.

I probably look as worn as the jacket tonight, he thought.

The bartender walked off, to return with another glass of amber liquid. "Drinking Olde Henley, huh?" he asked. "That stuff will kill you."

"I'm not that lucky," Fenaday said.

A couple of businessmen came in. The bartender, apparently smelling better tips, moved off, leaving Fenaday to his drink. He lifted the glass and held it at eye level, studying its shifting amber color in the low light of the bar, but didn't raise it to his lips. It wasn't alcohol he wanted; it was distance and numbness. Distance from the memories of a lost home and a lost love. Thoughts of Lisa crowded close and jagged tonight, and the traditional medicine of the Irish wasn't helping him. Maybe the ancient spirits of the island he knew only from books were having fun at his expense. The Sidhe loved tragedy and the struggle of mortals.

They must love me, he thought, *a lost man searching all of space for his wife. Show's over,* he thought to the spirits. His ship, the *Sidhe,* sat in dock, probably never to fly again. The end of the Conchirri War and the bounties it generated made it impossible to run a private warship. Backers in the syndicate that financed the privateer dropped off. *Sidhe* had made port on Mars with barely enough to pay off her crew.

Fenaday had spent the last few days looking for work in the bars and haunts of the huge spaceport, refusing to give up. Now he found himself alone in a Marsport bar, staring at the turgid liquor.

People began to fill in, office workers and maybe more prosperous spacers. Fenaday had posed as one of those more prosperous. The deception had failed. His last hope had just left. The shipping agent for a small firm plying part of the Fringe Star sector had expressed her regrets. With the war over and the Navy free to patrol again, her company no longer needed a privateer escort.

God, he thought, putting the glass back down, *there has to be some way. Pick yourself up, man. Find something. Think.*

Nothing came to him. A warship or exploring service would not take him on as a passenger. He was only thirty, but there were hundreds of younger, regular Navy captains looking for berths in the rapidly contracting Confederate Space Force. Merchants rarely traveled in the Fringe Stars, and then only to the settled worlds he'd already searched for any sign of Lisa or her ship, the *Blackbird*. *Sidhe* was the only instrument for his search. Now he and the ship lay useless on Mars.

Fenaday dropped his head on the table so no one could see his face. "You can't cry," he whispered. "You can't start; you're a tough pirate captain." Lost in his own private misery, it took him a while to notice the being who walked up to his table, to react to the sudden drop in the noise level of the bar. Only the rare and bizarre drew attention in a place as blasé as, Luchow's Marsport. The hush finally drew Fenaday's head up from the table. He met the alien's stare with a startled expression.

The being stood slightly over a meter tall, resembling a large otter, save for the face that suggested a human ancestor, Homo Habilus.

"You grieve, human," the alien said. Its voice was low for the small body and whistled in parts, but it spoke Confederate Standard clearly. "Enshari understand grief."

"With enough cause," Fenaday said, regarding the small being with wonder.

"Ah, then you know the story of my people."

Fenaday straightened in his seat, glad for the distraction. "I can't imagine that there's anyone who doesn't."

"You might be surprised by the shortness of memory for tragedy," the Enshari said. "Tell me of what you have heard." It seated itself unbidden at Fenaday's table in a fluid motion that heightened its resemblance to an otter. "Please."

"All right," Fenaday replied slowly, trying to guess the other's motives. "Three years ago, while we were scrubbing the last of the Conchirri out of the universe, they struck at Enshar. A freighter discovered the disaster—"

"Yes," the alien said, "disaster, the very word, complete and utter disaster." It seemed to fold into itself a little, as if in remembered pain.

The bartender appeared at the Enshari's elbow. It seemed that Fenaday's stock had risen. The alien pulled himself together and ordered a wheat beer. Fenaday waived another drink.

They waited for the bartender to return. In the background,

music started. Mercifully, it wasn't the crap teens listened to, but a blue jazz piece. The bartender returned with a large bottle of nut-brown beer and an Enshari-scaled mug. Fenaday poured for the Enshari, who nodded his thanks. They listened for a minute while the small being drank some of his beer. After a few sips, he looked up at Fenaday. "Yes, Captain, please continue."

"The Confederacy," Fenaday began, "sent a fleet, which was very nearly destroyed by some form of electronic attack. Anything and anyone who tried to land was annihilated. Not that it stopped returning Enshari ships from trying."

"Like moths to a flame," murmured the small alien.

"I guess so," Fenaday said. "The fleet dropped guard satellites and fled. The government banned travel there. The only contact is a warship dropping into the system to pick up the guard satellite's information. Even that is done from the system's edge. No vessel has entered Enshar's orbit in nearly three years."

The Enshar made a whistling sound in its own language. "Just so, Captain Fenaday. You know the tale of our grief well, far better than most. That grief brings me to you. I'm Belwin Duna, Scientist of the First Order of Enshar."

"You know my name, Mr. Duna. Which means this is not a chance meeting. What do you want with me?"

"I'm going to Enshar," Duna replied. "I want you to take me there."

"Whoa," replied Fenaday, raising a hand. "Let's back up here. You may remember there is a death penalty for taking an Enshari to your system, Mr. Duna."

"Of course," Duna replied, "I have obtained permission for such travel."

"Can't be—" Fenaday said.

"Please listen, human," interrupted the Enshari. The Enshari's alien face and eyes conveyed no cues Fenaday could interpret. Yet, the tension in the small body, the near desperation conveyed itself. It was almost a smell. "I alone, of the remaining eleven-thousand survivors of our species, have received authority from the Confederate Government for this final attempt to determine what destroyed us."

The past tense sent a shudder down Fenaday's back. "How did you manage that?"

"Very simple," the alien said. "My surviving people have our compound, where we are cared for and protected, but they announced to their wardens that unless I was permitted to make the attempt, we would begin mass suicides. After the first dozen, we gained permission for one Enshari and one attempt. I am the foremost scientist and scholar left to my people. I've studied every scrap of information that could conceivably be related to the disaster. I have every authorization; you may check that with your government."

"A dozen suicides with so few in the gene pool," Fenaday murmured.

"You do not understand grief as well as I thought," Duna said. "The grief of the Enshari is itself a waking nightmare."

"My grief is my own concern," Fenaday growled.

"But known," replied Duna. "You seek your mate, a naval officer, lost in the long and dangerous borders of Fringe Space where only warships go. Your ship sits in a launch cradle. A private warship is an almost impossible expense, even to one with your former wealth and contacts. Your quest ends soon."

Fenaday passed his drink from hand to hand. "Soon," he acknowledged softly. At the bar a couple of young women laughed brightly, as if pain and terror didn't exist in the universe.

"Perhaps not," Duna said, leaning backward, confusing body language to a human. Fenaday, suddenly intent, leaned forward.

"All Enshari property off-world is owned by the Exiles, as we call ourselves. In the material world, we are all wealthy, for the little consolation that gives. Take me to Enshar. The wealth we will bestow on you and your crew will allow you to fly forever. We will help you in your search for Lisa Fenaday in any way possible."

Fenaday's bark of disbelieving laughter startled the alien. It curled defensively. From the corner of his eye, Fenaday caught a sudden shift among several humans and a tall, elfin Denlenn, standing at the now-crowded bar. Their attention fixed on him. As he suspected, the Enshari had not come alone. Duna was a VIP.

13

Fenaday wondered if an Air Space Assault Team sniper had a bead on him.

"Apologies, gentlebeing," Fenaday said, sitting quite still. "That's not an expression of humor. You startled me. I sympathize with your quest, but it's even more hopeless than my own. Mine may lead to death, but yours does without a doubt. Nothing has survived the attempt to land on Enshar.

"Why talk to me anyway? Surely the Confederate Space Forces would do it. This is a fleet job. You need dreadnoughts, bio-ordinance specialists, and Air Space Assault Troops, not a privateer."

"The fleet that went did nothing, accomplished nothing and left," Duna answered.

"Leaving three shuttles, a destroyer escort and later a dozen Enshari vessels behind, lifeless," the human retorted. "All we could do is die alongside them."

"Perhaps not," Duna repeated. "The fleet and other landings occurred just after the disaster, when whatever happened was still in effect."

"You have reason to believe this has changed?" Fenaday asked.

"We do not know, but it's been well over two years since the last landing attempt. There is no way to tell. Animal life survived on our world as did test animals from other worlds when they were crash-landed on our world. Your government would not allow our volunteers or condemned prisoners to be used in such fashion."

"What makes you believe conditions are different?" Fenaday asked.

"Perhaps after almost three years...it sleeps," Duna said.

Fenaday stared with pity at the poor creature. He'd often feared his own grief would end in madness. It chilled him to see it in another's eyes.

"Bio-ordinance," he said, looking away, "doesn't sleep."

"Nor does it destroy space stations and ships," Duna replied.

"The Conchirri..." he began.

"Were never there," Duna stated. "We studied every record from the war, including theirs. The Conchirri Xenophobes did not do this. We do not believe it was bio-ordnance."

"Then who or what?"

"We don't know, but such ordnance would kill all life, not just sentients, ours and yours," Duna replied. "Like all other survivors, I was off-world, on sabbatical, when the disaster struck. I am old and past fathering offspring, though we live much longer than your species. I know Enshar, our people, our world, better than any creature alive. I'm best suited to chance a landing and find some defense against whatever murdered our world.

"The peoples of the Confederacy are weary of the expense and disruption of war. They are demobilizing quickly, too quickly in a universe containing the Dua-Denlenn and the unknown. Your fleet and your people will not risk lives and treasure on the closed book of my race. I cannot go unless I hire a vessel. You have a powerful warship and a reputation for escaping tight spots and, finally, you may be the only being I can find who is as desperate as I."

"And if you cannot find someone?" Fenaday asked.

The alien leaned back again. "The Confederacy has been kind, particularly your species and the Denlenn, as if they feel they have to make up for their half-brothers in their systems, the Dua-Denlenn. Even the Moroks have helped." Duna hesitated. "But you are aliens and you cannot understand, though you mean well. Without our homeworld, we will not survive. There is no separate word for our homeworld and the members of our race. Without Enshar, there will be no Enshari people.

"If we fail, I at least will leave my bones on Enshar," Belwin Duna whispered.

The eyes showed no emotion, but the human could see the fur ripple and twitch. *Enshari tears?* he wondered.

The Enshari produced a data disk from its jacket. "So, human, here is everything: the contract, payments, authorizations, and a file marked confidential that I would ask you to read before you reject my offer. You may reach me at the Hotel Paradise. Think hard on it, Captain. For if you and I do not hunt the same trail, then it may be that we will hunt no trail separately. Humans do not live long, as we measure it, but you may live long enough to see the last of my kind.

"Good night, Captain." The Enshari slid out of the chair and left without looking back. Four large humans quickly flanked him.

15

Fenaday looked up and right to face a Denlenn, the same one who had stood at the bar earlier.

The slender Denlenn looked down at Fenaday from his nearly two-meter height. In low light he could almost pass for human, save for eyes that resembled those of a terrestrial cat, yellow or bronze, set in a tan face with skin that looked like supple leather. Those eyes caught and reflected the light, seeming to glow. His rough hair falling to his shoulders gave him a leonine look. This Denlenn wore a Confed flight jacket over civilian clothes. Badges and decorations spoke of hard service during the war.

"Help us," he said in a voice rich in alien accents. "Help Belwin. He is a fine being and night closes in on his people."

Fenaday shrugged. "If I even thought there was a chance..."

"I will tell you a thing that no one else alive knows," the alien said. "The zone of death does not reach a hundred thousand meters any longer."

As the Denlenn turned to leave, Fenaday seized its fine-boned arm. The Denlenn spun back, offended.

Fenaday stared at him, hard-eyed. "More."

The Denlenn studied him, then casually broke Fenaday's hold in a move that told of extra joints a human did not possess. Pulling back a chair, the long-bodied alien folded himself into it.

"A hyperbolic orbit," he began, without preamble, "low, not aimed for a landing, but low, at the maximum speed of a *Dauntless* Scout. The zone does not go a hundred thousand meters high." He paused, took a deep breath. "I made an illegal side trip when my ship was diverted to the Enshar system to pick up the last satellite data. I concealed my real purpose, allowing others to think I was gone on a joyride. In the months following the fall of the Conchirri, discipline was lax. I sabotaged my recorder, then made a run at the planet.

"I have breathed my last as a freeman if you are faithless," the Denlenn said. "My service would court-martial me at the least."

"Why didn't Duna tell me this?" Fenaday asked.

"He does not know and must not," the Denlenn replied. "If word leaked out, there would be no stopping his people. What if I am wrong? It would be by my hand that a whole race might perish. No. I must be certain."

"Why? What's this to you?" Fenaday asked.

After another long silence, the alien replied, "Belwin was my teacher at the university on Denla. We became great friends.

"Then the war broke out. I served on the fleet carrier, *Empress Aran*. During the first assault on the Conchirri homeworld, a particle beam hit my fighter and I was wounded. On my release from the hospital ship *Solace*, I was assigned to an escort carrier, the *Earhart*. I flew with the first Enshar expedition. Half my squadron died there, many shipmates, the brother of my best friend.

"I rejoined the *Aran* for the final assault on the Conchirri homeworld. I have watched a species wiped out of existence in this war. For all that the Conchirri richly deserved their fate, it is a terrible thing to behold. I will fight to not see such a thing again."

Fenaday studied the alien. "Big difference between a hyperbolic orbit and a landing."

The Denlenn stood, rising on his arms. The extra joints made Fenaday queasy just watching. "The zone does not reach a hundred thousand meters," he repeated. "Read the chip, read the confidential file on it. I risked my life to obtain both." He began to walk away.

"Are you going?" asked Fenaday.

The alien half turned. "My name is Telisan," he replied and left.

Chapter Three

Fenaday paid the tab and hurried back to his room at the Spacer's Lodge near the outer edge of Marsport's dome, facing the industrial zone. He locked the door, turning on the battery of jamming devices he kept secreted in the room. Only then did he pull out an unlinked portable computer to scan the data disk.

Authorizations came first. They looked authentic. He'd have them checked by a lawyer if need be. Next came the contract. Fenaday gaped at the figure, one billion Confederation credits, exclusive trading rights to Enshar, citizenship, diplomatic immunity, protection from extradition for any past misdeeds, free docking, and port privileges. All possible assistance in the search for Lisa Fenaday, including support for Fringe Star expeditions.

"Pity all I have to do for it is die," he muttered.

A knock at his door interrupted his reading. Fenaday cut off the computer. He picked up a lock-blade knife, snapped it open, and tucked it in his back belt, wishing he'd been able to smuggle in something more lethal. He checked the outside monitor. A middle-aged human stood outside, bulky, once very strong, dark-skinned, balding, and utterly unremarkable. With a pang, Fenaday remembered his wife telling him what great spies undistinguished people made. Somehow he knew this was such a person. It fitted too well with the night's developments. He opened the door warily.

"Captain Fenaday?" asked the man in a deep, pleasant voice.

"You know that," Fenaday countered. "Are you Foreign Office, or my wife's old service?"

The man smiled suddenly, teeth bright in the dark face. "Yes. The branch doesn't matter. You can call me Mandela."

"That's not your real name," Fenaday said wearily.

"Nope," said the man, "one of my heroes. Can I come in?"

"I suppose it could be worse," Fenaday said. "On second thought, I suspect it is worse."

"Captain Robert Fenaday," Mandela repeated, entering the room and examining it casually, "of the Fenadays of New Eire. That's quite a name. Your people turned their first-landing privileges into land and, later, into interstellar shipping. The Shamrock Line's banner became quite famous as your family clawed its way to wealth and power. Not too interested in sharing that wealth and power though. Your great-grandfather opposed the original Articles of Confederation."

"Did you come here to give me a history lesson?" Fenaday snapped.

Mandela seated himself on the most comfortable chair, placing his briefcase on the table. "Shall I cut to the chase, or do you want to go through the motions first?"

"The chase, by all means," replied Fenaday, leaning against a table where he could watch the door and the one window.

"Good. I may even get home in time for the game. I know you met Belwin Duna, and I know why."

Fenaday raised an eyebrow. "And you don't want me to help him."

"On the contrary, Captain. We very much want you to help him. We can't insist on such a suicide mission. However, we can give you additional incentives to go and additional resources, the like of which you never imagined."

"Why?" Fenaday asked. "No bullshit, why?"

Mandela smiled. "No bullshit. Every planetary government in the Confederacy worries about Enshar. We don't know what happened. We don't know if it will happen again. There's a threat out there, Fenaday. It has to be understood and if possible, controlled."

"Send the Space Forces."

"And risk having all those nasty pictures from orbit repeated for the folks back home?" Mandela returned. "All over the *Daily Vid* and the *Times*? Reporters and Congressman howling about why 'Our Boys and Girls' are being sacrificed for foreign worlds after all we lost in the war? Nope, it's an election year, Fenaday, bad for the President."

"Do it covert," said Fenaday.

"Plug in your brain, Fenaday. Every surviving Enshari is waiting on Duna's report. If he isn't allowed to go, or dies before he gets there, we face mass suicides, or they send another Enshari. Same problems for the President with the newsies."

"So," Fenaday began, "a highly expendable privateer, who you guys don't like anyway…"

"Civilians ships running around with chain-guns and mass drivers are a loose end and a menace," Mandela said. "Some have become private operators."

"Not me," Fenaday said. "My wife was…is Confed."

"Yeah," Mandela replied after a few moments. "Sorry."

"Spare me."

"Here's the deal, Fenaday. For what it's worth, I don't like it. You may not be a private operator, but you skate damn close. There is the little matter of a Dua-Denlenn freighter and a surrendered crew murdered while under parole."

Shock spread through Fenaday. Mandela knew *Sidhe's* deepest secret.

"I don't know…" Fenaday began.

"Now you can spare me," Mandela fixed him with a glare as he settled further into the chair. "Your pet amazon, Shasti Rainhell, polished off the crew. You covered it up, even hired her as head of security. I'm sure she is quite effective. Not many people can boast an assassin for their crew. Olympians are mercifully rare off their mad homeworld. Still, that's accessory after the fact for you, beingslaughter, at best, for her. We are aware of your relationship with her."

"Past tense," said Fenaday tightly, wondering how in God's name Mandela had ferreted that out.

"On the disk Duna gave you," Mandela continued, "are plans Telisan stole for a new stealth electromagnetic emissions masking program. Doubtless he hoped it might help you sneak up on Enshar and whatever killed everyone. He needn't have bothered. We'll give your ship a far better EME holosystem. All factory assembled, even has a warranty.

"You'll have trouble getting a crew and keeping it once they figure out where you're going. We will give you additional people.

"Finally, we'll add to that cash offer. We'll throw in pardons for anything you and your command crew have done to this point. Which is more than you have any idea of, in regard to Rainhell. It's that big, Fenaday."

"So, I take them within shuttle range of Enshar and stand off —" Fenaday began.

Mandela laughed. "No, Fenaday. It's too easy for an accident to occur. A shuttle explosion, perhaps? You're not going to drop a decorated war hero and a Nobel Laureate on Enshar and watch the show. You'll scout Enshar before they land. You personally, so we know there won't be any accidents."

"You think I'd do that?" Fenaday demanded, his lips drawn thin.

"No one pays me to think or to guess," Mandela said, his smile fading. "My job is to know. For what it's worth, I don't think you would do it, but there are others on your ship who might. One of them is very pretty and very tall."

"I could fight you in court," Fenaday said. He walked to the window, looking out of it in feigned indifference, but careful not to let Mandela see the knife in his belt.

Mandela looked amused. "You got any friends left, Fenaday? Big friends with influence? You got money stashed away for real lawyers? You'll be fighting us in our courts. I don't even have to rig it to convict you on stock and securities fraud, committed when you sold off the Shamrock line. Then there's the less savory stuff: gun running to Morokat, smuggling, illegal intelligence gathering, sheltering deserters, taking that condemned Frokossi prince off-world. He was declared a traitor. Do you want to be extradited to a Frokossi court on a political engineering charge and try out that defense?

"Of course you might win," Mandela continued, "but you'll be broke and disgraced. As for Rainhell, whatever she is or isn't to you, she goes away. The charges against her just start with murdering prisoners under parole. Assuming she decides to surrender into custody, which I doubt."

"Christ," Fenaday muttered, as Mandela put a data chip on the table.

"There's a number on that chip. Call it and say the word 'Faust' if you're going to accept. Our specialists will find you. You'll still have to recruit your own crew, but we and Duna will advance you sufficient funds to make it possible."

"Faust," Mandela repeated as he stood, "and we make all your problems go away."

"Lisa," Fenaday said suddenly.

Mandela looked back from the door. "I won't mess with you. You got everything we had. Lisa Fenaday was one of ours, one of the best. We looked, and we still keep an ear out. Didn't you ever wonder why your bribes and wiretaps worked?"

Fenaday snapped around, startled.

Mandela opened the door.

"You forgot your case," Fenaday called.

"It's yours," Mandela said breezily. "Your jamming equipment isn't worth jack. Instructions are in the case." He closed the door behind him.

"Son of a bitch," Fenaday said. After a minute, he went to the single window and sat on the ledge. For a cheap room, the view was not bad. He could see part of the sandy Martian landscape, sere even in the weak sun. A hundred years of terraforming had raised pressure, temperature, and oxygen levels to where a small rebreather mask allowed humans to endure the outside for short periods. The Martian sky remained pink in the daytime, and the stars blazed brighter than in Earth's night sky. Mars was still colder than hell.

He could also see the landing apron of the western edge of the port. A small freighter lifted off, the type the Shamrock Line used in another lifetime. He sat there for three hours watching the rusty sand blow and the occasional movement of ships and personnel in the distance.

Fenaday's thoughts roamed over the years, the ones past and the ones seeming to lie empty before him. He was broke and alone. Family and friends had fallen away over the years—due to the war, the bitter breakup over the Shamrock Line, or the natural drift when one leaves the mainstream of life.

"How did I get here?" he asked the room. "How in the world did I get here?"

Her face came to him as if in answer, the details blurry, which frightened him. He'd first seen Lisa standing on the veranda, at one of his father's legendary business parties. Slender, with blue eyes and dark red hair, she wore a filmy white dress that floated around her in the summer breeze. Everyone else disappeared, until all that was left was her face, her voice, and her laugh. They created a minor scandal by disappearing from the party into the gardens.

"More idle playboy nonsense from my spoiled son," his father had growled when he learned of their relationship. He was wrong. Lisa differed from everyone else he had known. She held a commission in the Confederate Space Forces, Field Intelligence Section.

His father opposed the romance. Fenaday's hands unconsciously clenched as he remembered the fury his father's belittling of Lisa brought out in him, a rage that daunted even his domineering father, "The Fenaday."

"Well and enough," the elder Fenaday said, just before it came to blows. "I should know better than to cross a man where his woman is concerned."

Not many people stood up to the elder Fenaday, and his son had been late in starting. Robert came to suspect that his father was secretly pleased with the changes Lisa wrought in his son.

They married in the fall of their second year together. Lisa stayed in the military despite his wealth. He accepted it as the price of having her. Then humans and the six other member races of the loose Confederacy collided with the Conchirri, a nightmarish species of intelligent carnivores, implacably hostile to all other life. Scientists speculated the behavior was sociological or religious. The explanation was what sophisticated people, afraid to believe in true evil, fell back on.

When Lisa left for combat duty, Fenaday stayed to help his father keep the Shamrock Line afloat. Losses in ships and lives mounted. The elder Fenaday, in bad health from a lifetime of hard living, aged rapidly before his son's eyes. Decisions fell to Robert more and more often.

In the second year of the war, Fenaday saw a Confed aircar land and raced to the door, reaching it before the butler. A nervous young officer in dress-blacks stood there.

"Lt. Commander Elizabeth Fenaday," he said, voice cracking with strain, "is three months overdue and presumed lost on a classified mission. The *Blackbird* left a forward base just before a Conchirri cruiser attacked the outpost. The base and the reasons she left charted space are gone.

"The Secretary of War wishes to express…"

Fenaday stared at him. *This isn't real,* he said to himself. *I'll wake up any second now. I always do.*

The young officer left the letter and a neatly folded gold flag with the butler.

Fenaday's father died two weeks later. Robert buried him on the estate. A few friends came by and offered useless advice and hollow comforts. Most had gone, fled to the safer inner worlds. Fenaday had no brothers or sisters; his mother had died when he was three. A throng of lesser relations came to the estate seeking advantages under the cover of consolation. He sent them away.

His uncle Patrick had glared in contempt before leaving. "Aye, go sulk. Your old man would have got a gun and bagged a Xeno."

The words raced round and round in his mind till the early hours of the next morning when he stood on the veranda where they first met. "Lisa," he said finally, "I think I'll go get that gun now."

At sunrise, he put everything up for sale. The government and the Shamrock board tried to stop him, but now he was "The Fenaday" and forced the sale through. He learned of a captured starship languishing in a Confed yard, a Conchirri *Tokkoro* class Frigate-leader taken in a raid. Fenaday christened her *Sidhe*, after the ancient elvish spirits of Ireland. He ordered her painted in the cheapest color the dockyard had. In bitter irony, the color was blood red.

Letters of Marque and Reprisal followed and Robert Xavier Fenaday became a privateer. Fenaday, who had rarely gone without anything, learned about want as everything went for the ship. He signed whomever he could, paring the misfits, at least those that he could live without.

Sidhe launched into the war as a hired escort, priority cargo runner, anything that kept Fenaday near the Fringe Stars where Lisa disappeared. Two years passed in his search, but he found no sign of Lisa or her ship. Fenaday lost track of the spaceport bars in which he hunted wild rumors of lost ships. Handling a board room or trade negotiation hadn't taught him how to live in the world he now sentenced himself to.

Confed fleets beat the Conchirri out of the lost colonies, back into their space and finally to their homeworld, where the Conchirri fought until exterminated. His enemies were extinct, but Fenaday was no closer to learning Lisa's fate.

Fenaday shook himself out of remembrance to find that Sol had long since set. He finally turned on his private computer and spent an hour reading the data chips. Afterward, he walked to his dresser and fished out a tiny, precious possession. He opened the small silver box and gazed at the photo of his wife, studying her dark red hair and startling blue-gray eyes. He returned to the window and set it there.

"What should I do, Lisa?" he asked. "Mandela's offer seems like the only way to carry on. It also seems like certain death. Where, Lisa? Where do I go from here?" The picture gave back only silence now, where once it had spoken hope to him. Fenaday slowly closed it and stood turning to the desktop communicator.

He made two calls. The first was brief, to the number Mandela left him.

"Faust," he said. The videophone emitted a beep, and the words "video denied" flashed on the screen. Then the line went inactive.

He let out a long, shuddering breath. One way or another, life as he knew it had just ended.

He placed the second call to the suite of Belwin Duna at the Paradise. He wasn't surprised when Telisan's image flicked on the screen. Duna appeared on the screen a second later. "Yes, Captain," said Duna.

"If I can get a crew," said Fenaday, "we go. I'll call you in two days. We'll meet Friday at twenty hundred hours at the Excalibur near Dome Top. You're buying."

"God bless you, Captain Fenaday," Duna exclaimed. "You will not regret this."

"I know," Fenaday said. "Only the living have regrets."

"Now, now I can sleep," Duna said. "Enshar…Enshar." He wandered out of view of the monitor.

Fenaday found himself looking at Telisan.

"Hyperbolic, huh?" Fenaday said.

The Denlenn smiled, human-like. "As your people used to say in the war with the Xenos, 'Hoo-rah.'" The screen faded.

Fenaday put his head back and laughed for the first time in weeks.

Chapter Four

In the morning, everything seemed less amusing. Fenaday made his next call with a certain amount of dread. After he identified himself, Shasti Rainhell's image appeared on the screen. Mandela had called her his pet amazon, and she looked the part. Jade-green eyes looked back at him from a perfectly symmetrical face of imperious beauty. Her ivory skin contrasted with night-black hair. She wore a judo gi and had evidently been working out. Not that she'd broken a sweat in Mars' low gravity.

"Found other work?" he asked.

Shasti gave back her usual impassive gaze. Steady, impenetrable, betraying little. *Like a statue,* he thought, *the eyes reflect light, but not warmth or depth.* Shasti was all surfaces. In the two years he had known her, she'd revealed almost nothing of herself or her past.

"Haven't looked," she replied in a surprisingly musical voice. "Have you left the privateer business? Should I start?"

Fenaday sighed. "I am into a new business that is very much an endgame, one way or another. If it works, your and my problems, the ones about the ship and money, end. If it doesn't, the problems end anyway."

Shasti looked at him without speaking for some seconds. He

could almost feel the distance grow. "What have you gotten yourself into?"

"Meet me at the ship in an hour and I'll fill you in."

For a terrible second, he thought she might say no.

"Should I bring anyone?" she asked.

Fenaday thought for a second. He had high turnover among officers and crew for one reason or another. He didn't trust most of them. "Do you know where the Exec went?"

"To jail," she replied. "There was a manslaughter charge waiting for him here. Evidently Romola isn't his real name."

"How distressing," he replied. "Just come yourself then."

She nodded, giving him her most enigmatic look. The screen faded.

Fenaday leaned back with a sigh. Shasti was in. His odds of survival had just doubled. Unfortunately, twice zero was still zero.

———

An hour after his call, Shasti Rainhell's two-meter-plus shadow fell on the gantry leading to the silent *Sidhe*. The frigate lay in a takeoff cradle, secured by the Marsport Authority. Shasti gave them a wide berth, having already passed a security checkpoint and, as always, wary of police. A few dock workers labored on the cradle or the ship. One, she noted, appeared to be watching her sidelong. Men often did. It was not unusual for one to be surreptitious about it. Her size and obvious strength kept catcalls stilled, but she sensed other intentions and trusted her instincts.

Shasti paused on the catwalk leading to the ship. Leaning back against the slim metal rail she looked up, pretending to study the ship. Not that she needed to. The vessel had been her home since her escape from Dua-Denlenn cutthroats.

Sidhe sat with her four hundred and eighty meter, blood-red hull engulfed in the launch cradle's embrace. Wings, set far back on the hull, held two black *Wildcat* fighters. Far over her head hung the turrets for the chain guns. *Sidhe's* big punch, the mass acceleration driver, ran the length of the horizontal interior axis of the ship. Her crew of two-hundred fifty was largely dispersed through Mars by now.

The spot she'd stopped at allowed her to study her watcher from the corner of her eye. He was using some hand tools to work on the scaffolding, bolting and unbolting the same piece of decking. *Confed police*, she thought, *and that means big trouble. Maybe coming was a mistake. What the hell has Fenaday done now? And why do I keep staying to save his ass?*

When she had seen enough of the man's face to remember it, Shasti started back up the gantry. A personnel lift took her up to the main gangway. She used her ship's officer pass to enter the secured airlocks and boarded the turbovator. The door to the spade-shaped bridge opened.

———

F enaday looked up from his command chair as Shasti walked onto the bridge and cocked an eyebrow at him. He didn't rise or reach out a hand. Shasti hated to be touched. For a while, he'd thought her uninterested in men, until she proved otherwise one spectacular night.

"I've checked the ship out," he said. "I've got every anti-bugging and white noise device we have working," he said, "I think it's secure. No guarantees."

"In this or anything else in life," she replied. "I assume you didn't bring me here for a sparring rematch." She dropped into a bridge chair at her security station with an easy grace.

"No, no rematch," he replied. It took him ten minutes to lay out the details of the meetings with Duna.

"Enshar? Why would you even consider this voyage?" she asked, looking at him as if he'd gone mad.

"I had another visitor later, a man calling himself, Mandela. He's with Confed Intelligence. He knows about the day we met. Someone talked."

Shasti did not yell, scream, or curse the unfairness of the world. "Inevitable." She shrugged. "Three people can keep a secret if two of them are dead. I'm surprised it didn't come out earlier."

"There were too many eyes," he agreed, standing and stretching. "You never would tell me how you ended up a prisoner on a Dua-Denlenn pirate vessel. Shoddy treatment for the man who rescued you."

She cocked her head. "You had no idea I was aboard. You were after a bounty as always."

"And for my troubles, you nearly brained me, ran off my guards, and shot up my hold full of valuable prisoners. Next thing I know, my landing force is running, I'm looking at a pile of dead Dua-Denlenns and the barrel of my own pistol."

Shasti leaned back in her chair looking pleased with herself. "It showed you why you needed to hire me. As for the rest, my solution took care of the need for paroles."

"Yep," Fenaday agreed. "Less paperwork, clearly. I suppose you had your reasons."

Something flickered in her eyes, quickly suppressed. "I was working as a bodyguard," she finally said, "when the Dua-Denlenn struck my employer's compound. Someone hated her to have commissioned such an expensive raid. The cook drugged my food and they took me alive. My patron and her children died badly. I had to watch."

"My only regret about the Dua-Denlenn," she continued, "is that I didn't have time to kill them slowly. Torture is part of the Dua-Denlenn culture, almost an art form. I'd have made each one of them into a masterpiece. But with you there, I had to settle for just dead."

He looked at her sidewise. It was the most she'd ever said on the subject. "I don't disagree," he replied, "but it put us in the trap we're in." He drew a deep breath and came to a sudden decision. "Or at least, it's the trap I'm in. I'm too well known to run, and where would I go? I put most of my family into bankruptcy when I sold off the Shamrock. I have some money in a small emergency fund. It's not enough to lift ship, but it's enough for you to run."

Shasti stared at him. "You'd do that, for me? They'll jail you on that basis alone."

He shrugged. "There are worse things."

She stared at him, then shook her head. "No, I'll stick with you."

"Shasti, I'm going to die on Enshar. There's no chance. It's a fool's errand. They're sending my ship because they have to send something, and no one cares if we die."

To his surprise, she gave a small smile. It was the first he could recall. "If we don't survive," she said. "I'll never have a chance to meet this wife of yours. A woman who could so obsess a man might teach me a thing or two."

He laughed ruefully. "If that happens, I may end up with some explaining to do."

"Is that why you stopped?" she asked, catching him off guard. Her expression closed up again; the glimpse into the depths suddenly shuttered.

Now he was in uncharted space. "I don't know," he sighed. "I thought our affair meant I was giving up. After all the things I did to start my search, I can't do that. A lot of people were hurt when I sold the company. My cousin's father shot himself... Then there's all I've done since. Maybe some of the people I've dealt with had it coming, but that doesn't seem to square somehow. If I give up, then I did it all for nothing, and I'm not sure I can live with that.

"There's something else..." He hesitated, then plowed ahead. "I wasn't sure if you were with me because you felt you needed to be..."

She shook her head; her long, glossy, black hair shimmered.

A knot released in his chest. He hadn't realized it until then, but it was important to him that it had been more than business. Vanity, he supposed. "I'm not free to give more. I felt bad about that."

Shasti smiled again. It seemed the day would be full of such surprises.

"You're an anachronism, Robert, a throwback to the days of white knights. Even now, with Enshar staring us in the face, you're thinking of ways to keep looking for her. Why? Tell me why?"

He looked at her blankly for a second. "She's my wife."

"Wife," she said with surprising bitterness, "just a word. It tells me nothing, Robert. You've searched for years for a woman whose ship disappeared in unknown space. When the ship doesn't come back, the crew doesn't."

"Yes," he replied. "I know all the sayings. Your life is the ship's plus the air in your suit. I've heard them all."

"Yet, you continue," she said.

He looked at her intent face and gave a small sad smile. "Do you know what I was before I met Lisa?"

Shasti shook her head.

"Lonely," he said. "Living a life without purpose or passion. Never had to struggle for anything, everything was handed to me because of my family's wealth. I never knew if someone loved my wallet or me.

"Then I met Lisa. She wasn't impressed with the name Fenaday. I found I had to be more than a spoiled rich kid to keep her. She told me once that I was her world. That's a lot to live up to.

"When her ship disappeared, I wasn't prepared to just stand there and take it. I wasn't prepared to be reasonable.

"I may not be the toughest, or the brightest. God knows nothing I'd done before prepared me for this life. I'd be dead a couple of times if it wasn't for you and dumb luck. What I am though," he added with a grin, "is what the Irish are best at, stubborn and unreasonable."

She stared in frustrated incomprehension. "Words and words. They mean something to you, born-human. To me, created and engineered, they convey nothing. The meaning seeps out of them. All I have left are the sounds."

Fenaday looked at her tentatively. *Created? Engineered?* Her past was something she'd never discussed, a place barred and warded. Today, Shasti seemed so different, so much more approachable. "You've never told me about your life on Olympia. All I know is the same wild rumors—"

She stood abruptly.

Too far, he thought. *Damn.* He waited, dreading that she would storm out.

After a long, dark moment, Shasti sat back down, as if she'd forgotten the reason for rising. She dusted imaginary lint from her sleeve.

"Sorry," he ventured.

She nodded, not looking at him.

32

"For now," she said, before the silence could lengthen again, "since neither of us wants to spend the rest of our lives in a cell, we need to focus on how to do this and survive. You know they're watching the ship."

"Yes," he said, equally anxious to get back to neutral territory. "I've spotted several of them on the external monitors. As obvious as they are being, I suspect they want us to know they are there."

"We'll need a crew," she said. "We are not going to find a lot of people in our situation."

"How about you taking the executive slot?" he asked.

She shook her head. "I don't have the navigation math or the certifications, but I wouldn't want the last fool back even if he wasn't locked up."

"No, I don't want him back either," Fenaday mused. "I'm promised a number of people by this Mandela, specialists he said, and better than what we could find, but still..."

"We don't want them in charge," she warned. "God knows their real agenda."

"Agreed."

"We need an X.O. who isn't in their pocket," she continued.

"I met a hot pilot with Belwin Duna," Fenaday said, "Navy-trained and a Wing Commander. For some reason—and it is just a hunch—I feel he is trustworthy, at least where it doesn't cross Duna. His name is Telisan, a Denlenn."

She stiffened.

"Denlenn," he said, "not Dua-Denlenn."

"They look much alike," she growled, "but a hot pilot you say?"

He nodded.

"I can live with it," she said, standing. "I'll start rounding up a crew. The usual wages won't attract anybody."

"Tell everyone it is a high-risk mission," Fenaday said, "with an extremely good chance of not coming back. No details, don't mention Enshar. It will get out eventually, but I don't want to deal with the press if I can avoid it. Tell them it pays a hundred thousand credits for able-bodied spacemen and twenty-five thousand more for every grade over that. It goes to their dependents if we don't come back."

She blinked. "We have that kind of money?"

"Yeah, but on a very short leash. Otherwise we'd be lifting for the Fringe at maximum delta-v. We are not dealing with fools."

"Be nice," Shasti sighed, "if it was easy once. Just once."

"Where's the fun in that?" he asked

Shasti gave him a mock glare, shaking her head. "Standard humans," she muttered.

Chapter Five

S hasti and Fenaday spent the next thirty-six hours looking through the low places of Marsport for their crew, trolling through bar after bar and less savory dives and flophouses. *Sidhe* was crewed normally with two hundred-fifty spacers and her own Landing Expedition and Assault Force, nicknamed the LEAF. Fenaday wanted a full contingent of ground fighters on this trip. He'd need fewer regular crew, since they'd carry no cargo or trade goods. This was a military mission, and Fenaday planned to take as few to death with him as he could. As for Mandela's people, they were not his responsibility.

Fenaday finally located Carlos Perez, *Sidhe's* chief engineer. Ironically, he found him in Luchow's, where Fenaday had carried his own sorrows the day before. His wife had already thrown him out. Again. Fenaday explained about the upcoming voyage.

"Sounds like a suicide mission," Perez said, dark eyes blazing. "That is exactly what I want, provided *La Bitch* gets nothing in the event of my death." Fenaday clapped him on the shoulder and sent the engineer back to the ship to start coordinating repairs and maintenance.

Moshe Karass, pilot of the *Sidhe's* shuttle *Banshee*, was maintaining Marscabs in a garage. Karass was one of the few of Fenaday's crew in whom he had much faith. The Israeli was a good pilot and loved spacing. Karass looked pleased to see him. He wiped his hands on a rag before shaking Fenaday's hand.

"Hey, skipper," Karass said. "What's the good word?"

"There's work, Moshe. It pays four hundred thousand credits for a top pilot, but I can't recommend it."

Moshe whistled in astonishment. "Four hundred thousand credits? Where are…never mind. If you could tell me, it wouldn't pay such a mint. Well, I'm no closer to getting a decent spacing job. Pan World's frame job on me for that moon shuttle collision is still fresh in the minds of prospective employers. My only way back into space is with you. If we live, I'll have enough money to clear my name."

"Okay, Moshe. Get down to the ship as soon as you can."

Meanwhile Shasti had found most of her LEAF troops in bars or jail cells. Some were working as leg breakers, bouncers and such. A few had found respectable work; those she left alone. This mission was suicidal and only the desperate, or those they desperately needed, were invited.

One of the respectable turned up at the ship anyway.

Shasti looked down from the gantry to see a familiar, tall shape, striding between lines of supply carts. "Johan," she muttered to herself and took a work elevator to the ground.

Johan Gunnar had served in the LEAF with her since she arrived on *Sidhe*. He'd landed a job with a shipping warehouse as a manager. Glad of it, she'd not contacted him.

He smiled when he saw her open the elevator cage. "I hear there's a mission," he said, his eyes level with Shasti's. Breath steamed from his breather unit as it whiffed O2 to him.

"I heard you had found a job already," she replied.

"Bah," he growled. "A few days behind a desk and I begin to think death might be preferable."

"You're being a fool," Shasti said. "This is a voyage for the desperate and the damned."

"You're going," he said. "That's good enough for me."

"I qualify on both grounds," she snapped.

"My choice." He shrugged. "For my own reasons."

"As you say," she said, "your choice." Angry for reasons she couldn't quite understand, Shasti spun on her heel and left.

She spotted Fenaday by the front landing jack. As usual he had a preflight list in his hand. He and their tactical officer, Katrina "Cat" Micetich, were talking to an engineer and pointing at the immense jack towering over them. Fenaday spotted her and waved her over, handing the comp to Micetich, who walked off with the engineer.

"What's our status on ground troops?" he asked, adjusting his breather and zipping his leather jacket. It was bitterly cold in the ship's shadow.

"Pickings have been better than I expected," she said, putting Johan out of her mind. "With the war over, the economy lousy, there are lots of hard cases available: LURPS, Commandos, and Air Space Assault Team troops. Mars seems full of people with little concern for life and hungry for money." Shasti knew the type too well, having been raised from childhood as an assassin in the Denshi Order on Olympia. She'd developed an eye for the good, for the ones putting up a front, and for the plain crazy. She made her picks, hoping she read people—standard humans as she thought of them —correctly.

Fenaday grimaced. "Great. Well, the contractors showed up an hour ago and began the most extensive maintenance *Sidhe's* ever received. I'm glad Mandela's footing the bill for it. We'll have ship-wrights around the clock. I'm having them pay particular attention to our shuttles and fighters."

Something tickled Shasti's senses, and she turned away from him. In the distance, just coming around a machine shed, a group of people came into view.

Fenaday's stepped forward to stand next to her, eyes narrowed. "What's that?"

"Must be Mandela's contingent. About fifty of them," Shasti said.

"I wish I knew how you do that," Fenaday muttered.

"Just rely on it that I can," she replied.

The group passed the gate to *Sidhe's* launch pad, led by another forgettable individual.

"I do like punctuality," Fenaday said. "Let's go meet the latest members of the legion of the damned."

Shasti nodded, trailing him in her customary position to his left and slightly behind, opposite his gun hand. She shot equally well off either her left or right.

———

They walked over to the loading platform in silence. Fenaday waited, trying to look relaxed as the newcomers came up to them. A breeze from the terraformed desert tugged at his brown hair. He shivered again then put on a cap bearing his ship's name and identification numbers.

The nondescript man came forward, the group pausing behind him at a hand signal. He walked up to them slowly. "Good morning, Captain Fenaday, Commander Rainhell."

"Just Rainhell," Shasti said. She didn't look at the man; her eyes searched the people behind him for any threats.

"Who are you?" Fenaday asked.

"Mr. Gandhi," he replied. "Mandela sent me."

Fenaday grinned mirthlessly. "Your boss has a hell of a sense of humor."

"I assure you that you have no idea. Be glad of it. I'm bringing you the promised help, all sworn to secrecy, of course. A damn sight better than anything you're likely to find." Gandhi turned and waved at the group. A small woman, bundled in an ankle-length blue Marscoat, led five other people up to them.

"This is Dr. Shizuyo Mourner," Gandhi said. "She has a Ph.D. in Enshari biology. Dr. N'deba, also an MD and familiar with Enshari biology, Dr. Fierman, Dr. Hecht, their assistants Yamata and Vashti."

"Pleased to meet you," said Mourner, a woman with an intense, almost predatory look. "In case you're wondering, I agree with Mr. Duna's speeches. No Enshar homeworld, no Enshari. I'd hate to see my specialty become a study of corpses."

"You come on this voyage," Fenaday replied, "you're apt to end up a corpse yourself."

Ignoring her shocked look, Fenaday turned to Shasti. "Call Quartermaster Dobera to the dock."

"Dobera will see to getting you settled on board, Doctor," Fenaday said. "Afterward, he'll show you the Sickbay."

Shasti popped out a pocket com and relayed the order. The medical party walked to the place Fenaday indicated.

A group of five advanced on Fenaday and Shasti. They were enough to startle even a seasoned traveler. The man was about Fenaday's age, though taller and gaunt. Half his face was covered with a ceramic and metal skullcap that included a prosthetic eye. Most such surgeries were far less obvious, and Fenaday wondered why the man wore the disfiguring headpiece. Then Fenaday looked more closely at the man's companions. They were HCRs—Human-form Combat Robots—inventions of the closing days of the war. The clear filament hair they used for transmission, ECM, and cooling was long and gave them a feminine look.

Actually, he thought after a few seconds, *they don't look all that female. It's a first impression.* The machines stared back at him with doll's eyes. They wore black jumpsuits, identical, save for a color strip running sash-like across the chest.

Their human controller strolled up. "Kyle Mmok," he introduced himself, ignoring Gandhi, who returned the favor. He introduced his team. "Cobalt, Verdigris, Magenta, and Vermilion."

Rather horribly, the robots bowed as he called their name-colors. Worse, Magenta curtsied. A sardonic smile passed over Mmok's pale face. Belatedly, Fenaday realized Mmok was communicating subvocally. He probably had almost as much machinery in him as the HCRs.

"I have thirty crab-style assault robots and a half dozen general purpose models in a warehouse nearby," Mmok continued. "We all come combat tested on Conchir itself. Isn't that right, girls?"

They nodded in unison.

Fenaday kept his face a mask, though the HCRs raised the hair on the back of his head. "Wonderful act. I didn't realize there'd be a floor show." Fenaday gestured to the spot where Dobera and Mourner stood. "Over there."

Mmok nodded without looking at him and moved on.

Dobera, a Frokossi of about middle height for his reptilian people, stood by the first group, scratching a clawed hand over his head. He held a portable computer. Mourner pointed to something on it, doubtless looking at details of the sickbay. Two of Dobera's assistants showed up. One went over to Mmok, looking somewhat nervously at the HCRs.

Gandhi introduced an array of shipwrights and engineers whose names Fenaday didn't bother about. He'd get the list later from Dobera. Before Gandhi finished, another group showed up. Twenty-two ground troops, in black and green Air Space Assault Team uniforms, followed a tall, lanky human and an ape-like Morok.

"First Sergeant Daniel Rigg," said the big, gray-eyed human, "reporting aboard the *Sidhe*—"

"It's pronounced *Sheeee*," Fenaday interrupted. "The *d* is silent."

"Then why put it in?" asked the blue-skinned Morok, giving Fenaday a fang-filled grimace.

"So we can tell who isn't Irish," Fenaday said.

"This is my assistant team leader, Sergeant Rask," Rigg continued, ignoring the by-play.

"Welcome aboard," Fenaday said. "You're a long way from Morok, Sergeant Rask."

"Nah," the red-eyed, apish alien said. "I'm a local boy, born on Mars."

Fenaday barked a laugh. He took an immediate liking to the Morok, if only because he was shorter than Fenaday. Mmok, Rainhell, Telisan, and now Rigg made him feel dwarfish.

The last to be introduced was a petite, striking woman of about twenty, with dark red hair and an olive complexion. She wore a Confed flight suit, discoloration showing where the uniform insignia had been recently cut from it.

"Pilot Angelica Fury," she said.

"Did your parents hate you or something?" Fenaday asked.

Fury glared at him. "Fourteen combat drops in *Dakota* shuttles, two confirmed kills air to air," she replied woodenly, ignoring his joke.

"Welcome aboard," Fenaday said. "The *Pooka* doesn't have a regular pilot. She's yours."

She snapped a salute and joined the others.

Gandhi handed Fenaday a data chip. "We've kept this under wraps so far, but the press will get wind of it shortly. Even if they don't learn it's about Enshar, which they shouldn't, they can be trouble. How soon can you lift?"

"Normally, I would have said two weeks," Fenaday replied. "With you footing the bill and the twenty-four- hour full shifts you've put on her, I can take *Sidhe* up in about three to four days."

"That may be too long. There are people who would like to stop this mission."

"Me for one," Fenaday snapped. "How about some details?"

"None to be had for now," Gandhi lied, having the grace to look somewhat uncomfortable about it. "We'll get you what you need, when you need it. The disk contains a number to reach me at. Be alert, be wary, and get off Mars as soon as you can." The bland man turned and quickly walked away.

Fenaday turned to Shasti. "Put Mmok and Rigg's team in separate compartments where your people can watch them. We'll be safer that way, I think."

"Yes, then what?"

"Then," he said with a smile, "get ready for dinner."

———

Belwin Duna and Telisan waited for them at a private room in the back of the Excalibur. Dinner at Mars' premier restaurant would be staggeringly expensive, but Fenaday didn't care. If ever anyone was entitled to live by, "Eat, drink, and be merry, for tomorrow we die," they were. Fenaday decided to stick Mandela with the tab instead of Duna in a small bit of revenge. He also planned severe depredations on the wine cellar.

Fenaday had worried about Shasti's reaction to Telisan. However, the tall Denlenn, still five inches below Shasti's height, managed to charm even her. He held out chairs and poured wine for her while they waited for their table in the exclusive elfin towers the Excalibur was known for. Fenaday was surprised by the slight stab of jealousy he felt while watching the two of them. He began to understand why Telisan made Wing Commander. The alien's natural diplomatic skills and easy manner made Fenaday envious.

A waiter took them upstairs to their private table in the tower with a fantastic view. They could see most of the Mars colony spread beneath them. Lights moved everywhere in the purple-red dusk. In the far distance, the occasional flare of spaceship engines threw harsh glares and shadows.

"Beautiful," Duna said. "It is good that life holds such sights."

"Quite," Shasti added, to Fenaday's surprise. "A cold beauty, but a beauty none-the-less."

Words that might apply to Shasti herself, he thought. She looked at him and he wondered if she had somehow divined his thoughts.

"You must see Denla sometime," Telisan said. "There you will see warmth and beauty combined."

They looked out over the shrouded world in companionable silence for a few more seconds.

"I had a visitor two nights ago," Fenaday began. "He uses the name Mandela." He glanced at the others. Either they were good poker players, or the species difference made their surprise invisible. "Does the name mean anything to you?"

"No, Captain," Duna replied. "Does it concern our business?"

"Yes. Mandela isn't his real name. He's with the Confederate Government, one of those nameless and faceless who wield the real power."

"If he is trying to stop us—" Telisan began.

"Quite the opposite," Shasti said, watching the Denlenn narrowly. "He's the reason we are going." This time the old professor and the ace pilot did look surprised.

"Yes," Fenaday said. "He is most persuasive." He repeated the speech he had earlier given Rainhell.

"This Mandela is unknown to either of us," Duna said after Fenaday finished, "but all you relay is logical as to the Confederacy's motivations. I am sorry that this has happened to you. I hoped this would be your free choice."

Fenaday shrugged. "The government would put me out of business one way or another. I'm lucky to get as far as I did." For all the sympathy, Fenaday noted that Duna didn't offer to go to Mandela and get them off the hook. The Enshari was a desperate being. In his place, Fenaday wouldn't have let them off either. Accustomed as he was to enlightened self-interest, Fenaday didn't take it personally.

Waiters—actual people, not servos—showed up with their meals. Fortunately, Fenaday and his companions were all omnivores with sufficiently similar tastes that nothing disgusted the others. In his previous life as a merchant, Fenaday had learned to have a strong stomach. He was glad not to need the skill tonight.

As he looked at the others in the soft candlelight, a feeling of unreality gripped Fenaday. *I used to live like this,* he thought with a faint shock. *Evenings in good restaurants with intelligent, decent people for company.* That life seemed so far away, as if it had happened to someone else.

They made an interesting sight at the table. The tiny Enshari sat on an elevated chair, next to Fenaday, who wore his best ship's uniform. Shasti wore what Fenaday always referred to as her "vampire" outfit: a black, V-necked, form-fitting bodysuit with a gold sash under a red bolero jacket. On her chest rested a ruby of eye-catching proportions. Her skin looked all the more white and flawless against the clothes. Telisan looked somewhat incongruous in a human-cut suit. Handsome even by human standards, he still bent in all the wrong places. The Denlenn waved his overlarge hands as he spoke with animation about flying in the war against the Conchirri.

Fenaday asked everyone to hold off further discussion of their mission until after dinner. The hour gave him an appreciation of why Duna and the Denlenn pilot were friends. Belwin Duna was the image of a genial grandfather, for all that he looked much like a large otter. Over eight hundred years old, the Enshari's store of knowledge seemed endless. It complemented an empathy that crossed barriers of culture and species. Duna drew out of Fenaday things he usually tried not to think of: the family bankruptcy, the suicide of the chief financial officer and his father's best friend, other even more painful things. Duna listened sympathetically until Fenaday pulled up short.

"My problems," Fenaday said, "must seem trivial to you with all you have lost."

"One can only feel so much pain," Duna replied. "If one cares passionately about a person, their death can weigh as heavily as the death of a species. After a point, numbers become meaningless. Is not each person a unique universe, never to be seen again in all time?"

Fenaday thought briefly about the unique universes he'd ended and nodded.

"It's time to get to business," Fenaday finally said, glad to switch the subject. "Enshar: theories on what happened, approaches to the planet, weapons, tactics, any information you have that might give us a chance of survival.

"You've seen my ship. She's powerful for her size, but nothing compared to a cruiser like the *Bengal*." He spent a few minutes relaying the capabilities of the *Sidhe*, mostly to Telisan, who made notes in a pocket comp. Fenaday then gestured to Shasti.

"Our Landing and Expedition Force," she said, "is handpicked and trained in light weapons. I've managed to get back the core of that group. They're the equals of any ASAT or Marine platoon except for the lack of heavy weapons. I've picked up about twenty newcomers, all with equivalent backgrounds. By the time we reach Enshar, I'll be happy with them or they'll be sucking space."

Telisan looked at the big Olympian.

"She's mostly kidding," Fenaday said. *I hope*, he thought.

She sipped her wine and gave him another of those enigmatic looks reserved for when she felt he was being too squeamish about the business they were in. Fenaday knew he was a disappointment to her in terms of sheer ruthlessness.

"We know what this Mandela has given us," Fenaday continued. "His stringers arrived today. They're the sort of professional people we'd never normally have a chance at—doctors, engineers, and scientists. You may even know some of them, a Dr. Mourner and her associates?"

"Mourner," Duna said in evident excitement. "Yes, I know of her. I have read her papers. A brilliant mind."

"Why they're so willing to throw their lives away," Fenaday said,

"I have no idea. He also delivered twenty-two ASATs. To crown it all, there's a cyber-force of robots under a human controller. He's even got four of those humanform combat robots we heard rumors of at the war's end. Well, they're real."

"I know." Telisan nodded. "Confed used them in the final assault on Conchir. I never saw one, but I heard much of them. They are deadly."

"Yes," Fenaday said, "they looked it."

"Machines," Shasti said, an undertone of contempt in her voice. Olympia, the homeworld of human perfection, did not allow robots. "Just slightly better toys."

"It's the human who worries me," Fenaday said, as he reached for a wineglass. "Their controller is a cyborg named Mmok. I figure him to be Mandela's lead watchdog. Somehow I have to integrate this mob into a proper crew."

"And keep them under careful observation," Telisan finished.

"Just so."

"Like you, I do not trust this Mandela and his largesse," Telisan said. "The government only agreed to this mission in order to prevent the suicides and the embarrassment. If we disappear en route, they could always claim the Enshar plague got us and fake whatever evidence they need."

"The thought occurred to us as well," Shasti said.

"What steps have you taken to guard against such an eventuality?" Duna asked. The Enshari's fur twitched and rippled with anxiety.

"There's little we can do," Fenaday said grimly. "We're a privateer, not a Navy ship, or even a company ship, where the crew and captain might have served together a long time. We draw self-interested adventurers, people with blots on their records of one nature or another—drunks, druggies, and dregs. I have a few officers I trust. Shasti leads the list. Karass, my lead shuttle pilot, follows. Then there's Chief Engineer, Carlos Perez, within limits, and a Frokossi ex-princeling named Dobera. He serves as quartermaster. On a regular mission I might trust some of the others, but not under these circumstances."

"My people," Shasti added, "are a little better. The nature of ground fighting is such that it builds some bonds, at least in the squads. Again, as the captain says, there are more we could trust in less desperate circumstances. On my side I count on: Gunnar, Li, Bernard, Connery and the two Morok brothers, Hanshi and Lokashti Tok."

"What of your Number Two?" Telisan asked. "Or does our formidable lady take that role?"

Shasti shook her head.

"You bring us to my first point," Fenaday said. "I need an Executive Officer for the voyage. My last one ended up in jail. I don't want him back anyway. You ran a fighter wing. I looked up your record, very impressive."

The Denlenn looked oddly disturbed. "Thee would trust me?" he said, suddenly formal, his accent deepening, as if his mastery of Confed Standard had slipped.

For a second, the switch to the archaic version of the language threw Fenaday, then a memory surfaced from his days as a trader. Denlenn used different versions of their language for different things. Low Denleni for commerce, Middle for everyday and High for important matters. It would discomfort a Denlenn to speak the same way on every subject, even in an alien tongue. Telisan's use of the old human form meant he was dealing with a matter that touched his personal honor.

"Not entirely," Fenaday said, "but I know who you are and what you want. It may sound funny coming from someone who's essentially a legalized pirate, but my instincts tell me that you can be trusted. Shasti agrees, and she doesn't like anyone."

The Denlenn smiled. "High praise indeed."

"You do not know how high," Shasti said dryly. "You're regular military, good family, never any trouble with the law. Add to that, this is your insane idea."

"So," Fenaday added, "I feel I can trust you in matters that do not cross Duna's interests."

"But can I trust you?" replied the Denlenn, his face gone hard, flat and alien. "The weak link in our plan has always been you. What prevents you from dumping us in space the minute we leave atmosphere? Your ship is reconditioned. You could flee to the Fringe

46

Stars again. Bad odds with Confederate forces in pursuit, but better than what you face at Enshar."

"Thought of it," Fenaday admitted, to Telisan's evident surprise, as the Denlenn tensed visibly. "Again, this may sound funny coming from a legal pirate, but I wouldn't do that sort of thing. At least not to people like you. To some of the scum I've faced over the years, yes. It's how they play the game, and I'll use their rules.

"Don't worry about it," Fenaday continued, raising his glass. "It doesn't do me much good to run. I can't search for my wife with the Confed Navy hunting me down. It's been nearly impossible to keep *Sidhe* working when I didn't have to face active government hostility.

"Also, those government stringers aren't going to just let me go, and I suspect we'll be escorted from a distance from when we lift. As Executive, you'll be in the middle, able to secure yourself by playing one side against the other. I'm not telling you anything you don't already know."

"All true," the Denlenn said, "but I want one more guarantee. I want your word of honor, Fenaday, sworn on your hope of ever finding your wife, that there will be no treachery. Give me that and I will serve you as I served my captain on the *Empress Aran.*" The Denlenn drew a small, concealed blade slowly, so as not to provoke Shasti. He placed it on the table then covered the blade with his hand and looked expectantly at the human.

Fenaday looked at the knife for a few seconds then touched the hilt. "I swear," he said, feeling faintly ridiculous, "on my hope of ever finding Lisa again that I will take you to Enshar and if possible, bring you back alive."

The Denlenn placed his big spidery hand over Fenaday's; it felt feverishly warm. "To Enshar then, I am your officer. You may count on me, from this point in any matter that does not affect the safety of my patron, Belwin Duna. My life is otherwise of no account and is yours."

Duna looked at his young friend, then at the human. "Do you know any Denlenn, Captain Fenaday?"

"No, not really. I've met one or two briefly in business. I couldn't say I know much about them."

"Then you will have to take my word for the great honor that it is to have a Denlenn of the Selen family in your service. Once upon a time, they ruled Denla, and the faithfulness of their house is the stuff of many legends."

Telisan smiled at his friend and bowed his head. The blade went back to its concealed pocket.

"Well," said Fenaday, "that's settled then. Now to you, Mr. Duna, I've read everything on your data-disk, as has Shasti. Most of it is familiar to anyone who was flying at that time. We have nothing new to go on."

"I am afraid that it must stay that way," Duna replied. "My only hope is that whatever inimical force struck my planet has either left, passed away, or relaxed its guard."

"You speak as if you think some alien race destroyed Enshar," Shasti observed. "No trace was seen of any ships or any ground personnel. You know that, Telisan. You were there."

"You forget the call from the *Flamme*," Telisan reminded her. "There was a call of boarders on ship."

Shasti brushed the comment aside with a hand gesture. "Hysteria. Nothing was near the *Flamme*. Unless you believe someone secreted themselves on board a destroyer escort, light years away... an intruder makes no sense."

"But still, the call was made," the alien insisted.

"Invisible aliens?" Fenaday smiled.

"Who can say?" Duna answered. "With all we have seen in the last ten years, is it such an impossibility?"

"One hopes so," Shasti said. "How can we kill what we can't see?"

"Our only plan, then, is to attempt a shuttle landing and see if something tries to kill us," Fenaday said. "What a lousy situation."

"I, of course," Duna announced, "will go in the shuttle making the attempt."

"I shall pilot," Telisan added.

"I'll make those calls, gentlemen," Fenaday said. "You work for me once we lift ship."

"Of course, Captain." Duna nodded. "It seemed only honorable to offer."

"Of course," Fenaday returned.

"What do we do now?" Telisan asked.

"Dessert?" Shasti said.

Fenaday twisted in his chair, to look at her deadpan face. "Don't try to tell me that wasn't a joke."

Shasti sighed. "You know I have no sense of humor. I'm simply still hungry."

"Hah." Fenaday turned back to the others, who seemed amused by the unexpected exchange. "What happens next is that we continue to prepare to lift. Keep your bags packed. I plan to lift in five days, but things could develop. Telisan, I need you at the ship immediately, but we can't risk Duna being on board just yet. It wouldn't take a genius to connect a suicide mission and Enshar if the crew sees him. Even though I don't intend to land the *Sidhe*, or even take her within the so-called 'zone of death,' we'd lose most of the crew if they learn of our destination."

"I do not like leaving you, Belwin," Telisan said.

"Go, youngling, go. I'll be fine. Confederate security should be more than adequate until you come to collect me. I shall be careful."

"Very well, but I will see you to your quarters tonight. If I may, Captain?"

Fenaday nodded.

They stayed a while longer for Shasti's dessert. Her legendary sweet tooth, in a gross unfairness, never seemed to deposit an ounce of fat anywhere. Perhaps it was as she said, she simply wasn't made for obesity. Fenaday suspected her heavy workout schedule helped. He long ago learned never to get between the Olympian and chocolate.

When she finished, Fenaday drained his coffee, and they bade Duna and Telisan good night.

———

After they left, Telisan turned to Duna. "You are not going to tell them?"

"Tell them what, youngling? The mad musings of a lonely old scholar? I have no shred of proof for this suspicion. It is not even an old story, but the corruption of a story so old even the Enshari have forgotten the tale. How would it help them to know?

"I do not believe either of them would heed such a warning. You've spoken to them both. Do they strike you otherwise?"

"No. Yet, already I feel my oath bent, if not broken," Telisan replied distantly, as if in some small pain. "He took me unaware with the request to be his officer and I do not believe that he has any idea what he has asked of me. I saw no honorable way to decline as they have been forced into serving our needs, something I would have stopped if I could. Now I must balance my duty to my captain with the secret we share."

"Let them prepare for such enemies as they can imagine," Duna said. "We will be there if there is anything to my thoughts, not that I have any idea what to do about it.

"Yes," Duna continued, "you will find yourself, as you grow older, burdened more and more by the necessity of keeping secrets."

"I have already found it so," Telisan said sadly. "Come, let us go to rest. We begin the final leg of our journey in the morning."

Chapter Six

Telisan appeared outside *Sidhe* in the bitter cold of early morning. Fenaday met him at the main hatchway. He saluted Fenaday in crisp Navy style. "Reporting aboard, sir." Breath steamed from his breather.

"Glad to have you aboard, Mr. Telisan," Fenaday replied, returning the salute. The Denlenn followed him, and they resealed the hatch. Fenaday knew the Denlenn had other names, but only his closest family would know those. To others, the Denlenn would be known only as Telisan of the Selen clan.

Telisan immediately took charge of the thousand details of preparing a starship for deep space. The Denlenn displayed a solid working knowledge of the Conchirri Frigate-leader's design. *Of course*, thought Fenaday, *he'd attacked enough of them during the war.* Fenaday's opinion of the Denlenn went up a notch after he discovered Telisan had been studying the interior design of the frigate for over a month, since he and Duna settled on Fenaday's vessel as a candidate for the desperate voyage.

Since Mandela's contingent knew of their destination, Fenaday kept them off the ship. After stowing their equipment and belongings, the scientists occupied an entire floor of a nearby hotel, kept under guard by Rigg and his Air Space Assault Team. Fenaday posted Mmok and his various robots, including the HCRs, around the ship's exterior as guards. He also sent out Shasti's best Landing Expedition and Assault Force troops: Gunnar, Li, Connery, and the Toks to keep an eye on Mmok.

Reporters began to catch wind of unusual doings at the port. Telisan and particularly Duna were too well known to escape attention entirely. Apparently the bartender had talked to someone about Duna's meeting with Fenaday at Luchow's. Fenaday despised reporters and knew that if word of their destination got through to the regular crew, he would never find enough people to lift ship. Shasti doubled security and referred all calls to Duna. The Enshari's staff issued innocuous press releases about an archeological dig in the Altair system. Fenaday hoped the ruse would gain him the few days he needed to escape their attention. Mandela wanted the government's involvement concealed, which meant there was some force, either public or within the government itself, that opposed the expedition.

Regulars among the crew tried frantically to discover the real destination while they could still jump ship. Money drew back all the people Fenaday needed, but they remained skittish about the secrecy and his vague warnings of extreme hazards ahead. Of *Sidhe's* regular crew, only Fenaday and Shasti knew their destination. Mandela's people stayed out of reach in the hotel and none of *Sidhe's* crew ventured to question Mmok. New crewmembers grilled the old. The veterans knew nothing—but for the sake of their pride —pretended to be in the know.

———

S hasti finished her stowage check in the LEAF bunkroom and walked toward the exit. A few troopers worked on their personal equipment or lounged about. She spotted Gunnar talking with the Morok brothers, Lokashti and Hanshi. She'd finally forgiven Gunnar for abandoning a decent chance at a normal life and coming. She nodded when he waved.

"Commander Rainhell," said a voice, "got a minute?"

Shasti turned to look at a new member of her expeditionary

force. His name popped into her memory, Heaton, former Confed Marine Commando. One of the last people she'd hired as she ran short of time. The barrel-chested man leaned closer than he needed to.

"What?" she asked. Something about the scent of the man bothered her.

"How about a break? We've been cooped up shipboard for days. Why? What do you say to some liberty?"

"No," she replied, annoyed at being asked.

Heaton's face darkened. "Then how about some break in this bullshit security? Where are we going? Huh?"

"You'll be told what you need to know when you need to know."

"This ain't the real fleet, you know," he said. "It's a fucking pirate ship—that's all. I don't need to put up with this crap from you people."

Shasti studied him and it clicked, the jittery posture, overly bright eyes, and the scent—adrenaldust. A common vice among combat troops, the chemical antidote to fear made dusters fierce but unstable.

She looked at him without expression. "Twenty-days double duty," she said. "More if you don't shut up. And you've had your last dust on this ship, hophead." She turned to leave.

"Damn you, don't turn your back on me," Heaton yelled. He grabbed at her. Maybe he was reaching for her arm, but his hand closed on her breast instead—hard.

Shasti spun back and punched. Heaton flew backward, but not faster than Shasti. She followed the fist with a kick, hitting him while he was still in the air. The man landed flat on his back. She stood in the center of the bunkroom, waiting. Around her, people scrambled to their feet. Before anyone could intervene, Heaton roared and threw himself at her. She blocked his powerful arms easily, contemptuously parried a kick, then stepped into the big man. He grappled, relying on his size and bulk. She pulled him off the floor and threw him into a bulkhead. He clambered back up, shock on his face, finally realizing that he was up against something more than human. She lunged at him, hands moving almost too fast to see.

In seconds, the fight turned into a beating. Shasti's beautiful face stretched taut in a silent snarl. Heaton collapsed, and she started kicking him to death.

"Boss, boss," Gunnar shouted. He, Hanshi, and Lokashti rushed up to stop her.

Shasti flung off all three, but they managed to break her murderous concentration. She paused. Gunnar climbed to his feet, moving between Shasti and the wreck of Heaton.

"Boss," he said. "It's me, Johan. Come on. Look at me. It's Johan."

Shasti stared unblinking at him.

"Boss," Hanshi called in Morok, "this dung is nothing. Do not dirty your hands. My brother and I will do this for you."

"I need no help," she growled, but the madness receded from her eyes.

"Of course not," Gunnar said. "Of course."

"No one touches me like that," she gritted. "No one. Not ever."

Lokashti walked over to Heaton and stirred the bleeding man with a foot. "Certainly not twice," he said.

"Leave it to us," Gunnar said.

She shook her head. "Fight's over," she replied, anger vanishing as if never present. "Call sickbay, I'll report to the captain."

"No need," said Fenaday from behind them. He stood in the hatchway. "Heard the donnybrook," he added.

She looked down at Heaton, then back at Fenaday.

Fenaday shrugged. "There's always one who seems to feel the need to test you on each voyage. We got it out of the way early this time."

Shasti nodded stiffly. She suspected that he wasn't pleased with how she'd handled the situation, but wouldn't reproach her in front of the others.

"I'll call Dr. N'deba to the ship," Fenaday said. "Gunnar, get a med-tech up here."

Fenaday looked at Shasti. "Are you all right?"

The question surprised her. Couldn't he see she was unhurt? "Yes."

"Good," he replied. "I'll see you on the bridge later. Get this cleaned up." He left.

Shasti looked at Lokashti. "First aid," she said. "Hanshi," she added, "get the newbies to clean the deck." She looked around at the faces in the compartment. "I won't be so gentle with the next person who crosses me." People nodded or looked away. No one met her eyes.

She walked to the hatchway. *No one touches me like that,* she thought. *Never again, never again, never ever again.*

———

H ours later, Shasti joined Fenaday on the bridge. She was her usual cool, controlled self.

"N'deba patched up Heaton," she said. "I arranged with Gandhi to transfer him to a military hospital where he can recover under wraps until we leave."

"Good," Fenaday replied. "I understand Hanshi and Lokashti wanted to cut him up and process him through the waste system."

Shasti nodded. The Toks long ago bestowed a *nom de guerre* on her, "Death's Angel." The name stuck, and Fenaday knew the Toks would make sure it circulated among the new members, especially the ASATs. Shasti never acknowledged it, but Fenaday suspected it secretly pleased her. The Olympian Assassin had brought the Morok brothers aboard. She had saved their lives somewhere long before she joined the *Sidhe,* and they were fanatically loyal to her. He doubted there'd be any repetition of the hospitalized spacer's mistake.

"Did you call for me, sir?"

Fenaday turned to see that Daniel Rigg had entered the bridge. "Yes," Fenaday replied. He nodded toward Shasti.

"I'm going to break your squads into fire teams," Shasti stated. "I want to match one of yours with one of mine to integrate the force."

Fenaday expected Sergeant Rigg to protest the dispersion of his ASATs. He didn't. Rigg simply smiled, as if acknowledging the point scored. He measured both of them with cool, gray eyes, seemingly unconcerned. He gave Shasti a look—one reserved for a respected opponent, wary, yet confident. Fenaday would have been happier if Rigg shot his mouth off.

"That will be all for now," Shasti said.

Rigg left without a word.

"That one is no dumb grunt," Fenaday said. "Watch him and never turn your back. He believes he can take you."

She nodded. "He believes it, but he'll have to bet his life to find out."

"I'm not worried about his life," Fenaday replied. "There are twenty-four ASATs. I've only got one of you."

Shasti's teeth flashed briefly. "I like the odds."

———

Shasti and Fenaday met with Duna for a late dinner at the Marsport Hilton. Telisan stayed behind in the port office, straightening out details of the initial flight plan to exit Mars's congested orbit. The evening, like several before it, turned into a working dinner held in the Enshari's spacious rooms to avoid notice. Shasti perched on the window, staring up at the top of Marsport dome, as Fenaday and Duna reviewed progress on the ship, stores and crew.

"I received this from my Confederation security this morning," Duna said. He pressed a switch on the tabletop causing a large viewscreen on the wall to flick on. Shasti left her spot at the window to join them.

"Here is the latest data on Enshar from the Confederate destroyer *Quicksilver*," Duna began. "She uploaded the monitoring satellite's information about six months ago."

On the screen the image of the planet's night side appeared as seen from the satellite.

"Not much has changed," continued the Enshari. "At night, less artificial light is seen, as one after another, the power plants go off-line. Cities continue to decay or become infested by wildlife and flora. Massive fires rage unchecked in some cities and forests as some untended device made by my people fails, causing ignition.

Most of the derelict shipping has sunk. There is no sign of any intelligent life."

"Not at all encouraging," Fenaday said. Enshar had been abstract to him until now. He felt as if he was looking at his own gravesite.

"Captain," Duna said. "It's evident from what my security tells me that reporters are becoming more suspicious about my stay. We've used our cover story as best we can. The ruse seems to be working for now. Should they put two and two together, as you humans say, with the unusual doings at the port and your ship, we could have trouble. Your government's aid to me is conditioned on the expedition remaining secret. I also fear that others, some from only the best motives, will interfere or seek to cancel our mission.

"There's considerable opposition to this trip among your government. Some feel that I am raising my people's hopes only to dash them. They think our only hope for survival is to forget our homeworld and fear I may bring on the very extinction I seek to fight."

"I can't imagine," Fenaday said, "that Congress would be glad to find out the government put an eminent scholar into the hands of a privateer under suspicion of criminal activity and sent him on a suicide mission."

"Please stop using that expression," Duna begged, visibly upset even to the humans. "I wouldn't have agreed to this voyage if I thought there was not at least some chance."

Fenaday shrugged. "As you wish."

"I think the time has come," Duna added, "to move me to the ship. I will remain in my cabin until liftoff. Mandela can arrange a story about my going off to a university on Earth, or some such cover."

"Very well," Fenaday said. "Shasti, call ahead and tell Mmok we are coming in by way of the emergency hatch and to keep the area clear."

She nodded and pulled her pocket com, speaking quickly and quietly into it. Fenaday could hear Mmok's voice rasp out something from the other end. "It's set," she said, snapping the device closed.

Fenaday turned back to Duna. "I am afraid you'll have to ride the last couple of hundred yards in a sack. One sight of an Enshari, and we might have a half-empty ship."

"A sack?" Duna repeated, looking a little ruffled.

"Don't worry." Fenaday grinned. "We even have one with us, just for the eventuality. Shasti will carry you on board on her shoulder. She's quite strong. Carried me for two miles when I was shot on Morokat."

Duna looked up at Shasti, who gazed down impassively. "One would be quite far off the ground on such a shoulder," he said. "I am from a species that prefers underground dwelling. Perhaps you could…"

"I'm the captain," he replied. "She carries the sacks."

They were saved from further argument by the arrival of Telisan with their final approved exit papers. Security had admitted the Denlenn, who joined them for coffee, as Duna gathered up his belongings. Fenaday handed Duna a package Telisan brought from the quartermaster's stores. It held a ship's uniform tailored for the little Enshari. Duna seemed touched by the gesture.

"Well, I shall be quite in fashion," Duna said, looking at the black leather jacket and sage-green clothing.

"There's a uniform for you in your cabin, Telisan," Fenaday said. "For now, we wear civvies until we get to the starship."

"About this sack," Duna said, "I hope you wouldn't mind if Telisan carried me in it?"

Telisan sputtered into his coffee. "Sack?"

"I'll explain on the way down," Fenaday sighed. "Grab his suitcase, please."

Exiting separately, they took different cabs. The yellow and black robot cars dropped them at the edge of Marsport proper, the great dome that provided Earth-like warmth and conditions. From there they traveled in separate cars on the transport tubes, taking the train-like machines to the commercial and industrial sections. They rendezvoused at the entrance to the freight area of the port where *Sidhe* lay docked. From the tubeway exit, it would be a walk on Mars's own cold surface.

After donning insulated Marscoats and putting on breathers, they set out. The small devices whiffed enough oxygen in a nose tube to keep anoxia at bay. As they stepped out onto the frigid surface, Fenaday was glad for the terraforming that raised the equatorial temperature to about ten degrees Fahrenheit.

"This way," he said. "No fancy passenger terminal for us privateers. We live a hardy life."

"I think I would like to get into that sack already," Duna said.

"Sorry," Fenaday said. "You'll have to suffer like the rest till we get nearer the frigate. Besides, what are you complaining about? You have a fur coat on under there."

"Wait till you are eight hundred years old," the tiny Enshari groused, "then you can tell me about how much you feel the cold."

Fenaday grinned. "I'll see you get a cognac in your cabin after we are aboard."

Fenaday's chronometer indicated well after midnight as they trudged toward *Sidhe's* cradle, passing silent warehouses and small docker bars. Fenaday began to feel like a child trying to sneak around the schoolyard after closing.

They boarded a slidewalk to take them the final leg to the cheap-seats—as Fenaday referred to the area around the frigate. Sodium floodlights illuminated some of the port, barely holding the darkness of the Martian night at bay. The stars shone down brilliantly with hardly a twinkle in the thin air. Phobos, larger and closer of Mars's moons, rolled through the sky above them only six thousand kilometers away. It looked like a chunk of reddish rock, but glittered with lights from homes and installations on its airless surface.

The slidewalk ended. From there they trudged on pavement covered in part by the grit of the Martian desert, which crunched under their insulated boots. They passed older warehouses with field equipment parked about them. Some smaller freighters sat on their own gantry-aprons. Occasionally, a light glinted from a port or hatchway. For the most part, the ships in this area sat sealed tight against the inhospitable air.

Duna spoke in his soft small voice about his last time on Enshar. Fenaday listened with half an ear, thinking mostly about a few hours of sleep in a warm bunk. The others trailed behind them.

"Look out!" Shasti yelled from behind them.

From the shadows of a warehouse and from between parked trucks, figures sprang at them. Suddenly the Martian night was full of bodies, making impossible jumps in the low gravity. Knives glinted, clubs and batons waved. Had there been guns in the attacker's intentions, Fenaday's people would have been cut down. Fortunately, it was near impossible to get firearms in and out of Marsdome proper.

Shasti intercepted an attacker heading toward Duna. Her booted foot flashed out in a flying side-snap kick. The man's breath left in an agonized whoosh and he rocketed away, crashing through an aircar window. Shasti landed upright and immediately exchanged a blur of ferocious blows with a Morok. The apish alien backed away from her, blocking as best he could. A roundhouse kick caught the Morok in the midsection, and he folded like a wet bag.

Fenaday sidestepped a baton, moving to a hook stance, as the wielder struck at him sideways. He merged with his attacker, a bearded human with wild eyes and the stink of liquor on him. Fenaday seized the baton with his right hand, continuing its motion with his spin, ripping it free of the other man's hands. Reversing the circle, he smacked the baton into the bearded man's gaping face. One down.

He caught the glint of a knife from the corner of his eye and swung the baton down in a block. A Dua-Denlenn with a knife pulled the thrust as if it had been a feint and lunged as the club swept past. Fenaday dropped into a back stance, swinging the baton back in a wing block. As his left hand touched the knife arm of the attacker, he clamped on it and pulled the alien forward, off balance. Fenaday slammed the baton into the Dua-Denlenn's armpit and ribs then went for the head. He snap-kicked the side of his opponent's knee and heard a rewarding crunch. The knife flew away as the Dua-Denlenn screamed and fell.

Fenaday's head snapped around. Assailants charged from everywhere. The fight seemed to slow in his eyes, taking on a preternatural clarity. Telisan, fifteen feet away, fended off two attackers trying to reach Duna. Another man lay on the ground with the small knife Telisan had sworn allegiance to Fenaday with, sticking in his throat.

The Enshari wisely dodged behind the big Denlenn. Fenaday

could see that Telisan was strong and fast, but not a trained hand fighter. His barroom swing knocked one man back, but the knife-wielder closed in. Telisan blocked awkwardly, avoided being gutted by a hair, and backed up with cut hands. Fenaday lunged toward him, but too many opponents stood between them. He shoulder-rolled to get clear, came up, and flung the baton. It cracked the knifer in the side, startling more than disabling him. As the knife-wielder staggered, Duna leapt onto the man's arm. An enraged Telisan followed up, hitting the knifer hard and downed him.

Someone jumped on Fenaday's back, applying a full nelson. Fenaday reached down with his left hand and found groin. The grip loosened. He grabbed the sensitive inner thigh, gouged, and the hold loosened more. Slipping a leg behind his attacker's leg, he twisted and flung him free.

Another man hit Fenaday in the chest with a flying tackle. Fenaday flew over backward, falling as best he could. The man landed on his chest, raising an arm. Shasti appeared suddenly over the thug's shoulder. She dropped on him, wrapped an arm around his neck, snapping it and shoving the body away. A baton wielder struck her, and her block did not quite stop the blow. She dropped away sidewise but gathered herself almost instantly.

Fenaday rolled and tangled the legs of her attacker. The man fell to his knees, and Fenaday's knife-edge palm landed on his neck. He sprawled bonelessly. Fenaday scrabbled forward, snatching up the dead man's weapon. *I have a club again*, he thought, as he lunged— not bothering to come to his feet. Telisan struggled in the grip of three men. Duna lay on the ground, kicking upward at a man who was striking at him with a club. The Enshari locked his hands protectively around his head and pedaled his feet at the attacker, preventing him from getting in a good shot.

Fenaday slammed into the club wielder. The thug swung wildly with the club as he staggered. Fenaday parried at the forte of his own club. He kicked the other man's arm up, thrust into his solar plexus, and followed with a savage blow to the skull. Another man down.

Shasti lifted one of Telisan's attackers over her head and dropped him to her knee. His scream cut short as his spine snapped.

Telisan put his back to hers and inexpertly boxed with another brawler. Duna stood between them. At least six of their attackers lay unmoving. More hung back, injured. But reinforcements rushed from the shadows.

Fenaday ran, hopping over a club and parrying a knife to get back to the others. The situation looked grim.

"Come on," shouted one man. "Let's get them." He leaned close, swinging a crowbar. Shasti grabbed, pulled, and seized him by the neck, twisting in one fluid move. She flung the body, tripping up a big-bellied thug who rushed toward Fenaday.

Suddenly new figures appeared in the fight—thin, slender blurs. Men screamed briefly as the shadowy forms raced among them. A few turned to run. They didn't get far. The figures cut them down with single blows. In seconds, only Fenaday and his party still stood. Silent, feminine figures formed a motionless ring around them, facing outward.

Mmok walked out of the darkness, his stiff-legged limp betraying him even in the low light. "It appears," he said, "that not everyone wants to run the risk of the Enshari getting their planet back."

"No," Fenaday huffed, trying to catch his breath, "but they didn't want us dead either. Just disabled. These aren't assassins. They're bar toughs, leg breakers. Pros would have used guns. Or at least they'd have been better hand-to-hand."

"They were good enough for me," Telisan gasped. The Denlenn had the worst of the fight, trying to protect Duna. His hands were badly cut, and he was covered in bruises. "I am apparently better in a *Spacefire* than a brawl."

"Cobalt," Mmok ordered. "Med kit."

The machine turned, detached a small package from its utility belt, and held it out.

Duna snatched the kit from the machine and began frantically bandaging Telisan's cuts. He spoke softly, consolingly, in his own tongue to his friend.

Like the robots, Shasti stood facing outward, face calm and still, eyes searching for opponents. The similarity between the machines and the Olympian chilled him. It was almost reassuring to see a trickle of blood on her ivory skin. Shasti didn't bruise worth a damn, but even she could be cut.

"Let's move it," Mmok said.

Fenaday shook his head. "Things will go better for us if the Port Police find us here."

"The Port Police aren't coming," Mmok growled. "Someone else is. You don't want to be here when they arrive. All this is going to disappear and what you don't see, you can't be asked about later. We have to go. Now."

Fenaday stared at him for a few seconds, trying to read something in the one human eye and failing. "How did you arrange that?"

The half machine man looked at him coldly. "I uplinked to Mandela as soon as I saw trouble. He's sending the cleaners."

"Let's get to the ship," Fenaday decided. "Telisan, can you walk?"

The Denlenn nodded and they started off, keeping the best speed they could. The HCRs paced them at a distance.

"How did you know we were in trouble?" he asked Mmok.

Mmok gestured upward. Fenaday looked up to see a small, saucer-shaped object floating silently, about thirty meters over them.

"Reconnaissance robot," Mmok grunted. Despite the limp, he had no trouble keeping the pace. "Didn't see the ambush. They were undercover in the cars and buildings. Saw the fight. Me and the girls came as fast as we could."

"It appears that you will be useful to have around, Mr. Mmok," Fenaday said.

Chapter Seven

Mourner and medics greeted them at the gantry to *Sidhe* and rushed them to the sickbay. The brightly lit bay looked more like a hospital suite now then the rudimentary space it had been only days ago. Medics checked everyone, but Mourner herself examined Duna. Secrecy about the Enshari was going out the airlock.

Fenaday was glad for her expertise. Mandela would take any harm to Duna out of his hide. Fortunately, the old scholar had taken little injury, thanks to Telisan. Mourner decided to keep him in sickbay for observation, assigning a medtech to watch over him. The old Enshari, spent from the fight, dropped off to sleep almost immediately.

With the adrenaline rush of the fight over, Fenaday's bruises and cuts asserted themselves. In some cases, the bruises went to the bone. Telisan's cuts looked deep and painful, but well within the skills of Doctors Mourner and N'deba. The transformation in his sickbay amazed Fenaday. He had a full medical staff of a quality a regular Navy vessel might well envy. Mourner's skill with a tissue regenerator awed anyone watching. She fluttered about them like a small, active bird.

"Your injuries barely need attention, Commander Rainhell,"

Mourner said, clearly fascinated by the Olympian. "They already look days old and are well on their way to healing. I'd love to do some lab studies of your—"

"No," Shasti growled.

Mourner looked as if she might press the point, but Shasti fixed her cold, empty, jade-eyed stare on her. The doctor found herself suddenly without words, something Fenaday suspected seldom happened to her. Shasti stood, slipping her jacket back over her shoulders.

Fenaday looked past the two of them toward Mmok. Fatigue weighed on him like a sodden blanket. "We have a few hours to sunrise. See that the ship is secure, Mr. Mmok."

Mmok grunted, his chief form of communication.

"I'll be in my cabin," said Fenaday, standing and barely suppressing a groan. "Wake me only if the Conchirri attack Mars."

———

S unrise came, but the Port Police didn't. Shasti woke him, bringing a message that appeared on *Sidhe's* computer, untrace-able, though they had no doubt of its origin. "Press getting wind of the mission, get off Mars."

"What now?" asked Shasti.

"We move up the clock for liftoff," he replied. "Call everyone to the ship after sunrise. Order them to come in groups of ten or more. Once aboard, everyone but you stays aboard.

"I want you to scout the area of last night's fight. Don't take any risks. If you see anything suspicious, pull out. Use our private chan-nel." He hesitated for a second. "Take a weapon, screw the regs."

She nodded with her usual economy of speech.

Two hours later, Fenaday stood on the bridge, working through the prelaunch checklist with Katrina Micetich when his private com beeped. He walked into his ready cabin off the bridge and clicked on the com.

"All evidence of the attack," Shasti said without preamble, "including the blood, has disappeared. Mandela cleaned up our mess very professionally."

A chill ran down his spine as he wondered what'd happened to the unconscious and dead they'd left behind. "Okay. Get back here as soon as you can."

The next twenty-four hours became feverish as Fenaday made one day do the work of two. The crew came aboard, resigned it seemed, to blasting off into the unknown. Duna stayed secluded in the med bay iso-lab. Dobera and the stores crew finished loading at two a.m. local time. Fenaday ordered the last connections to the docking cradle severed with relief. *Sidhe's* own power came completely online. The ship sealed for space.

On the bridge of the former Conchirri frigate, Fenaday sat in the center seat. Shasti stood beside him. She had no flight duties, but a monitor gave her details of the ship's security functions. Liftoff was her favorite part of space flight. She always watched from the bridge.

Fenaday clicked on the monitor in the arm of his chair. Perez's face appeared. He and the ship's engineers, the so-called "black gang" as engineers were called in the day of coal driven ships, manned the reactors far aft in the ship.

"All engines ready for all power settings," said Perez.

"Excellent," Fenaday replied. "Standard Mars launch settings then."

He looked over at Micetich and a new crewman seated at the ship's controls. The gunnery stations remained unmanned. Mmok appropriated a seat there, a chill and unwelcome presence. Fenaday forbade him to bring an HCR to the control center. The cyborg was bad enough.

He turned to the radar and communications specialist, Sharon Hafel, a gray-haired, stocky woman, one of Mandela's people. "Keep scanning and stay alert for any out of pattern traffic."

"Aye, sir," she replied without taking her eyes from the instruments.

He noted Shasti's curious gaze. "Be a bad thing if we were hit by a conveniently out of control aircar."

"Not much we can do." She shrugged. "Mandela is not going to allow us to arm weapons anywhere near Marsport."

"Captain," Telisan called from the companionway entrance

behind them. "The port pilot is here. We are cleared for lift." The port pilot, a rotund fellow, followed him in. His arms were full of forms and a portable com. The pilot would unlock Fenaday's weaponry and leave in his little cutter after *Sidhe* cleared atmosphere. The port pilot walked over to Micetich's station and gave Fenaday a questioning look.

Fenaday nodded. "Take her up." He hit the klaxon, which hooted three times. "All hands, this is the bridge. Take hold, take hold, take hold. Stand by for artificial gravity to cut in at ninety seconds after liftoff."

Around the bridge, people buckled into seats or belted themselves to takeholds mounted in consoles and walls. After the ship's AG came on, the precaution would be unnecessary.

The port pilot displaced Micetich, who moved to stand behind him, a slightly disgusted look on her heavy-featured Slavic face. Fenaday understood her feelings. He hated the arcane port procedure. Fenaday believed it existed to give the Confederacy an excuse to implement fees.

The red frigate shuddered in her cradle as the power came on. Slowly, she began to lift against Mars's still formidable gravity. The pilot put her into a forward ascent. *Sidhe* derived lift from her wings and aerodynamic hull to save on reaction mass. The starship reached high Mach numbers quickly, flying into orbit like the space planes of the twenty-first century. After they reached orbit, Fenaday thanked the port pilot and put him off in his cutter.

Once free of the drag of Mars's atmosphere, *Sidhe* rendezvoused with an automated tanker platform, replacing fuel used in lifting out of the gravity well. After that Fenaday set course for the system's edge where the FTL drive could work. The inner system was far too dense to allow the FTL drive to be effective. Fenaday enjoyed the freedom that came from Mandela's checkbook and burned fuel at military levels to speed them on their way. Another tanker station awaited them at Sol system's edge.

"Radar contact," Hafel announced calmly, "bearing, two hundred seventy degrees and zero degrees relative. Distance, thirty thousand kilometers, relative speed...dropping to zero."

"Let me guess," Fenaday replied, "a Confederation cruiser, Battle or Nova class."

"Good guess," Hafel said with a sidelong glance of her almond shaped eyes. "IFF shows Confederation Battle class cruiser, *Rourke's Drift*. Shall I raise them?"

"Negative. If you start to transmit, she'll jam us," Fenaday replied. He turned a sour look on Telisan. "Your friend Mandela doesn't want you to get lonely or talkative."

"I am no more convinced he is my friend than that he is yours," the Denlenn said. "People like him fly whatever flag suits them. I saw my fill of them during the war. Killers, not warriors. They use us like the clip of a tri-auto."

"True enough," murmured Fenaday, a little surprised. Telisan was regular Confed military. "Is it different among your kind?"

Telisan made an odd gesture that Fenaday felt might be a sigh. "Yes, or rather it was. A Denlenn leader is expected to lead from the front. To be bravest. So we were when this war began. Our methods cost us many of our best fighters and leaders. Your kind told us this was foolish, but we would not listen. These ways served us during our wars with Dua-Denlenn. Our cousins have no honor, but at least fight with civilized restraint. Why lay waste to a world and lose the value of it for all time?

"Nothing prepared us for the Conchirri. Honor and restraint were unknown to them. We lost many battles, even some worlds, before we resigned ourselves to changing to your methods, as the Moroks already had. Your kind makes war almost into a business, a matter of calculation."

"It had been a long time since we'd had to fight," said Fenaday distantly, thinking on the long history of humanity's wars. "The big ones ended centuries ago, as the stellar Diaspora allowed many of Earth's adversaries to gain sufficient distance from each other."

"It came back to you quickly," Telisan said.

Unable to decide if this was an accusation or a compliment, Fenaday opted for silence.

Three days out from Mars, Fenaday decided to break the news of their wild venture to the crew. First, he filled all critical stations with either Mandela's people, or the few reliable members of his own crew. He ordered Shasti, Gunnar, Li, Mmok, and his HCRs into the central shuttle bay, where the rest of the crew gathered. Rigg dispersed his Air Space Assault Team troops throughout the ship to provide security.

Fenaday met the others outside the bay. Shasti had put her port clothes away and wore the same loose, sage-green, fatigue uniform as the ASAT troops. Simple and functional, it hid her fascinating curves, making it easier to concentrate around her. She carried a baton as well as a short-barreled riot gun. He assumed she'd loaded it with plastic bullets. Connery, Gunnar, and Li carried similar arms. Telisan, an expert shot, carried a laser, as did Fenaday. Mmok wore no obvious weapon, though Fenaday felt sure the cyborg had something secreted on him. His four HCRs stood around him. Magenta wore a plastic flower in her hair, more of Mmok's sardonic humor.

I would hate to believe he sleeps with the damn things, Fenaday thought.

Shasti raised an eyebrow at him. She did not smile, but again, her quirky way of looking at him made him suspect she knew what he was thinking and that it amused her.

Fenaday took a few deep breaths and led them into the shuttle bay. The buzz of conversation lowered as he mounted the hastily erected dais. Shasti stood on the deck before him, her head still level with his. The HCRs fell in on the corners of the dais. Mmok and Telisan joined him on it. Shasti's best Landing Force troops took up strategic spots in the bay.

"Not like the old days, when you could have taken the bay by yourself," he murmured, just softly enough for Shasti to hear. The barest hint of a smile touched her lips, then her face returned to its usual mask-like calm.

He looked at the crew, as unusual a collection as had ever flown space. They ran from dedicated professionals from the shadow side of the military, to adventurers, to the desperate. They all stood staring at him.

Fenaday keyed his throat mike. "You're gathered here to find out the destination of our mission. All of you signed up for the voyage knowing this was a high-risk mission. It is for this reason that the least ranked of you will make most of a lifetime's earnings on this one voyage.

"You know we are government sanctioned and sponsored. The point is—we are legitimate. We are doing something the government wants done, but does not want to risk regular forces to do."

He drew a deep breath. "We are on our way to Enshar."

The reaction was as bad as he expected. One female crewmember screamed and others cursed. Fenaday looked at them, seeing wide eyes, open mouths, terror stamped on every face.

"Silence," Telisan roared in his best parade ground voice. As if to emphasize his point, the HCRs snapped from parade rest to attention in absolute unison.

"We're dead," one crewman sobbed into the wary silence.

"We are not," said Fenaday sharply. "The command staff has no more desire to die than you do. We have brilliant doctors and scientists on board, the best robots and equipment the Confeds have and an ASAT team. They did not come here to die."

"They had a whole planetary military on Enshar," called one man. "They were wiped out. Just like the fleet that came after."

Fenaday recognized the man after a second, Greywold, a bar tough hired by Shasti to pad out the landing force. She'd been unhappy about him afterward, but they needed the gun.

"The fleet was not wiped out," Telisan replied. "I was with it. The attack on us ceased as we drew away from the planet. I will also tell you something now declassified. I took a scout below the so-called line of death. I descended to the height of the *Flamme's* orbit. The zone of death is not there."

"*Sidhe*," Fenaday said, "will not approach the planet closer than the point at which the attack on the fleet ceased. I'll take a single fighter on an atmospheric entry. If I'm not attacked, the three *Dakota* shuttles will come in for a planet landing. I'll ask for volunteers, but if I nominate you as necessary for the mission, you go.

"Understand this, *Sidhe* is a military vessel. We are under Letters of Marque and Reprisal on a military mission. This means military discipline. I will brook no dispute with our mission. I will shoot space lawyers, plain and simple."

The crisis point seemed past. Many in the crew relaxed at the news that the starship herself would not land. Others, whose specialties meant possible inclusion in the landing, stood tense, their eyes flickering around the bay as if seeking escape.

"We didn't sign up for this," Greywold called out from the back.

"You are here, you signed, you go," Fenaday stated. "That is also the last outburst I will tolerate." Behind him, Shasti brought her riot gun up; its butt rode comfortably on her hip.

"While I command the mission," Fenaday continued, waving toward Duna, "I want you to meet the sponsor of it."

Belwin Duna entered from the passageway door where he stood waiting with Li. He walked with apparent ease to the dais and stood on a box Fenaday set up for him.

"Greetings, crew of the *Sidhe*," said Belwin. "Though you do not believe it now, in times to come, each of you will be venerated as heroes among my people for participating in this great cause."

Duna delivered an impressive collection of indirection and platitudes. He acquainted them with the facts of the disaster and reminded them that in the time since the attack on the fleet, there had been no sign of any hostility on the planet. All this glossed over the fact that nothing remained on the planet to attack. The little scholar's speech calmed the crew at least for now.

Duna made much of Telisan's flight. The scholar had only learned of it after liftoff, one of Mandela's conditions on Telisan's pardon for stealing the stealth programs. When Duna learned of Telisan's flight, the hope that shone in the old scholar's eyes was painful to see. Fenaday realized that Telisan had been right to keep the information secret.

"Let me guess," Fenaday whispered to Telisan, "that sometime in his long life, he was a politician."

Telisan did not nettle as expected. "It has been a long life, as you say. He has been many things in it. Here, I think he means just to comfort. They must go to Enshar. Perhaps they go less afraid now. I tell you that he believes there is a chance, or he would not do this."

"A leader can deceive others," Fenaday replied, "but he should not deceive himself."

71

"As you wish," Telisan said. Manners forbade him to argue with his captain.

The meeting broke up, and the crew went back to their stations. For the rest of the ship's day, Fenaday worked the crew as hard as possible with maintenance, fire drills, everything else he could think of to keep them busy.

That evening, Quartermaster Dobera made sure dinner was the best food *Sidhe* could boast. Fenaday met Duna and Shasti at the entrance to the mess, leaving Telisan on the bridge standing watch.

Sidhe didn't have an officer's wardroom, but Fenaday sometimes used a large table on a raised area in the back for official functions. A steward greeted them, rushing out drinks.

"The condemned will eat a hearty meal," Johan Gunnar said.

Duna overheard the comment and looked over at Fenaday. "Your cook is good?"

"My cook," Fenaday said as they seated themselves, "insists on being referred to as Chef Marcel. He affects a terrible French accent, but he's no more French than Shasti. He's a deserter from the War. He is also a trained chef, so naturally the Confederacy drafted him for the infantry, the service arm with the highest rate of casualties."

"Yes," Shasti added. "Claiming he'd trained to prepare meals, not risk becoming one for the Conchirri, he deserted. We were refueling on Morokat when he tried to sneak aboard *Sidhe*. I caught him immediately."

"She brought him to the bridge," Fenaday said as plates were set about him. "I was reaching for the com to call MPs when he asked me if I was a betting man. He made a wager that if he could serve me one meal, I would never turn him over to the MPs. He won."

Duna laughed, his small, furry body shaking.

"The chocolate soufflé garnered him Shasti's support," Fenaday continued, reaching for a glass. "I figured hiring him was a good chance to bank a favor with my formidable new security chief. Food on *Sidhe* had been miserable."

"Good thinking," Shasti said, with a casual wave of her knife.

"At times like this," Fenaday said, "when I need to pump morale in, I'm glad to have him. Terrible accent notwithstanding."

Normally Fenaday didn't eat with the crew, but tonight it seemed best to see and be seen. Marcel, crowned with his pleated, white chef's hat, brought their food, too busy with the special meal to subject them to much of his fake French.

Fenaday scanned the room. He frowned at a group of crewman clustered around an animated Greywold. Katrina Micetich caught his look and slunk sheepishly away. Greywold held his eye for a second. He felt Shasti shift beside him. The man's eyes dropped as he suddenly discovered an interest in his meal. Fenaday turned to look at Shasti. She nodded and he knew she would keep an eye on him.

"Captain," Duna asked, missing the by-play. "How long will it be to Enshar? I keep forgetting to ask Telisan."

"Always an interesting question," Fenaday replied. "Hyperspace itself has no analog with normal space, so distances in jump don't mirror those of the normal universe. A voyage between two relatively close stars can take months of objective time. Yet, others separated by hundreds of light years, take only weeks. Hyperspace is 'thicker' or "thinner' between certain stars. Even in those jumps, the currents of hyperspace can change the length of the trip, depending on where you enter. Between some stars there is an express pipeline, as if a river's raging current helps the ship's drive. The jump to Enshar is one of these, shorter than many jumps, for all that it's over six hundred lights to your system."

"Which means?" prompted Duna.

Fenaday laughed. "Forgive the lecture, Professor. The voyage will take four weeks of actual time. We will be in hyperspace for thirty-eight days universal time."

"Not that we will experience that," Duna mused. "It never fails to amaze me how one experiences nothing in hyperjump, not even dreams. I think that thirty-eight days will bring us to the city of Gigor in the spring."

"Yes," Fenaday replied, butterflies hitting his stomach at the thought. In Gigor sat the dead Confederation shuttles. They lay there now, awaiting him.

S*idhe* accelerated outward from Sol system. Onboard, Fenaday and Telisan continued working up the crew. Belwin Duna did all he could to restore morale. Always available, he spoke to everyone and answered every question. Fenaday's instinct proved correct, the old scholar had once been a politician. He worked the crowd. Before long many of the crew began to see themselves as heroes on a quest.

Wherever the little scholar went, an HCR, or Mmok himself, followed. Clearly the cyborg had orders to keep Duna safe. Fenaday worried about the Enshari's safety as well, but there was no one better suited to protect Duna than Mmok and his unsleeping watchdogs. Mmok's sentry duty also freed up Shasti's limited number of reliables to watch Mmok, Telisan, and everyone else.

Sidhe reached the edge of Terra's system and the FTL drive began its buildup. The small quantum singularity that provided the ship's artificial gravity now bent the fabric of space time. *Sidhe* breached that fabric and leapt into hyperspace, heading outward to Enshar.

Chapter Eight

Fenaday groaned as reemergence brought him back to the land of the living. "I think living," he muttered, fighting dizziness. He sometimes felt that he left larger and larger pieces of himself in hyperspace each jump. Maybe one day he wouldn't come back at all. Vision returned slowest, lagging sound, which started as a roar in one's ears then muted to the normal operating sounds of a starship. There was nothing to smell but canned, tasteless air. Gradually, shapes began to form before his eyes, followed by a gray light and finally color.

"Status," he croaked.

"No targets on scan," Sharon Hafel said, her own voice rough and hoarse.

"Ship speed is .66C," Nye added. "Momentum from Sol system is still with us."

"Weapons armed and ready," Wardell said.

"Engines and ship systems nominal," Telisan said.

Fenaday's stomach lurched, and he only partly smothered the groan.

"The long fast ones are the worst," said Telisan, standing beside him.

"At least have the decency to look ill," Fenaday groused. The

Denlenn seemed fresh and ready for anything. Fenaday, as usual after a jump, wanted a shower and some sleep. Jump was hard on the human body. Why, no one knew. Dobera and his department would be running through the ship, handing out food and drinks laced with restoratives. Sickbay would have a few people overcome by jump sickness.

"Well," Fenaday said, "no immediate threat nearby. Still. Bernard, Hafel, do you have that holographic camouflage online?"

"Aye, sir," Bernard answered. She was one of Mandela's people, a brilliant young comp tech. "System just came back up. Wish I'd been able to look at the machinery itself, though."

A thought Fenaday shared. Mandela's shipwrights had cannibalized a large forward compartment and sealed it. He had no idea what was in it. Gandhi had told him on his final call that if the seal was broken, they might as well not come back.

"Engage holographic camouflage. Let's see if Mandela's expensive toy works," Fenaday ordered.

Sidhe went into stealth mode. Her holographic generators slowly cloaked the warship's hull with the appearance of an asteroid. Other stealth devices installed by the Navy reduced her radar signature by fifty percent. *Not invisible, but comfortingly obscure*, Fenaday thought.

"Helm," Fenaday said, "put this solar system on the main screen. I want constant update from scan."

Micetich manipulated controls, and *Sidhe's* main screen fractured into a computer schematic overlaid with multiple views in long and short scan. On it they could see their ship, arrowing in from beyond the orbit of the twelfth world. Star charts listed the primary as Britton 335, known locally as Mur. A G5 star, larger and hotter than Sol, it sleeted out more radiation. Moonless Enshar orbited farther from Mur than Earth did from Sol. Duna had told him that the higher radiation count factored in the development of burrowing creatures on Enshar.

"Communications have interrogated and received a microburst data dump from the master satellite at the system's edge," Hafel advised.

"Okay, shut down," Fenaday said. Other than that microburst

with the satellite, *Sidhe* emitted no radiation. Fenaday wanted to run silent.

"Pass the information to Duna and the science team," he told Telisan. "I'm sure they're clawing the paint off the lab walls."

Behind him, Dobera and a steward entered the bridge accompanied by Shasti. As usual, Shasti showed no sign of any discomfort from the star jump. She pulled a coffee and protein bar off Dobera's cart and handed it to Fenaday. His stomach rebelled at the idea of food, but he welcomed the coffee. Taking the cup, he sat back with a sigh. There'd be little to do until the scientists finished their initial work on the satellite information.

Answers came back quickly. The information, only minutes old, added nothing to what Mandela supplied them.

"Well," Fenaday said, looking at the screen. "Lafayette, we are here."

———

The starship began braking gently. Fenaday aimed for the two large gas giants in mid system. *Sidhe* would use their gravity to brake further in order to enter the inner system at a sane speed. Star systems change and the charts on Enshar had not been updated since the disaster. Fenaday didn't plan on inhaling a chunk of rock at relativistic speed, so the voyage to Enshar from the system's edge would take two weeks. Two very long weeks.

Fenaday again sought to fill the time with drill and work. Distractions only helped a little. As they neared their destination, Duna found much of the friendliness toward him evaporating. The crew no longer felt heroic; they felt cold, scared, and mean. *Sidhe* began to wind like a watch spring.

———

The sound of shouting brought Shasti running toward the mess hall. She raced in, spotting a mass of struggling men and women around the bolted-down tables. Before she could even shout an order, a slim form burst in from the opposite hatchway, slamming into the knot of crewman and scattering bodies with bone-breaking power.

HCR, she realized. "Freeze," Shasti shouted. "Freeze, now!"

The room stilled immediately. The HCR held one man down, his arm levered into an agonizing position.

"That was good advice," said a droll voice. Shasti turned. Mmok had entered from the other side, trailed by another of the deadly machines and by Daniel Rigg.

"It wasn't advice," Shasti growled, stalking forward. "That was an order. Stand at attention." She looked the group over. To her annoyance they were mostly her LEAFs, though all were new hires. One of Rigg's ASATs, a powerful looking, shorthaired man stood facing them. From the bruises on the Landing Force Troops, he'd given better than he'd got.

"What the hell is going on here?" Shasti demanded. They all looked at the floor, like children. But there was nothing child-like in the danger of riot and disorder in the small, delicately balanced ecology of a starship. Men died for upsetting it.

"I won't ask again," Shasti said, walking among them. She smelled fear on one woman and turned to glare into her eyes.

The trooper couldn't hold her stare. "It was Greywold, Commander. He said that the ASATs were talking us down. Saying that we were trash…"

Greywold, Shasti thought. *I am going to regret not trusting my second guess on that one.* She scanned the LF troops. "Excellent," Shasti observed. "You took advice from a man who cut and ran on a fight." The chagrined troopers looked about. Greywold was nowhere to be seen.

"And what's your story?" Dan Rigg snapped.

Shorthair snapped to attention. "Provocation, sir."

"Soldier, when you are provoked, you come see me. You don't go hand-to-hand on duty and in space."

"Sir. Yes, sir. No excuse, sir."

Mmok laughed silently. "Doesn't look like your fellow was doing too badly, Dan. Maybe Commander Rainhell ought to thank you for giving her slackers a lesson."

"Shut up, Mmok," Shasti said. "And get your machine off that man."

Mmok's lips thinned. His one eye narrowed.

"Orders on punishment, ma'am," Rigg interjected. "Or do you want to leave that to me?" He moved to stand next to Shasti and stared at Mmok. "Discipline needs to be maintained, now more than ever. Right, sir?"

Mmok glanced away from Shasti. His sardonic face slid back into place. Behind him, in response to an unseen signal, the HCR released the trooper's arm. It walked up to stand at Mmok's shoulder, in a not-so-subtle warning not to push him.

Shasti considered. Rigg was ostensibly her number two and he'd just backed her. She and Fenaday suspected that Mmok had been given authority to command the ASATs if it came to a break, but until then, both Rigg and Mmok reported to her. Still, the ASAT was clearly the more approachable and used to dealing with standard humans.

"That might be as well, Mr. Rigg," she said. "My plan was to space all of them and use the food and air on the more deserving." Her cool eyes rolled over the pale and nervous crewman.

"I'm sure Sergeant Rask and the Toks can find a lot of double duty for them," Rigg said. "Maybe with five hundred laps in full gear around the hanger as well." He turned to the ASAT. "You got any complaint about leading that little run, mister?"

"Sir. No, sir," said Shorthair.

"Lead them down there. Double time, mister." The ASAT saluted and the LF troops shuffled out after him, leaving the three humans and two robots. Stewards appeared from the kitchen to clean up the mess.

"The next person," Shasti said, "who breaks discipline is going to take a bullet to the skull. I am not losing control of the deck of this ship."

"Agreed," Rigg said. "Hard though it may be for you to hear, if there's a problem, it will be among your new people. Your older hands, particularly your trouble team, are as reliable as my folks, but the newbies..."

Shasti nodded. "I've got my best people dispersed at all critical areas."

"May not be enough," Rigg said.

"My people," Mmok said, grinning and stressing the word people, "never sleep and they never stress. They're the happiest of warriors."

"Keep one here then," she said, feeling ambiguous about having to rely on the cyborg. "Cover Duna, the bridge, and engineering. I'll get Captain Fenaday to clear an HCR for bridge access."

He gave her a sloppy salute.

"We have another problem," Rigg said. "I was coming to see you when I heard the scrap."

"What?"

Rigg looked embarrassed. "I'm afraid that I didn't list a weapon when we logged them into the arms room."

"You mean the personal .38 slug-throwers you and Rask hid?" she asked.

Rigg's mouth hung open. Mmok gave a low whistle, seeming to enjoy Rigg's discomfiture. "You're busted," he observed.

"If you think you can hide something from me on my own ship, you're mistaken," she said, her face cold and foreboding.

"Yes, ma'am. My weapon is missing. I kept it locked in my personal locker. Someone picked the lock and went through my stuff last night."

"Twice," Shasti said, folding her arms across her chest. "The first time it was me. Last night was someone sloppy."

"So we have a loose gun aboard," Mmok said. "Suspects?"

"Greywold," Rigg said. "His record shows priors for theft. It got him thrown out of the Deutsche Brigade. I searched his locker, but he's not dumb enough to keep it there."

"HCRs can find it," Mmok said.

"Get them on it," she said.

"We'll turn both weapons in to the arms room, after mine's found," Rigg said.

"Keep them," she said. "But keep them on you at all times from now on." She walked toward the entrance, then paused. "Just like Mr. Mmok keeps his palm laser on him."

Mmok looked startled for a second. "One for you."

Hours later the pistol showed up, hidden behind an air duct.

The thief had been careful enough to keep prints off of it, but Shasti had little doubt of the thief's identity. It didn't take her long to make up her mind about what to do about it.

———

Two days before Enshar orbit, Fenaday was on his way to the bridge when Shasti called him on their private channel.

"Fenaday here, secure."

"Meet me in Arms Four," she said and clicked off.

Worried by the cryptic call, he hurried to the arms room near the main hanger deck. Their combined landing force, including Mmok's robots, had suited up and was outside on the hull, practicing ship-boarding tactics. Shasti should be with them.

Instead, he found her in her small office near the weapons storage area, suited up but with her helmet off, watching a security monitor. She looked up from the monitor as he entered. On it he could see ASATs and LEAFs scrambling over the ship's hull.

"What's up?" he asked.

She gestured at the screen. "Greywold."

"Damn. He acting up again?" Fenaday said wearily.

"For the last time," she said grimly. "I have him out on the tail end of the ship, alone. I need you to make it sound like I'm still onboard. I'm a simulated casualty in the war game. They won't be looking for me. I'll need a minute to get there, kill him, and get back. I'll make it look enough like an accident so we won't have problems when we get back to the Confederacy. People will get the message anyway."

Ice formed in his stomach. *I've grown too comfortable around her,* he thought. *She's not people, as I know people. Christ, I used to think the corporate lawyers were cutthroats. I wonder if someday I'll find myself on the losing side of some such calculation with her?*

"No," he blurted.

"What?"

"You can't just kill him," he said, trying to keep the shock out of his voice.

"He's a liability," she said impatiently. "You know we stand

81

balanced on a knife's edge here. We need control and he threatens that control. He also provides me with a tailor-made chance to enforce discipline and lose nothing more than a weakling."

They stared at each other.

"Find another way," he said.

"You're being a fool," she said. "He's more useful this way."

"No," he said quietly. "Don't bring this up again." He turned and left, knees shaking.

———

On the eleventh day of the voyage in from the system's edge, they came within direct range of Enshar with their own more sophisticated instruments. Fenaday stood on the bridge, with a full crew, plus Duna, Mmok, and Rigg. Shasti was also there. She and Fenaday were still recovering from the proposed assassination of the day before, carefully stepping in the delicate dance they'd done before when one or the other overstepped a boundary.

The main view screen lit. Simultaneously several parts of the screen began to display different views, some visual, some radar or infra-red.

"Enshar," Duna said raptly. The word held a devotion about it. "Enshar, with my own eyes."

"Massive radar contact," announced Hafel, "right where expected." The screen switched to a debris field. Nothing recognizable showed, just points of reflected light.

"My God," Katrina Micetich said. "I saw *Bifor* Station once from a freighter. It was huge. You could see it from the ground in daylight. What could destroy something like that? *Murbicko* was even larger than *Bifor*."

"And it's gone too," Fenaday snapped. "Ancient history, Micetich. I want a geosynchronous orbit over the city of Gigor in the Northern States. Coordinates are in the computer. Set up the course, Mr. Nye, and transfer it to her station.

"Hafel, keep a close eye on radar. There's a lot of junk in orbit. I don't want to be holed.

"Gunners, keep a radar lock as well. Open fire on anything

vectoring in on us that does not emit current IFF. Weapons are free."

Twenty minutes of maneuvering inserted *Sidhe* into orbit at a height of one hundred fifty kilometers. She ghosted over a world emptied of intelligent life. Animals moved on the face of the world, infesting its cities and fields. The domed cities stood largely intact. Little of the ruination could be seen although rents and burned places marred some domes.

"We're coming up on initial orbit over Gigor base," Nye said. "Gigor was home to Enshar's space forces and it's where the Confederate fleet's shuttles landed."

Shasti gestured with a long, elegant finger. "There they are."

"Maximum magnification, Hafel," Fenaday said. *Sidhe's* optics could focus on a can of rations from her height. Three *Wolverine* assault shuttles from the original landing force Telisan had accompanied, leapt into stark focus. Other than being overgrown by grasses, they seemed unchanged from the moment of their landing over three years earlier.

"Deploy probes," ordered Fenaday. These dropped from *Sidhe*, parachuting to landings around Gigor and other locations. It took the rest of the first orbit to deploy all ten of them.

"The only remarkable thing about the probes," Mourner announced after the second orbit, "is their survival. They've landed and begun sensing—air: normal, water: normal, radiation: normal, soil: normal, no detectable biohazard, and no detectable chemical weapons. It seems that, other than for the overnight extermination of the Enshari people, Enshar itself is a normal world."

As they continued to cruise over the planet-sized tomb, Fenaday watched Duna's joy at seeing his home evaporate. The old scholar gazed at the world that gave birth to his species and then murdered its offspring. Telisan stood next to him, a hand on the Enshari's shoulder, his face drawn with worry. Duna had not left the bridge since they reached instrument range ten hours before.

"Belwin," Telisan said, "perhaps some rest—"

"No, my young friend. I am here to fight whatever it is that has taken our planet, and that means a study of the disaster. I draw great solace from the fact that our probes, unlike the fleet probes, have not gone inactive. Still, against the weight of the empty world below, that fact seems a slim reed on which to rest one's hope for survival."

The two walked over to Fenaday's chair. "What now, Captain?" Duna asked.

"A proper government research vessel," Fenaday said in a low voice, "might spend weeks or months studying Enshar before attempting a landing. Even as well-equipped as we are, we don't have those resources. I also have doubts about keeping *Sidhe's* crew in line while so close to Enshar for an extended period. The ship is a powder keg. In the end, regardless of tests, only one thing will tell us if Enshar is habitable—a landing."

"I fear that you are right, Captain," Duna said.

"We'll see what the scientists have after the first day's orbit," Fenaday concluded.

———

Another day passed. They learned nothing they did not know before. After the end of their second day in orbit, Fenaday called a staff meeting. The doctors, scientists, and technicians gave sometimes lengthy reports. The information summed up easily.

"We're getting nothing from orbit," Fenaday said. "Animal tests won't tell us anything. We can see plenty of animals from orbit. The sole new factor is the continued existence of our electronic probes on world. That fact does not change my opinion; it's not safe to land the *Sidhe*. We will proceed with the final plan. I'll take a *Wildcat* fighter and attempt a landing. If anything threatens, I'll abort, if I can, and that will be the end of this attempt on Enshar. If nothing goes wrong, then I'll go for a landing. Provided I am not attacked within an hour of that landing, the shuttles under Commander Rainhell will land three hours later. Our force will establish a perimeter on world and begin the investigation."

The room stirred at his announcement. Some faces bore eager expressions; others looked at him as if he was already dead.

"Any questions?" he asked.

"Yes," began Telisan, "though it is not a question. There are two fighters on the *Sidhe*. I wish to take the other one and accompany you. One man alone cannot face whatever is down there."

"If there is something down there," Fenaday replied, "all you could do is die with me. One is enough to find out."

"No," replied Telisan equally firmly. "You signed me as executive officer based on my experience as a wing commander in the war. Take my advice now. I would never send a single pilot on such a task. You cannot watch your back and perform a mission. That is what wingmen are for.

"There is an old saying among my people," Telisan continued. "'One man alone on a wall is half a man. Two men can be an army.' I tell you," he finished, with more passion than Fenaday had seen the easy-going Denlenn exhibit before, "that you cannot face this alone. There is no one else aboard who can handle a fighter with a tenth my skill. You need a wingman. I am that wingman."

"Makes sense," Mmok chipped in.

"It does," Duna added. "I wish it did not."

"I know you lost friends there—" Fenaday began.

"This has nothing to do with that," interrupted the Denlenn. "I swore I would serve the *Sidhe* as I served the *Empress Aran*. I am of the Selen clan, which would mean little to you but much among Denleni. I have striven all my life to meet that standard. This is my first chance to begin to make payment on that promise. For the sake of my own soul, I must begin to make good on my oath.

"We fight to save a race from extinction. I will not have it said that I held back any measure of strength or will in such a cause. My life is of no account against what we seek to accomplish. I would give it gladly to advance our cause but an inch."

There was silence in the room. Fenaday looked the Denlenn in the eye. *I forgot such people actually exist,* he thought.

"Telisan," he said, "I would be honored to have you on my wing. Thank you."

———

The Denlenn inclined his head, mostly to hide his relief. He had given an oath both to Duna and to Fenaday and been caught between them. He had done little on his pledge to the human. Now, at last, came a chance for redemption. If Fenaday died because Duna's suspicions—mad though they seemed—were true, he would not die alone. If anything could be done to save his captain, Telisan would be there to do it. Selen honor demanded nothing less.

Fenaday and Rainhell stood at the same moment, exchanging a long glance. She seemed on the verge of saying something, then turned away.

———

A fter the staff meeting, Fenaday retired to his cabin. In fourteen hours, he would drop into Enshar's atmosphere. He tried to read but could not concentrate. Sleep eluded him.

He paced in his cabin, the largest on board but still small. In one corner of the bedroom hung a beautiful photo of Lisa, taken soon after their marriage. He looked at it for several minutes. Sometimes, he could almost feel her presence in the room. Better media existed for such images. For a while, he had a holographic imager that would show her walking and talking from tapes they made. One day he caught himself talking to the image as if it were real. A pleasant little fantasy, he told himself, he'd only indulge himself for a few seconds. The holo played for hours before he recognized it as the first step in a descent into madness. Tonight, he looked, remembered and felt nothing. The picture remained just a picture on a wall. He was alone, and the room was too quiet.

"I'm never going to find you," he said to the picture.

Fenaday fled the room. He began to walk the *Sidhe's* corridors. The ship ran on night watch with its smallest crew. Torn between his desire to see people and the need not to be seen in this state, he drifted through the vessel. He dropped in on some stations pretending to be inspecting. He didn't stay long or talk much. For a vessel that looked so big from the outside, *Sidhe* held few places to go. He stopped in the mess for a cup of coffee and found no one there he could talk to.

Eventually, he ended up in the corridor outside Shasti's cabin on

C deck. Fenaday stood there for a few minutes, irresolute. Then he turned away. *It's not fair and it's not right,* he thought.

The door whooshed open behind him. He turned to find her standing in the doorway. She wore a kimono-style robe, black silk pants, and looked at him with no readable expression.

"Hi," he said, feeling foolish. "I was just walking by."

"You've been there for nearly three minutes," she stated. "Did you think I would leave the corridor outside my own cabin unmonitored? That would make me a rather poor security chief, don't you think?"

"Come in," she added, when he did not respond.

"No. No, it's all right," he said, embarrassed. "Not your problem."

"Robert," she said, quietly but with force, "come in."

He entered the cabin, and the door sealed behind him. They stood in the low light by the doorway, looking at each other.

Fenaday dropped his eyes, then sighed. "I think," he said slowly, "I am going to be dead in a few hours." He looked up. "I don't want to be alone."

Shasti said nothing, but reached forward for him. He tilted back his head to kiss her. His arms wound around her body.

"No pasts," she said, when they separated, "no tomorrows, and no promises. Just tonight." He nodded and she led him to her bed. They lay side by side, touching. More than two years had passed since they'd been together. He wanted to take his time; it might be the last chance for any tenderness.

Shasti's body was as splendid as he remembered. Night black hair cascaded to her small waist. Her perfect symmetry kept her powerful body from appearing over-muscled. Nearly seven feet of goddess and here with him. Fenaday was glad for the low light. He felt ape-like by comparison.

She opened her robe, guided his hand inside, filling it with a full breast. As his fingers slowly caressed her nipple, she made a soft sound of pleasure. Her mouth came against his and their breathing quickened. Clothes dropped to the floor and their bodies began to move together as one.

She drove all thoughts of the future from his mind as he reveled in the warmth between them. Shasti responded as if they were created only for each other. The times before were exciting, but not like this. *Perhaps,* he thought, *it's the nearness of danger.* He didn't care. He'd gone so long without anyone's touch.

They made love s over the next few hours. At first tenderly, then a frantic mood seemed to take Shasti. She growled, even biting a little. Her legs clasped him with their full strength as if she wanted to pull him into her forever. The next time she was more careful, as if to display her skill, her almost perfect muscular control.

She wanted to start again. He smiled at her. "I'm not eighteen, you know."

"No," she replied, nuzzling him. "Not very breakable either."

"Good thing," he said fighting a yawn. "Or you'd have broken something on me the second time."

"That a complaint?" she asked idly.

He smiled. "God, no. But I could use something to drink."

Shasti slid off him, heading for the small refrigerator in her cabin. *Just watching her walk is an experience,* he thought. For the first time, he noticed the room. It had changed from its formerly Spartan look to something surprisingly feminine. A katana and wakizashi sat in their traditional holders by one wall, but draperies and indirect lighting softened the room.

At that point he noticed an easel and, curious, slipped out of bed for a closer look. He saw a forested, wintry landscape. In the middle of it padded a wolf, threading his way through the trees. The animal seemed to watch him wherever he moved. Brushes below the unfinished piece made it unquestionably hers. The style matched that of the two other landscapes on the walls.

She came up behind him, stretching an arm over his shoulder with a Bellerian fruit drink. "They aren't very good," she said.

"Not true," he protested. "They are. I can almost feel his fur."

"I've tried to learn," she said. "I take lessons when we are not on board, and there are disks for the voyages. I realized one morning that all my training—all my life—was about killing. I wanted something else, something of my own. I want to be more than a bio-weapon."

He looked up over his shoulder at her but could think of little to say.

She moved past him and picked up a brush, seeming to study it. "I have a question for you."

"Ask away."

"I wanted to resolve our discipline problems by eliminating Greywold. It's a sensible move. Eliminate a malcontent, quell further dissent. I didn't understand your reaction. I know you were upset. Why?"

Fenaday sipped his drink before replying. "I'm not judging you, Shasti. You've never told me much about your past, but I see who you are and what you do. It tells me about a hard life. Who am I to judge anyone anyway? I used to be a spoiled rich kid. I didn't learn about want until...well you know about that.

"Despite everything that I've survived in the last few years, I'm not really tough enough for this job. I just can't have a man killed in cold blood. This isn't the sort of thing I learned growing up. I studied how to run ships, balance trade ledgers, make a profit for the line. Murder's not in me. Maybe it should be. In a lot of ways, you're more fit to command *Sidhe* than I am. I guess it's not the sort of thing I could do and look in the mirror each morning."

"I still don't understand," she said. Sadness underlay her words. "I'm almost an artificial life form, Robert. I sometimes wonder how much of what makes a real human has been left out of me."

He smiled. "Being ordinary isn't all it's cracked up to be. I'm plenty ordinary. Sometimes I think it might be great to be one of the men from your planet. Wouldn't you prefer a partner more in your scale?" He stopped. Her face had gone rigid.

"No," she said in a harsh whisper.

"Sorry, I didn't mean to upset you."

"No," she repeated much more softly. "No pasts here tonight. Not yours and, assuredly, not mine."

He finished his drink quietly.

"I feel I could sleep for a few hours now," he said trying for lightness.

"Good," she replied, also trying to close the awkwardness of the moment.

"Do you mind sharing? I don't think I snore."

Shasti gave him a frank look. "I want you to stay. I don't want to be alone either. I guess I am at least that human."

They slid back into the bed and lay next to each other. Fenaday dropped into sleep almost immediately.

Shasti, who needed far less sleep than an ordinary human, lay awake for a while. Memories she had never shared with anyone, surged in her, tearing at her nerves. Finally, she invoked mental disciplines learned long ago and banished her past. She altered her body chemistry and entered REM sleep by an act of will.

Shasti woke, her mind sharp and alert, at exactly six a.m. as she'd ordered her body to awaken. She rose out of the bed smoothly.

Fenaday stirred next to her. It took him longer to wake up and his head ached. He had that skittery feeling of too little sleep and too much caffeine. Morning seemed somehow unreal.

Shasti finished in the shower before he could get his mind together. He smiled at her wanly. As usual, she didn't smile, but she seemed well-pleased with the world. Looking at her he thought, *One wouldn't think extinction might be only a few hours away.*

Fenaday got into the shower, letting hot water beat down on his head. He wanted to stay there forever. The idea of taking a fighter down seemed insane. More than ever, he wanted to live. Despite everything, he wanted desperately to live.

Shasti pulled the curtain back. He looked up at her.

"Time to go?" she asked, as if it were out to a movie. Then he noticed her flight suit.

"Where do you think you're going?" he asked, turning off the shower.

"One of the *Wildcats* is a two-seater," she replied. "We'll take that one."

"No, you don't," he said. "There's no reason for you to get killed in this."

"Assume we aren't killed," Shasti said, throwing him a towel. "Once down on the planet, it'll be hours before the shuttles arrive. Telisan is incompetent in ground fighting, and you need me to watch your back."

"No," he said, firmly.

"Has it occurred to you," she replied, "that arguing with me while you are stark naked and soaked doesn't enhance your authority? See you on the flight deck."

Before he could summon a reply, she left. He could either run naked down the corridor after her, or have a major blowout with her in front of everyone on the flight deck. She had him mouse-trapped.

Fenaday found his clothes and returned to his cabin to get into proper gear for the flight. A cup of Irish tea sufficed for breakfast as he didn't want much of anything on his nervous stomach. Fenaday considered adding a shot of courage to the tea, then decided against it. Rummaging through the weapons locker a cautious captain learned to keep in his quarters, Fenaday chose a heavy laser pistol and a tri-auto carbine. Then he reached for his father's ancient Scottish dirk. It seemed a pitiful weapon to take against what had devastated the planet below, but there was no guarantee that more modern weapons would fare any better. Perhaps, as his father had thought, there might be luck in the ancient blade.

Fenaday looked around the cabin, realizing he would probably not see it again. He walked to the bedroom and looked at his wife's picture. "Goodbye," he said, silently adding a plea for forgiveness. Then he left for the flight deck.

When he got there, he found Shasti on a ladder, making alterations to the ejection seat in the stubby matte black *Wildcat*. Her oversized frame meant he would have even less leg room than usual in the small fighter.

A sizable crowd gathered in the hanger bay. Hangar crew prepared the fighters, which had been brought in from the wing mech-link stations for a thorough check. The other shuttles, large *Dakota* class transports stood ready as well. They'd launch and assume an orbit for a later landing if disaster didn't overtake the fighters. A number of the crew gathered to watch them launch. This deprived Fenaday of his last chance to have a quiet battle with Shasti.

Not, he reflected, *that it was likely to work*. He walked up to her. "You fight dirty, you know that."

She looked down at him. "It's how I was raised," she replied in all seriousness.

Chapter Nine

"Ready?" he asked Shasti as he tightened the straps on his helmet.

"Always," she replied.

Fenaday pulled back on the stick, and the *Wildcat* fighter lifted from *Sidhe's* main shuttle bay. He deftly piloted the fighter out the pressure doors midway up on the frigate's blood-red hull then rolled the *Wildcat* on her side. Fenaday looked back at the ship where he'd spent the last few years and felt a pang. *Sidhe* was the closest thing he had left to a home. The frigate floated above him, beautifully lit by Mur's starlight. Right now, with Enshar so close, he wished himself safely back aboard her.

"Perez to Fenaday."

He keyed open the mike. "Fenaday here."

"Communication check."

"I read you five by five, *Sidhe*. Scramblers on, we should be secure." He'd left the engineer in command. Perez was not trained to navigate a ship, but Fenaday considered him more reliable than the inexperienced Micetich. In any event, he'd taken the precaution of locking the ship's computers with codes to prevent anyone from taking *Sidhe* out of orbit for several weeks.

"Telisan to Fenaday, checking in."

"Read you, Telisan," he said, concentrating on the entry window for the dead world below them. He planned a steep and fast approach.

"He must be a good formation flyer," Shasti said.

"Why do you say that?" he asked absently.

"Because I can see the color of his eyes from here, kind of a yellow gold," she said.

Fenaday looked over his shoulder at his wingman. "Eek."

Shasti was slightly exaggerating, very slightly. There was at least a five-meter separation.

"Fenaday to Telisan."

"Read you."

"I'm not used to being much closer than a few kilometers to another object in space. Much as I appreciate the company, how about one hundred meters separation?"

The Denlenn's laugh sounded over the headset. "One hundred meters? I'll have to fail you out of flight school. Why, we are so far apart now, I am deprived of much of the view of the beautiful Shasti Rainhell. Still, I swore an oath to obey you, so one hundred meters it is. I only hope that no one I know sees me in such a sloppy formation." Telisan's fighter slid smoothly out of view.

"Is everyone enjoying this trip but me?" Fenaday muttered.

"I could use more leg room," Shasti said.

"You can keep quiet," he snapped back. "You should be safely back on *Sidhe*."

"I am where I chose to be," she replied unperturbed. "There is little point running from death. It finds you anyway."

"If I had my choice," Fenaday said, "death would have to spend a good deal of time looking and wear out a few sets of boots chasing."

Telemetry from the frigate showed their fighters on course for the landing window. Fenaday engaged his heat shield, watching it slide over the canopy. He readied the fighter for atmospheric entry. With her nose pointed toward Enshar, the *Wildcat* began to heat from atmospheric friction. Communications cut out due to interference. They slipped into the quiet time of entry. Whatever happened now would be known only to them.

They rode down in silence and the increasing heat that the fighter's life support could not entirely dispel. Finally, the temperature began to lessen, and the canopy automatically retracted. They'd entered the ionosphere of Enshar about one hundred and twenty kilometers up. The fighter's nose lost its cherry glow as its superconducting material shed heat. They coasted high in the clear sky, still a midnight blue due to the nearness of space. Fenaday had timed their landing for ten minutes after sunrise at Gigor. They were coming in from the west, so the land below them lay shrouded in darkness.

"Fenaday to Telisan, status?"

"All in order."

"Fenaday to Perez. Any reaction to our entry?"

"Negative and you are well below the height at which *Flamme* was destroyed. So far, so good, Captain."

They continued their downward path. As they came into thicker atmosphere, the shuttles began to cut silver contrails through the starlit sky. Fenaday smiled as he looked back at his wingman. Telisan's *Wildcat* looked brave, riding its contrail. A last moment of beauty to take with him if they were struck down.

———

Thousands of feet below the *Wildcats* lay the tiny, desolate remnants of a farmhouse in the town of Smarr. The night lay cool and still. Suddenly on the edge of the field, dust, twigs, and leaves stirred as if in a storm. For only a second, the whirling debris formed a shape. The shape faced heavenward, as if looking at the contrails. Then it dissipated, as if it had never been. There was not a breath of wind in the night. All returned to stillness.

Traveling eastward, the fighters raced over the horizon.

———

"There's Gigor," Fenaday said. The sun cleared the horizon, and its rays lit the tops of trees and buildings, leaving the field still cloaked in purple shadow. He heard Shasti's seat creak as she leaned

94

forward to look beyond the backrest of his seat. Fenaday put the *Wildcat* in a slow circle at a height of four hundred meters. Shasti and he looked out at the devastated base. Gigor base extended for tens of kilometers. The beige and yellow Enshari buildings in the distance had the squat and unlovely utilitarian look favored by governments. Beyond them, toward the city proper, lay the domes and half-domes preferred by the Enshari. Shattered glass in those buildings splintered and threw back the sunlight.

"Looks worse than it did from orbit," she said.

"Yeah," Fenaday said. "No question that the base was attacked. By what, I can't imagine. The pattern of destruction doesn't resemble that from an airburst nuclear weapon. Nothing else I know of—not even a mass driver—creates destruction like this."

"Only a few military spaceships were based at Gigor," Shasti said. "Most Navy traffic used the port at the capital city of Barjan."

Fenaday pointed. "There's the Navy area. It's completely destroyed." They had seen all this from orbit, but it lacked the effect of viewing it with their own eyes.

"Notice something?" asked Shasti.

"Yeah," Fenaday replied. "Those shuttles on the apron look like they were cut down by a laser fired from ground level. See that neat slice on the metal of that green and white hospital shuttle? It's cut almost in half. Whatever it was started striking the ground at a low angle, bubbling the apron."

"Energy weapons don't work that way," Shasti said. "Why use massive quantities of power to cut metal when a kinetic weapon does it cheaper and faster? Lasers are for burning flesh, starting fires, and damaging sensitive instruments—"

"These are a few of your favorite things," Fenaday murmured.

Shasti ignored the comment. "Well, this isn't Conchirri work. If they had energy weapons like this, we would all be dinner."

Fenaday brought the *Wildcat* to a hover near the edge of the apron close to the barracks. The sun had risen enough to light the field. A brilliant, dark-blue ground cover, reminiscent of pansies, dotted some of the nearby tarmac.

"Let's get this over with," he said tightly. "Are you ready, Shasti?"

"Locked and loaded," she said, putting her tri-auto in her lap.

"Telisan, this is Fenaday. I'm going in. Keep circling. If anything happens, run for it. That is an order."

"Of course," replied Telisan. The Denlenn's easy answer made Fenaday suspect Telisan was simply humoring him.

"Fenaday to *Sidhe*, we are landing."

The fighter landed smoothly, blowing dust and debris away from the *Wildcat*. Fenaday throttled back the engines, but didn't cut them off. He kept the HOTAS stick, which controlled thrust and weapons, in his right hand. Fenaday looked to starboard, Shasti to port. The fighter's swivel-mounted guns followed the motion of his eyes. The Confed shuttles from the first expedition landed only sixty-three seconds before being overwhelmed by whatever killed their crews. Fenaday didn't look at the clock. He scanned every shadow, dreading the sight of a dust cloud similar to the one that enveloped the Confederate shuttles three years ago. Telisan circled above, equally vigilant.

From Perez's station aboard *Sidhe*, the engineer announced, "Thirty seconds."

Fenaday kept his eyes on the ground. His heart pounded, and his mouth felt dry. "Nothing in sight," he reported. To his own surprise, his voice sounded calm.

"All clear here," Shasti said. She didn't even have the grace to sound concerned.

"Same," Telisan reported. "Nothing on motion sensors."

"Forty-five seconds."

For an instant, Fenaday thought about saying something to Shasti, something about the night before. He snapped a quick glance into the one of the mirrors. She stared out the canopy, catlike, intent, totally focused on here and now.

He returned his attention to the field.

"Sixty seconds."

Fenaday held his breath, his finger on the trigger.

"Seventy seconds, Captain. Congratulations on a new world record."

The breath left his body in a whoosh.

"Okay," he said, voice shaking slightly. "I'm heading into over-heat, initiating engine shutdown."

"Telisan, keep circling. Perez, start the shuttles down. Tell Karass he is to abort if at any time we lose contact before landing."

"Pop the canopy," Shasti said. "I'd like to breathe some fresh air."

Fenaday hit the release, and the canopy whirred upward and back. He unbelted, then removed the bulky flight helmet and stood in the cockpit of the fighter, drawing his laser pistol. A breeze blew across the ruined spacefield. It felt wonderful, sifting through the flight suit to reveal that he'd been sweating. The wind also brought the sounds of trees and leaves but nothing that spoke of animal life.

He stretched stiff muscles. Mur climbed overhead into a partly clouded sky, its light still stronger than Sol's. Fenaday put on an unbreakable shooting visor and a ship's cap. Shasti did not need a visor; her eyes could cope with greater extremes.

The first thing that hits you on an alien world, he thought, *are smells. Not because they are alien, but because they are absent from ship air.* Enshar smelled like trees, rain, and dirt. Brilliant, lush green foliage edged the spacefield. The soil, what he could see of it, looked rather ordinary—if somewhat dark—compared to the brilliant vegetation in the distance. The apron of the field near the *Wildcat* seemed in reasonably good condition.

Sidhe's shuttles wouldn't arrive until they could line up on their own entry window, hours from now. Fenaday thought about staying in the fighter, waiting on the shuttles with their equipment and people to arrive. He also thought of other things. For the last few years he had shipped with people who did not mean a damn to him. The universe would generally be better off without most of his crews.

It's different now, he thought. *Sidhe* had accumulated some regulars he cared about. While he still hated Mandela's guts, the people the spymaster sent were good people, particularly Dr. Mourner and her team. Fenaday went first because Mandela did not trust him. Telisan came for honor. As to Shasti, only she knew her reasons.

Time to act like a real captain.

"*Sidhe*," Fenaday said, "we are going to scout around some. I don't want my people walking into a trap."

"*Sidhe* to Fenaday, recommend you wait for the shuttles," Perez said.

"Negative. I have over one hundred people inbound. If there's a trap here, I don't want it to spring on all of us."

"Good for you," came Telisan's voice. "Permission to land and accompany you. I can do nothing up here in the sky if you go inside. Three guns are better than two."

"Permission granted," said Fenaday. He and Shasti climbed out of the fighter using the kick-ins and dropping the last meter to the ground.

The Denlenn handled the fighter like a featherweight pleasure craft. He eased down within a few meters of Fenaday. Back blast from the VTOL fighter lifted Shasti's long hair. She scowled and pulled out a bandanna to tie it back. "Showoff," she said.

Telisan popped his hatch, leaping lightly from the fighter. Fenaday's knees ached just watching him land. "Showoff," he agreed.

The Denlenn strode. "We are on Enshar and alive. Another glorious day in the Corps, as you humans say."

"What do you want to check out first?" Shasti asked, looking about alertly.

"Those barracks are the nearest. Let's do those first." Fenaday turned, hitting the access panel on his *Wildcat,* which opened to a compartment holding a tri-auto carbine and some canteens. Telisan returned to his fighter, drawing out a similar weapon.

"Set them for AP bullets," Shasti said. "We don't want to use mini-grenades inside an enclosed space, and the flash of the particle beams can dazzle your low-light vision. It will be dark inside there."

Fenaday nodded but noticed that Shasti left her selector on full auto. *She probably regards Telisan and me as liabilities now that we're down. Of course, she's probably right.*

Everyone took a sip from the canteens, and they started toward the barracks. Their feet crunched on wind-blown grit and minor debris. They spread out, but with no cover, they just walked up, weapons covering windows and doors.

Up close they could see the signs of damage on the barracks

structure. Most of the windows were broken and doors hung ajar. Just as they reached the building, something black lunged into the air over them. Instantly, they dropped to their knees, weapons snapping up. With a beating of wings, three bird-like creatures climbed into the sky.

"Damn," Fenaday said, his heart beating furiously.

"*Sidhe* to Fenaday," called Perez, into their light headsets. "You gave us a bit of a scare there. We're going to lose you as you go inside. It'll be voice only."

"Acknowledged."

"A good point to remember," Shasti said. "This planet has gone back to the wild. The buildings are probably great denning sites for predators."

"It would be a bit of an anti-climax to come all this way, through all this, to be eaten by the local equivalent of a bear," Fenaday said. "Okay, let's go in slowly and carefully."

They reached the nearest door. While the Enshari were a small race, they were part of the Confederacy of Seven Species, with military and port facilities designed to Confed standard. Ceilings would be somewhat low, the doors small, but manageable. Shasti leaned past Fenaday before he could stick his head in, so he ended up covering her. They slid through the doorway into a corridor. There they saw the first bodies, or rather, pieces of bodies.

"We see bones in the corridor," Fenaday reported. "There's adequate light from some panels on the ceiling, so we haven't needed torches yet. Be damned if I know what's powering them."

"These bones are chewed," Shasti added, "probably by local animal life scavenging after the massacre."

Fenaday thought of the gruesome, planet-wide feast that must have taken place in the days after the disaster and shuddered.

"Proceeding down the corridor," he added. "If this is like most barracks, we will be in the main bunkroom shortly."

The main bunkroom sat at the end of the corridor. Bunks lay strewn all over the place; lockers had been torn off walls. Equipment and bones lay everywhere. If some giant had taken a big spoon and stirred the room, it might have looked like this.

"What in the gods' names happened here?" Telisan wondered, casting about with his torch. "More scavengers?"

"Big ones, maybe," said Fenaday doubtfully. He reported the sight to the ship. Telisan began filming with a small video.

"Don't do too much of that," Shasti warned. "Keep your eyes on the area." The Denlenn nodded, putting up the camera.

They moved through the building, up the stairs. Their hand torches lit places where daylight didn't penetrate. Sometimes a torch reflected off Telisan's cat-like eyes. *A major disadvantage in a night fight,* thought Fenaday, *and unnerving in itself.*

Fenaday jumped as he heard rustling and the scamper of small feet. Something small, fast and brown raced away from them through piles of paper and debris.

"Local equivalent of a rat," Shasti said.

"Most of the larger animals probably fled the noise of the fighters," Telisan said, lowering his weapon.

"Perhaps," Shasti said. "Count on nothing." Trailing her, they started forward again.

Everywhere that they found corpses, they saw the same sight, as if each room had been turned upside down and shaken.

In the non-coms quarters, they discovered a new piece of the puzzle. The walls showed scorch marks and spalling from weapon fire. The bodies in that room were more intact. Behind a bunk frame that had been dumped on its side, they found the desiccated corpse of an Enshar trooper. Shreds of uniform still showed on the gnawed body, and its bony hand clutched a standard-issue pistol. The Enshari had obviously jumped behind the bed for cover before being killed.

"Well, Sarge, at least you got a shot off," Fenaday said. "I don't know if it did any good, but well done anyway." He looked around and found a dusty, chewed blanket and gently covered the body.

They stalked the halls into another barracks. This one was even more thoroughly wrecked, with walls bowed out from some form of pressure. Shattered pipes still leaked water onto the floors. In places it cascaded down in small waterfalls that had eroded the walls and created mold gardens. They stepped carefully to avoid bones and debris. They took a dank corridor to the left, splashing through foul-smelling, ankle-deep water. At its end they found a gymnasium. Again, Fenaday's chief impression was that the space had been stirred with a stick. The room was a maze of torn-up chairs and fragmented skeletons. A game must have been going on when disaster struck.

They spread apart, facing outward. Fenaday caught sudden movement from the corner of his eye. On the second level, part of a stack of debris tilted forward.

"Shasti!" he barked. He swung his tri-auto up and peppered the area, aiming at a hint of a figure behind the stack. Shasti leapt away from the danger as the detritus smashed into the floor.

"Fenaday," Perez shouted from the *Sidhe*, "what's happening?"

Their eyes and torches searched the area of the slide. Nothing. Perez's voice became shrill with panic as he called to them.

"Take it easy," Fenaday said, with a calm he didn't feel. "Some stuff came down, that's all. Junk fell. We are okay."

"I would have sworn," Telisan said, his cat's eyes at their widest, "I saw a figure up there, only a shadow, but something."

"Yeah, me too," Fenaday said, "after the stuff started coming down. That's why I opened up. Shasti, did you see anything?"

"No," she replied, scanning the dark reaches of the building. "I was too busy getting out of the way."

They mounted the stairs to the area of the fall, weapons leveled. There was nothing, only more debris. Shasti checked the dust for tracks and found none.

"That pile sat still for over three years and came down just when you were under it," said Fenaday slowly, a hint of disbelief in his voice.

"Vibration," she speculated, "our voices or footsteps perhaps. Yet, both of you thought you saw something. Still, I can find no track of anything up here."

"Let's get back to the fighters," Fenaday decided. "We've pushed our luck enough for today."

They made their way to the nearest exit, carefully covering one another. With their investigation complete for now, Fenaday felt no need to go back through all the buildings. Shasti shattered a recalcitrant door lock with a kick, and they fled into the open air. They trotted back toward the fighters. Out under the bright sun of Enshar, it was easier to accept the incident as nerves and vibration. Yet, in Fenaday's mind lingered a fragment of an image, difficult for him to dismiss.

Perez raised them as soon as they stepped into the open. "Nice to have you back out under the ship's cameras," the engineer said. "The shuttles are only five minutes out from your location."

"Acknowledged," Fenaday said.

The breeze blew more stiffly now, and clouds piled in the distance. Fenaday frowned. There had been no forecast of storms in the intelligence report. Still, he heard a rumble of thunder.

"Wish I had a job where I could be wrong forty percent of the time," Shasti said, looking at the sky.

"There they are," Telisan said, pointing.

The three shuttles, painted the same Guard's Red as the *Sidhe*, came in slowly, in formation, dropping onto the tarmac near the fighters. Ramps opened. Mmok's robots, HCRs, and crabs, poured out to take defensive positions, followed by the LEAFs and ASATs. Shasti's small "trouble team" formed a circle around Duna, Mourner, and her people as the scientists and doctors came out of the shuttles. The relief pilots, there to take the fighters back to the frigate, walked over to the nearby *Wildcats* and began preflighting them.

Fenaday, Shasti, and Telisan trudged toward the arrivals. Belwin Duna had not gotten far from the shuttle. The little Enshari crouched, hands on the ground. They hurried over, Telisan in the lead, fearing the old scholar ill, but it was contact with his home-world that overcame Duna.

"Ah, Enshar," said Duna, as if addressing the planet, "I am here. Somehow, I will lead your children back to you." His small, furry hands caressed the tarmac. Fenaday looked away, embarrassed. He remembered the conversation in the bar. It seemed an age ago. Without Enshar, Duna said, there would be no Enshari. Seeing him now, Fenaday believed it was true. They needed their homeworld on a deep, biological level.

Rigg and Mmok walked up to Fenaday and Shasti. "Orders?" Rigg asked.

Fenaday gestured with his head toward Shasti.

"The tarmac won't allow us to dig in," she said. "I want a portable fence barrier constructed. Set the electrical current at lethal levels for Conchirri after nightfall. Make sure the scientists know the monofilament wire will cut skin at a touch and is difficult to see."

"We could leave the light source in the wires on active," Rigg said. "You can see it even in daylight."

"Agreed."

"Mmok," she continued, "put your crab robots on the perimeter. I'll keep gunners constantly manning the top turrets in the shuttles. You and your HCRs can escort the scientific party as soon as they unpack the motorized mules from the shuttles."

Rigg saluted and left. Mmok grunted and followed him.

The sky clouded, but the rain held off as the science teams investigated Gigor. Duna and Mourner sampled and analyzed, visiting the destroyed ships and barracks buildings as engineers tried to revive some of the port's computers. Despite their efforts, they learned little. A concentrated force had struck the ships and shuttles at the center of the base, though it appeared not to have been an energy beam. Gigor showed evidence of seismic shock in some areas and none in others. Often, they encountered what they began calling "the stirred effect."

As night fell, so did the weather. A furious lightning storm broke over the field. Everyone retreated to the shuttles, save for Landing Force Troops on guard duty. They sat in the mules, which were grounded by their tires, putting up the plastic tops that gave only an illusion of shelter. Guards in ponchos cursed their commanders for not simply relying on Mmok. The robots were capable of grounding themselves and stood indifferent to the storm. The torrent blew out quickly, as if it had spent its strength. Half an hour after it began, the stars came out.

Fenaday ordered everyone not on guard back into the shuttles. It was tight, but manageable with mules and other equipment off-loaded. Beyond Duna, no one felt much like sleeping out under the stars. Enshar's animal life, especially the birds, manifested itself more with the setting of the sun. The robots and the gunners loaded infra-red prints of the native life in their weapon computers. It was probably the only way anybody would get any sleep. Nervous sentries, he did not need.

Fenaday sat with Shasti and Telisan in the left side hatchway of the shuttle *Pooka*, each too keyed up from the day's events to sleep yet. They kept their weapons with them, but nothing seemed threatening. The light element in the barrier wire made a delicate tracery of white light around their perimeter. It would make a perfect beacon had someone tried to range on them with a mortar, but as yet there had been no sign of any conventional enemy on Enshar.

"I didn't think I would be looking at stars tonight," Fenaday said quietly.

"We are okay so far," Shasti replied, "though no closer to finding any answer as to what happened and why. The scientists have been unable to find a computer with any useful information in it. They're shorted electrically, damaged by electromagnetic pulse, deteriorated due to lack of care, or simply show nothing useful."

"Still," Telisan said, optimistic as ever, "we are alive and nothing has menaced us other than the weather."

Fenaday shook his head. "Until we know what happened and why, no one dares bring the few remaining Enshari or anyone else back here. Our contract with you says we stay till Duna finds the answer or gives up. Who is to say what will happen tomorrow?"

"You arc," Shasti answered. "What does happen tomorrow?"

"The science team recommends we check out the *Earhart* shuttles," he replied. "After that, Duna wants to stop at his home. Beyond that, I don't know."

"Well, since I have the early morning watch," Telisan said, "I am going to get some sleep. Wake me if the world decides to end first."

Fenaday smiled at the retreating Denlenn. Shasti nodded pleasantly. She appeared to fully accept Telisan as a companion now, but Fenaday couldn't help but wonder if Mandela was right about her being capable of sabotaging a shuttle with Telisan and Duna aboard.

"That's probably a good idea," she said. "Why don't you do the same? I'll take the first watch. I want to get something else to eat any way."

"That reminds me," he said, with a smile. Reaching into the pocket of his flight suit, Fenaday pulled out a large chocolate bar. "It's broken, I'm afraid."

"Ah," she said, snatching it out of his hands, "it will taste just as good. I thought you were sure we would be dead after we landed?"

"Well, I wasn't sure what scared me more, Enshar, or being down on Enshar with you, without chocolate."

"Is there more?" she asked suspiciously.

"We'll see," he replied. "Good night." Fenaday's bunk was just inside the hatchway. He fell asleep the instant his head hit the pillow.

Chapter Ten

Morning is surprisingly chilly for this time of the year, thought Fenaday. He clutched his leather jacket a little closer and looked over his coffee cup at the lightening eastern sky. The sunlight of the big star made for quite a predawn show. He'd slept hard and deep, waking early, alert and energetic. *Maybe it's just joy at still being alive,* he thought. Fenaday stuck his nose in the plas-steel cup and breathed the coffee scent deep into his lungs.

"It is definitely not a good day to die," he whispered to himself.

"There are no good days for that," Shasti said from behind him.

He turned and smiled. "Good ears, Ms. Rainhell."

She arched an eyebrow at him. "The better to hear bad, ugly things sneaking up on you, Captain."

"Good. Listen very carefully," he said. "This could be a long day."

"If we are lucky," she replied.

The exploratory team broke camp after field showers and a hastily cooked breakfast, which were their only luxuries. The camp's defenders packed up the barrier wire and trooped into the big *Dakota* shuttles, which lifted off, covering each other.

Fenaday led the way in *Pooka,* though he left the actual flying to Angelica Fury. *Banshee* trailed with Karass at the controls, followed by *Farriq-Dar*. They maintained a combat-ready formation as they headed for the outskirts of Gigor base. The first Enshar expedition had landed twenty-one kilometers from the base. *Earhart's* captain had intended to do a long-range ground recon before moving into Gigor, but the Confed force was overwhelmed at their landing site.

Tension grew as they neared the site of the first landing. *Pooka* slowed, and the other two shuttles climbed for altitude.

"There they are," announced Telisan. His sharp eyes spied the camouflaged shuttles, set down in what was once a farmer's field. The Denlenn's face became grim, and his eyes glittered. Fenaday remembered Telisan had friends in those shuttles. He certainly had them among the fighters wrecked in the area. Mercifully, none of the *Earhart's* crashed fighters lay near the shuttles.

Foliage partially covered *Earhart's* shuttles. The three large *Wolverine* class assault-shuttles, many times more dangerous than Fenaday's old *Dakotas*, sat in a landing triangle. Each ship faced outward in the textbook deployment pattern. Their standard gray-green camouflage, dulled by years of sun and dirt, blended well with the local equivalent of wheat or corn. Vegetation covered the clear plas-steel gun turrets. Nothing could be seen of their interiors from the hovering *Pooka*.

Fenaday looked over Telisan's shoulders. "I don't fancy dropping into head-high ground cover. We won't be able to see a damn thing."

"There are a few ways to clear foliage," replied Telisan. "Daisy-cutter bombs, laser or chain gun fire, none of which seems practical."

"There's more than one way to skin a cat," Mmok quoted, "and they're all fun."

Telisan half turned in his seat, his eyes narrowing. "Does thee have something to say?" Clear warning sounded in the Denlenn's voice.

Mmok's half grin faded slightly. "The robbies can do it. We hover at ten meters as they jump in. They use monofilament to cut the grass and gather it up so we don't start fires on landing. The galaxy's most expensive weed whackers."

Telisan looked at Fenaday, who nodded.

"Do it," commanded Telisan.

"Fury, hover in the center of the landing triangle," Mmok ordered.

The HCRs jumped off the rear ramp of the shuttle *Pooka* as the crabs fell from their hookups under the shuttles. Shasti and her trouble squad, wearing hearing protection and secured to brackets at the hatchway, covered them. The robots quickly deployed and strung monofilament between pairs. They cut a huge swath through the area, uncovering each *Wolverine*, drawing no reaction. HCRs easily cleared the cut material. Fenaday ordered *Pooka* to land. As they came down, the robots stamped out any small fires that broke out and then fell back on the *Pooka*.

Hatches popped and nervous faces peered out over leveled weapons. Fenaday and Telisan joined Mmok and Shasti on the large rear ramp. One of the *Wolverines* sat a scant forty meters away. Fury stayed at the controls, ready to lift at the first sign of trouble. After a minute, Fenaday gave her the sign to cut the engines, and quiet descended.

Fenaday looked from face to face. Only Shasti and Mmok looked unconcerned.

"The robots report no animal life closer than four hundred meters, and those signals are retreating rapidly," Mmok reported.

Fenaday nodded, then turned to the radiotech, Susan Bernard. "Call the other shuttles down. Have them land close to us. We're going over to *Wolverine Six*."

He hopped off the ramp, followed by Telisan, Shasti, Duna, Mmok, and the trouble team. Everyone wore disposable chemical-biological warfare suits. The Confed shuttles had lain sealed for over two years. Their interiors would not be pleasant.

Sidhe's other shuttles grounded as Fenaday's party reached *Wolverine Six*. Telisan looked up at the gray-green hull and climbed onto its left thruster, reaching for the keypad. Before keying the opening sequence, he looked into the small battle porthole, shining a torch.

"Bodies," he said grimly, "lying around on the deck. Debris everywhere." He backed away and touched the keypad. Nothing happened. "As I suspected, power is out and the electronics are fried. I'm going to use the emergency lever."

Telisan reached down to a panel surrounded by yellow and black stripes, marked "Emer-Release." Everyone else covered the door. The hydraulics still worked, and the door whooshed open slowly, outward and down, forming a ramp. The smell that rolled out made them all seal their masks, not the sickly sweet smell of rotting meat, but a musty odor of mold and decay. Fenaday, Shasti, Telisan, and Mourner entered. Gunnar came as far as the door, looked in, and backed out cursing. He seemed happy to stand on the ramp. Fifty bodies lay inside the forty-five meter *Wolverine*. Most were in the back, where they formed an unpleasant mass on the floor. The bodies, sealed in the airtight shuttle, had not gone to bone or been devoured. Natural fungus and the microbes carried by all life had degraded them. They'd turned into mold gardens. Mourner called for Yamata and Vashti to get into suits and join her.

Bodies and equipment lay about the shuttle as if some giant had picked it up and shaken it. "Just like Gigor," Fenaday said.

"Look at this," Shasti called. She stood in the middle section of the shuttle, near the communications panel, pointing at one of the dead ASATs. The desiccated corpse lay on its back on the panels, a pistol still clutched in mummified hands. A space suit lay on top of the body, as if in some obscene embrace. The suit was the armored type used in boarding actions, and two blast holes showed in its back.

Fenaday looked at Shasti. "From the pistol?" he asked. Pulling out his long Scottish dirk, he tried to lever the encrusted space suit off the body. It stuck. Impatient at his squeamishness, Shasti simply grabbed the suit's shoulder with a gauntleted hand and pulled it off the corpse. It came free with a nauseating, crackling sound. She flipped it over, revealing larger blast burns on the suit's front. It had been shot from close range.

"Perhaps someone threw it at him?" wondered Telisan. The Denlenn had returned from the cockpit with dog tags clutched in his hands. His face looked drawn and tired.

"Or he held it up for defense and shot through it," Duna mused.

"Doesn't make sense," Shasti said, looking at the shuttle's interior with distaste.

The scientists plied their probes as the rest of them checked the shuttle's instruments. Gunnar ran a cable from *Pooka* to the *Wolverine's* ground power port to no avail. The ship was thoroughly dead.

Mourner came over toward them. The small, intense woman stood next to Shasti, who overtopped her by most of a meter. The Olympian and the doctor made for an incongruous sight.

"As near as I can tell," said Mourner, "most people in here died from blunt trauma. Bones are broken, skulls cracked. There are also indications on some bodies of stab wounds. Three, including the pilots, show signs of electrocution. The bodies are too badly decomposed for me to tell much in a field test. All this mold has screwed any chemical analysis."

"What the hell went on here?" Fenaday asked.

"I don't know, Captain," Mourner replied. "I can tell what killed them, but not who, or how they got aboard."

"I don't think any attack force was on board," Shasti said. "It doesn't look right for a gunfight or close-in battle. No burns on the bulkheads, magazines full of unfired rounds. They died quickly. Yet, who could surprise troops of this quality?"

"None of it makes sense," Telisan growled. "The shuttle doors never opened. How did attackers get in here?"

"I checked the hull floor-plates," Shasti said. "They're intact. Nothing came up from below."

"Maybe they went mad and attacked each other," Mourner said. "I just don't know."

"Any reason to stay here further?" Fenaday asked, fervently hoping there wasn't.

Mourner sighed. "Not without a real lab. I've taken samples, holos, and everything else I can think of. Maybe after we get back to the starship and I can use her facilities…"

Fenaday looked around the dead shuttle and shuddered. "All right," he said harshly. "Everyone out and back to our ships. We are pulling out and heading to Duna's home."

The crew left gladly and quickly. As they came to the hatch,

Telisan put a hand on his arm. "Help me reseal it. I want no animals disturbing their rest."

The hatch was clearly beyond the strength of the two, but they didn't call for the HCRs. This was a job for people. Shasti and Johan Gunnar threw their backs in as well, and the Confederate shuttle resealed. They made their way back to *Pooka*. As they crossed the open ground, Gunnar looked up. Clouds darkened the sky, and thunder rumbled in the distance. The big man scowled. "Does it rain every damn day here?"

"Maybe we landed in the rainy season," Shasti replied.

Gunnar, one of the few people who could small talk with Shasti, grinned at her.

Telisan and Duna listened to the conversation and exchanged anxious looks at each other and the sky. The Denlenn looked as if he might speak, but the Enshari shook his head.

———

I n *Wolverine Six*, behind the sealed hatch, something stirred in the darkness. From near the shuttle's communication panel, a shape humped itself painfully forward. The armored space suit Shasti had thrown to the deck in disgust rose from where she left it. It crawled slowly, seemingly with great effort, to the hatchway. Once there, it became mostly erect, propped against the hatch. It plopped its mass against the hatch several times, as if trying to pass through the obstinate metal. A slight electrical smell wafted through the fetid air along with the crackle of a tiny discharge.

The door remained sealed. Even Mmok's guardian angels did not hear the slight sound the suit made in the dead ship. The faceplate of the suit pressed against the porthole. It could not be seen against the shuttle's darkened exterior. Then, as if exhausted by the effort, it dropped to the deck like a puppet with cut strings. Utter stillness returned to *Earhart's* dead shuttle.

———

They lifted from the site of the Confed shuttles and their slaughtered crews, leaving the impending storm behind. Fenaday looked down on the shuttles sitting in the defensive triangle and shook his head. He turned to the pilot, Angelica Fury.

"Keep *Pooka* in lead, triangular formation," he said. "Maintain an economical cruising speed."

"Aye, sir, four hundred knots it is."

"Why so slow, Captain?" Duna asked "Aren't these *Dakotas* marginally supersonic?"

"Yes," Fenaday replied. "We have fuel-efficient reactor-based drives, but their range isn't infinite. The more propellant we use, the more often we have to either shuttle up or send the fighters down with tanks."

"Of course, Captain," Duna said. "Foolish of me to ask."

"Relax," Fenaday said kindly. "We'll be there in a few hours."

From the deck of the *Pooka*, Fenaday and the others watched the farmlands roll beneath them. Brilliant yellow crops topped with growths of swaying rusty orange filled the miles in a scene reminiscent of the American Midwest. Dark-hued trees, looking like Terran pines but studded with white flowers, marked the edges of the fields. Occasionally, the spacers saw farmhouses. Most were of the domed variety the Enshari favored, painted in light cream and beige. Duna pointed out some of an older style. Small hillocks of natural dirt poured over a modern construction, these resembled the early dens of Enshari farmers.

Other less pleasant sights presented themselves: crashed aircraft of various types, cars and trucks that had run off the roads. The shuttles flew over a wrecked Maglev train, its cars flung about as if by a maddened child.

The contrast between the pleasant countryside and the devastation became too much for Duna. "My poor people," he mourned. "What force is it that hates us so?" His small hands covered his expressive brown eyes. Telisan put a hand on Duna's shoulder, his golden, leathery face marked by concern. Shasti looked out of the canopy, uncomfortable. Fenaday, who had lost a home and family, felt a pang of sympathy for the Enshar.

"While we are still alive, there is hope," Telisan said.

"Hope is a thin meal," Duna replied, uncovering his eyes.

For the first time, Fenaday drew a sense of age from the Enshar. Duna always seemed energetic. It was hard to believe the little alien had lived for eight hundred years. Now Duna looked every one of those years, old and tired. For some reason, it frightened Fenaday. He wished desperately for something comforting to say but could think of nothing that did not seem trite in light of the tragedy.

Li, one of Shasti's trouble squad, came up with a cup of hot tea. Shasti had assigned Li as a bodyguard to Duna. Duna looked up at the tea and the concern on Li's hard-bitten face. The scholar took the tea and bowed his head against the cup twice in an Enshari gesture of respect and thanks. Li bowed gracefully from the waist.

Fenaday shook his head. Li, like most of his crew, had never shown a sign of giving a damn about anyone. Somehow Duna seemed to bring out the best in people.

Li caught his look. "I learned it from the old movies," he said. "I grew up in Stockholm."

There was a brief laugh from the humans, even Mmok. Duna and Telisan looked puzzled. Telisan made the Denlenn equivalent of a shrug, a gesture Fenaday had learned meant, "Aliens, who can understand them?"

People settled in. Mmok, Rigg, Rask, and some of the other troopers folded down enough of the seats to play cards. Some talked, cleaned weapons, or slept. Fenaday and Shasti stayed by the canopy, watching the world roll beneath them: beautiful, mysterious, and alien. One could almost forget the disaster that had brought them here.

Three hours later, the shuttles began circling a huge house on the outskirts of the town of Pelen. The sprawling structure was painted a mustard-yellow with an olive-green roof and cream trim. Duna's home sat on a cliffside, its back to the eastern sea of Canelda, with its dark, almost black waters. It fronted a wide lawn where the shuttles could land without difficulty. Two smaller cream-colored domes of typical Enshari architecture sat on the grounds as well. The staff and groundskeepers had lived there. Duna's home was only for the family and guests. The house was not typically Enshari, as befitted its unusual owner.

"Pelen is where I was born," Duna said. "I met my wife, Medu, here. We made it our home for three hundred years. She passed away years before the disaster and is buried on the property below, but my mission here is not sentimental. As one of the few of my kind to spend much time off-world, I enjoyed a quasi-ambassadorial status. My home, which I've not seen in fifteen years, also acted as an intelligence gathering station. The staff maintained an extensive bank of computers, recordings, books, and periodicals, sending me material on all manner of current events.

"My hope is that the computers in the building survived whatever happened. They were electronically protected from snooping, and the building has its own power supply. We may find some clues within."

"It's beautiful," Telisan said, looking at the huge building.

"Medu," said Duna, "trained as an architect. She based the design, with a few Enshari refinements, on homes found on the North Atlantic coast of Earth's North America. The building style is similar to a New England telescope house, though she added another story. Oh, how proud she was when it was finished..."

Duna's home reminded Fenaday of his own on New Eire's rugged seacoast. An unexpected feeling of homesickness swept through him. He turned away from the view outside the canopy for a few moments.

They flew in over the lawn, dropping in a triangular formation. Robots sprang from the shuttles, forming a perimeter. Rainhell's and Rigg's people fanned out, more confident now, also taking defensive positions. Fenaday held the shuttle engines at low throttle for a minute. Annihilation did not threaten. He joined the others on *Pooka's* rear ramp.

Fenaday tilted his head back and let the sunshine fall on his face with its gentle warmth. The breeze from the ocean brought a fresh, clean scent to them, cooling the air and stirring the evergreen-like trees, making their white flowers bob almost cheerfully. The lush growth of the interior had thinned out in the windswept coastal area. Leaves and plants appeared darker and more subdued, less dazzling to human sensibilities. The grass they trod on looked similar to Terran fescue, though shaded a darker green and with metallic hint to it.

The spacers started up the crushed-rock path toward the door. Duna, Mmok, and Telisan walked beside Fenaday. Rainhell and her trouble team guarded their right. Rigg and a fire team of ASATs paced them on the left. They walked at an easy pace, looking over the beautiful grounds.

"My home," Duna said simply.

Magenta and Cobalt moved at a distance from them, patrolling farther out on the flanks. The crab robots and the HCRs Verdigris and Vermilion circled the shuttles with their firepower.

A sudden movement from the forest's edge caught Shasti's eye. "Down!" she yelled. The spacers threw themselves flat. Magenta flashed into sight, firing a tri-auto. In the background came cries and yells. The shuttle's engines coughed into restart.

Fenaday rolled upright, his laser pistol clearing the holster. No less quickly, Shasti dropped into a firing position with her tri-auto rifle. Magenta stood triumphantly over the smoking remains of the menace: a late-model garden robot. It lay on its side, sparking fitfully. Its hedge trimmers and clippers seemed comical compared with the deadly efficiency of the HCR. Fenaday looked around with more attention. He was chagrined. The erratically clipped grass should have told him something. The solar-powered mechanism must have operated irregularly, soldiering on whenever the weather allowed it sufficient charge to go about its work.

"Captain," Angelica Fury shouted into his headset, "what's happening? Do you need support?"

"Negative," replied Fenaday drolly, standing and holstering his laser. "Mr. Mmok just made our first bag of the voyage. A three thousand credit garden robot, by the look of it."

Laughter barked out over the net and Fenaday saw quick, nervous grins on the faces of the spacers near him. Mmok ignored all of them, his throat moving as he subvocalized. Fenaday wondered if he was chewing Magenta out or adjusting her programming. In the background the shuttle engines wound down again.

Duna picked himself up, dusting off his ship uniform. He

headed for a small tree to the right of the house as if nothing had happened. As they neared it, a small headstone became visible. Everyone held back as Duna spent a few moments at his wife's graveside. He leaned forward to embrace the stone. Fenaday looked up at the house, fighting to keep his vision from blurring. He knew what it felt like to mourn a lost wife. Finally, Duna stood and walked, very deliberately, back to the house.

Fenaday realized that the little Enshari might find the bodies of friends or family on the other side of the door. He signaled Shasti to stop Duna and waved to Telisan.

"Does he have anyone in there?" he whispered.

Telisan looked at him for a second, then smiled. "You are very considerate for a pirate."

Fenaday wasn't sure why the comment warmed him, but for the first time that day he managed a smile. "I don't want the old scholar to go through any more than he has to. He may have gotten us into this mess, but I've grown kind of used to him."

Telisan looked up at the big, cream-colored house. "Medu passed away long before I met him. He has many children, some survived off-world. Of the ones who died on Enshar, I do not think any lived here. They were all grown. He had many friends, but I doubt they would have been at the house while he was away."

"Yeah. Well, I think we'll go in first anyway," Fenaday said.

They walked up to the door.

"Shasti, Mmok, Morgan, Li, Connery, and Rigg, you're with us. Gunnar, you stay with Duna. Send the HCRs around the back," Fenaday ordered.

He keyed his mike. "Fury, come in."

"Fury here."

"Send a squad to secure the area between the shuttles and the house. We got sloppy, not noticing the mowed grass. It didn't cost us. Let's not get sloppy again."

Fenaday drew his laser in a fluid move, aiming for the door lock.

Duna made an apologetic noise. Fenaday looked down. The little Enshar offered him a sonic key. Telisan and Mmok grinned. Shasti pretended to study a cloud formation. Fenaday sighed, took the sonic key, and unlocked the door. It swung open easily. He reached in, bending low, to find the light switches. About half of them came on. Some flickered. He noted panels in the ceiling. These glowed softly as he opened the door.

"Bioluminescent fungus," Duna said, catching his glance. "We developed it to a high art. Enshari do not require darkness to sleep. There will be light in every room. The panels require no maintenance and get all they need from the air."

"Good to know," said Fenaday. "Less shooting at shadows."

He stepped into the room. The ceilings were low, a little over two and half meters. Shasti did not actually have to stoop, but she was clearly unhappy about it. She stood at eye level with a ceiling fan.

Duna's home ran off solar power, with a backup generator. Surprisingly, the house was in good order, even the air-conditioning still worked. The spacers split into teams of four to search the house. They found water damage in the kitchen from a burst pipe; otherwise everything seemed intact and in good condition.

Li and Telisan called Fenaday and Shasti up to the study. They found the Landing Force Troops standing in front of a locked door that the sonic key would not open. Fenaday burned through the lock as the others covered him and kicked the door open, but Shasti cut in front of him, leading with her tri-auto. The room they entered was particularly cold. In the middle of it, lying on the floor, lay the intact body of an Enshari, nearly buried under a mountain of books, tapes, disks, and data crystals. Fenaday and the others looked around the room. All the windows were sealed from the inside. On the far side, a connecting door led to the computer room they had come so far to investigate. Fenaday leaned in; there was no other exit from the computer room.

With reluctance, Fenaday turned to Telisan. "Duna should see this body. He may have known the person."

The Denlenn nodded. "I'll prepare him for it."

Telisan returned with Duna in tow. Duna approached the body and looked at it. Fenaday held his breath. The Enshari made a few small hand gestures while speaking in a low voice. It reminded Fenaday of Father Luxor saying last rites over his father. He wondered if in addition to his other careers, Duna might have been a pastor.

Duna stood and turned to look at Fenaday. "I do not recognize the body, though it appears from the uniform that she was on the staff here." He waved a hand at Telisan. "Come my friend; the data banks are back here."

Duna and Telisan disappeared into the back room and began working on the equipment. Fenaday and the others returned to the body. Fenaday had no idea of the corpse's age. Enshari looked much the same for most of their long lives. The corpse had been mummified by the cold, dry, air-conditioning. Shasti and Fenaday exchanged puzzled looks.

"Great," he said, "a locked room murder mystery."

"She came in here," Shasti mused, "locked the door, sealed the windows from the inside, and then buried herself under books and junk?"

"Doesn't make any damn sense," he replied.

This time Fenaday leaned over the body and searched it. He pressed his lips firmly together and tried not to think. He found a wallet in the overalls. He pulled it out, breathing hard, and did not protest when Shasti took it from his hand to briskly empty the contents. She pulled out a hand comp from her harness-pack, running it over the cards she extracted from the wallet. It interrogated the chips in the cards and yielded the details of an ordinary life—as collected by bureaucrats galaxy-wide. The little speaker on the hand comp converted the Enshari language into toneless Terran.

"Barsta Ucout, 169-3 Beltway Street, in Hardin Town, Deieppen Province: married female; age, one hundred and twenty-seven Terran standard years; two children; employed as a domestic." It added phone numbers and other such details, a pitiful summation of a life.

"Apparently, she was the housekeeper," said Shasti. She turned to Gunnar. "Show this to Duna. He may have known her."

The big man nodded and disappeared into the other room.

"Fenaday to Fury."

"Fury here."

"Send Dr. Mourner's team up under escort. Tell her we found a body in a sealed, air-conditioned room. It's in good condition. I want her to check it out."

"We copy, sir. They're on their way."

Johan Gunnar returned. "He said it was a cleaning service, no one he knows."

Doctor Mourner arrived with N'deba and the rest of her team. Fenaday sent most of the trouble team outside to keep the perimeter. Mourner and her techs set up a bewildering array of instruments delivered by one of the crab utility robots. The small cargo carrier looked a lot like its namesake. Fenaday, who did not like bugs or shellfish, ordered it out of the room after it unloaded. It lumbered out on its six sturdy legs, unoffended, followed by Gunnar.

Mourner set about her medical butchery with an unsettling clinical efficiency. Shasti watched with her usual detachment, doubtless memorizing how Enshari came apart in case she ever needed to kill one. Fenaday looked out the window at the ocean.

Telisan appeared from the other room. "The equipment looks intact," he said. "It was all off-line at the time of the disaster, for some reason. It may be that when the main power failed, no one reinitialized the system. I need a power generator from the shuttle. The house system is not generating enough reliable power."

"Order it," said Fenaday.

This time, it was Fenaday's tech people who showed up with the crab robot and a small portable generator. They dropped it off in the study and headed back to the shuttles.

Dr. Mourner came over to Fenaday, snapping off her gloves. Her team packed up and moved downstairs. There were more bodies to check in the outbuildings.

"I figured you would like a preliminary report," she said.

"Yes, Doctor."

"The subject is a young Enshar female, overall premorbid health appeared good, prima gravida one—"

"Please, Doctor," said Fenaday, exasperated.

Mourner smiled. "Sorry. The short version is death by multiple, severe, blunt trauma. I believe the trauma was inflicted by the objects covering the body. I base that on the force with which blood and hair is driven into the material of the books, tapes, and disks used."

"Beaten to death with books," Fenaday said in disbelief. "They can't be that heavy."

"No, they aren't," Mourner agreed. "I found a lot of fractures, indicating heavy blows. I doubt an Enshari could inflict them using such an implement. It would take someone quite powerful."

"Or mad, crazed on some drug or something?" he asked.

The doctor shook her head. "Enshari physiology doesn't work like human. There is no adrenaline, no hysterical strength mechanism. They evolved with a low rate of predation, so they're long-lived and with slow reproduction. Enshari maintain the same level of vitality for most of their lives."

"This makes less sense the more we work on it," Shasti complained.

Telisan leaned out of the computer room, ducking because of the low opening. His face lit with excitement. "Everyone come in. We have the computer up and have found something."

Mourner quickly followed Shasti and Fenaday into the computer room. The screen cast an eerie glow in the room, turning Duna's face into an animal-like mask. He stared, unblinking, at the monitor's flat screen. Fenaday edged behind Duna to get a better look.

On the screen he saw the image of a male Enshari. The small, alien face filled the screen; it seemed to speak urgently. Smoke drifted in the background. Flickering flames lit the area erratically. Duna slumped in his chair, speaking a few soft words in a low tone to himself.

Fenaday looked at Telisan impatiently. "I don't speak Enshari."

Without looking up, the old Enshari stirred, tapping the curiously shaped keypad. The image reset to start and began speaking. A computerized voice came out of the speakers, in the same cold uninflected Terran their own comps used. The voice overplayed the Enshari's own.

"Duna, are you there, Duna? This is Creda. Everyone's dead. It's killed them all. The whole world is on fire. Everyone's dying. What have we done?

"We unearthed ancient machinery in the Barjan Deep. We didn't know. They were just legends, just old tales. Legends like the ones you taught. Stories to frighten children. We thought it was dead. It came back, drew on the power sources. Then came the manifestations. You kill them, but there are always more.

"We thought we could control it. We were fools.

"Duna! The power is going. Can you hear me? Duna!"

On the screen, the Enshari's eyes turned from the monitor and beheld some horror. "No. No, go away," came the mechanical translation. It did not convey the terror in the Enshari's voice. The terrified squeaking of its native voice offered a chilling counterpoint. Creda fled the monitor. They heard a shriek, the dull, meaty impacts of blows, followed by the sound of objects falling to a hard floor. Then, there was only silence and the snapping sound of fire burning. The screen faded automatically, and the message began to cycle.

They stayed silent for a few seconds.

Duna spoke slowly. "Creda is…was a student of mine at the university. He became a full professor some time ago. We used to talk history until the early morning hours. Medu would get cross with him for keeping me up so late."

"I am sorry, Belwin," Telisan said.

"I think you may have a connection problem," Shasti said. "I'm getting a burning electrical smell."

Dr. Mourner shrieked. They whirled at the sound.

A monstrous figure filled the doorway, lurching toward them. Fenaday's brain refused to process the image. *It's made of books,* he thought, *books in the shape of a man. What's holding it together?*

The thing flung itself at the knot of paralyzed explorers. Even Shasti was too stunned to get off a shot. It knocked her and Telisan flying as it charged. Mourner stood paralyzed. Duna dove under the computer table. The thing crashed into Fenaday. Years of martial arts reflexes triggered, though his conscious brain refused to work. Heavy blows fell on him. He blocked, rolling away from the worst.

Fenaday hit back with all his strength, then grappled, trying to tie up the thing's arms. Its substance was more than just books and tapes. It felt as if there was some thick gel around the physical material. He could see nothing other than the paper and office debris making it up, but he felt a cold weight, like the body of a heavy snake. As he grappled with it, a consciousness seemed to invade him, inchoate, hungry, and angry. He felt a sense of age, desperation, a longing for past strength. More sensations ate into him, and his mind grew numb under their weight.

Fenaday's reflexes slowed, and this saved him. The thing batted Fenaday from its path. Arms made from books, tapes, and curios slammed into him, cutting through the tough fabric of his leather uniform jacket. Fenaday hit the wall, sliding down limply. He looked up, numb and stunned, sure the creature would finish him, unable to even attempt to draw his laser. Instead, it turned and lurched toward Duna, who stared at the oncoming nightmare with huge eyes. The sense of rage in Fenaday's mind flamed, driving out all other thought.

Shasti and Telisan's guns filled the room with flash and roar. Books, tapes, curios, the gel holding it together, flew into pieces. Abruptly, the hate in Fenaday's mind became an image of age, feebleness and despair. The thing came apart, and the detritus of its body tumbled to the ground, inanimate.

They stood frozen, staring at the debris. Mourner's harsh tearing sobs were the only sound. Telisan, covering the mass on the floor with his laser, reached out and shook her. Hard. Shasti rushed over to the cut and dazed Fenaday, seizing his shoulders, looking into his face.

She is beautiful, he thought, distracted and confused.

Shasti took his chin in her hand and searched his eyes for signs of concussion. Her touch seemed to break the fog clouding his brain.

"I'm all right," he said. "The... the thing... it was in my mind."

"Can you stand?" she asked, concentrating on the essential.

"What was in your mind?" Duna demanded. "What did it tell you?"

"Later," Shasti snapped.

"Yes, later." Fenaday struggled to his feet. The thing had struck him harder blows than he had ever felt in any tournament or fight. He felt bruised to the bone.

Gunnar and the trouble team burst through the door, followed by Mmok, Rigg, two ASATs, and the HCR Cobalt. Fenaday realized the fight had taken only seconds. His connection to the thing made it seem longer.

"It's all right," he said as their guns searched everywhere for targets. Mmok, Rigg, and the HCR covered Shasti and him. Connery and Gunnar targeted the Confed agents. Li eyed Telisan.

"Put your weapons up," Fenaday ordered. "Now, goddammit."

Fenaday flicked on his mike. Karass's and Fury's voices immediately spilled out, calling for instructions. He schooled his voice to calm. "This is Command One. Clear the net. All personnel fall back into defensive perimeter on the shuttles."

In the background, Fenaday heard Shasti and Telisan explaining the nature of their attacker to the others. He saw disbelieving looks, even as Duna and Mourner confirmed it.

"Rask," called Fenaday, "acknowledge."

"Here, Captain," Rask replied.

"Keep the area from the house to the shuttles secure. Fire on anything that moves. Mmok will back you up." He looked at the cyborg, who nodded and disappeared. Mourner and Duna were running their instruments over the mass on the floor, taking samples.

"Drop those," he said, "something knows we are here. We're going to break contact with this area and disappear. It might be able to follow a piece of what was itself." They looked as if they might argue until they caught the glare in his eyes.

"Take every record and recording you can," he continued. "Duna, download that computer disk. We're getting out of here. Gunnar, cover that mess on the floor; if it stirs, blast it. Mourner, get back to the ship. Li, take her there."

"Mother of God," Connery said, "it's like the Shellycoats of my grandfather's old stories."

"What?" Fenaday asked. Connery, a former Shamrock employee, was a native of New Eire. What he said triggered a memory in Fenaday as well.

"Ah, you've forgotten that one," Connery said, "of the Sidhe; there were Drows, Pookas, Banshees, and Shellycoats. Shellycoats

123

were spirits, manifesting as creatures of rock, shell and wood. Anything you might find in a stream."

"We have such legends too," called Duna, from the computer.

"Shellycoats," Fenaday repeated, remembering the legend. Enshar's nemesis now had a name. "Are you through, Duna?"

The Enshari nodded, picking up his case.

"Let's get out of here," Fenaday said. They left the room with Shasti and Connery bringing up the rear, racing down undersized stairs and out the front door.

The sky above them darkened as the wind began to strengthen. Telisan and Fenaday exchanged worried looks. "This is more than coincidence," Telisan said.

"Remember the port," Shasti called over the gusts, "the blast damage. Can the thing call down storms?"

"God knows," Fenaday said, as they neared the shuttles. "Let's think about it after we're airborne."

They raced aboard *Pooka* as the first raindrops began to pelt them. The other shuttles had already sealed their hatches. Fenaday hurried up to the control deck. "Take her up," he ordered Fury. "Head out to sea. I want to find a nice, uninhabited island at least two hundred kilometers from here."

Telisan reached past him to flick on a screen. As the shuttles drove up and sped away, they could see lightning begin to flash around the home of Belwin Duna.

Chapter Eleven

The shuttles climbed to five thousand meters over the weather, heading out to sea at four hundred knots. On the flight deck, Fenaday tried to calm his speeding heart. Mourner came up and made him sit while she used a regenerator to close the cuts on his face and reduce the worst of the bruising. Fury cast him sidelong glances as they climbed for altitude.

"Bernard," Fenaday said, turning to the radio operator after Mourner finished, "call *Sidhe*. Find out how widespread the storms over both Gigor and Duna's home are."

"Aye, sir." The answer came back in seconds. "Both storms were small, sudden and very local. The one at Gigor dissipated shortly after we left. The one at Duna's continues."

"I see," he said grimly. "Call Mr. Duna up to the cockpit."

The old Enshari appeared, quickly flanked by a worried Telisan.

"Your planet seems to be haunted, Mr. Duna," Fenaday began. "Storms and now apparitions seem to be plaguing us. What do you make of these phenomena?"

"I truly do not know, Captain," Duna answered. "Enshar's atmosphere, stirred by its powerful sun, is well known for storms. This is especially true in the spring, and it is now mid-spring on

Enshar. Our violent weather is one of the reasons life on Enshar developed with a predilection for burrowing."

"There was that burning electrical smell," Shasti said, "just before the attack." As usual she managed to arrive unobserved.

How the hell does someone so big manage to do that? Fenaday wondered.

"It could well have been the computer," Telisan countered, "damaged as it was."

"Could have," she said, clearly unconvinced.

"That's all," said Fenaday, eyeing Duna and Telisan.

After they left the deck, Shasti turned to him, keeping her head near his so their voices wouldn't carry. "Do we head up to the ship?"

He shook his head. "Without a proper launch window, the shuttles could exhaust weeks' worth of atmospheric operation and still not reach a stable orbit. There's little chance of arranging an orbital window to *Sidhe* inside of twenty-four hours. Shuttles and ship have changed their positions relative to each other too much. We need a place to hole up till you and I decide what to do next."

"And them?" she said with a slight inclination of her head in the direction Duna and Telisan had gone.

"They know, or suspect, more than they're telling," he replied. "Watch them."

She nodded and slipped away, leaving the small flight cabin to Fenaday, Bernard and Fury.

"Updated forecast from the ship," Bernard said. "Big storm front ahead, looks natural though. Meteorology on *Sidhe* says it has been there for days."

"We'll have to chance it," Fenaday decided. "Even with our reactor drives we can't keep flying forever. Find me a nice island, something with no habitations on it."

Fury checked the shuttle's computer and triangulated with the frigate. She pointed to the map display on her flight panel. "An island suitable for our purposes is about two hours' flight at cruising speed. It will get us down and in cover by nightfall."

"Shape course for the island," he ordered. "Bernard, alert the other shuttles."

After two hours of flying over the featureless ocean, Fury pointed over the shuttle's blunt nose. "Land ho."

Fenaday looked out to see a large island, divided by low hills and windswept on the deep ocean side. After circling the area, Fenaday decided on a clearing on the lee side. A small forest offered cover there, though the trees were short and scrubby compared to those by Duna's home.

The shuttles landed in their usual defensive triangle. This time there was less of a casual air as the troops piled out, accompanied by the robots. Gray clouds heavy with rain scudded over their landing site. Shasti and Fenaday stepped out as the shuttle ramps went down onto stony soil. The smell of ocean greeted them, along with a cool breeze.

"Looks like New Eire, or pictures I've seen of Connemara," Fenaday said.

"Be a bitch to dig in with all this rock," Shasti said, looking around the landing sight.

He glanced up at Shasti, as the wind stirred her tied-back hair. *She so rarely sees the beauty,* he thought. *I wonder why. What sort of life did she lead before I knew her?*

Shasti flicked her mike switch. "Rigg, Mmok, Rask," she said, "we're going to fortify the encampment tonight. I want barrier wire strung, floodlights placed, directional claymore mines, and the crab robot guns sited. Mmok, get your utility robots to dig firing slits and foxholes. Human guards will accompany HCRs on regular patrols."

"Acknowledged," Rigg said.

"Yeah," came Mmok's raspy voice. "I'm going to send Airbot to scout the rest of the island before the storm. It's an experimental model with a limited charge and requires a lot of my attention, so I'll have to ground it at night."

"Agreed," Shasti said.

On their own, the crew began to gather wood for a series of cheery blazes using the cargo robots and their cutters to fell trees. The clearing teams opened up fire-lanes. For those who had not seen the Shellycoat, the evening acquired something of a holiday air, despite the tense precautions.

Shasti and Fenaday walked the perimeter, checking the defenses.

"What's the plan?" she asked, when they were out of earshot of the others.

"Simple," he replied. "Break contact with the enemy, bunker up, and regroup. We need time to assess what we've found, or what's found us. I'm going to call a war council at sunset. I need to find out where the diverse parts of my 'command' stand."

"I'll make preparations," she said.

He smiled. "I count on it."

———

All the factions gathered on the open rear ramp of the *Pooka* just after sunset. The shuttle's lights on their lowest setting and a nearby campfire provided soft illumination though there were still banners of light from the sunset on the clouds above them. Shasti quietly arranged to have her trouble squad nearby. Fenaday knew the others would take similar precautions. There was no way of telling how much of what they thought secret reached Mmok through his web of robots and electronics.

Rigg showed up with Rask. Mmok brought Magenta, who wore one of the local white flowers in her polymer hair. Fury, Karass, and Nusam, the shuttle pilots, followed them over. Johan Gunnar poured coffee all around before retiring to the side of the shuttle to watch. The crowd of people stood in a semi-circle facing the shuttle, looking at either Fenaday or Duna. Shasti perched on a shuttle engine, a carbine resting on her thighs. Telisan sat near the fire and stared into it.

Without preamble, Fenaday launched the question. "Mr. Duna, today we got a small glimpse of what happened here nearly three years ago. It wasn't pretty. I suspect you know more about this apparition than you've told us."

The group stirred. Shasti quelled it with a cold stare. It always amazed Fenaday how her beautiful face could generate so much menace without a trace of expression on it. It felt like having a loaded weapon track over you.

Duna looked steadily at him. "Captain," he said, equally formal, "if I told you an army from the Atlantis of Earth's legends had overwhelmed my people, would you not think me mad? In truth, did you not think I was mad when we first met? I had suspicions of what might have occurred. These suspicions made me doubt my own sanity. The truth is—I feared to confide my thoughts to your government or anyone else. It would have given them the edge they needed to deny my quest and destroy the last hope of my people."

"Good counterattack," Fenaday said coldly. "However, we are here now, and I want to know what you know—all of it—and I want it now. What attacked us at your home?"

"A thing indeed," Duna responded, stepping up onto a broad flat rock as if it were a podium. "A creature, if creature it is, from the stories used to frighten naughty children. It is, well, the word won't translate into your language. An analogy would be to the demons and spirits of Earth mythology. They are creatures of air, taking their physical form from whatever lies around them."

"That thing that attacked us," Shasti said, "was real."

"Let me begin at the beginning," Duna said. He seemed to draw comfort from sliding into a scholarly role. "We Enshari are an old race, compared to most others. We are very long-lived. Our history is so lengthy it can literally be the study of a lifetime. There are seven thousand years or so of well-recorded history on Earth's China. Is that not so, Mr. Li?"

Li, looking surprised at being addressed, nodded from the shadows where he and the other trouble team members waited. "That's what Mom used to say."

"The cave drawings of your ancestors are about fifty thousand years old, Captain," Duna continued. "Our recorded history dates back a hundred ninety thousand years and our prehistory goes back further still.

"My specialty is the study of that pre-history, what we call the 'Unearthing.' It was the time we left burrows and caves and began to build towns and cities. We developed science at an astonishing rate compared to the other species of the Confederacy, and there are schools that contend we did not make that leap by ourselves, that we were helped by a beneficent alien race. I am one of those partisans.

"At the time of the 'Helpers,' as we call them, my people were primitive; little better than savages. The highest society was the kingdom of Barjan. It was pre-technic but had developed some science and writing.

"The most ancient records we have, which are themselves copies many thousands of years removed from the originals, and hence less reliable, tell of a terrible war of gods and demons fought on Enshar. Much of our race perished at the hands of such demons, or in the storms they raised.

"Then came the others, the Helpers. They destroyed or chained the demons and storm monsters, seizing their leader. Legend has it that the chief among the storm gods, for whom we have no name, was chained in the depths of the Barjan Mountains. What we now call the Barjan Deep."

"That's the name I heard your friend Creda say," Fenaday interrupted.

"Just so," Duna agreed. "The story is that the Chief Demon was one of the Helpers turned to evil, or perhaps something created by them. The Helpers could not, or would not, destroy it. They pursued the demon from a distant land, in long-running battles. Legend says that they did not intend for Barjan to become a battle-ground and they sorrowed for it. In penance, the Helpers taught the Enshari science and technology, turning our face outward to the stars. Then they left. Within a few hundred years, we broke out into space.

"No record survives of what the Helpers actually looked like. Apparently, they manifested themselves as giant Enshari, though we doubt this was their real appearance."

Silence fell, broken only by the sounds of the sea. Camp lanterns and the lights of the shuttles themselves began supplanting twilight as the sun disappeared.

"You believe this tale?" Gunnar laughed.

Fenaday glared at him and started to speak.

Shasti preceded him. "Quiet, Johan," she said softly. The big man subsided.

"No," Duna replied politely, "not in the literal sense. It is one of the creation myths of my people and not an uncommon one among the seven races. We think of it as a tale for children, or a fable, like your Noah's Ark.

"Many of my colleagues thought me a fool for studying it. They claimed the leap to the stars is simply an example of Enshari superiority. The tales were mere monster stories, perhaps like those you cited, Mr. Connery. What did you call the thing?"

Connery looked back at the Enshari. "The one most like your monster is a Shellycoat. It's a Sidhe, an Elf, like the ones all our ships are named for. The Pooka was a horse you rode to your death, the Banshee's wail foretold doom, and the Shellycoat would form out of anything near a stream bed."

"Very similar," Duna said. "Perhaps we will use that for a translation and call them Shellycoats."

"I remember the stories," Fenaday added, "though the Shellycoats from those legends were more mischievous than deadly. They were also called Bogles. I thought it was a Scottish legend."

"I'm Scots on my mother's side," Connery confessed.

"We won't hold that against you," Fenaday said, drawing a quick nervous laugh.

"Whatever we call them," Fenaday said, turning back to Duna, "what the hell made you think this had something to do with now?"

"A few weeks before the disaster," Duna replied, pacing on the broad rock, his hands clasped behind his back, "I was at the University on Denla. I received a communication chip from my old friend, Unam Bela, an associate of Creda's. He told me that Creda had called him to the site of a new municipal construction in Barjan. City planners decided to ignore the old tradition about not digging in the Barjan Deep. The work uncovered many old artifacts, but recently at the deepest levels, they uncovered fragments of ancient metal, an alloy of an unfamiliar type. MRI and sonic scanners revealed a sub-cavern below. He was going to join Creda on the dig. The disaster occurred two weeks later."

Duna stopped pacing for a few seconds. "I did not believe it myself at first. Like most, I thought the Conchirri engineered it somehow. Gradually, I began to wonder if there could be something in the old tales of an evil buried in Barjan Deep. After I discussed my thoughts with a few of my fellow survivors, I became so discouraged that I told no one but Telisan here. I swore him to secrecy long before we met you, Captain."

Fenaday looked at Telisan. The Denlenn did not meet his eyes, but said, "I have carried the burden of two secrets; this and my knowledge of the zone of death. I no longer bear either weight but feel no lighter." He threw a small log on the fire, as if it mirrored the disturbance in his soul, it cast a shower of sparks upward.

His head came up, and he looked squarely at Fenaday. Light from the camp lights flared in his alien eyes. "I fear I have not fully kept my oath to serve you as I served the captain of the *Empress Aran*. You may have my resignation if you wish."

"I'll take it under advisement," Fenaday said, expressionless.

"So where does that leave us?" Mmok interrupted.

"Pulling out," Fenaday said. "We've landed on Enshar, survived, gathered more information than has been learned before. We are even on the scoreboard, actually one up. I don't want to give whatever the hell is down here the chance to start a tally. I think it's time for the Confederacy to take over."

"With respect, Captain," Duna protested, "everything we have learned here has been transmitted to the starship and the satellites. And what is it we know? An inimical force haunts Enshar. It hates my kind but doesn't care who else it kills."

"It's confined to Enshar," Fenaday said, leaning back on the shuttle and crossing his arms.

"Do you know that, Captain?" Duna asked. "Will you chance that the creature will never get off my world? It came from outside, if the legends are true. And you met one of those legends today.

"What if there are others out there? This one must have been in a weakened state. Else, why do we live? Now is our chance to try and destroy this enemy, to free Enshar, and give my people a chance for survival."

"I vote we stay," Mourner said, obviously moved by Duna's speech. "I know the whole medical staff is with me." Behind her, Dr. N'deba nodded. A few others murmured assent.

"This isn't a democracy, and you don't get a vote," Fenaday snapped. "We have a contract, Duna."

"You may be the captain, Fenaday," Mmok said, "but you're not the owner. You know Mandela's conditions. You pull out now, and he is not going to regard that as fulfillment of the bargain. What good does Duna's agreement do you without Mandela's?"

"Some of us have orders in such an event," Rigg said reluctantly, and evidently surprising Mmok, who looked displeased but said nothing.

"Do not threaten the captain," Telisan rapped.

"Whose side are you on?" Mmok said.

"I wish to stay," Telisan said, "to defeat this evil that has very nearly murdered a race. My life is sworn to this purpose, and I will use every honorable means to stay. But do not threaten the captain, or my hand is against you."

Fenaday felt the situation slipping from his control. Shasti coiled, cat-like, on the wing next to him. He could see the other HCRs in the dimness beyond the shuttles. Shasti's trouble team stirred as well. Some additional LF troops, sensing the trouble, looked warily at the ASATs near them. The situation headed for explosion.

"Captain," Duna said in calm, measured and pleasant tones, "may I make a suggestion?"

Fenaday nodded warily.

"We are fortified in a strong position here. Let us sleep on it, as you humans say. Perhaps the sun will bring us new counsel and wisdom."

Fenaday looked around, as if weighing the odds. The old Enshari had been a politician, and he was providing Fenaday with a way out. Clearly he could not force the expedition off-world just now. Perhaps he could at least engineer a temporary retreat to the *Sidhe*.

"Very well," Fenaday said. Tension in the area collapsed visibly, hands slid off weapons, and people breathed again. "We don't have a good launch window till mid-morning anyway. We could make a low orbit tonight, but there'd be risks.

"When we reconvene in the morning, we'll consider a temporary pull back to the ship, while we figure out what's going on. I don't think that's unreasonable," he added, pleased to get a few spontaneous nods.

"Shasti, Telisan, and Duna, please stay. Everyone else, dismissed."

The others drifted off. Mmok looked unhappy about not staying, but he'd probably bug them anyway.

Duna studied the human. "Captain," he said slowly, "you may have a political future yourself. All you intended was a temporary retreat. Very clever. Advance a proposition you cannot defend and replace it with one more reasonable."

Fenaday yawned. "It also served to clarify the sides." He looked up at Telisan. "So, whose side are you on?"

"I gave you my word," Telisan said, his face drawn and tight. "So long as you got us to Enshar and made no move against the personal safety of my patron, I am your officer."

"You disagreed with me a minute ago," Fenaday said.

"Forgive me," Telisan said, "but I hate ambiguity. I disagreed but made it clear that I am your man. I will follow your orders, even if it means killing."

"Yes," Fenaday said, more gently. "Thank you, Mr. Telisan. As regards the matter of your resignation, can I rely on your giving me fair warning if I encroach on your oath to Duna?"

"Yes," Telisan said, clipped and tense.

"I believe you," Fenaday said. "Please retain your commission."

"I also believe you," Shasti added, to everyone's surprise.

Telisan nodded, evidently not trusting himself to speak and looking almost weak with relief.

"Poor Telisan," Duna said, his fur rippling with anxiety. "It is I who did this to you. Blame me for any failure you feel there has been, Captain."

"We all do what we have to do, Duna," Fenaday said, "and justify it later. No one is pure here. At least I can understand and admire your motives; that's more than I can say for most people."

"Well, perhaps you can start calling me Belwin then," Duna said, hopping off of his rock podium.

Fenaday smiled. It was impossible not to like Duna, despite the predicament. "Good night, Belwin."

"Good night, Captain." Duna turned and walked out of the lantern light.

"I'll take first watch," Telisan offered. "I am too keyed up for sleep." He nodded to Fenaday and also vanished into the dark.

Fenaday turned to Shasti, anxious for her assessment.

"Do you have another chocolate bar?" she asked.

Chapter Twelve

F enaday's fortified campsite stood on the southeast coast of an island almost twenty kilometers long. Near midnight, on the northern side of the island, a huge mechanical shape drifted down toward the rocky beach. The name on the immense floating platform would have translated as *Industrial Seacatcher #14* had there been anyone to read it. Nothing warm-blooded had moved on the giant processing platform in nearly three years. Nothing since the nightmare of terror ended for her crew on its derrick and net-filled decks. Pitiful skeletons littered those decks, splintered and fragmented.

Seacatcher wandered with the current, much as her designers intended. A few functioning automatics and luck kept her from grounding. On her port side, a small ferry lay wedged and partially submerged—a companion in death also crewed by bones—collected on some unwitnessed occasion.

The heart of her automatics had now failed, and *Seacatcher*, which floated over the horizon when Fenaday's force landed, drifted into shore. High above, *Sidhe* orbited. The starship noted the approach of the derelict. Despite the upload of the attack at Belwin Duna's home, it never entered Perez's prosaic mind that the derelict could pose any threat. The chief engineer lived in a secure world of math and science. Imagination was not his strength. He noted the powerless derelict's drifting approach, but ignored it. It was, after all, merely another dead wreck.

Seacatcher came to rest on the other side of the volcanic ridge that bisected the island. The pounding roar of the surf masked much of the grinding, metallic cacophony of its arrival. Distance and the heavy night air attenuated it further.

On the derelict, a shape formed, taller than an Enshari, nearer the height of a man. It drew its substance from paper, plastic, and bits of bone and metal. The shape canted across the deck, heading toward land. As it moved, pieces dropped off and new ones took their place. The gusting wind seemed to shred it at times, as if the energy or attention keeping it together waxed and waned. When it reached *Seacatcher's* landward edge, it simply toppled over into the surf. Fragments washed up along the beach, and it took some time for the manifestation to collect itself. It moved on, pulling sand, driftwood, and shells into its body. Down the windswept beach it danced, with only the rustling sound of wet paper and sticks. It slipped along lightly, now with greater speed, now with lesser. Sometimes, it came close to dissipating, as if its outraged component parts demanded rest, a return to their natural state. The shape negotiated the open areas of the island, avoiding the heavy forest where it could. Eventually, it reached a point on the headland, above the spacers' encampment. It stopped in line of sight of the camp, but not near. Having reached its objective, the collection of bones and bits settled lower to the ground. Its substance became denser, whirling with less energy. It called.

On the deck of *Seacatcher*, unlife stirred. An army, resting from its previous mission of slaughter, reassembled. It incorporated its previous victims' bones, metal, plastic, anything handy. They varied in size, but six giants made from girders and scaffolding stood like field marshals in the midst of the resurrected force. The ghastly army, its mission renewed, began to disembark. Above it, as if in cooperation, the heavens joined the assault with a rumble of thunder and a deluge of rain.

———

F enaday's people slept comfortably, under cover from the rain and the lightning. This time only the robots stood out in the storm, on watch. Their airborne sister, the scout robot so useful on Mars, sat in a shuttle, grounded by the wind and rain.

The HCR Magenta detected movement and sound beyond the perimeter. A draw ran from the valley, and by design or luck, the Shellycoat army had marched down it. It allowed them to close to within several hundred meters of the camp without detection. The defenders had not been blind to this danger, lacing the small canyon with mines. At its end, the draw left any attackers facing a hundred meters of open terrain, under every gun of the camp. In a millisecond, the robot checked its target profile and came up with "Unknown." Fortunately, its programs contained a new instruction. "Unknown" meant hostile.

Magenta signaled an alert to Mmok back in the camp. In the same instant, she commanded the mines to detonate. Her steel sisters joined her in a blur of flashing metal, leading the reserve of crab robots to the section of barrier wire facing the attack.

In the camp, Mmok leapt to his feet, yelling warnings.

Fenaday sat bolt upright from a deep sleep, grabbing his jacket. Moments later he and Shasti stood on the ramp door of the shuttle, looking for targets in the driving rain. Troops spilled out from shuttles and shelters, running for firing slits and foxholes. Fenaday popped onto the net, hitting his command override button. "All section commanders, this is Fenaday. Hold fire until we have a target. Mmok, your robots may fire at will."

Telisan and Duna joined them on the ramp, both with sidearms. Shasti left his side, racing around the encampment. He heard her calling for everyone to look to their front. Mmok's robots opened up on the prepared killing ground at the draw's exit. Anti-tank munitions flashed and boomed, giving hints of what lay beyond the barrier wire. Fenaday saw something that looked like a crane toppling into the dirt.

The Shellycoat army, its size more than quartered by the ambush, burst out the sides of the draw. A wave of creatures charged at the barrier wire, far faster than a man could run over such ground.

"Weapons free," Fenaday yelled.

Shasti called for fire, and everyone, including the top turrets of the shuttles, opened up at once. The Shellycoats seemed to have no sense of survival. They hit the barrier line and flashed into nothing.

"Floods," Fenaday shouted over the net. The downpour made it impossible to see clearly. Actinic bursts of light from explosions and energy weapons didn't help.

The floods clicked on, revealing a scene undreamed of even in Dante's nightmares. Beyond the barrier wire, the ground seethed, alive with thousands of horrific, man-like shapes of all sizes. They lurched forward, made from metal, plastic, wood, and rock. The most terrifying had skulls and ribcages whirling in their interiors.

The weaponry of the spacers cut huge swaths through the oncoming mass. Shellycoats exploded into mere debris. Barrier wire began to short under the press of material, throwing brilliant sparks to add to the confusion.

Fenaday moved to the front, flanked by the others. He saw Shasti repositioning the ground troops. He didn't interfere; she knew more of war on planets than he did. Troops ran, slipping and cursing the mud and rain. Mmok's utility robots began to scramble out from the shuttle area in response to some silent call for ammunition.

Fenaday turned to Telisan. "Get the doctors and the techs to pass out ammunition."

Telisan nodded and ran off. Duna accompanied him.

Fenaday hit the net. "Pilots, fire up your engines. We may have to withdraw."

"Karass, roger."

"Fury, roger."

"Nusam, understood."

Fenaday, laser in hand, rushed forward to help in the fight. Out of the corner of his eye, he saw *Farriq-Dar's* turret swing upward. His eyes followed the gun's track, and he saw the giant.

It stood sixty feet tall, in an ape-like shape. Behind it came four others, made of gantries, scaffolds, and cranes. They strode out of the draw like colossi, eating up ground in huge strides. Weapons fire switched to them. *Farriq-Dar's* chain gun tore the first one apart.

Then the shuttle switched to the second, which was already taking fire. The giant exploded. Parts of it struck the barrier wire and scattered the defenders. Fire slackened momentarily under the shower of metal. Girders struck *Farriq-Dar* as the thing toppled forward. The sound of metal crashing on the shuttle added to the confusion of gunfire and screams.

A third giant fell to combined fire as the weapons disrupted the unlife holding it together.

The fourth stepped over the wire as lesser Shellycoats raced through the gaps. Magenta, Cobalt, Verdigris, and Vermilion charged in, blazing away. The crab-like robot guns and utility robots also swarmed to the breakthrough engaging the Shellycoats. It gave some of the cut-off troops a chance to run for the shuttles or better positions. Shasti reorganized them quickly and the spacers' enormous firepower began to contain the threat.

———

On the *Farriq-Dar*, Pilot Officer Nusam looked out at the mass of wreckage on his canopy in dazed terror. Debris hadn't penetrated the ceramic steel of the canopy and turret, but the concussion had. His gunner hung in the belts of her seat, unconscious. All he could hear over the communications net were screams and desperate orders. His shuttle sat where the breakthrough was worst. Outside the cabin he could see monsters made of wood, steel, and bone skittering over the shuttle's sides trying to reach him.

Nusam's nerve failed, and he rammed the throttles forward. *Farriq-Dar* began to lift. Its thrusters tumbled men and Shellycoats alike.

———

Fenaday looked up in shock at the desertion. "Nusam," he yelled into the headset. "Get that shuttle back down here. Nusam! Acknowledge!"

Farriq-Dar rose slowly, thirty feet, forty. Then the fourth giant struck at it with steel arms that had once drawn fishing nets through the deep ocean. Her armored hull withstood the blow, but the port engine nozzle did not. It crumpled, cutting thrust from the engine. Unbalanced, with the other engine running full blast, *Farriq-Dar* flipped over.

Fenaday was on his headset, still demanding Nusam's return, when he saw the shuttle turn over and start down directly toward him. "Down, everyone down," he screamed into the command override. "Everyone drop."

Something hit Fenaday, throwing him backward, the breath rammed out of him. *They got me*, he thought numbly as he hit the wet ground. Long, fine, black hair fell into his face. He realized Shasti had knocked them both into a partly rain-filled ditch. They lay face to face—for a second. Then the sky over her shoulder lit up with an orange flash; the ground bucked as the shuttle exploded. They clung to each other, gasping for air. For a moment, it was simply enough to be alive.

Shasti heaved off him and lunged out of the hole. He followed with less grace, half soaked. They hit the ground running, looking for targets.

The shuttle lay upside down and burning. Its blast must have hit *Banshee* badly; her top turret had stopped firing. *Pooka* and her gun still blazed away. Bodies lay everywhere. Fortunately, the blast did their enemy worse harm; *Farriq* fell on the main breakthrough. The giant that had struck the shuttle stood wobbling as if wounded. Fenaday ran forward, scooping up a fallen tri-auto. He fired a weapon from either hand. The laser set the giant ablaze as the tri-auto ate at its substance with explosive charges, bullets, and energy blasts. Other fire joined his, and the giant toppled. Fenaday turned, looking for targets. He saw the last giant moving toward Shasti.

She stood at the perimeter, gunning down a group of Shelly-coats trying to surround survivors fleeing from the front trench. Her hearing, more sensitive than a normal human's, must not have recovered from the blast. She did not hear the clangor of its approach, too intent on the enemy before her. She did not hear Fenaday's scream as he raced forward, firing. He was too far away. Too late, she felt or saw something and began to turn. Forty feet tall and made of suspended debris, the giant swung down a girder arm.

Johan Gunnar sprang from a foxhole, almost at Shasti's feet. The big Swede hit Shasti with a shoulder, sending her sprawling face down in the mud. The girder missed her by inches. It hit Gunnar squarely. He didn't even scream. His body lofted into the air, flung like a child's toy into the forest beyond the shattered perimeter.

Fenaday grabbed another weapon from the bodies on the ground, put it on full auto, and fired. It emptied its ammunition in a rush; the particle accelerator spat out metal and energy fitfully. He continued charging, firing his hand laser at what he thought of as the thing's face. The giant stood, its head a mass of flames as the laser refracted off metal, igniting anything flammable. Even the metal began to glow. The weapon, made for short bursts, grew hot in Fenaday's hand.

The giant backed away as its girder arms came up to shield its face.

Oh my God, he thought, *this one is aware.* He shifted to fire around the shielding arms. Shasti appeared at his side, face bloody, eyes wild. Death's Angel, the crew called her. Now she looked the part. She held tri-autos in each hand and fired them with a scream of hatred. Explosive bullets began to detonate in the giant. Cobalt appeared next to them, firing her heavier weapon. The thing continued backing, then came apart, its pieces thundering into the mud, splashing them with its death throes.

With all the giants down, the smaller Shellycoats' attack became disjointed, as if the will or intelligence had gone out of them. They skittered around at random. A counterattack would rescue the situation. Fenaday turned to find Shasti, only to see her race through a section of downed barrier wire into the forest, heading for where Gunnar's body had been flung.

Fenaday was torn. The camp needed him, but Shasti was running heedlessly into the dark. He heard Telisan's strong voice and decided the Denlenn would take care of the camp. No one else could cover Shasti. He raced after her, leaping over a body he couldn't recognize. He spotted movement heading for her back and snap fired from long range. A Shellycoat flared and disintegrated. Shasti's long legs ate up ground. He lost her in the rain for a few seconds. Then a power gun flared in the distance, and he ran to the spot.

Shasti knelt over the crushed corpse of Johan Gunnar, cradling him in her arms. Fenaday saw from his injuries that he must have been killed instantly. He stood by Shasti's side, trying to look in all directions at once. They were too far from the camp site—alone. In the downpour, he could not tell a Shellycoat from foliage.

"Why, Johan?" she asked of the corpse. "Why die for me?" To Fenaday's surprise, she ran a gentle hand over the bloody face. It flicked into focus for him. Johan had always been special to Shasti. He'd even heard a rumor of a romance but had dismissed it.

"We've got to get back to the camp," he yelled. "We're dead out here."

"Fool. I told you not to come," she scolded the corpse. "You had a good job on Mars. You could have had a real life. This is stupid, Johan. "

Fenaday's skin crawled at her too reasonable tone. He looked down at her through the pouring rain. He could not see tears. Her face seemed as calm as always, but her eyes were bright and strained.

Behind them, he heard more firing and screams.

"Shasti, I realize he was something to you, but we've got to go."

She didn't react, only stroked Johan's face as the rain poured down.

"The living before the dead," he shouted at her.

He reached down, seizing her arm, hauling her back from the body. Shasti fell backward as he dragged her for a step. She convulsed with a scream of rage and blurred into movement. Fenaday doubled over as the barrel of her tri-auto slammed into his stomach and stayed there.

She stood, glaring. Death's Angel, with her weapon leveled, white knuckled, at him. "Never," she snarled, "never touch me like that. You go too far with me."

Fenaday fought for breath. "Apparently, I went too far in relying on you."

He straightened, backing away from the barrel. She leveled it at his face. He saw hate and death in her eyes, and a coldness spread through him. Her finger stayed tight on the trigger. "Our crew is fighting back there," he said. "Dying. They need us. But you stay. You fight your private war with the universe right here. If any of us live, you can tell us how it went."

He spun and ran back to the embattled campsite, wondering if he would feel the one that hit him. *They say you don't,* Fenaday thought, but he no longer believed in even small mercies.

He came up on the campsite. Telisan and Duna were forming the survivors into a square, firing volleys in all directions. The robots became the ramparts behind which the spacers stood. Three of the HCRs stood shoulder to shoulder in the thick of the attack, fighting with palm blades and kicks against the man-sized Shellycoats. People raced toward the square, firing as they ran. Mourner and Yamata fled from the side of the burned out *Farriq-Dar*, Shellycoats in pursuit. Fenaday realized that Telisan could not see them from his position. He sprinted forward, firing the last shots in his laser. Shellycoats flashed and melted into fragments. He reached the doctors, covering them as they ran for the square.

The Shellycoats came straight on at the spacers, only to be mown down by disciplined fire. Finally, the last one fell the wood of its substance burning. The spacers stayed in the square for some minutes as the rain tapered, making rushes to recover any wounded they saw, or to check bodies lying nearby. More spacers appeared, breaking out of cover, yelling out their names as they ran for the safety of the square. The explosion had not caught as many as Fenaday feared. Firing pits and bunkers protected most from the attack and the blast.

Fenaday felt a hand on his shoulder. He turned to face Telisan. Smoke stained the Denlenn's face and blood trickled from his hairline. "Thee lives. Good. When I could not find you, I feared my poor service ended. What of Shasti?"

Fenaday turned away. "She'll show up. She always does."

Telisan blinked, too startled to respond.

"Get that barrier wire restrung," Fenaday shouted. "Mmok, position your robots on the perimeter to cover the wire crew. Connery, form a fire team to back them up. Rigg, pull two teams together. Collect all the wounded. Fury, Karass, grab what you need and check the shuttles. I need barrier power and shuttle guns."

The camp came back together quickly. After reestablishing minimal security, Fenaday grabbed Mmok's arm. "Shasti's out about a hundred meters that way. Send an HCR to bring her in."

"What the—" Mmok began.

"Shut up and do what you're told," Fenaday snapped. For once, Mmok had the good sense not to push further.

Cobalt returned in a few minutes with Shasti. She carried Gunnar's body on her shoulders, wrapped in a poncho. Fenaday suddenly remembered another day, when she had carried him in over some dangerous miles on Morok. Now, all he felt was a coldness and a distant relief that she still lived. The big man's corpse joined nineteen others stretched out beside the overturned shuttle with its two corpses.

Telisan walked up to Fenaday. "I have the list," he said. "Twenty dead: Gunnar, Dr. N'deba, Nusam and his gunner, nine from the Landing Force, six of Rigg's people, and an engineer. Fifteen seriously wounded, a quarter of the robots and Magenta were destroyed."

"God," said Fenaday. "God." He turned away so Telisan could not see his face. *I am supposed,* thought Fenaday, *to shrug it off. Tough privateer captain, that's what I am supposed to be. Twenty dead. Twenty dead people. A mother's pain, a father's hopes, all gone. But gone to where? Where do you go to when the dark comes? Did a kindly god greet them? Or is it just the dark?*

"Captain?" Telisan asked, concern in his voice.

"I'm all right," he said, his voice thin and strained.

Fenaday drew a deep breath and turned to Mmok. "I remember Creda saying something about the things regenerating, about coming back from being killed. Put your crab robots in the middle of the Shellycoat debris. Order them to fire on any pieces of material that rise off the ground but shouldn't lift under the ambient wind. Maybe they are easier to disrupt if they are shot early."

"Hope you're right," grunted the older man. Mmok turned to subvocalize to the HCRs and stopped, clearly startled. The movement caught Fenaday's eye. He looked in the same direction.

Verdigris, Vermilion, and Cobalt stood behind them, looking down at the remains of their sister, Magenta. The wind stirred their monofilament hair. It was macabre, as if they were mourning.

Fenaday and Mmok walked over to the battle-damaged robots. The HCRs should have been on the perimeters, per their last order. Apparently their programs were more flexible than Fenaday realized. The HCRs looked up at their approach. Smoke stained the artificial faces and the hair they used for antenna and for cooling. They might resemble dolls, but the spacers owed their survival to them.

Mmok stared at them, as if having difficulty believing his eyes.

Fenaday called out to one of the nearby LEAFs. "Morgan." The man, dirty and bandaged, but otherwise whole, hurried to him.

"Yes, sir."

"Magenta goes into the grave with everyone else," Fenaday said. "Handle the body properly."

Mmok snorted. "You're a proper maudlin Irishman, Fenaday. It's just a machine."

"You heard me," he said.

Before Morgan could do anything, Mmok turned to the HCRs. "Vermilion, retrieve Magenta, then follow this human. Take his orders regarding disposal of the parts."

Vermilion bent down to retrieve the identifiable parts of Magenta with apparent gentleness.

"What the hell," said Mmok. "She ought to be carried by her own."

Fenaday turned and nearly walked into Shasti. They stood eyeing each other for a few seconds. Her face betrayed nothing, remaining icy and remote. He nodded at her. She said nothing. He did not know when she'd arrived, but realized she was back in her accustomed place behind his left shoulder. It might be a tacit apology. Still, all he could remember was the look in her eyes and the whitening of her hand on the weapon's pistol grip. His ribs still ached where she had slammed the barrel into him. The cold spot in his chest did not warm either.

Fenaday moved about the camp, resetting their defenses, checking on the wounded. Dawn broke. Its warmth brought relief from the night's cold rain. Shasti and Fenaday traveled the camp in frozen silence. Seeing this, Duna and Telisan exchanged troubled looks.

————

F ar above the embattled camp site, the frigate *Sidhe* had watched the battle, helplessly. Perez heard the panic and confusion over the tactical net and cursed his inability to help. The fight was far too close to the camp for the starship to fire. Scanners could barely cut through the storm. Flaring weapons fire was all he could see of the battle. Then one of the shuttle's engines gave off an infrared bloom. The bridge crew sat spellbound and watched as *Farriq-Dar* exploded. As the battle ended on their screens, casualty reports began coming. All three shuttles had been hit.

At the back of the starship's spade-shaped bridge, one of ASATs standing security watch slipped out the pressure door. Sergeant Diron Naks quickly made his way to the quarters of Lt. Katrina Micetich. He buzzed insistently.

Micetich opened the door. "Diron, what are you doing here? I thought you had watch?"

"Let me in," he hissed. "It happened. They were attacked."

Micetich paled. She grabbed his arm and pulled him into her cabin. With so much of the crew off the ship, the remaining spacers had moved into unoccupied cabins for the rare pleasure of privacy. The two young people embraced fervently and kissed. They'd fallen in love on the outbound voyage. Both volunteered for the mission, but now, in love, they were reconsidering the risks of the voyage. While only the landing force stood at risk, they were content to sit it out in orbit.

"What happened?" she breathed when they pulled apart.

Naks described the disaster planetside.

"You know what this means," he finished.

"Yes," she said, "with the shuttles damaged, Fenaday is going to bring us down."

"The fool," growled Naks. "It's probably a trap to get him to do just that, to bring us in range to be finished off. If we go down, we'll be wiped out like all the rest. We've got to protect ourselves. This isn't our fault. No one said anything about Enshar when they asked for volunteers. They tricked us."

"Yes, darling, they did," she agreed. "Get our people together. We've got to move now. We have to get Perez first. I'll call him here as soon as you get back."

He raced out the door, and the mutiny began.

Chapter Thirteen

On the planet, the landing force made flight preparations, shifting the wounded into the shuttles and drawing in their perimeter.

Fenaday returned to the *Pooka* to find an exhausted Telisan and Belwin Duna.

"Captain," Duna began, "please forgive me. If I hadn't argued against you..."

"Ancient history, Mr. Duna," Fenaday replied. "I'm in charge. Whatever happens is my responsibility."

"So many dead and hurt," Duna mourned.

"Telisan, what's our situation?" Fenaday asked. Painful-looking flash burns marred Telisan's leathery face and his usual optimism seemed absent. He stared hard-eyed at the battlefield. *It's nothing new to Telisan,* Fenaday thought.

"Twenty dead," Telisan answered. "Fifteen badly wounded, two of those are critical. Almost everyone bears some small wound. Half our ammunition is gone, as well as a quarter of our robots. The big problem lies with the shuttles. *Farriq* is a total loss. *Banshee* took the worst hit, but she is flyable, as is *Pooka,* though both are holed by shrapnel. We couldn't take them into the high atmosphere, much less space. I think if we can find a machine shop, we might repair

Pooka. I suspect it will take a shipyard and some live shipwrights to repair *Banshee.* The pressure door is blown in, and I have no idea how to fix that."

"We cannot even retreat to space," Duna murmured, "and I have killed you all."

"Belwin," Telisan said gently, "you forget. We can bring the ship down."

Fenaday nodded. "I didn't want to if I could avoid it, but we have no choice now."

Li walked over to them with some coffee. Steam rose out of plas-steel cups. Fenaday reached for a cup gratefully. "Good man."

"Well," Li said, "if you ain't dead, you need coffee, and maybe even then."

The gallows humor drew grins, save from Shasti, who sat a few feet off and declined the coffee with a shake of her head.

"Telisan," Fenaday asked, "are you sure *Banshee* is airworthy?"

Telisan nodded wearily, his bright yellow eyes on the horizon. "The blast went mostly upward. *Banshee* sat partly hull down behind that little rise of ground, so the debris hit her mid and upper hull. The thrusters, drive units, and controls run through the armored floor. It was simply bad luck that a large piece of *Farriq* hit both the pressure door and the turret. Otherwise, she would be in better shape than *Pooka.*"

"Damn Nusam," Fenaday said.

"Are thee so immune from fear?" Telisan snapped.

Fenaday started to reply, but Telisan, his leathery face suddenly turning pale, stood up and bowed.

"Forgive me, please," Telisan asked. "I forgot myself."

"It's all right," Fenaday said, putting a hand on the tall alien's shoulder.

"Okay," Fenaday continued, "so far these things don't seem to show any sign of regenerating. We don't know if they do. We bugged out of the library too fast to see if that one came back. We know that when we killed the self-aware one last night, it had some effect. Maybe it was some sort of subcontroller."

"Certainly the attack fell apart after it did," Duna added.

"I don't want to be here at nightfall to find out. We will pick a landing site and bring the *Sidhe* in. Then, it's back to orbit and maybe just home. We appear to be overmatched. Meanwhile, Telisan, go get those burns attended to."

The Denlenn looked as if he might protest; but Fenaday cut him off with a raised hand. "No argument, Mr. Telisan. I need reliable people around me."

He regretted saying it instantly. He hadn't aimed the comment at Shasti, but she could only think she was the target of it. *Well,* he decided, *it might not be the worst thing.*

"Mr. Duna," Fenaday said, "stay close to Telisan, please. We will call the ship from *Pooka.*" He started off, half expecting he would be alone, but Shasti trailed alongside him. He searched for something to say, could not come up with anything, and damned himself for it.

As they passed two of the Landing Force troops, Shasti stepped aside to speak to them for a second. They hurried off in the direction of *Banshee.* She caught up to Fenaday effortlessly, her long legs covering the ground quickly.

He looked over at her. In the morning light, her face seemed colorless, except for the lustrous jade-green eyes. "Anything I should know?".

"It is going to occur to people," she replied tonelessly, "that wherever Duna is, the things strike hardest. The monsters will clearly not stop with him, since no outworlders survived on Enshar, but we have many frightened people here. Someone may figure it increases their own odds of survival if the last Enshari on the planet is dead."

"Very sensible," he said. It sounded stilted even to him. She did not reply. It struck him with a sudden clarity. She looked and sounded the way she did when they met in the shuttle bay, years ago. His anger at her actions in the wood had ebbed, replaced by the memories of all the times she'd saved his life.

Years wiped out, he thought, *me and my damn mouth.* Still, he could not bring himself to approach her. The familiarity they had shared was shattered, and he above all others knew how lethal Shasti could be when provoked. For now it seemed best to walk on the eggshells and let matters settle.

They reached *Pooka.* A weary Angelica Fury looked up from

under a panel as they entered. She held a micro-torch and battle patches of malleable ceramic. Fury was smart enough not to bother him with questions. He walked over to the communications console, passing one of Rigg's people in the top turret. Susan Bernard, one arm in a sling and looking like death warmed over, set up the call to *Sidhe* without his asking.

"Fenaday to Perez."

After a brief delay, a response came back. The screen did not light up with an image. Fenaday assumed it was due to damage to the shuttle's com system.

"This is Micetich on the bridge."

"We've had a bad night down here, Micetich. I assume you received a situation report."

"Affirmative."

"We can't come up, so we are going to bring *Sidhe* in for a water landing. Give me an ETA for a planetary landing at my location. If you can't make it before nightfall, we will be relocating."

"Please hold, ground base."

"Micetich," Fenaday snapped, "you're supposed to have that figure at your fingertips at all times."

Silence greeted him. He repeated the call several times. He could see dismay on Bernard's face. "They are receiving you," she whispered.

"I know they are," he said. He turned to Shasti. "Get Telisan, Duna, and Mmok. We have trouble."

Shasti vanished out the door. She'd long ago mastered the art of covering ground without looking as if she was in a hurry. Fury, Bernard, and the gunner stared at him, something like panic in their eyes.

"Do your jobs and keep your mouths closed," he ordered. They returned to work, but Fenaday knew they would listen to every word.

He heard boots on the deck ramp as Shasti returned with the others. Telisan arrived first, looking a question at him. Fenaday shook his head. Mmok was plainly furious. At that moment, the speaker crackled.

"This is *Sidhe*," came Micetich's voice, it sounded shaky.

"Put Mr. Perez on."

"Captain, Mr. Perez is unavailable," Micetich answered. "It's this way, sir. We will do everything we can to get you off the planet, but the ship isn't coming down. We don't want to be added to the body count on Enshar."

A coldness spread through Fenaday's belly. "Micetich," he said, "get Mr. Perez to the screen before you do something you may not live to regret."

"Forget it, Captain," came a new voice. "We are not going to take any chances. You've been down there seventy-two hours and you've gotten a quarter of your command wiped out. If we come in, it will be just like the *Flamme*. Anybody who doesn't agree with us is under lock and key."

"Naks!" Mmok exploded. He started swearing.

Fenaday's shoulders sagged. Naks commanded shipboard security. He was an ASAT and part of Mandela's team. They'd thought him reliable.

"Shut up," Fenaday ordered Mmok.

Fenaday considered, rubbing his hand over his face. He had no leverage in the present situation. If he pushed too hard, he might even lose the slender thread of the help she'd offered. "Micetich, if you attempt to break orbit, the ship's engines and power will go offline."

"Yes, sir, very clever. Mr. Perez explained quite thoroughly that we can't leave orbit for four weeks due to the safeguards you rigged. We can wait."

At least Perez is still loyal, thought Fenaday. Still, he was glad he had not given him the access codes.

"A Confederate Naval Court will stretch your neck and that of anyone with you," Fenaday stated. "Mutiny and marooning are death penalty offenses."

"We doubt it, sir. We were brought into this under false pretenses. Nobody told us about Enshar. We are only contesting your illegal order to land. Otherwise, we will still take your orders. In any event, we'd rather be judged by twelve than carried by six, not that we would even get that on Enshar."

"Very well, Micetich. You mentioned help. What do you have in mind? We can't climb out of this gravity well in the shuttles. I've got critically wounded here. How do I get them out?"

"Can you reach the spaceport at Barjan?" she asked. "There may be ships there."

"Try harder, Micetich. Those ships haven't been maintained in years, even if they are undamaged. Add to that, most will be Enshari and unfamiliar. It could take weeks to get one flyable. There are people here you are going to kill in twelve hours if we can't get them to better facilities. So add murder to your list of accomplishments."

There was the sound of a scuffle and some unintelligible shouting over the speaker.

"Stand by, Captain," Micetich said and clicked off.

"She is very polite," Shasti said, leaning against the bulkhead, her green eyes chill with promise. "When we retake the ship, I want her. I'll be sure to apologize as I slowly strangle her."

Fenaday shook his head. "Hold that thought. She may not be wrong about a board of inquiry finding them not to be mutineers. The government won't want the public to know we launched our little expedition without telling everyone where we were going.

"Also, she didn't have to even return our hail. Once they knew what happened to the shuttles, all they needed to do was sit tight for a few weeks and then leave. They could then make up their own story. Probably most of the crew doesn't know for sure what's going on.

"If it weren't for the presence of Duna and Telisan here, she might have opted for it. No one gives a rat's ass for the rest of us. We're all expendable, but Telisan's a war hero and Duna's a Nobel Laureate."

Fenaday leaned back in his seat. "She's walking a thin line. She has to help us or face the probability of prison for life—or life on the run. I think we can rely on her in anything that doesn't bring *Sidhe* into atmosphere."

"Fenaday," came the speaker voice. It was Micetich again, sounding out of breath. "Do you have any suggestions as to how we can aid you?"

"I do," he replied coldly. "Let's start with the preliminaries.

First, you and your fellow mutineers are under arrest. I will reserve the decision to proffer charges, at this point—that will depend on your cooperation."

"Fenaday," Micetich said, "we will want your assurances, on the record, that if we get you off-world, my people go to the Confed Navy, alive. I'm sure Death's Angel has already been making plans for me. We just want to live. Some of us have followed you into a lot of tight places, and we won't abandon you here—"

"For four weeks," Mmok muttered. Fenaday glared him into silence.

"—if we can avoid it," Micetich finished. "What do you have in mind?"

"I need evac on my wounded, fast. I want both *Wildcat* fighters sent down. You will find two stretcher pods in Stores Bay Five. I want full reloads sent down in the fighters, along with every land mine and all the barrier wire there is. Also, three days rations. Send the wire and ammunition first. We have enough food and medical for a few days. Dr. Mourner will give you a list. Telisan will give you a list of spares we need for equipment. I want that drop ASAP, Micetich. What's the orbital window?"

"By the time we get this together," she responded, "daybreak tomorrow. Even if I just send the fighters with what can be scraped together fast, the earliest window is for nineteen hundred standard."

"Damn," Fenaday said. "We are not going to weather another night here. We are moving to an island closer to the mainland. Fury, get the coordinates of the first one we flew over coming out here. Micetich, schedule your arrival at the coordinates she gives you."

"Wait one, Fenaday," Micetich replied. Two long minutes passed. "Okay, ground base," she responded. "I have volunteers, one of yours and one of ours. Only one fighter will land at a time. The one flown by your guy will be unarmed.

"Understand this, Captain," she continued, "we don't want a fight. Don't load the stretchers with anybody who isn't wounded. It won't work. We will get you all off, but you and Rainhell come up last and the HCRs do not come at all. We will surrender once you're on board, provided we get your recorded assurance you will turn everyone over to Confed Navy. I want it witnessed by Duna and Telisan."

"Affirmative. Fenaday, out." He sat back in the flight chair, resisting the urge to begin swearing.

"She planned it well," Duna said quietly, "poor frightened child."

Mmok made a sound of disgust and turned his back to them.

"The Shellycoats," Telisan began, "are becoming smarter and more numerous. Something on this world is waking up and becoming more aware of us. Not all at once. It seems to be working in fits and starts, else we would all be dead. It is, however, waking. It will take weeks of landings to evacuate this way. We will not last that long."

"We won't make it," Shasti added without any evident concern, "even with resupply and better tactics."

"Unless," Duna said, "we carry the fight to the enemy. Our only chance is to go to Barjan and destroy it."

"Destroy what?" Mmok snapped, turning to face them. "We don't know what it is, or where it is. Whatever force is operating here destroyed an entire planetary defense establishment and part of a fleet. We have a crew of cutthroats, screw-ups, and a few pros. We are fucked."

"I have a theory about our opponent," Duna said, raising a hand. "I will not know much more till we get to the Barjan Deep excavation where poor Creda died. What I know is what I see. Our enemy is stupid and aimless. We were only unlucky last night. But for the poor fool in the shuttle, we would have stood off the attack, powerful as it was, with little loss."

"There was the aware one at the end," Fenaday said, as if reluctant to even remember the image.

"Yes," Duna replied. "I believe the force that released itself from the Barjan Deep and spread over the world did not do so instantly, but over the space of a few hours. For all we know, the Shellycoats, as you call them, were moving for days, unseen and unfelt.

"Then it struck with near simultaneity over the globe. I think it reserved its greatest powers for the space stations and the military bases. Later, it struck against the fleet. These attacks were well planned and coordinated."

"What explains our survival here?" Shasti asked. "Why aren't Shellycoats manifesting themselves inside our perimeter? Why not inside this shuttle?"

Everyone but Duna and Shasti looked around the shuttle's interior nervously.

"That may be what happened on the *Wolverine* shuttles," Duna replied. "The same fate has not overcome us because, as Telisan suspects, the central guiding intelligence that assaulted the planet is not active. Perhaps it no longer exists, or is damaged. Or it may be that the central directing authority is not as yet aware of us. We are facing lesser parts of it, lesser forces perhaps.

"I believe we are presently below the level of intelligent awareness of our enemy. His automatic systems, or outposts if you will, attack us when we encounter them. The longer we are here, the more of them we provoke. As we provoke more reaction, higher levels of the enemy become aware and attack us more effectively. As these fail, they call on higher levels still. Eventually, the guiding intelligence that directed the original strike, if it still exists, will be awakened. We will be destroyed almost immediately afterward, I fear.

"These Shellycoats are only one manifestation of their powers. A massive electromagnetic pulse was used on the planet and later against Telisan's fleet. We have seen evidence of its ability to influence storms, perhaps to direct lightning. Some such weapon was used on the ships of Gigor base. I have no doubt that the efficiency with which it works goes up many hundreds of times if the directing mind comes on line."

"So," asked Telisan, "how long do we have till the Thunder God wakes up?"

"I do not know, youngling," replied Duna, "days, weeks, never? I have speculation based on ancient legends and incomplete observation of our circumstances."

"Days, I think," said Fenaday. "Just a feeling I have," he added, as the others looked at him, "maybe from being in physical contact with the thing. It's also the only prudent option for planning."

"We can't get off-world in days," Mmok growled.

"Maybe if we get to Barjan spaceport——" Telisan began.

"And trust ourselves to unmaintained and unfamiliar ships?" Shasti said. "It took a full dockyard of two hundred shipwrights, plus our full crew, working round the clock to get *Sidhe* ready for space in five days."

"True," Fenaday said, "but we are not talking about interstellar travel. We just need to hop far enough out of this gravity well for the ship to pick us up. Launch is the most dangerous part of the voyage to be sure, but if we could make a vessel space-worthy for an eight-hour flight, it would be enough. We might also find human-built ships at the port; that would make things easier."

"What of the Confed shuttles?" Duna asked.

Telisan waved a dismissive hand. "The electronics were fried; nothing worked on them. They are of a much newer variety than these *Dakotas*; the equipment is incompatible."

"Why would it be any different at the port?" Shasti said.

"Remember my computer," Duna said. "It was off-line at the time of the EMP. It does not appear that the EMP blast hit all places on the planet or hit with equal strength. The EMP appears to have been directed—though how such a thing is possible, I do not know.

"We might find functioning equipment in Barjan. Remember the lights on the night side? They were reestablished by secondary systems after the mains were knocked out. Perhaps the various embassies, with their reserve power sources, would be a place to start. We need a vessel that either was not hit by EMP, or where the essential equipment was off-line at the time," Duna concluded.

"Telisan," Fenaday said, "get a download from the ship. See if there is power operating in Barjan." The Denlenn nodded and headed for the communications panel.

"Back to defense," Shasti said. "Do we take a force into Barjan, leaving the others in some more isolated location?"

"Will that help?" Fenaday said bitterly. "I thought we were isolated here."

"There is an answer to that too," Mmok said. "I sent my air scout out after the weather broke. It was too stormy last night to keep the thing in the air; they are rather fragile.

"Anyway, some sort of immense, ocean-going platform fetched up on the other side of the island. It wasn't there when we came in. It doesn't register any power. Those imbeciles on the *Sidhe* must have seen it drifting and didn't regard it as a threat. More damn bad luck."

Telisan returned. "There is some power showing in Barjan," he reported, "mostly lights. I have satellite photos on their way. It will take a few seconds."

Fenaday thought for a minute. He rubbed eyes he only belatedly realized were very sore. "I am not going to split the force," he decided. "I want to pull out of here for the other island we overflew coming out. We will overnight there and come into Barjan in the early morning. Then we make for the port and establish a defended site. Search parties will look for a likely ship to get us out of here."

He paused. "A small party using all of our robots will accompany me as we attempt to locate our enemy's headquarters, point of origin, whatever, and blow it to hell." There was quiet at the table as he finished. Outside, the rain started again, lightly. Fenaday felt very alone.

"How will we attack it once we find it?" Telisan asked. There was a slight heartwarming stress on the "we."

"Yes," Shasti said. "We will likely have only one chance. It must be carefully planned." She didn't look directly at him.

"I'm going to order *Sidhe* to soft-land a nuclear warhead from a Mark Nine missile on Barjan field tonight," Fenaday said. "They can use an escape capsule with a homing beacon. We'll pick it up when we go in."

"Why not fire on the target from orbit?" Fury asked from the pilot's chair.

Fenaday frowned at her for speaking, but answered anyway. "It's the Barjan *Deep*, Lieutenant. Enshari dig their cities in. The best protection in the universe is a couple hundred meters of earth and rock. Even a mass drive has trouble with hardened underground targets through atmosphere. Besides, what would I use for a target?"

"Barjan is a huge city," Duna added, "occupied for many millennia. It is wide, and by our standards, somewhat shallow because of the taboo on digging in the Deep itself. Still, it is more than deep enough to be considered a hardened site. A mass driver would destroy the fragile ships at the port long before it got anything far underground. I am afraid the captain is right."

"A hunting we shall go," Fenaday said.

"Tally-fucking-ho," Mmok added.

Chapter Fourteen

Shasti and Fenaday kept their distance from each other the rest of the day, even visiting the casualties separately. One of the critically wounded died without regaining consciousness. She joined the others in the mass grave dug alongside the *Farriq-Dar*.

Fenaday walked over to the graveside carrying a small Bible. *They call it a soldier's manual*, he thought, full of the *"Yea, though I walk through the valley of death"* passages someone in the Confed Chaplains Corp thought would comfort believers. *I must not count as a believer. They don't comfort me.* He squinted up at Enshar's fierce sun. *Is there a God up there*, he wondered. *Is someone, anyone, looking down? Can you hear me? Where's Lisa? Why did all these people die? Why?*

"Captain?" Rigg said, giving him a concerned look. "We're ready."

"Yes, of course." He glanced around. Those not on guard or repairing the ships stood around the huge hole dug by the utility robots. Fifty people, many wounded, looked at him expectantly, waiting for the words to sum up the lives ended in that hole. Waiting for him to chant the magic spell that would somehow make sense of it all. Suddenly, he wanted to scream at them, wanted to tell the terrible truth that it didn't make sense, that he didn't know why those in the pit were dead and they were still alive, didn't know why the guardian angels of the fallen had failed to guard.

He drew a deep, shaky breath, looking at their expectant faces, then opened the small black book. "Man that is born of woman has but a short time…"

He finished the inadequate words, and Rigg's ASATs fired a volley. People picked up shovels and put the dirt in, very gently at first, till the wrapped bodies disappeared under the soil, then with more of a will. They had no markers, but *Farriq-Dar* would guard their sleep.

The survivors packed themselves into the two airworthy shuttles and headed for the inner island. Shasti rode in *Banshee*, ostensibly to keep an eye on things in the more damaged shuttle. Fenaday did not object.

He sat in the shotgun seat of the *Pooka*, looking down at the deep ocean. Mur's brilliant light splashed among the waves. The sight should have cheered him. As it was, he was merely grateful that the storms plaguing them had subsided. It seemed impossible to reconcile last night's battle with the bright sanity of day.

Fenaday looked over at the *Banshee*, thirty meters away and slightly higher. The Guard's Red paint on her upper hull was scorched and chipped. He could see some evidence of structural damage by the airlock door. Telisan and the aircrew patched it so air did not blow through the hole, but the shuttle's speed was down to two hundred kilometers an hour.

Fenaday unconsciously rubbed his ribs where Shasti hit him with her weapon, forcefully enough to break skin. Telisan noticed his movement and looked over at him. "Is something broken?"

Fenaday did not look back. "I'm afraid it might be," The Denlenn waited, but Fenaday said nothing further, he just looked out of the canopy. Telisan shrugged and returned to his instruments.

———

The spacers reached the smaller barren island after several hours travel in the protesting shuttles. The shuttles landed back to back. Nervous spacers hastily erected defenses. All the wounded remained aboard while the able-bodied set up camp.

Just before sunset, the *Wildcats* arrived. The appearance of the *Wildcats* cheered the defenders as the fighters circled the encampment. *Wildcat 1* balanced shakily in VTOL mode, then bumped down on the cleared field. Fenaday winced reflexively, praying nothing failed in the landing gear. *Sidhe* shipped few pilots; most of them were already down-world with the expedition. Clearly the *Wildcat's* pilot was not familiar with the fighter. The canopy rose on the stubby fighter. As Fenaday expected, Hanshi Tok climbed out. The Tok brothers were Moroks of the same blue-skinned humanoid race as Rask and among the most reliable of the crew. Fenaday knew Hanshi to be trustworthy, especially as his brother, Lokashti, was on-world with the landing force.

Hanshi climbed out. Lokashti walked over to him and gave him a very human-like embrace. Then Hanshi hurried over to Fenaday. "Captain, it is good to see you. I am your man. I spit on all mutineers." The Morok's smile, with its pointed teeth, was a fearsome thing.

"Thank you, Hanshi. It's good to see you too."

Telisan and some of the crew began unloading supplies from the ambulance and stores pods, as well as the small internal cargo space. Mmok and the utility robots immediately took some of the boxes out to the perimeter. Mines and robot spares, Fenaday imagined.

The other fighter continued to circle. Fenaday scowled up at it, noting the point-to-point missiles nestled under the wings. "Who's the watchdog?"

"One of Mr. Perez's new engineers, Tolk by name," Hanshi said. "Gods rot him. I would give much to shoot him from the sky."

"Another one of Mandela's," Fenaday murmured to himself.

"They don't seem to have been as reliable as he assured us," came Shasti's voice.

Fenaday turned. She'd slipped up on him again.

"Yes," he said stiffly. "I don't think anyone counted on the Special Forces people going bad." She walked up to stand near him.

"Ah," said Hanshi, delighted to see Shasti, "you live. This is good. We shall have much fun retaking the ship."

Shasti nodded. Hanshi did not seem offended by her cool greeting, doubtless used to her reticence.

"How does it stand on the ship?" Fenaday asked.

"Balanced on a razor," Hanshi replied, looking around at the campsite. "Micetich and her lover, Naks, lead the mutiny. The supply crew is in with them. Dobera remains loyal. You took most of the regular landing force down with you. The few who remain are worthless and do what Micetich tells them. The only other armed people on board are Naks's ASATs. Half follow him and half are in the brig. He arranged to have all their people on duty just after the attack. *Sidhe's* security systems are designed for operation by a small loyal cadre. This time it is a small disloyal cadre. Most are just waiting it out to see who comes out on top, especially in Engineering. They support neither side. They just keep the ship running and obey the nearest person."

"So there is no chance the vessel will be retaken?" Fenaday asked. A gust of cool wind slapped at him and he put his hands in his jacket pockets.

"No," Hanshi said, "not unless you and Death's Angel are there. Most would follow you if you were there, but they will not fight to come down to the planet."

"I never figured Micetich for something like this," Fenaday said.

"Naks," Hanshi said, "has turned her head. All she sees now is him."

"So what do I bring back to the ship, Captain?" Hanshi asked hopefully, looking at Shasti.

"Just the wounded," Fenaday said. "Deliver them to sickbay, then go spend some hours in the simulator. You nearly pancaked coming in today. We don't have spare ships."

"Captain," Hanshi begged, "if we are not going to attack, do not send me back to the ship. Send Karass. As you saw, I am a lousy pilot. I can do more good here."

"I would like to have him," Shasti said.

"It would make the likelihood of surviving the flight higher, I suppose." Fenaday grimaced. "Hanshi, call Tolk on the ship's radio; see if you can set it up. Shasti," he almost stumbled over her first name, "tell Karass to get ready."

"Yes, sir," she replied woodenly and stalked off.

They made the transfer. *Wildcat II*, its armed and suspicious pilot watching them intently, also landed and off-loaded. Fenaday wished he had bought more of the ambulance pods, but there were only the two. The small fighters, loaded with three wounded in their pods, headed back to the frigate before the flight window closed. The better part of a day would pass before a second landing could be attempted.

Night began to fall around the tense camp. This time the starship remained alert to any object on the sea, with orders from Fenaday to fire on anything that approached. Mmok sent out his air scout. Beyond rolling waves and thundering surf, it saw nothing.

Shasti came over to where Fenaday, Telisan, and Duna studied maps of the area by lantern light, trying to assess their next move.

"Captain," she said, "would you care to inspect the perimeter defenses?"

Fenaday looked at her, his face carefully free of expression. "I'm sure your arrangements are satisfactory, Commander."

"As you wish. With your permission, I'll take the first watch."

"Very good, Commander. Mr. Telisan will relieve you."

Telisan smiled at Shasti. She registered no reaction, just nodded and walked off toward the barrier wire. Fenaday returned to the map. Duna looked thoughtfully at Shasti's retreating back and excused himself from the others.

Mmok had watched the exchange from a distance, eavesdropping with the aid of his mechanically enhanced hearing. As Shasti passed by the mechanical man, out of sight now of Fenaday and the others, he whispered "Trouble in paradise? Lover's tiff?"

Shasti blurred into motion, seizing Mmok by the throat and lifting him off the ground before he could react. She banged him up against the shuttle's hull.

"Who gave you permission to talk to me?" she said in a silky, dangerous voice.

He glared back, started to move, and stopped abruptly as the pressure on his trachea doubled. "One call to an HCR," he choked out, "and you're history."

"Make the call," she dared him. "You'll be there to greet me in hell."

"Perhaps," came another voice, "it would be better if neither of you did anything further." Duna padded up to them. "Please let him go."

Shasti stared down at the little Enshari, then let go of Mmok, who slid down the shuttle's side. The two tall humans stood, stiff-legged, eyeing each other.

"Mr. Mmok," said Duna, "I believe Captain Fenaday wanted to see you. Something about the robots. I am afraid with my old brain, I can't remember the details."

Mmok sidled by Shasti, his face murderous. Shasti looked back, calmly, no trace of emotion visible. Mmok disappeared around the shuttle.

"I don't recall asking for any help," she said.

"No," Duna said, looking up at her. The Enshari came barely to the top of her hip. "I'm sure it is a rare event when you find yourself in need of help. You have always seemed very self-sufficient."

"I've had little choice in that," she replied with a hint of bitterness.

"Still," the Enshari mused, "it does seem you have had a friend in our captain."

Shasti appeared to draw even more into herself and turning away from Duna. "That's none of your concern."

"As you wish, my dear girl. I wish only to help."

There was a hesitation, almost a lack of firmness, in her for a second. "I don't think it's something you would understand."

"Perhaps not," Duna replied. "I have studied alien species for several hundred years, but I fear I remain dreadfully ignorant. Why, I was even married to the same lovely lady for four hundred years and never knew everything about her, either. She was always a source of delightful surprises. Of course, it might not be important that I understand. Perhaps it is important that Robert understands. He seems confused, a bit lost."

"The attacks keep escalating in size and intelligence," she replied, bitterness ebbing, leaving an undertone of sadness. "We aren't going to last much longer. We'll probably all be dead tomorrow, then it won't matter."

To her surprise, Duna reached up and patted her hand. His small paw felt warm and leathery. "That is why," he said, "it matters so much today, dear girl." The little Enshari turned and walked away. Shasti watched him go, then looked heavenward at the early evening stars and sighed.

———

Fenaday groaned and rolled upright in his sleeping bag. All the available floor space in the shuttles went for the wounded. He lay under the *Pooka*, on ground that appeared to grow rocks. Early morning light was falling, and people were beginning to stir. One or two got up briskly. Fenaday hated morning people.

He stumbled to his feet, fighting off the usual headache that he got from sleeping on anything other than a regular bed. Every muscle and bone ached from the battle.

Telisan sat at the nearby campfire, having had the last watch. Without a word, he handed the human a cup of coffee. Fenaday managed a grunt.

Telisan looked at him. "Perhaps it would be better if I went to get the breakfast crew started."

Fenaday grunted again. Morning was difficult enough to deal with without being hungry as well.

The ships had grounded near some small freshwater pools. After draining the coffee, Fenaday felt the urge for a bath. He headed down past the guards and the barrier wire. Cobalt stood by the outer barrier and dropped the lines for him.

"Morning," Fenaday growled, before realizing it was only a robot next to him.

"Situation normal," the robot replied.

Fenaday made his way down to the streamside. Water poured over shallow, rocky basins, almost perfect for bathing. He walked down the slight hillock and saw Shasti, wearing only dark-gray underclothes, sitting on a towel spread over a broad flat rock. Her long white limbs caught the sunlight as she brushed her black hair.

She looked neither sore nor bruised. Any artist would have sold his soul to paint her sitting there.

She spotted him and he nodded at her. Things were settling between them, but the strength they provided as a team was gone. To leave seemed to risk their fragile peace. So, he said nothing, just stripped out of boots and uniform, cooling sore, abused feet in the pool. He stood at its shallowest edge for a few moments.

He was relieved to hear other feet coming. Turning, he saw Brian Connery walking down the trail. Connery spotted Shasti, and a black glare from her caused him to veer away to find a pool at the far end of the glade.

Shasti brushed her waist-length hair for a few moments longer. Then with a curse, she threw down her brush. Fenaday looked directly at her for the first time, surprised.

"My ex-husband used to do that to me—drag me backward like a doll," she said softly. "It meant pain for starters and much worse to follow."

For a second Fenaday was lost, then realized she was referring to his pulling her away from Johan's body. He sat down on a rock, looking back in stunned silence. "I'm not sure what's the biggest surprise," he finally managed, "that I didn't know you'd been married, or that someone could manhandle you and live."

She looked at him obliquely and shrugged.

"We've shipped ten voyages together," he said after it became obvious that she would say nothing more. "Fought side by side, been lovers even. I haven't forgotten that you carried me out on Morokat, but I don't really know you at all. Do I?"

"I've never let you," she replied, picking up the brush and inspecting it. "You've never met anyone else from my world?"

"No," he said. "Olympians are a secretive lot. They rarely go off-world and don't encourage visitors or trade. From what I have heard, it's not a place I would want to visit anyway. "

"A hard world," she said bitterly. "A place for supermen to measure themselves.

"His name is Jalgren Pard, of the House of Denshi," she continued, with obvious reluctance. "Denshi specializes in assassins and bodyguards and controls the government. Pard is much older than I am, big, even for one of us, strong, cruel, and very rich.

"We Olympians worship a new god. His altars are laboratories, and we sacrifice original humanity on them. Did you never wonder why I'm so tall, so strong, so perfect?"

He nodded carefully. Silence seemed best.

"Olympia was settled by people who wanted to guide natural selection, to breed better people. Careful programs mated the best people, producing superior children—each generation slowly building toward the ideal. They're called the Selected. But that was too slow, too chancy for some people. About a hundred years ago, a faster road beckoned: bioengineering. Who needs parents when you have artificial wombs?

"I came out of one of those, Robert. I was made."

"What?" he said.

"We build people on Olympia," she continued, "taller, stronger, with perfect features and no diseases. We're called the Engineered. Pard used to say that our existence rendered the Selected obsolete. I know that gradually the Engineered are displacing them from government and the military on my homeworld.

"My body builds muscle at a rate no standard woman's body can. My bones are twenty-percent denser than a human male's and more elastic. That's why I weigh more than a human my size. I should live to be at least a hundred and seventy years old."

She took the brush to her hair, stopped, and held some of its glossy length in her hand. "Even my hair doesn't require the care of a regular woman's. Tailored genes keep it soft, not oily, and ten times stronger than human hair. Makes a good garrote."

She looked away and resumed brushing. "Pard ordered me created," she continued softly. "I'm designed to his taste: color of hair, eyes, skin tone, breast size, height, even length of leg.

"He had others before me but never another Engineered. I was an experiment for him. I even trained in the house of Denshi as a bodyguard and assassin, so I could be useful for more than bed warming. He wanted me to be self-reliant. No clinging females for Jalgren Pard.

"I'm an expensive toy, Robert, built to spec and just for him to play with. When I reached my early teens, he claimed me for his bed. It began well. Ignorant child that I was, I was even honored. But it became…very twisted and sick. One day, I decided I did not want to be a toy anymore. I escaped. Sometimes, when he finds out where I am, he tries to have me killed. Wounded pride, I suppose.

"My world's dirty little secret," she ended.

"My God, Shasti," he said, shaken. "I didn't know. In all the time we've known each other, you've never found a time to tell me this? I don't think you've ever told me anything about your past, never anything personal."

"No, I haven't," she said, "but neither have you. You've never even shown me a picture of your wife or told me much about her."

"It seemed, somehow wrong," he said slowly, confused.

"Why?" she asked simply, turning back to look at him.

He looked into her face, there was no mockery there, just a child-like lack of comprehension. It suddenly struck him. Shasti had never been close to another human being before. She had no mother, father, brother, or sister. Her sexual experiences began badly, with a cruel, older man. The greatest trust Shasti could show was to allow herself to be vulnerable. She handed him that trust now.

"Because of what happened between us," he said, groping for words.

"You have been good to me, Robert. Few have. But I don't love you. I've never loved anyone. They left it out of my design.

"I like being with you. Enough to say these things. Enough to want to buy back last night. But, I could never give you what you are searching for in your lost Lisa. I wish I could hope to learn to give it. I wish I understood what makes a man do everything you've done for her. Even after years of watching you, I still don't." Her eyes shone bright with tears she would not shed.

"How old are you, Shasti?" he asked, wondering why he did not know.

She blinked and thought for a second. "Around twenty-four in standard years."

"With a life span of one hundred and seventy, or more? That's a long time to live without love," he said.

She looked down, pensive. "Can you miss what you do not know? So much of love is pheromones, hormones—intense feelings I simply don't have. My systems are designed to suppress most strong emotions. Everything, except," she hesitated, "rage. Rage is useful for survival, useful for a warrior. They left me that. I've tried to learn to control it on my own." She looked at him sidewise. "I'm still working on it. Perhaps that is the worst of it. Death's Angel they call me. It may be true because it's the only time I'm truly myself."

"And when we were together?" he asked.

Again came the bitter smile. "Oh, I enjoy that too, as you should be able to tell. Remember, I was made to enjoy physical sex. The rage is all my own."

Fenaday felt a deep sadness unlike anything he had felt before. When he lost Lisa, a soul-tearing grief and anger had overwhelmed him. He'd declared war on the universe and the God he believed had turned his back on him. His feelings for Shasti were less fierce, yet deep and tinged with pity.

"There is more to what happened out there in the woods than this," he said, moving over to share the rock with her. She did not look at him. "You and Johan? It always seemed as if he was special to you."

"Yes. Once, between missions," she replied. "It meant more to him than to me. I didn't understand what he wanted of me. I don't even now. I didn't want it to go further. It was a bad idea, in a moment of weakness."

"We all have them," he said.

"I am afraid it killed him," she said, eyes downcast. "When this voyage came up, he threw away everything he had gained. I fear that I'm the reason he joined up. Perhaps he hoped to restart things between us. Asking me for things I do not understand and cannot give. So you're right, it is both things."

Fenaday shook his head. "I don't think he's unhappy with his choice."

She looked back uncomprehending. "He's dead."

He could find nothing to say to that.

"I want to go back to what you and I were," she said. "You

171

won't see last night's side of me again. I want you to count on me as you did before."

He nodded. "I never really stopped. I guess my feelings were just hurt." Abruptly he leaned forward, taking her hand. She looked away, but held tight to his hand.

"One thing I've learned in life is that there are roads to places that no roads lead back from. Everything is different now," he said. Emotion welled up in him. He felt unbalanced, like a man reaching for a handhold and missing it.

"Has this Pard tried to kill you since you joined *Sidhe?*" he asked, switching back to firmer ground.

She shrugged. "Twice on Bandish, once on Morokat. I think he was behind our troubles there. I handled it."

"Then he knows you belong to the *Sidhe* and will try again."

"He doesn't pursue me full time," she replied. "It would be beneath his dignity. But yes, he'll try again."

"Then that is war with House Fenaday, if we get out of this alive, we'll deal with him," Fenaday said, "together."

"Make no rash promises," she warned. "Pard is the head of Denshi and deadly. I bested him once by sheer surprise and barely escaped alive."

"It's been said and cannot be unsaid. Besides, I'm pretty formidable myself, you know," he said with an ironic smile.

She shook her head, looking him in the eye. "You would look like a child next to Pard."

"The bigger they are, they harder they fall?" he added hopefully.

"Well," she said, with the barest of smiles, "maybe we will get lucky."

Fenaday and Shasti walked back to the camp, side by side, talking quietly. Duna and Telisan watched them return and exchanged their version of smiles of relief.

"I think our chances for survival just went up," Telisan said.

Chapter Fifteen

Sidhe slid closer in orbit to Enshar, recovering her _Wildcats_. The fighters' running lights glinted as they lined up for entry into her hangar bays. With recovery complete, the frigate altered orbit with a quick burn of engines. Fenaday's security protocol allowed the starship's engines to be used to change orbit, but the mutineers' best efforts had failed to find a way to use them to break out. She moved to an orbit sufficiently close for a parachute drop on Barjan Field.

A brilliant yellow escape capsule popped from the frigate's side. Inside it sat a Mark Nine one-kiloton warhead, the largest the Confed Navy permitted a private warship. The capsule fell through the atmosphere until its onboard computer finished analyzing wind, height, and trajectory. A parachute deployed much later than would have been the case with live cargo. The warhead, well secured and incapable of going off by accident, slowly sank through the quiet of Enshar's night. At a thousand meters, it disturbed a flock of migrating unbars. The giant bird-like creatures squawked and dodged the capsule. The deadly load landed between the wrecks of two in-system freighters on Barjan Field. Emergency and rescue lights began their automatic plea for help pulsing brightly at intervals. On the half-hour, a siren sounded for a few minutes. Wildlife fled the area in alarm.

———

"Barjan," announced Duna, pointing at the horizon with a small furred hand, "a city with a longer history than some species, far larger even than your Tokyo or Peking." He drew his otter-like body up in evident pride.

Fenaday and the others crowded the flight deck. As the shuttles came in from the ocean, they could see the city in its ruined majesty, stretching out in all directions back from the coastline. From the air, it looked like a froth of bubbles of different sizes and shapes, burying the low mountains of the coastline. They could see domes of white and a variety of metallic colors shining in the sun. Shaftways lined with windows and balconies allowed light to plunge into the depths. Some of the domed exteriors showed rents and signs of explosions. Several new-style towers visible in the distance looked ragged, uneven, as if they had attracted some form of explosive weapons fire.

"The mansions and the more desirable properties are down those shafts," Duna said. "Barjan's upper regions were reserved for commerce, sanitation, industry, the poor, and those young non-traditionalists influenced by other cultures."

The shuttles approached the immense Barjan Spacefield, a proper complement to the huge city. Fenaday could not tell where the city began and the space/airport ended. They'd flown over the seaport side on the way in, passing over dozens of half-submerged wrecks, long broken free of their moorings. At the quays sat more vessels, including a huge submarine transport lying on its side.

"Are there undersea cities?" Fenaday asked Duna.

"Several major ones and a number of other installations," answered Duna, absently staring at the horizon-filling city.

Fenaday imagined being hunted by Shellycoats through the streets of a city beneath the sea. The thought filled him with a deep horror, as did the sight of the half-sunken ships. Fenaday feared little in space or in the air, but for some reason, the sight of a sunken vessel always made him uneasy.

"Radio direction indicates we are nearly on top of the capsule," called Bernard. They all pressed against the windows, searching for it. Fenaday saw the bright yellow capsule first, pointing it out to Fury. The shuttles sank to the concrete of the field. This time Fenaday didn't tax the engines by running them for a possible escape. The damaged shuttles couldn't take the strain, and in truth, they had nowhere else to go.

The *Dakotas'* still-functional ramps dropped. In a well-rehearsed drill, the remaining robots, led by the three HCRs, came out, forming a perimeter. The ground troops followed warily, taking cover around the shuttles or behind the robots. In a deliberate display of nonchalance, Fenaday and the command staff sauntered out of the shuttles and into the open.

Sweat popped out on his forehead as Fenaday stepped into the enervating heat of the spaceport apron. He unsealed his shirt, glad he had left his leather A-2 jacket in the shuttle. Shasti walked beside him. She'd torn the sleeves out of her shirt. Her well-muscled arms cradled a bipod-mounted tri-auto, the same heavier caliber the HCRs used. He admired the way the shirt stretched over her chest, then mentally kicked himself for being distracted from the task of surviving the day. He wondered if she had noticed.

Telisan had noticed and he smiled to himself. The Denlenn was an essentialist, having seen so much cut short in the war. He lived for the moment. *A pity,* he thought, not for the first time, *that there are no Denlenn females along.* He found human females attractive enough, but there were compatibility problems in physiology and psychology. He sighed. Two particular faces occupied his mind, a female and demi-female of his species. He wondered if he would ever see them again.

The spacers stood in a circle, surveying the evidence of their unknown enemy's work on the field. Some ships were scorched and flayed open as if by a tremendous heat, perhaps the whips of lightning from Duna's ancient stories. Carbon scoring defaced the hulls and the concrete apron. Glassy trails lay melted in the permacrete. In the far distance, the remains of a large vessel rested where it careened into the ground on that fateful day. Her shattered inner structure resembled an enormous ribcage.

Telisan followed Fenaday's gaze. "At least it was quick on her."

The permacrete apron stretched before them, littered with smashed helicopters, aircars, and lesser modes of transport, as if they'd been struck down in a single instant. The characteristic debris piles typical of a Shellycoat attack were curiously absent.

Fenaday raised field glasses to the city beyond. Several fires burned in the distance, trailing plumes of smoke into the bright blue sky. He didn't know if these were natural or the result of some power short or failed machinery. Batteries, solar power, and self-repairing machinery had kept Barjan full of mechanical movement since the Enshari perished, but it was a dance of the dead. Out in that foreboding city, robot domestics tended rooms filled with bones of their masters or perhaps cleaned them away as mere refuse. Repair robots without central direction attempted to keep the city lights working. Gradually, each hit a problem only solvable by the living and failed. Still as seen from orbit, many machines continued to move in the city's bowels.

"The amount of mechanical and electrical movement in Barjan," Duna said, "makes me doubt that the EMP effect was used near the city."

"Let's hope so," Fenaday replied. "It will be hard enough to get a ship operational without having to replace the computer system as well."

Fenaday turned his eyes away from Barjan's ruins and walked over to the nearest crashed vehicle. The others trailed him. Shasti gestured to Connery and Daniel Rigg, who spread their squads out further to cover them.

They examined the wreck of a small helicopter. The black and orange machine lay badly crumpled, though there had been little fire. Human and Enshari bones rested intermingled in the cabin; the remains were in poor shape from animals and heat.

"Christ," Mmok said, "can you imagine what this slaughter-house smelled like for the first few weeks?"

"No," said Fenaday quietly, "I thank God I can't."

"The bodies are all gone to bone or less by now," said Shasti, as if to reassure him. Fenaday smiled to himself. She knew he was somewhat squeamish, at least by her standards.

Over twenty spacecraft lay in this section of the port. They ignored four more, smashed onto their sides by the attack or perhaps, merely toppled by storms. These were clearly shattered and beyond hope. Of the others, about half were military, or of a commercial type for rough, semi-prepared fields. The rest sat on the field, in vertical take-off cradles like the ones on Mars. Several of the nearest ships were burnt out hulks. Another looked as if it had been in the advanced stages of a refit never to be completed. A few promising prospects existed: a small in-system sloop and a huge liquid-hauler—both looked undamaged. Fenaday made a mental note of their positions.

"All right," Fenaday said, "enough sightseeing. Let's get that nuke and find the Terran Embassy."

Mmok pointed to an area between two badly damaged in-system freighters. "Signal came from there," he said laconically. Mmok stripped out of his shirt and tossed it to Cobalt. His one cyborg arm gleamed as the sun bounced off metal and polymer, contrasting with his pale white face and other natural arm.

They walked into the shadow of the freighters, grateful for the shade, and spotted the capsule immediately. Mmok unsealed the hatch, cutting off the lights and siren before it could blare again. The warhead and the detonation kit were bundled in with additional supplies.

"Dinnertime," Mmok called out as he passed fresh charges to Cobalt and the other HCRs, which in turn loaded them and other supplies on the three utility robots. The larger unarmed versions of the crab robot handled the equipment easily.

"There's a groundcar park over near the port buildings," Rigg said. He'd pulled out his field glasses and scanned toward the control tower area. More cautious than some of the others, he'd only unsnapped the body armor over his chest, and sweat stained his green uniform shirt.

"Let's check it out," Fenaday said.

As the landing force moved, the gray crab robots skittered over the permacrete, keeping an unvarying distance from Mmok. Cobalt and Vermilion also paced them, though closer. Verdigris returned to the shuttles with the utility robots and the warhead under the watchful eyes in *Pooka's* top turret.

"Wouldn't it have been faster if we landed near the embassy?" Duna asked. On his shorter legs he had some trouble keeping the pace. He was also struggling with a silvery tube that he'd brought from the shuttle.

"We passed over the embassy on the way into the spacefield," Fenaday said. "The helipad is blocked by a crash. I want to scout the site from the ground before trying to move into the legation. Automatic defenses might still be operating, and we need to clear landing areas of debris before bringing in the shuttles."

"Ah," Duna said. He popped a seam on the silvery tube, and it unfolded into a silvery parasol that Duna raised over his head.

As the spacers slogged over the burning apron, fitful breezes from the ocean provided them some relief. Fenaday was glad for the brim of his hat and the sun goggles he wore. Rask walked next to Fenaday. His blood-red eyes were hidden behind goggles; otherwise, the heat didn't seem to bother the blue-skinned, goblin-like alien. A breeze lifted Shasti's long mane of hair, and the sun created flashing blue highlights in it. It also raised bright, metallic highlights on Mmok's ceramic metal skull in a far less charming effect.

Reaching the vehicle-park, they bypassed the smaller Enshari vehicles, heading for others of Terran design. Several of the largest vehicles bore Confederate Military markings. Rask greeted these like old friends. "Well, well," he crowed, waving his ape-like arms, "good old reliable M-2 multi-fuel armored transports."

"You think they're usable?" Rigg asked dubiously.

"Hell, Sarge, the damn things run off of any liquid you can get into the converter. Engines will be gunked up, but we aren't buying them. Gimme about twenty minutes with some help, and I'll have at least one of them running."

Rigg looked at Fenaday. "What do you say, sir?"

"How many of the mules do we have left?" Fenaday asked.

"Just three. They can only take four people each or the equivalent in equipment. We could put everybody in the scout force into two of these. They also have armored sides."

"You've got your twenty minutes," Fenaday said.

"I'll give you a hand," Mmok added. "I'm pretty good with engines, being half one myself." The rare evidence of humor drew a few grins.

The spacers settled into whatever shade was available. Telisan radioed Fury, relaying the reason for the hold-up. In the shade, it was cool enough to make sweat-soaked shirts suddenly cold. Shasti sat next to Fenaday. Despite all the improvements of genetics, Shasti shared something in common with most women. Her body temperature ran on the cool side. Fenaday, who radiated heat cheerfully, provided a comfortable place to put her back against. He smiled at the liberty, taking it as a sign that things were healing between them.

Shasti looked at Duna sitting near them, studying the city.

"Belwin, how are you doing?" she asked—in a rare display of concern.

The Enshari looked back at her with his large dark eyes. "I am all right, Shasti, though I cannot help thinking of all that is lost and can never be made good. I keep my mind focused on the task to be done here."

"Revenge is a powerful motivation," she said.

"Revenge, my child," Duna said gently, "is a luxury, and an expensive one. I am only interested in re-establishing a home for my people. Life is more important than revenge. Nothing brings back the dead. Nothing makes them rest any easier. I would forego revenge for a home."

Fenaday tensed a little, expecting Shasti to take offense at being called a child. No rebuke came from the Olympian, who only replied, "Interesting thoughts, though foreign to me. On my world, people live by the blood feud, and revenge is an everyday occurrence. I was raised in a guild of assassins."

"How terrible," Duna said. "It sounds as if much that is precious is wasted on such a world."

Fenaday listened to the discussion with bemusement. Shasti was not by nature chatty or empathetic. Somehow the Enshari had made a connection with her. Fenaday felt grateful for it. She needed more friends.

Rask and his crew were better than their word, getting two of the large M-2s running in the twenty minutes. "If my old motor sergeant saw the abuse I put the engines through in startup," a gleeful Rask said, "he'd die of apoplexy. The engines need a tear down and clean out, but there's no time for it now."

Rigg and Shasti's best troops boarded the multi-fuels, leaving the remainder under Fury's command at the shuttles. Fenaday and his command staff rode the second vehicle. Rigg and his ASATs took the point, flanked by the HCRs operating as a skirmish line. Crab robots, lacking the HCR's foot speed or heat endurance, latched onto the vehicles as Mmok's air scout circled overhead. It transmitted the best views of the way ahead to Mmok so they didn't waste time on blocked streets.

Multi-fuels proved a good pick for the trip. They could go around—or in some cases up and over—the debris. The big machines headed up the on-ramp of the airport freeway, slowly wending their way through the wreckage of the last Enshari rush hour.

"Could all this have been done by Shellycoats?" Shasti wondered.

"I doubt it," Fenaday said, grabbing onto a side rail as the multi-fuel shoved a wreck out of its way. He avoided looking into the wreck but couldn't miss the flash of white bone within.

"Why?" Telisan asked, looking at the cars dotting the roads all around them.

"Yes indeed, Captain," Duna said, intent. "Why?"

"What would the Shellycoats form from in a car on these highways?" Fenaday said. "Nor do we see any sign of chained lightning or extreme heat. I fear our enemy has other ways of killing than what we have seen. Something that killed people over a wide area all at the same time."

"Ah," Telisan said, "you cheer me. I was afraid we had seen all there was to see. Now you tell me there are new amusements ahead."

Fenaday snorted. "Let's hope we don't experience those amusements."

"Hmmm," Shasti said, "neutron radiation, a massive EMP, nerve gas?"

"The God knows," Duna said.

Near midday, they finally reached the embassy. The building resembled a fanciful castle with a crenellated roof and heavy stone facade. Lesser buildings, barracks, tool sheds, and the like surrounded it. The embassy sat on a greenish-blue lawn, secure behind an ornate wrought iron fence.

"Mmok," Fenaday called, "send the HCRs to scout and have the crab robots open the gates."

Mmok nodded, and the machines skittered over to the main gate, slicing through the locks and pushing them open. Nothing fired on the machines. HCRs raced into the grounds spreading out to counter any threat. The spacers proceeded carefully onto the lawn, weapons at the ready.

"Look at that," Rigg demanded, rare excitement showing on his lean face.

A circle of Marine and ASAT corpses, identifiable only by the remains of their uniforms and weapons, lay around a cluster of civilian corpses halfway to the helipad. The spacers trotted over to the scene of the final stand.

"Whatever struck the Enshari down at the same instant did not seem to have been at work in the embassy," Fenaday said, observing the circle.

"We can't leave them like this," Rigg said, his jaw knotting. "I'll get a burial detail together."

"Later," Fenaday said, looking up at the big man. "We need to make the embassy ready for the rest of our force." Rigg and Rask looked at him, both clearly upset.

"These were our people," Rigg growled.

"The living take precedence over the dead," Fenaday snapped. He regretted the words as they left his mouth. Shasti stood right next to him; Johan had to be on her mind. "We will attend to them when we can. Our own wounded come first. Right?" The ASATs nodded reluctantly, walking off to join the others on the first multi-fuel.

Fenaday looked up at Shasti and searched for something to say.

She spared him the trouble. "It's all right," she whispered.

They avoided the section of the embassy gutted by fire, starting toward the main doors. Troops covered the door, while the HCRs and crab robots went up to the entrance. As they reached it, Mmok spun around. "Airbot spotted an incoming target," he hissed. "It's under vegetation, coming this way. No identification."

The HCRs and the crab robots dashed down the stairs as the humans scattered, seeking cover. Shasti dropped the bipod legs on her weapon, sighting in on the direction the HCRs were facing. "Everyone, look to your front," she called. "Rigg, keep a fire team facing the embassy. Connery, Li, back up Cobalt."

Vermilion stood next to Fenaday. "Distance to target?" he demanded.

"Target is approaching edge of the treeline," advised the robot, its flat voice gratingly calm, its weapon leveled and motionless.

"How many? How big?"

"Single target, approximately 1.5 meters."

"The size of one of my people," Duna cried. "Fenaday!"

Fenaday opened his command mike. "Attention! No one is to fire except on my direct order. Hold your fire. Hold your fire."

They covered the tree line tensely, every eye searching for a target.

It came out of the tree line hesitantly, on all fours, with ears up and its nose in the air.

"It's a fucking dog," cursed Greywold, the Landing Force trooper Shasti had offered to execute as an example. He aimed at the animal.

Fenaday spun toward him. "Freeze," he roared.

Shasti, moving as fast as thought, knocked Greywold flying.

"Hold your fire," Fenaday ordered. "Everyone on safe, now."

Shasti ignored the fallen Greywold and walked toward the animal. She stopped halfway, kneeling down to make her height less intimidating. She reached into her pack, pulling out a ration, popping the canister of food and holding it out to the dog. Her voice, always musical, coaxed.

Greywold glared at Shasti's back. Fenaday tapped his heavy laser pistol against his thigh twice. "You've already had two strikes, mister. Care to go for the third?"

"No," Greywold replied sullenly. The young tough climbed to

his feet, watching Fenaday warily. He safed his rifle. Telisan walked over and snapped it out of his hand with a glare. Greywold glared back.

"Would you care to try taking it back?" Telisan asked, golden eyes blazing in his leathery face.

Greywold stepped back, dropping his eyes.

The dog, a large but gaunt German shepherd, walked closer to Shasti, but still hung back, afraid. She continued to talk softly, throwing a small piece of food—hastily snatched up by the animal. The big shepherd looked at Shasti, sniffing the others beyond her. He whimpered and walked back and forth, wanting people, but afraid after so long alone. The dog crept closer to Shasti, who held still more food in her hand. He nibbled hesitantly, enjoying the food and the soft sounds that Shasti made. It was the old bond, being offered again. Shasti kept her hand out and the dog sniffed it, then licked. His tail began to wag and he moved closer, whining anxiously and butting his head against Shasti. She scratched the dog's ears, and he sat delighted. As far as he was concerned, happy times had returned to Enshar.

Fenaday walked up slowly and sat down a little away from the dog. The shepherd came over to him slowly. Fenaday held out a hand, speaking the way he would have to one of his father's hounds. The tail came up, and the dog practically jumped into his lap, knocking him over. Fenaday petted the animal, feeling its too thin body as it tried to lick him.

Shasti laughed. The dog, perhaps realizing the significance of the event, abandoned him to return to his first love. Shasti started talking to him. Fenaday handed Shasti a ration can from his pack. She opened it and dished it out for the shepherd's noisy enjoyment.

Shasti reached over and looked at the synthetic collar around his neck. This required more petting. The collar and its I.D. tag were nearly buried in his fur.

"His name is Risky, according to the collar, it's got a military ID. I thought he might be a K-9. They're genetically enhanced, bigger and smarter than a regular pet. He must have been assigned to embassy security."

Fenaday looked at her curiously.

"When I trained on Olympia, I worked with K-9s. They were the best friends I had." She stood slowly. The dog looked wary, his tail down. She stepped away then patted her leg and whistled. Risky trotted up and walked alongside her toward the others. She made several people come up, one by one, so as not to alarm the dog. Some offered snacks Risky happily accepted. Shasti quickly stopped that. "He won't be used to such rich food anymore. Let's not make him sick."

The dog greeted everyone with enthusiasm, even a chagrined Greywold. Duna and Telisan stayed back. Dogs meant nothing to either, and the shepherd was bigger than Duna. Fenaday couldn't blame him. He turned to Cobalt, the nearest robot. "Log this creature as a member of the landing force. Update all fire control protocols."

"Linked," the robot replied, "update complete. Please identify the new crew member." The breeze kicked up and lifted the robot's hair. For a moment, it looked nearly alive.

"Identify the new crewmember as Risky, a K-9 unit," Fenaday said.

"Acknowledged," Cobalt replied. The robot turned to the shepherd, which eyed it without much interest, having classified it as a man-made thing and hence useless as a source of treats or pets. "Arf, Arf," the robot said.

They all stared at Cobalt for a second. Fenaday snorted. "Very funny, Mmok. I have heard of living vicariously, but you take the cake."

With Risky on the team, they reentered the embassy. A familiar maelstrom had struck its interior.

"Shellycoat attack," Telisan said. Fenaday nodded.

"I don't know if it makes a difference," Fenaday said, "but I want all this debris moved out of here. It may be that if something was a Shellycoat once, it might make it easier to become one again. All the bones are to be buried and everything else, burned, buried, or put in the stream out back."

Telisan nodded. "After we check the place out, I'll have Mmok put the robots on it."

"Let the ASATs take care of the remains out front," Fenaday

cautioned. "They might not want the bones handled by machines. I don't need any trouble from that quarter.

"Have Rask hook up one of the multi-fuels to the helicopter wreck. Drag it off the pad. I want to bring the *Banshee* in back there. We'll put *Pooka* down on the front lawn."

Telisan nodded and went off to get Rask.

One of Mourner's medtechs came up the stairs and over to Fenaday. "The embassy follows the standard pattern," he said. "There's a good-size clinic in the basement for situations local doctors might not be able to handle. Unlikely that much of the drugs are usable, of course. The equipment and computers were off-line. They must not have had any medical emergencies that day."

"Good," Fenaday said. "Inform Dr. Mourner and prepare it to receive all our casualties."

He turned to Shasti. "First bit of good luck we've had in a while."

She nodded. "We were due."

Connery came up to them. The red-haired Irishman had a grin plastered across his face. "Whatever hit here got to them before the emergency power could go on. The units are still off and look to be in working order. The generator is a multi-fuel. Rask should be able to get it running. We'll need a portable battery pack from one of the shuttle's stores.

"The armory is intact. They must not have had time to use more than the weapons that were at hand. There is a fair supply of claymore mines, plastic explosives, and additional barrier wire. That means we have power in the building and for the exterior defenses. We'll also have more weapons than we have hands to shoot them. We'll be ready for a fight, Captain."

"The good news," Shasti said grimly, "is that we have power. The bad news is whatever hit these people took them out fast. Seconds, minutes tops."

Connery's face fell.

Fenaday shot her a warning look. "Good work, Connery. By nightfall, we'll be forted up so tight that the Conchirri fleet couldn't dig us out. Go get the equipment and tell Rask we have another engine job for him. He's in the back with one of the M-2s trying to clear the helipad."

"Yes, sir," said Connery. He headed for the rear doors of the embassy, casting dubious looks at the piles of bones on the floor and shining a pocket torch at any dark corners.

After he left, Fenaday leaned slightly toward Shasti. "Remember, everyone else here comes complete with fear and doubt. They need hope to keep their morale up."

"Self-deception," she judged, "but if it motivates them, so be it. I'll be more careful."

"Shasti," he said gently, "everyone needs hope."

She looked at him without comprehension.

They converted the embassy to a fortress in short order. Behind the main building, Rask and his M-2s cleared the landing pad. Telisan, their best pilot, drove a mule back to the airport to take *Pooka* in himself. Fury switched over to the *Banshee*, relieving Hanshi. She had the easy approach, a nice wide helipad.

The landing spot in the front of the embassy was far trickier. Fenaday and Shasti watched from the roof as Telisan brought the big red shuttle between trees, fence line, and the outbuildings. Fenaday's own hands unconsciously flexed as if he had the controls. The Denlenn zoomed up to the clearing, dropping the shuttle into the narrow landing site in a maneuver that made Fenaday cover his eyes. He opened them, expecting to see a smoking disaster. Instead, he saw Telisan smiling happily as he popped the cockpit door and jumped out onto the lawn.

"Do you think he actually waited long enough for the engines to switch off?" Fenaday wondered aloud.

"You said he was a hot pilot," Shasti said.

"God damn all fighter jocks," he griped. "We just made the last payment on that thing."

Shasti gave a brief laugh.

Fenaday and Shasti hurried down the stairs and out onto the lawn. A few of the landing force only now peeked out of their foxholes to see if it was safe. Dr. Mourner came out the back of the shuttle with the first stretcher case. She shot a venomous look at the unaffected Denlenn. As she went by, she poked Fenaday in the chest, "Next time, you fly it, or I'm walking."

Medics came out to help take the wounded to the basement clinic for better care than the shuttles could supply.

Armed with equipment from the shuttles and with the help of the robots, Fenaday sent work parties to get a suitable area prepped for the evening's fighter landing. At least three more of the wounded would be sent up to the safety of the ship. The area beyond the helipad looked best suited for the task. In three hours, they cleared a rough field on which the fighters could safely land.

Troops encircled the grounded shuttles and the embassy itself with barrier wire. A fire-team manned each small shuttle. Fenaday ordered mines laid in abundance down every likely avenue of attack. Crew-served weapons were set up on the roof and sighted in. Mmok positioned the robots for maximum effect. Quickly the force divided into watches. Those without immediate assignments did the sensible thing—they sacked out in anticipation of a long night. Fenaday, Duna, and the others nervously watched the sky. Bad weather could mean a return of the enemy's forces, but the sky remained cloudless as it darkened toward evening.

Before nightfall, the *Wildcats* returned. The more wounded crew went up in the ambulance pods. Another of the less wounded rode up in *Wildcat Two's* back seat.

Ninety-one of them remained on the planet, including six wounded, not counting the robots. They gathered close as Mur set in the west, taking with it the comfort of its fierce light.

Shasti reported to Fenaday as Mur's light began to fade. "Two fire-teams are on the roof," she said. "Additional guards man every window."

"We've never been attacked in the open, during daylight by the Shellycoats," Fenaday said. "All the attacks occurred in the dimness of buildings or at night."

"We don't know," Duna said, "if that's because we keep relocating too quickly to trigger a massive attack during the day, or if the things dread bright sunshine."

"That sounds too much like an old ghost story to me," Fenaday said. "I prefer to believe we've covered too much ground in the shuttles for our enemy to track us. On the chance that light does bother them, I ordered Shasti to have every light in the embassy switched on. One can only guess in such a battle."

"Did you find anything on the computers, Duna?" Shasti asked.

"Telisan and I have tried, without success, to find any part of the Barjan Computer Net that is still in operation, using the medical computers downstairs. All the other embassy computers are inoperable. After three fruitless hours, we gave up. Barjan's net is gone." He pulled out the data crystals he made from his home system. "We are going to devote our time to a detailed analysis of the video from Creda."

"You think it's particularly significant?" Fenaday asked.

"Yes," Duna said. "Barjan Deep is the name for a special area many miles long in the oldest section of the city. It had been underdeveloped for cultural reasons as I told you. In the last few years, it acquired a certain style as an address. This led to the digging boom that I believe uncovered the cause of the disaster. We hope to pin down the exact location using the video."

"I hope you're right," said Fenaday. "We have only one tactical nuke." He dreaded the prospect of crawling for days through the subterranean city, searching for the heart of the darkness that overwhelmed Enshar.

Tense hours followed, but there was no sign of any enemy. Fenaday reduced the alert so more of his force could rest, then summoned his senior officers. They gathered in the ambassador's office to review their plan of battle. Shasti attended, with Risky by her side. The animal had not ventured far from her since they found him that afternoon. Shasti had asked Dr. Mourner to examine the dog, who pronounced Risky healthy, just underweight and suffering from some vitamin deficiencies. The native bugs and parasites on Enshar had shown little interest in Risky, who was bigger than most of the wildlife he encountered.

Risky boosted everyone's morale. Everyone wanted to pet the dog, who reveled in the attention. They took his survival as a talisman that their luck had changed. Fenaday was glad for the effect, especially among the wounded.

Fenaday drained his coffee and looked at the others. "Well, we are in as good a situation as can be hoped for. We're in the capital city, dug in with all the supplies we need. The worst of the wounded are back on the ship. Tomorrow we start work on getting out of here and finishing off this...this...whatever the hell it is."

"If we last through tonight," Mmok said, sitting back in the chair with both hands behind his head.

Fenaday shrugged. He didn't feel the need to candy-coat the situation for this group, but he wanted no pessimism either. "We have a good chance. There have been no storms. We have relocated twice in the last forty-eight hours.

"If Duna is right in his theory that there is no central intelligence guiding the attacks on us, at least as yet, we may have slipped off the boards as far as the enemy is concerned."

"Yet, here we are in the middle of what may be its central location," Shasti cautioned.

"Remember," Telisan said, "the attacks have been disjointed, purposeless, stupidly done—if still terrifying. The thing may not have garrisoned this city; it does not act in what we perceive as a logical fashion. We do not know."

"We're not out of danger," Fenaday said, "but what point is there in planning for an overwhelming attack by an invincible force? If it happens, we die. If not, we are the first force to survive long enough to launch a counterstrike.

"Strike, we shall," Fenaday promised. "Mr. Duna."

"Every evidence we can find," Duna began, "indicates that the assault radiated out of Barjan. Here, the slaughter took minutes, if that long. The entire disaster was over, planet-wide, in hours. As the captain says, we are the first force to survive the initial attacks. We are in range of the enemy, alive and armed. There is—there must be—a chance."

Shasti looked up from stroking Risky's fur, as if to speak. Fenaday caught her eye and she subsided.

"We will attack in this fashion," Fenaday said. "Shasti, Connery, Li, Mmok, and the bulk of his HCR and crab robot force will accompany me as we descend into..."

"Captain," interrupted both Duna and Telisan simultaneously. Fenaday looked at them in surprise.

"I must go, Captain," Duna continued. "None of you has ever even been in an Enshari city. You cannot recognize the signs, much less read them."

"Duna," Fenaday said, "you could give directions."

"No, Robert," Duna replied, "not well enough to help, but there are other reasons as well. You were brought into this through my actions. We have lost a quarter of our force, killed or wounded. I bear the ultimate responsibility for this. I dragged you here to face monsters. I must stand with you when you do.

"Finally, I am the only member of my race on this planet. This is my home, the place I buried my wife, where we had our children, where some of them died. In the name of all who have died, in the name of all that we lost, an Enshari must be there to strike the blow.

"Give me a place in this fight," the Enshari demanded, his eyes brilliant.

There was silence in the room.

"It's not necessary for me to give you what is yours by right," Fenaday replied. "You fight with us in the morning."

The Enshari sat on the floor, his hand-paws covering his eyes. Telisan placed a long-fingered hand on his shoulder. Duna grasped it tightly.

"I too, must go," Telisan said, "for my comrades on the *Earhart*, for my friend Belwin, and to buy back a lie." He looked directly at Fenaday. "I demanded an oath from you, and you have been true in all things. I knew of Duna's fears that some ancient menace had been uncovered. I knew the stories of the demons and monsters, what you call the Shellycoats. I did not tell you even after I was your officer. I have not lied in any matter of honor before. I must go to buy back that lie."

"You don't owe me," Fenaday said. "I'm not some noble adventurer tricked into a quest. Shasti and I were forced to go by the government when our pasts caught up with us. Had you told either of us what you suspected, we would have thought you mad. Even if you'd told us and we believed you, what else could have been done?"

"Then it is myself I owe," Telisan replied.

"Who will command the team to go to the spaceport and find a ship?" Fenaday asked.

"Send Fury," said Telisan. "I am a fighter pilot. She actually served on freighters before the war. In any event, she knows ship systems better than I."

Fenaday looked at Telisan and smiled. "You're a damn fool, but I'll be glad to have you along. I'd rather be going anywhere else myself."

"For once we agree," Mmok added.

"All right, Fury will take Rask and half the ASATs and LEAFs back to the port, along with any of our engineers or other people she feels she'll need. Rigg, you'll take command here. I'm not going to give you any orders. Once we are gone, it's your shop."

"Mmok," Fenaday said, turning to the half-cyborg, "I assume you can rig a variety of different time delay detonation sequences for me on that nuke."

"In my sleep. How long a delay do you want?"

"I need four settings: three days, twenty-four hours, six hours, and one for two seconds."

The last fell on them all like a shroud. There was only one reason for the two-second delay, to replace a painful death with a quick blast of nuclear light.

"We'll take one of the multi-fuels in the morning," Fenaday continued. "Duna, draft a map of where you think the excavation might be. Everyone will carry one. It shouldn't take all of one day to get there and back. It's not much of a plan, but there it is."

"The underground will not be so bad as you all imagine," Duna said. "We Enshari evolved from denning animals, but we hunted on the surface. Our eyes see somewhat better in darkness than do yours, our sense of smell is better, but we do need light. In addition to all the shaftways bringing down light, there are bioluminescent panels almost everywhere. Remember, our genetic engineers developed them to a high art. They do not need replacing during their lifetimes and live twenty years or more, if tended properly. There will be sufficient light to see by."

"We will take torches and lanterns anyway," Fenaday said. "Daylight is 04:30 standard time.

"Mmok, prepare the nuke. Also, send that scout robot of yours out and see about securing us a decent route to the Barjan Deep. Duna will give you the coordinates.

"I suggest everybody check their equipment and try to get their heads down for a few hours. 'Boots and saddles' sounds at 04:30. Any questions?"

Mmok grunted as usual. The others shook their heads.

"Dismissed."

Chapter Sixteen

B efore seeking his bed, Fenaday made a tour of the guard posts. Nothing moved in the tomb Barjan had become. The sky remained clear. Stars formed unfamiliar constellations over his head, crowned by a view of the galactic core unblocked by nebula or clouds. Enshar's moonless but brilliant night sky gave him an extra feeling of security—their enemy seemed to prefer full darkness.

After he reviewed the defenses, he headed for ambassadorial quarters. Rank, after all, did have some few privileges still attached. He collapsed onto the bed gratefully. He was nearly asleep when he heard someone enter the room.

Without speaking, Shasti joined him on the bed. He turned toward her, looking a question. She laid her head on his shoulder and closed her eyes. With the padding of four feet and the clicking of nails, Risky joined them. He circled at the foot of the bed a few times before settling in with an immense yawn on the rug. Fenaday dropped off instantly.

When he woke some hours later, he reached for her, still half asleep, and said Lisa's name.

"No," she whispered.

It brought him fully awake. "God, Shasti, I'm sorry."

"Don't be," she replied. "I am not trying to take anyone's place. I am here, now, and for my own reasons." She reached for him. They made love, quickly and urgently, both believing it might be the last time, the last touch.

They fell asleep again in each other's arms. Then something wet and cold touched Fenaday's butt. He jumped. Claws clicked on the floor. Risky was awake, too. Shasti struggled to smother a laugh.

He glared at her in the semi-darkness of the room. "A thing like that can give a guy a complex."

Shasti lost her battle with the laugh and it burst out, a surprisingly high-pitched and girlish laugh for Death's Angel.

"Oh well," he grumbled, "I might as well get up. It's near three, and I doubt I could fall asleep again after that."

The showers at the embassy still worked. Embassies serving different species had to be, for necessity, nearly self-sufficient little fortresses. Even on a world as friendly and civilized as Enshar, the embassy followed the standard pattern with its own gravity-fed water supply. Shasti joined him in the shower. They enjoyed the utter luxury of being completely clean. When they came out, they dressed in the fresh uniforms that had been among the last supplies dropped in by the *Wildcats*. They left their old clothes in a pile for the laundry detail to collect, as no one knew how long they would be down-world. The little details of being alive, from toilet paper and soap to ammunition, all required tending.

Their personal weapons they kept with them. The rest of the gear they would pick up downstairs. It felt odd, he thought, sitting on the bed and sorting uniform parts. *Here we are getting ready to crawl into a dead city, on the hope of blasting some unseen monster to bits with an atom bomb, and the day begins with trying to find two socks that fit.* The ordinariness of it seemed bizarre. It felt more like going away on a camping trip. The heartsick fear that gripped him on the night before the landing was missing. He didn't know why; maybe it was that "good day to die" people talked about.

Shasti was her usual contained self. She gave him the look she sometimes used for a smile, though he could see her mind was already on the task ahead. Concentration was rarely less than total with Shasti. In that much, she proved true to the sports-minded founders of Olympia.

Risky wagged his tail, clearly figuring himself as part of the adventure, but they had no plans to take the dog. K-9s were highly trained, but Shasti had not had him long enough for the dog to recognize her as his handler. He might bolt. They could not afford such distractions.

As if reading his mind, Shasti looked up from petting him. "There's no reason he can't stay with us through breakfast."

"None," he replied, "provided he keeps his nose to himself."

They left the room, which had been a little island of warmth for them, and headed downstairs. Fenaday's chronometer read 2:17 a.m. The other members of the team would be awake soon. Telisan had organized a mess hall the day before. Food, and more important, fresh hot coffee awaited them. Fenaday grabbed a few sausage and egg sandwiches while Shasti made up a bowl for Risky.

Telisan, who never seemed to need sleep, sat at a table sipping coffee, a human vice he acquired in the Confed Navy. He smiled broadly at the two of them as they came down the stairs. Fenaday tried to forgive the Denlenn for his morning cheerfulness. At least he was quiet about it.

"Sleep well?" Telisan asked.

"Yes, very," Fenaday replied.

"Ah, good," said the Denlenn, smiling.

Shasti joined them on the couch. The Denlenn grinned even more broadly at her. She looked back at him. "Something?"

"Mere envy," Telisan sighed.

Fenaday began to wonder if he had their room bugged. To his surprise, Shasti returned the Denlenn's grin.

Duna padded down the stairs next. Fenaday did not know what a sleepy Enshari looked like, but he suspected it looked very much like Belwin Duna. Next came Connery, Li, and Mmok. Only the half-cyborg looked in any condition to face the day. He always radiated a metallic coldness, crisp and alert. Daniel Rigg walked in almost on their heels.

With the arrival of the others, the Shasti of last night disappeared, replaced by her expressionless, no-nonsense self. She finished her food and left to check equipment. Everyone began doing last-minute teardowns and cleaning of weapons. Fenaday checked each person for full canteens, a day's rations, reloads, flares, and torches. They went over the detonation procedures. Mmok made them simple but impossible to do by accident.

After everyone had their gear on, Rigg walked with them down the main hall to the front entrance. Guards on the windows called out good luck. Fenaday was surprised to see a cluster of people at the entranceway. The Tok brothers stood there. They had bitterly protested being left out of the assault force, but Hanshi was their only other pilot and Lokashti walked with a bad limp. Most of the medical team with Dr. Mourner showed up along with Rask, Bernard, Fury, and Morgan.

The Tok bothers took their leave of Shasti, gripping her by both arms. Fenaday shook hands with the doctors and the others.

"Go get 'em, skipper," Bernard said.

Angelica Fury looked at him. "I'll see to Micetich," she said, "if there's a need."

"Thanks, do that," he said.

"Best of luck, Robert," Mourner said, echoed by Yamata and Vashti. They shook hands with each member of the team.

Shasti held Risky's collar and snapped an improvised leash on him. She handed it to Daniel Rigg. "Look out for him if we don't get back."

Rigg nodded. "You'll do okay," he said with the casual assurance sergeants dispense before battles. "We'll see you on toward nightfall. I don't have to tell you anything. You'll be fine."

She nodded. "Look after him anyway, though."

"Yeah, don't worry about it. If you don't make it back though, he may be looking after us. He's got the track record on survival."

"I hate long good-byes," Fenaday said impatiently.

"Okay, let's go to work, people," Telisan announced, lapsing into Confed military slang, from his normally formal standard. They boarded the M-2 Rask brought to the front. All three surviving HCRs stood around the truck, motionless in the pre-dawn light. The utility robots, including the one with the bomb on board, latched themselves into position. Eight other crab assault models already hung off the truck. It looked as if flat-gray beach creatures were consuming the vehicle.

Fenaday and the other spacers boarded the M-2. Mmok's saucer-like reconnaissance robot circled overhead on guard. Duna, Telisan, Shasti, and Fenaday rode in the armored box of the cargo platform, glad for their leather flight jackets. Barjan had something in common with the desert: it was windy, and with the sun down, the wind was damn cold. Shasti slid up and into the ring containing the light caliber cannon Rask had mounted, hitting the charging handle on the weapon.

The M-2 hummed to life, pulling away from the embassy. A cheer went up from the spacers left behind. As the M-2 rumbled down the driveway, the gate guards pulled down the barrier wire to let them through the perimeter. Shasti's Landing Force troops joined the ASATs in a salute.

"There is rather an air of finality about these farewells," Duna observed pensively.

"Well, we have very little chance," Shasti said.

Fenaday looked at her.

"But maybe we'll get lucky," she added.

Telisan shook his head ruefully.

"It could happen," Fenaday insisted.

Duna grumbled something in Enshari that made Telisan laugh and went back to surveying the landscape. Fenaday rested his tri-auto on the cab, watching the HCRs pace the slow-moving M-2 as they wove around debris and vehicles, heading for the city.

The domes and half-domes of the city became clearer as the morning light strengthened. Half-domes were generally industrial or offices. They rose to considerable height but had none of the dizzying perspective of a Terran skyscraper. There were a few ruined towers as well. Up closer, the devastation was more evident. Bones lay everywhere. Empty window frames gave the domed buildings a skull-like appearance. They grew used to the crunching sound of tiny Enshari bones under the M-2's bulletproof wheels. Fenaday consoled himself with the knowledge that the dead wouldn't mind the desecration, knowing their mission of vengeance. Still, the scene was oppressive. The courage of morning coffee and a full breakfast faded before the evidence of their unseen enemy's power.

Fenaday turned to Telisan. The Denlenn seemed the most affected by the sight of the dead city. Maybe it reminded him of what he had seen, or perhaps even caused, during the war. The grim countenance of his usually optimistic and self-assured friend worried Fenaday. He had come to rely on the Denlenn's sense of humor when things looked dark.

"When we get out of this," Fenaday said abruptly, "we'll go up to where the fighters augered in. We'll locate your folks, your friend's brother, and give everybody a decent burial. Least we could do, I think."

The Denlenn turned his golden, cat-irised eyes toward the human. "I thank thee, my friend. If we live, we shall do that, but in truth I do not think we will live. A whole world fell to this enemy."

"If Duna is right," said Fenaday slowly, "if we're facing this ancient enemy he suspects, it must be very old. I've been trying to remember what I felt when I was in physical contact with the Shelly-coat we fought in Duna's library. I told you before that it felt like I was in communication, receiving something from it. It's difficult, like recalling a dream after you wake up. The more you concentrate on it, the more it fades. You're left with the doubt that you dreamt anything at all.

"I felt a sense of great age and a terrible anger. The anger, I think, was directed at the Enshari rather than any of us. There's more, much more, but that's what I have the most trouble remembering. It's easier to gather impressions than images. I recall a feeling of weakness and confusion, a lack of focus in the thing. Otherwise, I think it would have killed me."

Fenaday looked the Denlenn in the eye. "After two hundred thousand years, is it possible that our enemy might be senile?"

"Who knows?" murmured Telisan. "It might be. It just might be the case. The attacks on us have varied, some with intelligence and at least a degree of cunning, some not. None displayed the coordinated brilliance of the original two assaults."

"Let's hope the thing doesn't have a lucid moment while we're trying to put it to sleep permanently," Fenaday said. "It wouldn't take much more to finish us off."

They came to an area impassable to the vehicles. Bones and bits of bodies were strewn everywhere. Vehicles of all descriptions, from trucks and aircars to small motorcycles, formed a nearly solid mass.

"We're within three hundred meters of the main roadway leading down to Barjan Old Town," Mmok said. "From here, we walk."

Crab robots popped off the truck like fleas and moved up to join the three human-form robots. Utility robots, carrying supplies and the warhead, came off the truck more slowly. Fenaday and the others picked up their equipment and shouldered weapons. They formed up in the center of the robot force and began to walk down the sloping road to the tunnel entrance, where the roadway dropped into the earth.

As they reached the entrance, Fenaday stopped, looking around a last time at the sunlight and sky. Then, taking a deep breath, he stepped across the terminator thrown by the roof of the tunnel and into shadow. They started down the gentle slope, around wrecked vehicles and in some cases, over them.

The humans stuck close to the Enshari. He steered Mmok. Mmok steered the robots. Spotlights popped from the crab robots' bodies lighting up the area. The spacers saved their torches and lanterns for later need. The robot's power supplies were more than adequate for months of such use.

As Duna had promised, the lights proved unnecessary. The bioluminescent panels the Enshari were so fond of dotted the roof of the tunnel, though the light was dimmer than humans liked. As they crunched through a vast bone yard, hunting an enemy that might form around them in a nightmarish second, they were happy for the spotlights.

Shellycoats were not the only enemy to be feared. They faced bad footing, flooding, and decay in the city itself. Barjan had suffered many fires. Without intelligent agency to stop them, the fires caused widespread damage.

The smell of old smoke filled their noses, as did the smell of damp and rot. These eased only when they passed a shaftway. Fortunately, shaftways were common, both for light and ventilation. Some penetrated only dozens of meters. Others dropped off to unguessable depths.

They wound down the roadway until they reached a collapsed section. Then Duna began to take them down the side streets of the city. As they moved, Shasti drew luminous ranger marks at every turn. The robots and Mmok could find the way back with ease, but Fenaday wanted to take no chances of becoming lost.

Animal life constantly skittered away from them. Enshar's equivalents of rats, mice, bats, and other burrowing life had moved unchecked into the city's corpse. Mmok's robots could sense farther than the humans and were programmed to fire on moving targets closing on them or standing their ground. The non-enhanced members of the group found themselves starting at sounds, snapping up weapons at any sound or movement. Fenaday finally ordered everyone but Shasti to shoulder their weapons for fear of wild shooting.

"I thought it would be silent," said Shasti, at one rest stop.

Fenaday looked at her in surprise, realizing she was correct. His brain had tuned out most sounds, other than those of the animals. Barjan was far from silent. Metal creaked and groaned as it expanded and contracted. Water dripped. Air currents wafting past them emitted a soft sound as well, nearly flute-like. He looked up to see a small bundle of pipes on the ceiling.

Duna caught his gaze. "My people developed in caves and caverns," he said. "The song of wind through rocks is almost lulling, part of the ambiance."

"My people feel the same way about wind chimes," said Li, from his seat on a small powered cart.

"On Denla we prize the sound of the ocean," Telisan said. "We make many different types of machines and waterfalls so that the sound of rushing water is always near.

"What sounds are the Irish fond of?" Telisan asked.

Fenaday thought a moment. "Potatoes growing."

Shasti sighed.

"Now, Captain, you know it's the bagpipes that make the sound of Eire," Connery said.

"What does that sound like?" Duna asked.

"Imagine a man strangling a cat," replied Li, "while biting it on the tail."

"I will try," Duna said dubiously.

Fenaday smiled. "It's time to go." He turned to Duna. "Which way?" he said, looking at the bewildering maze of tunnels and caverns around them.

"We designed our cities for mass transit," Duna said, standing and brushing dust off his uniform, "with an abundance of walkways and trams. None of these still operate though. I fear we must simply travel by the underground streets."

The streets started off as broad thoroughfares in the commercial areas, where small carts supplemented pneumatic tubing as a means of delivering goods. As the spacers moved into residential districts in their downward course, they began to narrow. On either side of them, stacked up in the thirty-meter diameter passageways, stood Enshari apartments. Occasionally, a well-off family had a separate, circular home, with a small garden of fungus or other dark-loving plant life.

The thought of all the slaughtered families lying in the underground apartments nearly broke their nerves. They forged forward, close to each other, casting anxious glances in all directions. Only Shasti and Mmok seemed unaffected by the oppressive atmosphere. Mmok idly kicked bones out of his path in a move that made Fenaday's teeth grate.

"Have a care with your feet," he finally snapped at the cyborg.

"Quit giving me orders, pirate." Mmok glared contemptuously. "I work for Mandela."

Fenaday felt his own temper flash in response. He dropped a hand to brush the holster of his weapon. Mmok's single eye noted the gesture. He smiled coldly, but his wolfish grin dimmed as he noticed Rainhell's weapon already on him. Shasti smiled back equally coldly. The robots stopped moving.

"I fear," Duna said, "that you are not seeing Barjan at its best. It was not always such a darksome place. It was filled with light and laughter when I was here last. Very reminiscent of your Paris, Captain."

"Never been there," Fenaday said tightly.

"You should go, when we get back," said the little Enshari, as if nothing were wrong. "Mr. Mmok, if I read my map right, we go down this spiral stairway to the next level."

Mmok and the robots started moving again.

Fenaday spotted Telisan. The Denlenn had drifted to where he had a clean shot at Mmok. His heavy laser pistol sat in its holster, but Fenaday spotted something small and black in Telisan's long-fingered hand. The Denlenn palmed the device and walked up to pat Fenaday on the shoulder.

"He is good. Is he not?" Telisan said.

"He's got my vote," Fenaday whispered back.

Their larger feet managed the broad, shallow Enshari stairs easily, and they dropped another level. The side of the combination road-stairwell opened to the left. As if to back up Duna's earlier assertions of Barjan's beauty, it yielded a view of a wide cavernous space. In it they could see a formerly prosperous section of Barjan, lit by Mur's light pouring down the shaftways. Arches buttressed the roof sections. Hundreds of the larger Enshari domes dotted small plots of lawn, like delicate mushrooms in creams and gold. A fountain sparkled under a shaft of sunlight, too far away to be heard. Fenaday wondered what kept it going. Perhaps it was gravity fed, like the embassy. There was a hushed, cathedral-like feeling to the scene. It looked as if any moment, people would begin to stream, quietly and orderly, into view. The space was large enough for a cold wind to be blowing.

"Tis a damned shame," Connery said suddenly. Li nodded and zipped his jacket against the breeze.

"Yes," Fenaday agreed, shivering despite his jacket.

"Thank you, my friends," Duna said, his voice low.

"We should get moving," Mmok said. "We have to settle the hash of whatever did this so it doesn't happen again."

Fenaday looked at him. "No argument there."

They continued down the broad staircase with glances at the ruins of Barjan. The next level was particularly dark, and they moved through it cautiously, splashing through ill-smelling puddles when they could find no way around.

Duna turned, coming out of a narrow side street onto a broader roadway. "We are just above Barjan Old Town now. The area will be, for the most part, smaller and older. In some places, it will be uncomfortable for you, Shasti, because of your height. The temperature should remain fairly steady. Do not fear its older appearance. The area was always well maintained. Modern engineering supports the roof sections.

"I hope to reach the area of new construction soon. It will be more comfortable for you large folk. It will also mean we are near the site of the archeological dig. They were erecting new homes when they found the vault."

"We are going to feel real damn silly," Mmok said, "if we get there, and there is no bogeyman."

"It'll be worse than that," Fenaday added. "Where do we go looking for our enemy then?"

Mmok grunted.

They walked into the oldest section of a city built before the other species of the Confederacy discovered fire. An atmosphere of age was omnipresent. Carved or painted decorations covered every square inch of the walls around them. Smaller Enshari structures served as museums or shops and fewer Enshari dead lay underfoot here. The spacers saw no evidence of powered vehicles. Here and there, a cart or pedicycle stood among the bones of its former owner.

The team walked on for the better part of an hour, descending through levels in various stages of preservation.

"These levels were once very near the surface," said Duna, "back in Barjan's youth. Like Earth's Troy, the city has been built and destroyed several times and settled in on itself. The original rock and wood would have made for perilous mining, but there are no greater subterranean engineers than the Enshari. Look up."

They all gazed at the ceilings. Broad beams of metal ran through them, with spider webs of thinner metals radiating off them.

"Engineered lattices of nuclear dense metals," continued Duna, "indifferent to loads, hold up the city above. It is a very good thing that tectonic plate movements on Enshar are so docile. The rare earthquakes that have happened were utter disasters in our history, and one of the reasons the city had been rebuilt and re-dug several times."

The team broke out into a wider, open section, lit by the ever-present bioluminescent panels.

"Here is the new section I promised," said Duna. "You can see the homes here are of different styles than the usual domes."

"Yes," said Telisan. "I see one that looks like a Denleni design." He pointed to an elven construction of delicately carved wood and stained glass against one wall.

Fenaday saw a house that looked vaguely Colonial-human. The Enshari who had sought to recolonize the preserved and abandoned old town area were non-traditionalists in every sense.

"Open up your intervals," Mmok growled. "One grenade would get all of you."

They spread, out glad for the space. Mmok sent Vermilion, fleet and silent, ahead to scout. They walked on, alert, moving slowly.

Suddenly the robots stopped. Mmok raised a hand in a signal, sinking to one knee. Everyone's hands flew to weapons as they leapt for the nearest cover. Fenaday squatted next to Mmok. The man turned his metallic, artificial eye toward Fenaday. "I am looking through Vermilion's scanner. I see open ground and digging equipment."

"We have arrived," Fenaday whispered.

Chapter Seventeen

Ahead of them lay an area of flat, scraped ground over a thousand meters long and nearly as wide, dotted with construction equipment and small trailers for workers and archeologists. The cavern was dimly lit, more so than any other section they had been through.

"The bioluminescent-panels here are obviously temporary," said Mmok. He pointed. "Look, cart-mounted power generators. Bet they're dead though."

"Have the crab robots illuminate the area with red light," Fenaday whispered. "I don't want our low-light vision screwed."

Combined with the bio panels, the robots gave sufficient, if bloody, light to the area.

"I don't see anything," said Shasti. She had the best night vision of any, save Mmok with his artificial eye.

"There is a depressed area in the far distance," said Mmok. "The ground slopes down behind it."

"Send an HCR forward," Fenaday ordered.

Mmok nodded. His throat moved as he subvocalized to Vermilion. The HCR went forward without hesitation. Smooth and noiseless, the machine dropped into a crouch the humans couldn't match, keeping its Gatling tri-auto at the ready. Vermilion could barely be seen as the HCR approached the far area.

Mmok spoke up. "This must be the place, raw earth and a huge pit area. I see a wide, flat, metal section in the center, with a hole in the middle of a metal panel. Near that is a tall metal obelisk, I guess. It's huge. There's a derrick over a hole. It looks like it was used to drop people in... Wait a minute."

"What?" Fenaday demanded.

"Ah," Mmok said, "Eureka, I have found it. I have the image from your computer video, Duna. This is the spot. I can project a side-by-side comparison from memory. This is where Creda's call came from." The half cyborg hesitated for a second, then continued diffidently. "More confirmation. I just found Creda. The clothes are intact enough for an identification. Sorry."

"Thank you, Mr. Mmok," Duna said. "I knew he would be here."

Mmok looked at Fenaday, as did Shasti and the others. Fenaday hated this part. *As if I know what the rules are,* he thought. "Okay, let's go in. The objective is the pit area. Spread out, but always keep everyone in sight. Duna, stay next to Telisan and right behind me. We'll need your knowledge."

"Such as it is," replied Duna.

They started across the cavernous space, relieved to have a roof farther away from their heads. Small trailers and various pieces of digging equipment provided cover as they moved over the underground field. The ground ahead consisted of unrefined dirt and rock, clearly the site of the archeological excavation. Dig sites pockmarked the area, small depressions with grids of wire and hand tools nearby.

A vertical slab of dark metal, ten meters tall, dominated the area. It appeared to be covered by some form of script. Gleaming in the half-light, it looked new enough to have been placed there only yesterday. Yet, as they approached it, Fenaday felt an overwhelming impression of age.

Fenaday leaned against a trailer that might have belonged to Creda and looked up at the obelisk. "Can you read it, Belwin?"

Obviously the product of a high technology, it showed every sign of having been there since this level of Barjan Deep was inhabited. The bottom of it was not fully excavated. A resemblance to a grave marker suddenly struck him.

"A little," said the excited Enshari, back in his field again. The expedition was both a joy and a curse to the scholar. "It speaks of the burial of a great being. There is something I cannot translate, maybe a name. 'We could not destroy he who was the greatest of us.' More I cannot read. Ah, wait, this says, 'He saved us from darkness.'"

"*Darkness*" came the word, rumbling through their minds, accompanied by a sound like a waterfall in the distance. They spun back to back, hearts pounding, mouths open, eyes searching the dark. The robots did not react, though the HCRs turned toward the spacers, as though puzzled by their sudden movement.

Fenaday looked at the others. "You heard it too?"

"Yes," said Duna, Shasti, and Telisan simultaneously. Li and Connery nodded, eyes darting around as they stared at the shadows beyond the reach of their lights.

"The robots," said Fenaday.

Mmok looked at him. "They didn't hear it," he hissed. "They report no sound, no spoken word."

Cobalt stood next to Fenaday.

"Confirm," Fenaday demanded of the robot. "Did you hear a non-team member speak the word, darkness? Do you hear a sound like a waterfall?"

Cobalt turned soulless doll's eyes to him. "There have been no such sounds," replied the robot in its flat, metallic tones.

"*Darkness*," it came again, stronger. In their minds, faint and fuzzy images began to form. Words and concepts tumbled in a bewildering kaleidoscope. Fenaday saw a towering figure, almost glowing, standing on a rocky plain. He could not see any detail to the giant. Huge bolts of raw power rolled from the figure, filling up the sky, boiling away clouds and air.

Words came too. "*Darkness, darkness closes, the end draws near. Made the change, became the One. Raised the soldiers of light and air from my new mind. Slew the Others, the Dark Ones, drove them from our worlds. The final battle, the madness, the madness, the madness."*

It faded. For a second, Fenaday became aware of himself again, crawling on the floor like a child. He steeled himself to resist, but his consciousness fled as the thing spoke again.

"Madness... destroyed my own. Captured, buried." Suddenly it became a scream. *"Buried. The little people, deaf to me, buried, worse, worse...forgotten."* A blast of hatred filled him, a hatred of the Enshari. Suddenly, as if a switch were thrown, the psychic barrage ceased. Fenaday and the others lay on the floor, gasping for breath. The presence they felt was gone. No, not gone. As they struggled to their feet, they could hear the distant waterfall-like projection. It faded, quickly becoming so dim as to be nearly unnoticeable.

The robots, standing over the humans, aware of the assault on their soft-skinned companions, couldn't detect either a vector or a means. They could launch no counterattack.

Mmok began to update the machines. He was clearly rattled and whispered instead of subvocalizing. "Telepathic assault from the pit. No counterattack at this time." The robots accepted the impossible with mechanical equanimity. Extra-sensory perception was the stuff of labs and telepathy only a word, until this moment.

Fenaday looked at Shasti. She nodded back, her usual equanimity reasserting itself.

"Everyone else, stay where you are, especially you, Duna." Fenaday turned toward the hole. With Shasti on his left side, he approached the section where a hole had been bored through into the chamber below. They slid on their bellies as they reached the spot. Then, with a last look at each other and a nod, they peered over, shining their battle lanterns at the widest beam.

A Titan's corpse lay on a platform twenty-five meters below them. Had it stood, its head would have poked out of the hole, a head the size of an aircar, or a small truck. It had gone to bone an eon ago. Its skull looked up at them, from three empty eye sockets big enough for a man to step through. It had been bipedal, but nothing about the skeleton was familiar. Arms reached past the knees, the feet ended in disc-like hooves.

This was no ordinary casket. The chamber below them

stretched out for at least tens of meters, from all sides of the platform. Lights and mechanical movement played around some of the perimeter and near the platform.

"Perhaps," whispered Shasti, "it's some form of suspended animation or stasis. It has the look of such equipment from the early days of spaceflight."

"Or a diagnostic bed," he whispered back. "It looks like that as well."

"Whatever it is," she continued, "it failed our friend down there. He has been dead for an age."

"Yet, something down there is still alive somehow. You felt it too. The body may be dead, but something is still active in the chamber. Look at the machinery."

"The ceiling of this chamber is two meters thick," added Shasti. "I've never seen an alloy like this. I assumed they used a heavy military laser to cut this meter-and-a-half hole."

Fenaday waved to Mmok. The half-cyborg came up to the hole the same way they had. Mmok looked into the hole only briefly. He cursed and drew back from it, unnerved.

Fenaday began to fear the nuclear device they brought with them might be inadequate. He had never believed in ghosts—despite his Irish heritage—and didn't now. He thought some vestige of the life force of the Titan might exist in the computers and machinery shifting around the monster's bed. Perhaps the attacks originated in the machinery, but he didn't believe it. There was too much malice and hatred in what he felt from his encounters with their enemy.

"Mmok," he asked, "if we fire off the bomb outside the chamber, will it do the job?"

"How the hell should I know?" Mmok snapped. "This metal is meters thick so the blast will go up and out easiest. That's physics. The hole should still admit plenty of blast, but I don't know anything about this equipment. I can tell you this metal is harder than anything we make. I've had Cobalt doing a spectral analysis. I don't know what they used to cut this hole with, but it would normally be mounted on a battlecruiser.

"This is new alien equipment, from a race we don't know. Something spoke to us telepathically. That's been bullshit until now. What else can they do that we don't know is possible? Force fields? How deep does this installation go? Maybe all the really critical stuff is below another floor made of this metal. If that's the case, then there is no way this small nuke can cut through another layer of this alloy. I'd need a shaped charge.

"The best way," concluded the grim half-cyborg, "is to put the bomb down in there. This is our one shot. It has to work. If you cook off the nuke up here and it doesn't do the job, then this whole area will be gone. We'll never be able to get back to this chamber to try again."

Fenaday lay on his back, away from the hole. "I was afraid you were going to say that." It was obvious to him now. They had to lower the warhead into the crypt itself. They had no idea how much blast was needed to accomplish their mission. Putting the weapon in the crypt, contained by the incredible walls of the chamber, would greatly increase the effect and perhaps even protect the areas of Barjan over them.

They retreated from the hole, rejoining the others. Fenaday sketched the details of what they had seen. He sent Telisan for a look. Connery and Li rested on their guns and stayed on guard for Shellycoats. Fenaday did not want Duna near the hole, despite the little scholar's curiosity.

"I want to put the warhead in there. We lower it in. I'll arm it, then you'll pull me out, and we run like hell."

Telisan stared at him as if he had lost his mind. "Why not arm it up here and lower it in?"

Mmok answered. "We don't know what sort of defenses are in that pit, either mechanical or cybernetic. The bomb might draw any sort of attack as we lower it in. Once it is armed, there is a distinct chance it could be triggered by an EMP, computer virus, or even mechanical damage. The other problem is this is a jury-rigged deto-nator, a bunch of cannibalized stuff from other systems. I don't want to lower it down there and have to wonder if it is going to go off because some bump or jolt on the way down disconnected some-thing. It would be embarrassing to be walking back here, wondering why it didn't go off, and get caught in a delayed blast."

"No, the only safe way is to lower it, check it, then set the timer once we're sure it's working," said Fenaday. "Can we use an HCR?"

Mmok shook his head. "No. They aren't made for that sort of work. I don't have that level of control over their hands. The interlocks on the timer are too delicate. If I'd thought of it before…" He shrugged.

"So," said Fenaday, fear drying his mouth, "down I go."

Mmok looked over at him. "Better you than me," he said with rare sympathy.

"*Madness.*" The word whispered through their minds. Terror returned, and they all froze. Only silence followed.

"I don't believe that the creature, the machinery, say the consciousness of this place, is aware of us," Fenaday said. "Else, why aren't we dead?"

"Your senility theory, perhaps," Telisan speculated.

"Whatever," Fenaday said. "Maybe it's recovering from its previous efforts. I don't think we have much more time before it becomes aware of us.

"Mmok, get the bomb rigged for the descent. We've got D-rings and rope in the supplies. Shasti, help me make a harness. The rest of you, lay low and stay quiet. Don't even think loudly. That goes double for you, Belwin. I don't want it to think of a live Enshari up here."

Mmok and his robot team checked the hoist and hooked up the bomb. They took special care with the bomb trigger. Fenaday and Shasti quickly rigged a harness and D-rings to allow him to slide down as well. She put a line on him so he could be pulled up easily. They moved over to the pit. He nodded to Mmok. The cyborg and Verdigris swung the bomb out with the derrick erected by the deceased Enshari archeologists. They stared anxiously as it descended into the pit. Despite their best efforts, the bomb oscillated on the way down.

Fenaday threw in his own rope. He wanted to wait till the bomb set down without drawing an attack before starting his drop. The bomb reached bottom, but one swing banged it into the side of the platform. Everyone but Shasti and Verdigris flinched away from the hole. It landed finally, canted at an angle.

"Just what I was afraid of," muttered Fenaday. He moved into a position to rappel into the pit. *The hardest part,* he thought, *is always the first lean-back, trusting the rope.* He eased into the proper stance and looked up, catching Shasti's eye. Her perfect face showed no emotion; he read anxiety in her anyway. He smiled reassuringly. She didn't return it, just watched him as he disappeared into the hole.

Fenaday spun slowly in his harness, then eased his grip and started dropping fast, hoping to present a moving target, in case the crypt had different defenses against biologicals. He reached the floor in seconds and crouched near the bomb, laser in one hand and torch in the other. One of the crab robots had extended a lantern into the pit. Its light didn't fully illuminate the chamber. He realized the chamber was far larger than he suspected. *Sidhe* could have docked in it. The light uncomfortably illuminated the immense skull, only five meters away. He tried not to look at it.

Banks upon banks of machinery hummed around him. Many seemed active at a low level. He saw an irregularity in the wall, well away from the platform. He spun his hand torch to a tight beam and shone it in that direction. The beam diffused over distance, but he could definitely see a section of the wall bowed in, though not breached. Fenaday remembered the stories Duna told of the rare, but devastating earthquakes that destroyed Barjan several times in ancient days. Perhaps some ancient earth movement had damaged the machinery. No lights flickered there.

This has to be a confinement, he thought with a shock. *Someone meant to come back for the creature but never did. Tended by the machines, yet somehow conscious, it died, waiting for a parole that never came.*

He jerked his attention back to the here and now and reached for the arming mechanism of the bomb, opening the first interlock.

The waterfall sound that had faded to background suddenly rose. Fenaday felt a consciousness fill the chamber. He heard a creaking groan, as of huge rusted hinges pushed from frozen disuse. Fenaday's head snapped around. The giant skull was shifting, turning toward him. Its eyeless sockets came to bear on him.

"*Who?*" hissed the voice in his mind, with a malevolence he never dreamt existed. Fingers of thought clawed at his brain.

Fenaday screamed, a high, shrill sound of pain and terror. He snapped up his pistol, firing convulsively, shot after shot, into the horrific skull's immensely thick cranium. Superheated bone chips flew.

———

"Get him out, get him out!" Shasti ordered. "The thing is alive." She hefted her tri-auto, but she had no clean shot. She feared severing the rope or hitting Fenaday with a ricochet. "I need a laser," she yelled.

Telisan, Mmok, and the others leapt to the tripod, hauling on Fenaday's safety rope. Duna raced to the hole, brandishing his energy weapon. He leaned in for a shot and saw the nemesis of his race stretched out in all its horror. And it saw him. The terrible head ceased moving. The triple eye sockets bore into him, devouring him with their emptiness.

A blast of hatred, so intense as to have flavor and color, burst from the pit, forcing everyone but Shasti back from the edge. Shasti held her ground, though it beat her to her knees. She put her head between her hands. For the first time in years and over a vow she had sworn to herself, Shasti screamed in pain.

The members of the landing force, wherever they were on the planet, heard the scream of rage sound in their minds.

———

On the deck of the bulk-fluid hauler, Angelica Fury and Rask stumbled to their feet, their eyes wild. They stood on the open cargo platform with the five others of Rask's fire team. The ramp was down. On the field they could see Shellycoats of many sizes forming from debris. One stood as tall as the giant marshals that had led the attack back on the island. Fury wheeled on Rask. "Oh my God, tell me you have the ramp's power restored."

Rask lunged for the portable generator and put it on maximum. The ramp began grinding upward, cutting off the view of the onrushing Shellycoats. Someone screamed, and firing broke out behind them. They whirled. Shellycoats had formed from the tools, fire extinguishers, and miscellaneous contents of the hold. Rachel Van Vugt, from Engineering, toppled forward, her eyes unseeing. A Shellycoat had impaled her on a length of pipe. The other ASATs backed away, firing furiously, dropping the things as they formed.

"We need a smaller place to defend," screamed Fury. Despair beat in her chest as she swept up Van Vugt's fallen weapon, blazing away, determined to sell her young life at the highest price she could extract.

Rask pointed to the raised area holding the cargo master's crane controls. "Only two ways in and out," he shouted. "We can hold there."

"For how long?" she asked.

"For as long as we got ammo," snapped Rask. "Come on."

They backed away, firing as they retreated.

———

Exploding claymore mines followed by gunfire told Daniel Rigg trouble had arrived. He bolted to the main verandah, where the guards were already firing out the windows. Shellycoats advanced from all directions on their fortress camp. Barrier wires sparked and blasted them, but as one vaporized, another appeared, incorporating bits of the destroyed one. The shuttle gun crews began to fire.

A whine sounded at his feet. Rigg looked down. Risky's tail was between his legs. Rigg reached down, patting the dog's head. "It looks like a fight, boy. We'll give them a good one. You look after yourself and wait for the next expedition. I promise you there will be one."

He drew his heavy sidearm, opening his mike on the battle frequency and started bawling orders. "Everyone keep your eyes on your own front. Cut the firing rate, controlled bursts. We ain't making ammo, so mark your target."

He looked up as a shadow fell across the room. A "marshal"

advanced toward the embassy. Made of cars, it towered thirty meters into the air.

Pooka's chain guns took it apart. It fell with a horrific crash. In the middle distance, he saw several cars on the freeway ramp stir and crawl toward each other.

Chapter Eighteen

enaday had dropped when the others let go of the rope. He was not conscious of it. His body splayed out in a rictus of pain. The laser hung from his hand by its lanyard. His eyes were open, but saw nothing of the pit.

But they did see. The alien consciousness of the pit grew. It reached out to him. His body arced in torture as the mind of the Titan, far too large and complex for his mortal brain, invaded. No longer conscious of himself, he became one with the dead thing in the pit.

He saw himself as a giant, proud in his service as the highest of the warrior monks of the Prekak order. His duty was to protect his kind and the lesser races with whom they dealt. War raged with a force of darkness inimical to all life. The Enemy was terrible, and the Prekak fell before them in desperate battles. Lesser races perished entirely. Soon, the Prekak fought the forces of darkness on the surface of their own homeworld.

Finally came a time of complete desperation, as defeat and extinction threatened the Prekak. The Order of Scientists conceived a last defense, the great machine. He, as the First, claimed the honor of the risk of being wedded to the machine. The telepathic powers of the Prekak, strongest in those chosen for the

Order, were all that stood between them and the darkness of the Enemy.

The machine worked. He went from monk to Godhead with a mind so powerful he could raise and animate matter with his own life's essence. He called these manifestations his soldiers of light and air. He gathered their remaining armies. With the deadly force of his mind, with the power it wielded over the very elements of the planet and with his soldiers of light and air, he descended on their enemies, driving them from the Prekak homeworld with great slaughter. There would be no escape from retribution. He was raised to love justice and to judge with mercy, but the Enemy's nature would not countenance clemency, and their sins demanded payment. He and the forces of the Prekak pursued. Their attack was made more bitter for all the helpless dead he and the Order had failed to protect.

Finally the Enemy was driven to their own homeworld, facing a maelstrom of destruction, wrought chiefly by his mind. Continents quaked and volcanoes erupted. He wielded lightning as if it were an energy weapon. The Enemy fell, but they too had their scientists, and their final weapon was also a psionic attack. As he closed in on their last fortress, it struck his mind with mental talons. He quailed under terrible blows. Soldiers of light and air faltered and flickered. The Enemy rallied, counterattacked. The battle hung on a knife's edge.

He reached deep inside himself, drawing on the discipline of a lifetime in the Order. He would not fail his people. He could not. Were the dead to be left unavenged? Were future helpless populations to suffer? He could not bear the thought. He drew the steel of his soul and steadied. Somehow he bore the unimaginable agonies and struck back with mighty blows. Despite terrible damage to his new mind, he hung onto the enemy, warping the very substance of the planet, destroying their evil for all time.

The agony grew unendurable. As he felt the last of the enemy die in despair, his own mind gave way. His comrades drew near to give him their love and praise, as the greatest hero of his race. He looked upon them and saw only more enemies. Death poured out from him. His mind was severely damaged, or none would have lived even for seconds. The soldiers of light and air turned on their former allies. They were now something lesser and needed to manifest themselves in physical form to do injury. As they originated in his mind and soul, their number was almost endless. The Order battled back in dismay, calling, pleading with him to return to those who loved him.

He fled into the reaches of space, pursued by his own kind. He landed on world after world and woe to the life of that world, in whom he saw only the enemy. His friends pursued, now in grief, intent on ending the terror caused by their fallen hero.

On Enshar, the Order caught him. He had begun his conquest of the tiny people of that world. His soldiers of air and light had grown weaker and lacked much of their former intelligence. In truth, they were effective only when he focused the strength of his mind on them. Even then, they were the merest shadows of their former selves, as was he. For subjugating the tiny primitives of Enshar, however, they sufficed even in their near imbecilic state.

The Order, led by a new First, landed and attacked. Relentless pursuit and battles had worn on him, and the scientists had made new arms for the Order. He was taken in defeat, pinioned, and brought to justice. Death was not in their judgment, for they were a just and merciful race. He had been the greatest among them and suffered unimaginably in their service. They still bore him love and honor for that. Yet, his crimes were severe. There were innocent, lifeless worlds behind him. He had to answer for all this.

They sentenced him to confinement and meditation. The machine and his powers were a part of his mind. They could find no way to remove either without causing his death. With the Order's new technology, his powers were repressed and confined. They hoped that, sealed away in a suspended animation chamber, yet conscious, the disciplines of the Order would restore his balance. They confined him in a chamber from which his power could not emanate to disturb the pitiful Enshari, the remnant of which the Prekak now took as their charge.

He was secured in his life-preserving chamber and left to ponder his sins. They would return for him when they judged his penance complete.

Though he could not control or influence the Enshari, as part of his penance, he was allowed to sense them. The Order hoped it would teach him remorse. Perhaps, at first, it did. Eventually, he came to see them as insects, scurrying above him, burying him in the excreta of their cities. In a few of their short lives, he was forgotten, reduced to mere legend. Eons wore on, yet there was no sign of a return of his kind. In loneliness and terror, he called to the Enshari, who could not hear him. Buried alive and forgotten, he grew to fear the Prekak were no more—that they had come to disaster out among the stars.

His hatred of the Enshari became all consuming, even exceeding what he had felt for the Enemy. He plotted their destruction, in infinite detail, over millennia. The plan became second nature.

The world moved in the greatest of the Enshar quakes. The walls of his tomb bulged, and there was damage to the system. He died and did not die. The machines and his powers did not allow him even that mercy. His body wasted, though enough remained to anchor him in space-time. The Prekak's mind grew more strange and bitter.

After an unimaginable time, a hole opened in the ceiling of his tomb. The Enshari had found him again. So far gone was he that a substantial period went by before what was left of his consciousness reacted to the fact he was free to strike. The vermin brought power into the pit. He seized their minds and took the power from them. The machines sucked at it greedily. He allowed no outward sign of the return of a measure of his strength. To the scientists and archeologists—now concerned by the strange behavior of their co-workers—he remained merely a colossal pile of dead bone.

Then the plan, laid down for epochs, burst outward in an orgy of devastation and death. The soldiers of light and air were once more raised. Many in Barjan, near the focus of his power, died merely at his mental command. He drew from the planet's electromagnetic forces; lightning became whips of energy and lethal radiation. He turned his mind outward to the giant stations. His soldiers attacked sensitive installations, appearing inside the most critical areas. Radiation and force whips struck the stations. There was no defense possible. Death scoured Enshar, without mercy, without distinction, in every corner. He knew of the other races, and though he did not hate them with the passion he reserved for the Enshari, no mercy was shown them either. In hours it was over.

He had nearly spent his final strength. For as Enshar died, much of his power died with it. The machines slipped back into lower modes, and his awareness faded as well. When the primitive warships arrived, his strike was feeble, barely sufficient to ward them off.

A slumber of exhaustion came over him then. Dissolute and ancient, he gnawed on the memories of his hates. Many of the soldiers of air and light faded entirely. Some continued to wander the world, unseen and unfelt, with little volition or intelligence left to them. Specters in the charnel house they had made of the world.

Tiny pinpricks impinged on his consciousness recently. They had not been enough to rouse him. Until now.

———

Fenaday twisted in the mental grip of his tormentor, but the thing focused its attention above. The soldiers of air and light formed beyond the lights and rushed toward the spacers. Cobalt and the other robots detected the movement, opening fire instantly, as Mmok cried a warning.

These Shellycoats were different, more dangerous and cunning. They ducked and dodged and used cover. As one shattered, another formed. It took more gunfire to break up these manifestations. They reached the line of crab robots and leapt on them. Electrical arcs lit the area as the Shellycoats, sucking power from the fabric of the world, grappled with the robots. Had they been even half as powerful as they were the night of the great slaughter, the battle would have lasted seconds. Ancient and enfeebled like their master, the Shellycoats could muster only a small fraction of their previous deadliness. The robots battled back, hand to hand, as the two forms of unlife tried to disassemble each other.

Cobalt fell as a large Shellycoat seized her in an electrical embrace. The HCR stiffened in a parody of human agony and dropped. The human defenders added their gunfire as the wave of enemies crashed through the sudden gap. Lasers, tri-autos, and grenades lit up the battle scene. Shasti threw flares as far and fast as she could. Parts of the ceiling started to fall, sparking fresh terror. Shellycoats absorbed the falling bits, using them for mass.

A rush of the creatures pressed in suddenly. One seized Mmok. He fell in a crackle of electricity. Duna and Telisan tried to reach him. Telisan blasted several Shellycoats before a flailing blow dropped him to his knees, blood cascading down his face. Another knocked Duna flying from off the back of a utility robot, and the Enshari slid, unseen and limp, into a small hole.

A Shellycoat leapt on the back of the cargo robot at the pit's edge. Shasti shot it to pieces. It fell into the pit, disintegrating into its components of rock, dirt, metal, and bone.

Shasti handed her heavier weapon to Connery. "Keep shooting." She turned toward the pit, seizing Fenaday's safety line.

"Did he set the timer?" Connery yelled.

"I don't know." Shasti bent her wide shoulders to pull Fenaday out of the hole. She could see him by the light of his torch, lying on the floor. His arms were rigid and his head thrown back. *He might be dead,* she thought.

Even with her genetically engineered strength, pulling the one-hundred-eighty-pound Fenaday out of the pit was difficult. He swung at the end of the cord, making the weight worse. Screams, gunfire, and the snapping of electrical bolts sounded in her ears. A thrown piece of something struck her in the back. Shrapnel stung her legs and arms. She ignored it all and pulled with quick, powerful tugs. Fenaday came out of the hole. She seized him and pulled him to her. His heart pounded madly; his eyes were open but unseeing. She untangled him from the rope and threw him up on her shoulders. Now she had hands free to fight. She grabbed Connery's carbine from where he laid it.

She turned to see Verdigris and three of the crab robots fall under a wave of Shellycoats. A bolt of electricity ripped from a Shellycoat and struck Connery. He flew backward past her and struck the ground, smoking, clearly dead. She could not see Duna.

Telisan, his face a bloody mask, struggled to his feet. Li fired frantically, trying to cover Telisan.

Vermilion appeared next to her, blasting the Shellycoat that killed Connery.

"Situation desperate," the robot stated in cool mechanical tones. "HCR controller is down. Unit being overrun."

"I know," Shasti snarled, cutting loose with the carbine. "Fight!"

Vermilion analyzed the situation. Her CPU determined their reduced firepower could accomplish nothing. They would be overrun and destroyed in eleven seconds. Mmok's last directions to the slender robot indicated the pit was the center of the attack.

"Auto destruct engaged," Vermilion said. Before Shasti could say a word, Vermilion leaped into the pit. She had no specific target and settled on an airburst, exploding in a deafening blast, high in the chamber.

A titanic moan filled their minds. Shellycoats faltered, some disassembled, but many remained, seemingly stunned. The sense of the alien consciousness receded greatly but did not disappear.

Shasti looked over at the others. Telisan regained his feet, leaning on Li as they dragged Mmok, unconscious or dead, along with them. She couldn't see Duna anywhere. The others were too far away, on the other side of a mass of milling Shellycoats for her to reach them. "Out," she ordered at the top of her lungs. "Get out as best you can. Run. I'll see you on the surface if I make it."

"Belwin!" Telisan called. "Belwin!"

A Shellycoat took a step toward Telisan. Li fired into it.

As if roused by the firing, about half the Shellycoats moved toward them. More began to form, though slowly.

"We've got to go," Li screamed. The last two crab robots screened them, but there was no question of holding their ground. They were forced away, heading back the route they came, firing. Telisan lifted Mmok off the floor as he retreated, still calling Duna's name.

Shasti took advantage of the distraction to make her own escape, backing away with Fenaday still balanced on her shoulders. She was cut off from the others, and now Shellycoats stood between her and the pit. Her night sight was almost as good as an Enshari's, and the bio-panels provided enough light for her to see by. She fled in the opposite direction, hoping to find another exit.

A small access roadway led back to the area of new homes. She climbed up whenever she could, heading for the surface levels. Fenaday's weight began to tax even her endurance. *Just like the Morok colony,* she thought, *only now it's a mile upward. Well, at least he isn't bleeding this time.*

Shasti rounded the corner and slammed into a Shellycoat. The monster, made of brick and other debris, fell backward from their combined weight. Shasti fell forward, losing Fenaday, who tumbled bonelessly to the ground. She hit the ground in a shoulder roll and blazed away with the carbine at point blank range. For once, the Shellycoat was brightly lit directly under a large bio-panel. She saw fragments of pale, almost translucent material shredding as the weapon tore apart the stuff of its body. *Ectoplasm or such,* she wondered, remembering Fenaday's description of the sensation of struggling with a Shellycoat in Duna's darkened library.

The Shellycoat fell apart as another lurched out of a darkened doorway. Shasti blasted it. Her carbine clicked on empty. Even the particle beam power-pack was exhausted. Shasti grabbed at her ammo pouch, empty and no time to switch batteries. She reversed her grip on the carbine, preparing to club with it as a third Shellycoat appeared.

Laser light winked into the Shellycoat, caressing it up and down its middle. It fell. She turned to see Fenaday, dazed but awake, up on one knee, the laser still tied to his wrist by the lanyard.

She ran over and helped him to his feet.

"What happened?" he asked hoarsely. "Where is everyone?"

"We've got to go, come on."

Fenaday followed, still shaky and uncertain. "Li and Telisan went back the way we came, dragging Mmok. I don't know if he's alive. We lost Connery and maybe Belwin. I didn't see him fall. All the HCRs are gone, and there are just two of the crab robots. The robots are with them, but so are hordes of Shellycoats."

"Did you set the timer?" she asked as they scrambled up the roadway.

"No," he replied. "I only opened the first interlock before the

223

thing moved. Then it had me in its control. Its mind linked to mine. I know who he is."

"Can that help us?" she asked eagerly.

"No," Fenaday said, a great sadness in his voice and eyes. "He was once a hero of his kind, the greatest of them, a decorated veteran of a holy war. But he was sick and insane before our ancestors drew on cave walls. There is no way to reach through that. Not even his own people could when they imprisoned him here.

"Shasti, I've got to go back to that chamber and try to set the bomb off."

She shook her head. "It's impossible, at least for now. It's alive with Shellycoats. Maybe later; this thing seems erratic."

"He's almost gone, senile, distracted and weak," Fenaday said. "At his full strength, he could rip up the crust of a world."

"He's still too much for us," she countered ruefully. The road became a steep spiral. They rushed up it, exiting onto one of the broader plazas, which usually meant a shopping district.

A dull boom sounded over them. Walls shook. The storefront alongside them bowed outward, then gave.

"Look out—" Fenaday shouted. The weakened sections of storefront and walls collapsed in with a spray of froth. A broken water main must have undermined it. The blast's harmonic finished the job.

Shasti moved, but for once, not fast enough. Falling debris caught her legs. She went down, and he lost sight of her as the passageway filled with dust. Fenaday scrambled back toward her, choking on dust, searching with his hands in the low light. "Shasti," he called in sudden terror.

"Here."

She lay under the deadfall. A metal beam pressed down on her leg.

"Is it broken?" he demanded.

"Doesn't feel that way," she gasped, struggling, "but I'm pinned."

She had little room to push at the beam, but lent her strength to his, as he struggled to shift it. It wouldn't budge. Fenaday searched around for a tool. He grabbed a piece of metal shelving and began digging under the beam. Careful as he was, an occasional indrawn breath by Shasti let him know when he was too close to her leg.

"Try and contact the others," he gasped. "My com unit is fried. Maybe they can find a way to us."

Before Shasti could say a word, a dragging, thumping sound came from behind them. Something was coming up the spiral way behind them.

"Shellycoats," she hissed.

He redoubled his efforts, knowing there wasn't time.

Shasti grabbed his shoulder. "Run," she demanded. "Run, now."

"No," he snapped, shaking her off and digging.

"God damn you," she said. "I'm dead already. You'll never find her if you die here. Go. Please, go."

The sound grew louder, metallic and dragging. *They must be at the last turn,* he thought.

"Go!" she screamed.

Fenaday stopped digging and drew his laser. There might be enough power for one or two shots, maybe three. He felt oddly calm. "I have a grenade left," he said, as if to reassure her. "We won't suffer. I just want to get a few shots off first."

Shasti looked back at him furiously, then her eyes softened and dropped. She touched a hand to his arm. "Robert," she said gently, "you were the only friend I ever had."

He smiled back, touching her hand, then passed the grenade. His laser came up aimed in the approved Weaver grip. Shasti closed her fingers on the grenade tab.

A shape came up the curved path in a disjointed rush. The bioluminescent panels illuminated the man-shaped target for him. Just as his finger tightened, he recognized the scorched and battered shape.

"Cobalt," he breathed. Reaction struck him. He sank against Shasti, eyes dimming for a moment. Shasti put the grenade into her breast pocket. Her hand might even have shaken a little.

"Affirmative," Cobalt replied. "I am damaged to level A-7 and out of communication with HCR controller. Request extraction and repair."

"Me too," Shasti said.

"Don't tell me that wasn't a joke," Fenaday said, gathering himself together. "Cobalt, get over here. Analyze this beam and lift it with minimum risk of bringing down the rest of it on Shasti. I will pull her directly away."

The robot's CPU analyzed the requests, and Cobalt bent over the beam. It began to lift. Shasti hissed in pain as more debris started to fall and shift. Fenaday seized her under her shoulders, pulling as soon as he could see clearance. She came free. He had to drag her backward as more of the wall came down, threatening to catch them again. Cobalt warded off the biggest pieces as they retreated. Fenaday got his shoulder under the tall woman's arm. They made the next crossway before stopping.

"Cobalt," Shasti asked, pain twisting her face, "do you have X-ray capability?"

"Affirmative. Left ocular only. The right is disabled."

"Scan my right leg. Don't exceed rads safe for a standard human. Is there a fracture?"

"Negative on fracture," Cobalt returned.

"Good," Shasti said. "Robert, help me up."

"Are you sure you don't need a splint?" he asked anxiously. He looked around for something to use as a crutch, but there was nothing nearby.

"Won't be necessary," she said, strain still present in her voice. "We Engineered have two settings: on and dead." She climbed to her feet with Fenaday's help. They started off with the robot trailing. Her height made it easy to lean on him, but she weighed more than he did, so they made progress slowly.

"No more chocolate for you, young lady," he said wryly. She rewarded him with a trademark Shasti glare. "Well, perhaps less pasta."

"Better," she replied. "I can lean on the HCR if you prefer."

"No," he said. "Cobalt, take my laser. Provide security."

Cobalt took the weapon from him, examining it. "Permission to direct feed to the laser."

"Huh?" he said, as they started forward again.

"The gun is nearly empty," Shasti reminded him, grunting a

little as she put more weight on the leg. "The HCR can run a power cable into it and power the weapon off its own reactor. You have got to learn to pay more attention to these details."

"Nag, nag, nag," he said. "Okay, Cobalt, permission granted."

They made their way through a cross-corridor. By the time they'd gone a mile, Shasti, to Fenaday's amazement, could walk on her own, though with a limp.

"My body is better designed than yours," she modestly reminded him. "I hardly have a shock mechanism. My metabolism generates its own anti-inflammatory agents, painkiller, and antibiotics."

"And you're pretty too."

"Nice of you to notice," she replied.

Aided by Cobalt, they continued upward. Shasti found a long pole for a combination of staff and cane. The robot's sensors made their path sure, saving them many a blind alley. No more Shellycoats attacked. The roaring sound of the monster's mind faded to where they were no longer sure if they hadn't imagined it. It seemed the Prekak had slipped into inactivity. For now Fenaday refused to plan further ahead than reaching the surface, sunlight, and air. They would somehow have to reattempt the chamber, when they were rearmed, healed, and rested. Yet, Fenaday doubted they would have the time or strength for a second attempt. He began to hope only to die in the open.

As they neared the surface, Shasti pointed ahead of them. "Look," she demanded, "Telisan and Li."

"Hey," Fenaday yelled. "Over here."

Telisan gave a cry of joy at seeing his friends. The two stopped dragging Mmok on a travois they'd improvised from their jackets. Gently, they laid Mmok down as Fenaday and Shasti hobbled up to them. The survivors all embraced.

"We feared thee both were dead," Telisan said.

"Hey, top soldier." Li grinned, slapping Shasti on the arm. She smiled back and thumped the man on the chest with a playful fist, almost knocking him down.

"How is Mmok?" Fenaday asked, kneeling to look at the unconscious cyborg. He seemed as burnt and battered as Cobalt.

"Still unconscious," said a clearly exhausted Telisan. "We fought our way back, pursued almost every step of the way. When the robots ran out of ammunition, we ordered them to self-destruct, collapsing the tunnels behind us. We ran into a few more Shellycoats, but we were able to destroy them. They're not as tough as the ones in the chamber, or we would never have made it."

"Let's get to the surface," Fenaday said. "We'll regroup up there."

With Cobalt's help, they picked up the travois and made their way to the surface. They came up not far from where they entered, though by another subsurface roadway that opened onto a hillside. Relief and joy at seeing the sun and sky temporarily removed the bitter taste of their defeat.

Telisan's com came to life with a crackle. "This is Duna. Is there anyone left? This is Duna."

The Denlenn's leathery face convulsed. "Belwin, where are you?"

"My son, my son, you live," came the whispered voice. "Oh, I am so glad."

"Where are you?" Telisan demanded. "We will come for you."

"No. No, do not move. I fell into a small pit, next to the main dig. I do not know how long I have been unconscious. I am out of the hole now. I can see the tripod over the pit. There are no Shellycoats in sight. Did poor Fenaday manage to set the bomb's timer?"

"I'm alive, Belwin," Fenaday said. "Shasti, Li, Cobalt, and Mmok made it, though Mmok is unconscious."

"Then I have even greater joy," replied the little Enshari, almost a mile below and away from them.

"I didn't get the timer set before the thing did something to me. I got the first interlock off. There are two to go, if the thing hasn't destroyed or removed the weapon."

"The blue button takes out the second interlock," Duna said. "The two yellows take out the third, then the red sets it off. Correct?"

"Yes," Fenaday said faintly, realizing the little scholar's intentions, "just as we showed you last night."

"No," Telisan said. "No, Belwin. Stay where you are. I am coming for you."

"I'm with you," Fenaday said. "Shasti, you and Li stay here. Cobalt, come with us."

"The hell you say," Shasti said. "I'm coming."

"Cease, cease, my brave, wonderful, young friends," Duna called. "The thing strengthens again, I can feel it in my mind. You will never make it to me. And we dare not risk a timer now that it is roused. We have only this one chance left."

"Telisan, my son, did you remember I told you I was once of the warrior class, like yourself?"

"Yes," Telisan answered, holding himself in check with visible effort.

"Time to be a warrior again, even if an ancient one," Duna said. "I shall descend into the chamber and revenge myself, my family, my kind, and our worlds."

"Duna," said Shasti into Telisan's mike, "you didn't even want to ride on my shoulder. It's twenty-five meters to the ground." Her voice strained, and Fenaday felt proud of her for it.

"I am past all that, my dear girl. I am a warrior on a mission. I will not fail."

Fenaday could stand it no longer. "Belwin, don't do it. We're coming." Before he could move, Telisan put a hand on his arm and shook his head once. Shasti looked down at the ground.

"No, my soft-hearted pirate. I attack…now."

They heard the sound of running feet and the huffing of Duna's breath as he charged the pit.

"No Shellycoats yet," Duna huffed. "I think they all went after you. Ah, a D-ring, good."

————

A mile below, the Enshari hooked himself to Fenaday's safety line and passed it through the D-ring. Duna's clear memory retained every detail of his training as a soldier, hundreds of years ago. He slid to the chamber floor, reaching it in seconds. The drop would have pleased his instructors. He lunged for the bomb, not stopping to detach the rope. To his utter relief, it was still intact. Vermilion's explosion had knocked over the weapon, but the body of the warhead protected the trigger. It had been affixed on the opposite side from the blast. Duna could hear the waterfall sound of the thing's mind very faintly, but the blast of mental violence he feared did not occur.

He slipped the interlocks in frantic moves, placing his hand over the red button. "Farewell my young friends. My blessings on you all and on you, Telisan, my son, most of all."

"Fare thee well, Belwin Duna, my honored friend," Telisan said. The Denlenn did not shed tears, but agony marked every inch of his leathery face.

"Go with God," Fenaday managed.

In the darkness of the giant vault came a creaking sound. It carried over the radio and froze Fenaday's blood. The giant skull was once more in motion.

"So, you are aware of me," Duna cried. "I am Belwin Duna, warrior of the Enshari. We have survived you. Terrible crimes have you committed on my kind and others."

In the chamber, the tiny Enshari seemed to grow in stature. His voice echoed like thunder. "You will not escape punishment. It ends now——" Duna's hand snapped down.

In the millisecond before the blast, the roar of mind-noise strengthened, a last clear thought rolled from the crypt into their minds.

"Good."

Chapter Nineteen

B arjan bucked beneath their feet like a pain-wracked animal. Glass and metal showered from the buildings around them, crashing into the street. Unable to shout above the cacophony, Fenaday gestured frantically at the tunnel behind them. Retreating back into the tunnel mouth, the spacers watched the shifting buildings in terror as dust and dirt fell on them. They covered Mmok as best they could and hugged the wall.

"This is more than our bomb," Fenaday yelled.

"Secondaries," Telisan agreed. "We've set off some power source in that thing's chamber."

"We're dead," Li cried.

"Look," Shasti said, pointing down the slope toward the center of Barjan. Two kilometers away, the surface of Barjan bulged and erupted, hurling debris thousands of meters into the sky. Towers tilted and fell, and the dome-shaped buildings twisted and collapsed. Smoke and dust filled the air, blocking light and vision. The ground rumbled and vibrated so badly none of them could keep their feet.

They wrapped shirts and jackets around their faces and tried desperately to breathe. Shasti grabbed Li's canteen and splashed water on the improvised dust masks then tended to Mmok.

Debris rained down, clanging into the street for what seemed like an age. Aftershocks went on for several minutes. Had they been directly above the Prekak's pit, they would have died, but their trek had taken them kilometers from the area.

Finally, they staggered into the open, struggling through the partially collapsed tunnel entrance. Dust filled the air as fading sunlight made for an eerie scene. With a slight shock, Fenaday realized most of the long Enshari day had passed. They were well into twilight.

Weary from injuries, shock, and loss, Fenaday picked up the travois. With Cobalt's aid, they struggled back to the truck, staggering over fresh debris, hoping to find the multi-fuel still operational.

"Cobalt," Fenaday said, spitting thick white dust to clear his throat and wishing for another canteen. "Check for radiation."

"Radiation levels are within human tolerance," the machine said as it limped forward, dragging a damaged leg. "Evacuation is recommended."

"Whatever power was added to the warhead was not nuclear as we know it," Shasti said. "Or the radiation would be far more intense."

She looked at Telisan. "Belwin never felt anything. It was instant."

Telisan, his eyes heavy with grief, nodded.

Fenaday put a hand on his shoulder, his own eyes hot. "I'd have gone. You know that."

Telisan managed a smile. "I know."

Shasti, who also could not cry, looked away.

Li stared vacantly at the rest of them. "I hope he got the damn thing," he said. "I hope it wasn't all for nothing."

"I don't know," Shasti said. "When Vermilion blew up in the chamber, the blast disrupted the monster's control."

"I think that whatever kept its consciousness in the universe was in that chamber," Fenaday added, straining with the travois despite the robot's help. "I don't know what death is for his race, but I think he longed for it."

The others stopped, looking at him.

"The thing entered my mind when I was in its chamber," he

said. "I learned his history. He was once a hero of his kind. I'll tell you more, later. If I can. Meanwhile, Mmok's bad, and we are beaten to pieces. Let's get back to the embassy."

They found the multi-fuel mercifully intact. Next to it, lay the inactive Airbot, where Mmok landed it before their descent. Most of the dome buildings near the machines had remained largely intact. They loaded Mmok in the back of the M-2, along with the inactive Airbot. They could do nothing for Mmok's burns and simply hung an IV of fluids for him. The M-2's armored hull shrugged off what little had fallen on it as it coughed into life and began to chug back to the embassy. Cobalt sat with Li in the driver's cab, lending its sensors and infrared sight to his human eyes.

A cloud of dust towered kilometers into the sky, but the ocean breeze blew it inland and away from them. Above them some of the stronger stars of the galactic core shone palely in the failing light, as the last banners of the sun faded in the west.

Telisan finally realized one of his arm bones was broken. Shasti set it and gave him a painkiller. Exhausted by injuries and grief, Telisan closed his eyes almost immediately. Shasti had a dozen small splinter wounds, which Fenaday patiently treated. Her leg, which should have been bruised black, looked nearly healed.

Li used the truck's radio to raise the embassy. He relayed to them, through the hatchway, the battles on the surface. "Fury and half her team, including Rask, survived. The embassy fared better. Only one dead there. The attacks have ceased, and there's no sign of Shellycoats."

Relieved, Fenaday and the others rode on in silence, watching the ruins of Barjan in the headlights.

"He called me, 'his dear girl,'" Shasti said.

He looked at her. As usual, her face gave little away.

"He meant it," Fenaday said.

She remained silent for a minute longer. "Robert, I have a favor to ask."

"The answer is yes, whatever it is."

"Good. I haven't had a dog since I was a child in K-9 training. I like Risky."

When he failed to respond, she looked at him. He'd fallen dead asleep. She shifted slightly so his head could rest on her shoulder.

They reached the embassy gates near midnight. The air rang with cheers. Hugs, handshakes, and Risky's barks greeted them, as well as anxious looks for the wounded. Mourner and her medtechs checked the surviving team for radiation and treated the injuries. All but Mmok were in decent shape.

"Mmok's burns aren't as severe as they look," Mourner judged as she and her tech fussed over him, "but much of the machinery implanted in his cyborg parts is shorted out. He's in a coma, though not in danger of immediate death."

"Do what you can for him, Doc," Fenaday said. "He's a son-of-a-bitch, but he's our son-of-a-bitch."

"Yes, sir." She nodded to her techs, who lifted Mmok onto a stretcher and headed for the infirmary.

A small celebration broke out in the ambassador's reception area. Cooks whipped up the best of the remaining food. The survivors sat, talking and joking in a subdued manner, their relief shadowed by the day's casualties, especially Duna. Despite the circumstances, Duna had been popular with the crew. Fenaday gathered the survivors, telling them of the scholar's magnificent attack. Everyone raised cups and glasses. "To the little Enshari professor and to Connery," Fenaday managed. "May they reach heaven half an hour before the devil knows they're gone."

After the celebration, Fenaday walked out to the *Pooka* to check with Fury on the message he'd ordered sent to the *Sidhe*. Passing a half-open door near the ambassador's quarters, he saw a reflection in a mirror. The room was lit only by starlight, but he could see Shasti sitting on the floor, holding on to Risky, her face buried in his fur. The dog tried to nuzzle her as his tail beat slowly. Fenaday heard a sound that might be crying. Might be. He hesitated, then fearing to make a mistake either way, he gently closed the door and padded away.

Fenaday found Fury just outside the shuttle *Pooka*, the incarnate personification of her name. She kept her voice low, but venom sang in it.

"I called to the ship," she said. "That cowardly bitch Micetich and her crew think it's a trick. They won't bring the ship in."

Fenaday leaned against a tree, too tired to be angry. After a few seconds in deep thought, he keyed his new communications unit. A vague, half-formed suspicion had just clarified in his mind. "Cobalt," he said, "report to Fenaday."

The damaged machine still proved quick, arriving in less than a minute. Its delicate, doll-like features were scratched and battered. With Mmok down, no one had the knowledge to work on the machines. They left them to their self-repair mechanisms.

"Cobalt," he said, "your HCR controller is comatose. To whom do you default on command?"

"Fenaday, Robert F.," replied the machine, "within guidelines and restrictions."

"Identify any Confederation forces in the Enshar system, other than ourselves," he asked.

"Information classified," stated Cobalt.

"Proof enough for me," said Fenaday. "Angie, begin broadcasting on all Confed frequencies. Request assistance. Explain that we've destroyed the force investing Enshar and it's safe to land. Better yet, have Dr. Mourner do it.

"My bet is your bastard boss has a warship in-system, waiting to see what happened. What do you think?"

Fury smiled wickedly at him. "Bet you're right. That'll fix Micetich's ass." She stepped out onto the lawn, heading for the surgery to get Dr. Mourner.

———

Fenaday's guess proved true. Fury's message drew an answer within four hours. Mandela had covered his bet with a small Confederate task force. The next morning the heavy cruiser *Challenger* and the Marine attack transport *Io* arrived from the far side of Mur's fourth planet. The high-speed courier accompanying them headed out to jump space to relay news of the success. Captain Altermatt, of the *Challenger*, had orders to stand off, unless called in by Mmok, or unless he had reason to believe the expedition had succeeded. Fortunately, the cruiser captain didn't care for skulking and followed his orders with the greatest of latitude.

With the *Challenger* and the attack transport closing in, Micetich's band of mutineers found the passive support of the crew vanishing. They couldn't break orbit. Despite the best efforts of the hackers among the mutineers, Fenaday's security programs kept the main engines locked. *Sidhe* stood no chance against a heavy cruiser even if they could maneuver. Figuring it was now only a question of being killed by her own crew or a Marine boarding party, Micetich surrendered to Perez. The mutineers went to the brig, and the frigate began the delicate task of lining up for atmospheric entry. She landed in the bay, just north of Barjan port, carefully making her way to an anchorage in the harbor itself.

The Marine transport *Io* landed on her jacks at the spaceport. *Challenger*, far too large for atmospheric entry, assumed orbit above Barjan. *Io*'s Marines arrived at the embassy, raising the Confederacy's green and yellow flag.

Mmok, Cobalt, and many of Mandela's specials disappeared into the attack transport for debriefing. Fenaday and Shasti exchanged warm farewells with Rigg, Rask, Mourner, and the others who had fought alongside them. To Fenaday's surprise, Telisan declared he would remain with the *Sidhe*. Before returning to the star-frigate, Fenaday sent the mutineers to the *Io*. He couldn't muster the energy to feel any hate toward them. Fenaday just wanted them off his ship and away from Shasti. Mandela had promised Fenaday and Shasti pardons and clean records, and he saw no point in taking risks.

At Fenaday's insistence, a ceremony was held at the embassy to honor Belwin Duna. The captains of the *Io* and *Challenger* attended. Crews from all three ships stood at attention as Enshar's flag climbed alongside that of the Confederacy, to the sound of rifle volleys. Fenaday added his own touch. From the bay, *Sidhe* loosed a three-second barrage of chain guns and lasers. The sky lit up in coruscating colors as the lasers, changing frequencies, struck the clouds. Telisan looked over at Fenaday, smiling.

The next day, Shasti and Fenaday accompanied Telisan on his mission to recover the fighter pilots from his squadron from the

Earhart. They buried them with honors at the embassy compound. The *Wolverine* shuttles from the first expedition, they left untouched and sealed for all time.

The courier returned two weeks later. Captain Altermatt relayed the news to them from the *Challenger*.

"You'll be pleased to know that the government of the Exiles has declared every member of the *Sidhe* crew, including, by accident, the mutineers, to be heroes and citizens of Enshar," he relayed from his ship. "I have a veritable heap of medals and orders being awarded you and your crew by transmission. It looks like you could spend the next few years traveling world to world for ceremonies."

"Excellent," Fenaday said, feigning an enthusiasm he didn't feel. He hadn't given a thought to what would follow. "Any word on Mr. Mmok?"

"No change," Altermatt replied. "He and Dr. Mourner are heading back to Earth on the courier. Maybe they can do something for him there. You can follow up with his boss when you return to Mars."

"Not in this lifetime," Fenaday said. "Thank you, Captain." He switched off the screen. *Return to Mars,* Fenaday wondered. *Is that what I do next?* He pushed away thoughts of a future that he hadn't expected to live to see. Shasti waited for him outside. For now it was enough just to take a walk by the seaside with a pretty girl. *No plans today,* he promised himself. *I'll decide tomorrow.*

He found Shasti by the *Sidhe's* dock, waiting.

———

The next evening Fenaday, Telisan, Shasti, and the ever-present Risky returned to the ship after yet another dinner with *Io's* officers. They settled into Fenaday's quarters with a bottle of Denebian flowerwine, a gift from *Io's* captain.

"I've been thinking about heading back to Marsport, then on to New Eire," Fenaday said after pouring the wine into a motley mix of glasses he'd scrounged. "Our job is done. There's no reason to stay longer. We're all well off now, and there are things, I'm sure, that we all want to do."

"What will you do?" asked Shasti. "Does the search go on?"

It took him a few seconds to reply. "I think..." he started, then stopped, as if the words themselves hurt. "I think," he repeated, "that she is... that she must be... dead after all this time." Now the words came easier, as the wall in his mind finally collapsed. "Maybe I always knew. As I look back now, maybe that's all it was, only my desire to hurt the Conchirri for taking her from me. Nothing nobler than that. I've killed hundreds, maybe thousands, of Conchirri with this ship. Now, there are none left. It still hurts as badly as ever.

"Duna said that he would forgo revenge for a home. Maybe he was right. I broke my home, many friendships, and my family when I started this. What do I have to show for it?

"I'm going back to New Eire to buy back my old home. I would like to put the Shamrock line together again. With the contract money and the exclusive trading rights to a resettled Enshar, it shouldn't be difficult."

"Will you keep the *Sidhe*?" asked Shasti.

"Yes," he said, patting the table affectionately. "She'll be the flagship. The old girl will have to work for a living, but I can afford her now."

"For me," said Telisan, "it is back to my world, to see my family and a young lady or two of my own kind. There are plans that have been on hold for far too long."

Fenaday looked at Shasti, the question lodged in his throat. *Is it right to ask?* he wondered. *There's so much between us, but is it something that can last? She'll live probably fifty years longer than I will. She's young, beautiful, and now rich. I'll never entirely get over Lisa. Shasti deserves someone of her own, without such unfinished business hanging on him.*

It was selfish to ask, or to offer, but he found himself speaking anyway. "What about you, Shasti? What do you want?"

Shasti looked over at him, her eyes shuttered, seeming to weigh something. "I have debts owed and owing," she replied. "I wish to deal with those."

Well, there it is, he thought.

"There is something I want to ask you," she continued unexpectedly.

"Like I said before, the answer is yes," he replied.

"I want you to keep Risky for me while I'm gone. I'd also like to keep my cabin on the *Sidhe*. It's the closest thing I have to a home."

He felt the knot in his chest loosen, glad she wouldn't vanish from his life.

"You'll always find Risky and your cabin safe with me," Fenaday said. "I'll go you one better. If I can get the old family home back, there will always be a place for you there for so long as you live."

"That sounds good," she said. Her eyes held his, the slightest of smiles played on her lips. "A rest, a time of safety, might be a good idea, before I attend to my other business. Perhaps it would be as well to let those matters wait a while longer."

"If it's the business I think it is, then you'll need my help," Fenaday said, unable to find more words.

Telisan looked at his two friends with more understanding than either would have been comfortable with. He sighed internally. He saw them caught between pasts they could not let go of and futures they wouldn't seize. Telisan feared for them both, but now was not the time to speak of it.

"Then we are decided," said Fenaday. "Homeward bound."

A day later, *Sidhe* pulled out of the harbor, painfully gathering enough speed to break free of the sea. With a roar of engines, the blood-red frigate shrugged free of the ocean, heading upward. She pierced the atmosphere of Enshar, returning to the icy embrace of space, bathed by the unblinking light of the stars.

On her bridge, side by side, Telisan, Shasti, and Fenaday looked into the brilliance of the stars and saw their paths.

The End

Afterword

Thank you, kind reader. Since you have voyaged so far with us, please enjoy another story set in Confederate Space. This one, "Beautiful Dreamer," won awards and was published a number of times. It's one of my favorite shorts.

Beautiful Dreamer

A CONFED SPACE STORY

Taluma Dekhara drew herself up to her full height of forty centimeters and stared at her rival, Sagawa of the Progressives. Sagawa glared back, her jeweled eye-shields glittering in the morning sun. Around the two antagonists stood a dozen Nateelians, some in the traditional robes and sashes and a few, Sagawa's people, dressed in miniature versions of the clothes the aliens, called humans, wore. The two groups had unexpectedly come on each other at the scenic overlook that faced the capitol. A bitter debate broke out immediately.

"It is change or die," Sagawa insisted. "We either master these new ways or we become a sideshow for tourists, irrelevant to the universe at large." The small intense Nateelian paced back and forth while arguing, causing the silver scales of her skin to coruscate. "Your childhood among priests and traditionalists has left you unfit to lead," Sagawa charged.

"Whereas," Taluma returned, "your rejection of our past, our traditions, values, and beliefs makes you fit?"

"Yes. Because I understand what you Dekharas fail to face. The roof has been blown off the world. Everything is changed, and the past cannot help us."

"This debate is pointless," Aveelo, Taluma's young cousin, interjected. "The matter will be decided at the Tol-kir-Kira. We will see who can offer the Concordiat a better dream."

Sagawa snorted in irritation. "Come." She waved to her followers. "There is no point to talking to these relics." Her coterie of the fashionable dutifully followed in her train.

"Rude fool," Aveelo fumed.

"Pay her no mind, dear cousin," Taluma said, projecting a serenity she did not feel. "Return with the others to the castle. I would like to meditate in this spot."

"As you wish." Aveelo made a gesture of respect and gathered the others, leaving Taluma alone with her thoughts.

With all witnesses gone, Taluma gave into the doubts that plagued her of late. Her thin-boned shoulders sagged. She walked up to the edge of the overlook to survey the jeweled and glittering city that lay before her, Donamore, capitol of the nation state of Truas, and most influential of the nation states of the Concordiat.

Once, she thought mournfully, *that meant the universe. Now there is a new scale against which Donamore and even the Concordiat are the equivalent of Poochberries.* She looked up, her gem-like eyes blinking independent of each other. Above was the sky, roof of the world, with its remote stars. Roof no more, as Sagawa had pointed out. The sky was endless and the lights were suns like her own, circled by many worlds.

The giants call my home, Wehardi IV, just a commonplace rock at the bottom of a gravity well. It's an uncouth name for something so important as my world.

Her eyes drifted to a sky-spearing pinnacle. A trading ship, one of the smaller interstellar vessels, sat on its fins at Skyport. Her courtiers had told Taluma it was named the *Cosmic.* The small trader still dwarfed her family castle or the largest ocean vessel the Nateelians had built.

The newcomers seem to threaten no harm in themselves, she thought, *but they bring new ideas, new perceptions, and a linear way of thinking so foreign that it frightens my people, to whom dreams are almost as real and sometimes more meaningful than the real world.*

To me they have brought something worse, doubt that dreams are worth anything at all. I'd been proud before the aliens came, she thought. *Now I can only wonder, proud of what? I cannot afford these doubts if I am to win the Tol-kir-Kira, the test of the beautiful dream. My father is old and doubts his ability to hold power much longer. Everything depends on my ability to project a vision of beauty before the Concordiat. The winner will be sovereign in this city, which leads the world.*

Before the arrival of the aliens, four years ago, I'd been favored to win. Even my rivals wept at the beauty of my visions, mystical animals, shining cities, wealth, and joy. But that was before Sagawa's Reform Movement, before alien thoughts and ways disrupted the stability of the thousand year old Concordiat. Dreams come rarely to me now, and they are confused pitiful things wrung out of my doubts.

Despair assailed Taluma. She had trained for a lifetime for this one test. Her clan and immediate family had invested so much in her. How could she fail them?

Taluma shook off self-pity. *Standing here*, she thought, *is answering nothing. I must see these aliens with my own eyes, speak to them. Learn why it is that they block my dreams, or another must be chosen to lead.*

With the decision made, she felt curiously lightened. Taluma quickly returned to the Dekhara castle, the formidable ancient pile of gray stone atop the mountain above her. Once there, she summoned her maid, and after borrowing the maid's less conspicuous cape and swearing her to secrecy, Taluma set out to leave the castle unobserved.

———

Brittony Janov tried to still the sobs that wracked her twelve-year-old body. She knew she shouldn't have run away, but disappointment had so seared her that she fled, deaf to her father's frantic cries. He and the crew of the *Cosmic* were probably turning Skyport upside down looking for her. Eventually they would find her by the shore road. It was a spot she came to overlook the sea, sheltered by the small copse of trees and not far from the outer trade gate. Another sob wracked her and tears ran down her nose. It had all gone so wrong.

Cosmic was on her fourth landing on Wehardi IV, ferrying in scientists and trade supplies for the Wehardians, or Nateelians as they called themselves. *Cosmic* had made the initial discovery of the new aliens, first to be found since the Voit-Veru. It made the family-run combine and its two trading vessels solvent and promised more wealth beyond. But for Brittony, it meant something special. The Wehardians were projective telepaths, able, with difficulty, to read consciously intended thoughts, even to project an image in the mind of another. She and her father had not been on the *Cosmic* when it landed on Wehardi but lived aboard the *Yukikaze*. When Brittony learned of the Wehardian's skills, she'd begged her father to take her on the *Cosmic* to Wehardi.

Brittony had a special reason. Unconsciously, she raised a hand to her head, feeling the slight scars beneath her dark brown hair. Skull fracture, the doctors said, with a small degree of permanent brain damage. A miracle really. The flitter crash that killed her mother should have killed her too, except that she was thrown free, landing in some bushes as the defective flitter cartwheeled. Somehow the nine-year old Brittony had survived, but when she awoke, it was if she had been reborn. There were huge gaps in her memory and into one of those gaps had fallen her mother. She could not remember her face, her voice, or her touch. Pictures and images could have been those of any stranger. The doctors told her father that her memory might return. It had not in three years.

"Are you ill?" said a small high voice in Tradespeak.

Brittony started and looked around. Next to her stood one of the little, lizard-like natives. Her eyes were faceted like Daddy's wedding ring gem. Her arms looked liked polished silver and ended in small claw-like hands. A cloak of dark green felt lay draped over the tiny native's shoulders.

"I miss my mother," Brittony whispered through teary eyes.

———

Taluma stared in surprise; the giant was a child! Somehow she had never thought of them as having children. This ugly tower of bone and flesh was still more than twice as tall as herself and many times her mass. Atop its head was an untidy mass of fur—no, hair. It did

246

have pleasing, bright blue-gray eyes, though these seemed reddened around the edges.

"Where is your mother?" she asked.

"Dead," said the child, distress obvious in her voice and manner, "a long time ago."

"I sorrow with you," Taluma said, "but why do you cry now?"

"Because," she said, "I had such hopes of seeing her."

"I don't understand," Taluma said.

"I thought," the child sniffled, "your people could read minds. My brain was hurt in the crash, and I can't remember my mother. One of your people in the trade port, Gawanis Defora, said that for a thousand credits he could reach my memory. I could almost see something....almost, then it was gone." Another shudder wracked the child.

White-hot rage lit in Taluma. The power to mindspeak lay in most of her race, the ability to project, to dream, was far rarer. To delve into the mind was a daunting task for even an adept, far more so with an alien mind. But to raise the hopes of a child and then dash them...unforgivable.

Taluma reached out with her gift, projecting a wave of soothing comfort to the child. It seemed to still the child's shaking. As her mind touched the child's, she felt a shock of recognition. The child was young, female, probably only ten cycles or so in existence.

Taluma's empathic nature reached out to the child, finding her "feel" to be surprisingly like that of her own young cousin, Aveelo. How could this giant seem so like a normal person?

"What is your name, child?" Taluma asked, though with a slight effort, she could have delved the child's mind for such surface information. Such an invasion, unasked for was unspeakably rude, even criminal. An adult could, with only a little training, block out most lesser talents. An adept like herself was another story.

"I'm Brittony Janov off the *S.S. Cosmic,* from the Janov Trading Family, out of New Eire," she said, with a hint of a defiant pride.

"Do you have a father?" Taluma asked.

"Of course," Brittony said. "Poor Dad. I ran off cause I was so upset. Oh, he's probably looking for me all over. He might even have called the captain. I had better get back before I cause more trouble." The girl turned to look at Taluma. "You were awfully nice to listen to my problems."

"I intend to do more than listen," Taluma said. "This Defora, who tried to read you, had no right to do what he did. You have been harmed by one of my people, amends must be made.

"I am Taluma Dekhara. I live there." She turned and gestured toward the castle overlooking the hill. She felt the girl's surprised reaction, tinged with alarm.

"Are...are you a princess?" stammered the girl, with wide eyes.

"Yes. Come to the castle tomorrow, with your father, at first bell and ask for me. Present this token at the gate." She handed the child her signet ring. "I am the strongest telepath of my realm. If it can be done, then I promise you it will be done. You shall see your mother."

"I will," the girl cried.

Waves of joy and gratitude flowed out of the girl, almost battering Taluma. *So like my little cousin,* she thought. "Till then." Taluma turned and started back for the counsel at a quick pace. The proctors must be summoned. Defora would be brought to her before sunset. He would bitterly regret his swindling when she was through with him.

———

"Brittony!"

She turned at the sound of her father's shout. He came pounding out the trade gate at a flat run. He raced up to her and grabbed her in a hug. "Darling, are you all right? Are you okay?" He stepped back still holding her to check that she had all her limbs still attached.

"I'm sorry, Dad," she began. "I shouldn't have run off."

"Damn right," he said, satisfied his daughter was not in immediate need of medical attention. "God, anything could have happened. I was worried."

"I'm sorry, Dad," she said again. "I was so upset."

"My fault," he said. "I should never have taken you to that being. I should take that little lizard and wring his neck."

"It's okay, Dad. That man was a fake. I met the princess. She told me."

"Who?"

"Princess Taluma, Dad." Brittony turned and pointed at the retreating figure of a well-dressed Wehardian. As if sensing his regard, the being turned and looked back steadily. It raised a hand in salute then turned and walked into the city gate.

"She's my friend," Brittony said. "She's going to show me Mom tomorrow at first bell."

Manfred Janov looked at his daughter and Captain Brantz, torn between hope and worry. Brittony was excited, animated even, a rare thing for his daughter since her mother's death. Yet he feared to see another tearful agonizing disappointment.

I could have crushed that little lizard for what he did to my daughter, he thought. Murder had filled his mind and it was fortunate for the alien fortuneteller that Brittony had run off at that moment and he'd had to chase her.

There was another concern. The discovery of a native race on Wehardi IV had helped reestablish the Janov trading family, but it had been more of a trickle than a flood. One reason was the restrictions placed on traders by the Confederacy, but it was more the official hostility of the ruling Wehardian oligarchy, led by the Dekhara family. Now Brittony was involved in ship matters way over her head and perhaps his as well. A Janov he might be, but only a very lesser cousin and counted not at all against Captain Brantz's authority.

Brantz had listened quietly as Brittony's tale had almost burst out of her. Her cool blue eyes studied the child and would suddenly shift to him. Brantz's chair creaked as she shifted back, running her hands through the silver-gray of her hair.

"Well," she said finally, "you've had quite an adventure, Brittony."

"Yes, ma'am. I hope I didn't cause much trouble."

"Trouble," Brantz said, "running off in an alien town beyond Confederate law? Arranging for meetings with a leading politician of a party opposed to the presence of traders?"

Manfred gulped, and Brittony looked at the floor.

His daughter's head came up, and the desperation in her face stabbed Manfred. "Can I see her? She promised me she could show me my mother."

Brantz looked at Manfred as if measuring some problem. "I don't believe that it would be prudent to break an appointment with the Dekharas. You and your father will go."

Brittony clapped her hands together in joy, then remembering decorum, quickly put them in her lap.

Manfred wasn't sure whether to be relieved or terrified. He caught the look on the captain's face. "Bree, wait for me in our cabin, then we'll go have dinner."

Brittony nodded and skipped out the hatchway.

"I'm sorry, Captain," he said. "I didn't intend for this to happen."

"I'm sure," Brantz said. "It may be trouble, but it might be something more. We've been here for years with only a trickle of trade. This may be a chance to break the stalemate. The wedge we've been looking for. So you go. You're training for cargomaster, so fortunately this is more or less up your alley. I'd rather have Master Speice handle this contact, but you are too involved. So it falls to you to make this work."

"Captain," he said, looking straight into her eyes.

"Yes?"

"I won't take a risk with my daughter's safety or health. Not even for the sake of trade."

The cool eyes measured him for a second, then seemed to soften. "If I thought otherwise, I'd kick your butt out an airlock. Spend some time on the books tonight, Manfred, you have a big day ahead of you tomorrow."

"Yes, ma'am." He stood, sensing the dismissal, and headed out.

"Manfred."

He paused at the doorway.

"It's good to see a smile on that child's face. It's been too long, and I've been worried. Understand that we are here for trade, but Brittony is *crew*. I want to see that child whole again. And if I don't hear from you by sunset, I'm gathering every man and gun and coming after you. Count on it."

He smiled. "Good night, Captain."

———

The following morning Brittony and her father stood under the fins of the *Cosmic* as she towered, blue-black and highlighted in yellow, into the sky. They both wore fresh dress uniforms of the same color, covered with half capes. Manfred rubbed his eyes. Cargo Master Speice had kept him up half the night relentlessly grilling him on procedure and protocol. The captain had handed him and Brittony small com units. Manfred turned down even a stunner, trusting more to his wits than to weapons.

Brantz wished him luck. "Remember, I hear from you before sundown or we are coming." To his surprise, she knelt next to Brittony and kissed her cheek. "Hope for the best, Bree," she said. "But know that it may not work and be ready to deal with that. Look after your father."

"Yes, ma'am," Brittony whispered, sober and contained.

One of Speice's trade crew drove them in a small "mule" to the spaceport's edge and dropped them off. From there they walked through the fairy-like city of the natives. It looked as if it had been carved from quartz and marble. Some buildings were trimmed in ornately carved dark woods. The small, brightly-colored aliens paused to watch them or scurried out of their path, seeming frightened by creatures four times their height, even after all this time.

The street of Donamore had gradually been widened, at least on the main roads. There were many areas where a human could hardly fit in the older sections of town. Manfred found himself looking in second-story windows of many buildings, to the evident discomfort of the residents.

Manfred huffed a little as they started up the hill toward the castle, glad for the half-cape that kept the morning chill and sea breeze at bay. Brittony, who skipped ahead impatiently, did not notice the climb.

They approached the castle's gray stone, outer walls which stood meters over their heads. Manfred ducked as they stepped through the gate. In the courtyard beyond, natives milled about a large blue tent. He recognized it from Master Spiece's description as the Trade Tent created to protect natives and spacers from the weather. Brittony might squeeze through some of the castle passages on her knees, but a grown human never could. So meetings were held in the courtyard tent.

Manfred looked at the soldiers standing around the tent. They held wicked-looking spears, about a meter long, and swords. He also noted small, but serviceable slug throwers on the belts of some of them. One, obviously an officer, stood directly in their path. His golden crested helmet contrasted with the silvery scales of his skin and the red of his uniform.

"Give him the token, Bree."

His daughter walked up slowly to the officer, who eyed her warily. He might be tall for his species, but he barely came up to his daughter's chest.

"Hi," Bree said in Tradespeak, then more formally. "We are here at the invitation of Princess Taluma."

"You are expected and welcomed," he replied, without a trace of accent. He took the token and nodded to the guards. They pulled back the flaps of the tent. The humans walked in.

————

Taluma looked up as the giants entered the tent. She had to catch her breath at the sight of the child's father. *He's as tall as a building,* she thought. *Well, not quite, but he's huge.*

She switched her attention to the less threatening visage of the child.

"Greetings," she said, "Brittony of the Janovs."

"Greetings, your majesty," Brittony said. "This is my father, Manfred Janov."

"Just princess, child."

"I want to thank you for offering to help my daughter," the father said. The deep rumble of his voice filled the tent.

"She was harmed by one of my people who broke our laws. The villain will make amends to our law with a year's service. I will make amends for the harm to your daughter.

"Please be seated on the pillows." She gestured. "It will ease my neck."

Brittony and her father sat on the thick cushions. Taluma walked up to Brittony. "I will lay my hand on yours," she said. "It helps on the initial stages. Do not grasp mine as I fear your strength and size."

"I would never hurt you," Brittony said.

"Of course," Taluma said, patting the child's warm soft skin, so different from the hard cool scales of her kind. *Perhaps you and your kind wouldn't intentionally,* Taluma thought, *but merely by existing you have the potential to destroy us.* "Now, relax. Let your mind wander."

Taluma began to infiltrate the child's mind. Again she was surprised by how similar Brittony's mind was to that of her younger cousin. She felt her own mind shift as she merged with Brittony. Suddenly the alien was no longer an ugly tower of bone and flesh but an adorable, passionate, stubborn, kind, careless child. Taluma gained confidence, finding the mental architecture more familiar than she dared hope. She delved past the child's love of her father, her ship, their friends to a well of pain and despair and pushed into the dark place...

She was in a flying craft, only something was horribly wrong. The sky pinwheeled over them, the ground came up hard. Taluma mentally braced herself for the impact though she could feel nothing. Darkness, then white, then blurry images, Brittony was outside the machine crawling back. There was fire and inside...

No! The child must not see this. Recklessly Taluma poured out her strength to ward off the terrible images. Unaware yet, Brittony's mind sought to focus on the powerful scene. Taluma struggled. *If I keep this up,* she thought, *I will never have the power for the ceremony, but if this is the image I leave Brittony with, then I will be a far worse criminal than Defora.* She put forth her full power. It barely sufficed.

On, she thought, *on to safer places, to warmth and love.* Now that she was secure in mastering the flows of Brittony's memory, she called the child's conscious mind to her. "Come, Brittony. Let's go see your mother."

"I'm here. I'm here." The urgent power of the child's mind caught Taluma off balance, and she had to refocus her strength.

A woman stood in front of them, holding a much younger Brittony. The woman was tall and pale; her hair was long and red. She sang softly, and the warm scent of her filled their minds.

Beautiful dreamer,
Wake unto me
Starlight and dewdrops
Are awaiting thee.

Sounds of the rude world
Heard in the day
Led by the moonlight
Have all passed away.

Beautiful dreamer,
Queen of my song,
List' while I woo thee
With soft melody.

Gone are the cares of
Life's busy throng.
Beautiful dreamer
Awake unto me.
Beautiful dreamer,
Awake unto me.

"Mom," Brittony whispered.

Images tumbled around them: Brittony's mother laughing and teasing, playing with her, teaching her, holding hands with her father as Brittony napped in her lap. On and on it went, coming out of the damaged part of her brain, out from behind the scars. Taluma wove the images into Brittony's mind where she could access them at will. There were other images as well, Brittony's mom scolding her, or having to discipline her. These too were truth and needed to be recovered, but today was not the day for these. She placed them where they would emerge slowly and much later.

Beside her, Brittony's emotions surged wildly between joy at what was recovered and raw pain over what was lost. Taluma sent a wave of comfort and concern muting the child's grief.

"See now," she said, astonished at the clarity of the communication between them. "Do not grieve. Your mother will be with you always."

"Thank you, Taluma," Brittony said. "I will never forget what you have done for me. You're my best friend." A wave of love such as Taluma had never experienced before rolled over her. She felt her own heart leap in response and a surge of protective emotion filled her. *Is this what a mother feels?* Taluma wondered.

"I must stop soon," Taluma said. "My powers weaken."

Brittony looked up at the image of her mother by a window under some alien star.

"So soon?"

"Yes."

"Then we must stop. I don't want you to hurt yourself."

Taluma severed the connection as slowly as she could, letting Brittony's mother fade into whiteness, not into darkness.

They were back in the tent.

"Dad," Brittony cried. "I saw her. I saw Mom. It was like she was right here. I remember everything!"

No, thought Taluma, *not everything, thank the gods. I will never regret the strength I expended to erase the last image of her mother. She will never see the fall or its terrible aftermath.* Dizziness assailed Taluma.

"Princess," Brittony cried. Her hands caught Taluma.

Taluma steadied. "I am all right, dear Brittony. But let us have no more of this princess nonsense between us. For you I shall always be Taluma." She sat on a cushion.

"Are you all right, Princess?" Manfred said. "Shall I summon your guards?"

When Taluma looked up at him, she no longer saw a monstrous figure but Brittony's dad. A man aged before his years by the loss of his beloved, who would do anything for his child. She remembered him dancing with his wife…

No. No more strangeness for now. I have fallen too far into their minds.

"I am all right, only fatigued. It has been the first time I was able to use my full mental powers in a long time."

"Because you are afraid of us," Brittony said.

"Bree," her father warned.

"It's true," Brittony said. "Not of you and me, Dad. But of all of us and what it means to her people's future."

"Yes," said Taluma, surprised. She reached back to Brittony's mind. *We are still in contact*, she thought. *How can this be? There is no effort, no strain.*

Is it wrong? Brittony mind-spoke to her.

I do not know. I have never heard of two who could remain in touch like this.

"I'm not afraid," Brittony said aloud. "So, I can hear your thoughts, the ones you are pushing at me now. You can hear mine?"

"Yes," Taluma said. "This is not like what I did in your mind. That takes effort and energy; this is like speaking without words."

"Can this be dangerous?" Manfred demanded.

"I feel no strain," Taluma replied. "I sense in your daughter a more adult mindset, a greater strength. It did not occur to me that while I was working in her mind that she might gain something from my own."

To Taluma's surprise, Brittony smiled at her. "Maybe I got some of your being more of a grown-up than I am. Hopefully you got some of my being a kid. You are awfully serious, Taluma."

Taluma laughed until her ribs hurt and Brittony joined in.

Finally when she had run down, Taluma said, "I have had little choice but to be serious. I face a trial in two days that determines the course of my life."

"Yes, I saw it in your mind, the Tol-kir-Kira."

Shock spread through Taluma. What else had Brittony learned?

"The what?" asked her father.

"The Tol-kir-Kira," Taluma said slowly.

"It means the test of the beautiful dream," Brittony interjected.

"Yes," Taluma continued. "My people had fought bitter wars till the gift of telepathic projection had arose in them. Since then, power has passed to the Dreamer, whose visions become the path for society. For there can be no deception in a dream. One's inner nature is laid bare for all to see. Wars became rare after the People chose the Way of the Dream."

The human child looked at her earnestly. "Taluma, you can't let Sagawa win. You have to dream." A determined look slid over Brittony's face. "And I'm going to be right there rooting for you."

———

I can't believe this, Manfred thought.

The two days since Brittony and Taluma had bonded had turned both the *Cosmic* and Nateel Concordiat on their ears. Taluma, to the shock of her conservative clan, demanded that Brittony attend the Tol-kir-Kira. Her family, caught between disapproval and forfeiture, could only agree. Now Manfred sat on the cushions along with Captain Brantz and the senior officers of the *Cosmic* facing an arena of white sand glittering in the moonlight. The stands around and above them were filled with thousands of Nateelians.

His daughter sat next to him, again dressed in her best ship clothes, but she had eyes only for Taluma, from whom she'd been separated only to sleep.

"She's got to win, Dad," Brittony whispered.

Does she? he thought. *She's from the party that disapproves of trade and wants to hold back the future.* He looked at his daughter, so passionate and happy again. *Trade and all be damned,* he thought. *Before Taluma my daughter was alive but not living.*

"We're rooting for her," he said.

Captain Brantz cocked an eyebrow at him. *Well, at least some of us are,* he thought.

"Sagawa's starting," Brittony said, grimness entering her tone.

On the sands before them, a vapor stirred. It formed a globe over Sagawa's head. It whipped faster and faster and suddenly there were images hanging in the moonlight. Nateelians dressed as humans, riding in flitters and spaceships, walking through buildings of Confederate design. The images were fuzzy and collapsed quickly into new ones along the same theme. Sagawa's arms dropped to her side as if in exhaustion. She staggered back to the tent of her supporters and collapsed into a wooden chair.

"Now it's Taluma's turn," Brittony said. "Oh, Dad, she's so afraid. I can feel it."

Manfred looked to see the tiny figure of the princess walking into the arena. She looked tired, hesitant.

———

In the arena, with ten thousand eyes on her, Taluma knew herself to be defeated even before she began. *Are the Progressives right? Do we need to cast the past aside and race into the future? What is the correct choice?* She tried to shake it off. *I must at least try.* She reached out with her mind. The sand began to stir, and vapors swirled up. Taluma fought to master them to force the inchoate images of her soul to take shape. But what shape, what image? She despaired.

Taluma's dream collapsed in her mind, the floating image over the arena dissipating before taking any recognizable shape. The bitter taste of defeat filled her, and she could feel Sagawa's glee at her failure.

I'm done, she thought. *I cannot envision my people's future. Power will pass to those who believe our traditions and culture have no value. I've failed all those who believed in me.*

Not yet, a voice cried in her head. Warmth and energy flowed into her. She jerked upright as if touched with an electric wire. She turned to face the flow of power.

Brittony stood, towering over the Nateelians and seated humans around her. She extended her arms toward Taluma. A murmur came from the assembled Nateelians. Some clutched their heads, and she realized that Brittony's mental shout had reached them as well. The spacers around Brittony shifted uneasily, looking at the assembled multitude but remained seated.

Brittony, Taluma sent, *you cannot help me.*

I have to! The child's mind pulsed back with fierce energy. *You gave me back my memory. You gave me back my mother. I can't stand by and let you fail.*

I cannot see the path ahead. How can I lead when I cannot dream for them?

With your heart, Brittony sent. *You have a great heart, big enough even for someone not like you. My father says that a good heart is all the strength one needs. Taluma, you and I are friends. That's the future.*

It struck Taluma like a thunderclap. *Yes,* she thought, *that is the future. Things can never be as they were before the aliens came. But there is a future. The child knows the truth.*

But I am too tired, Taluma thought. *I have used up my energy.*

Then take from me, Brittony demanded.

Taluma reached mentally for her friend and was astonished at the wild power of the child's emotions. She gathered in strength.

———

Brittony swayed slightly, then steadied. Manfred put a hand on his daughter's arm, his eyes anxious.

Captain Brantz looked at Brittony's father. "Manfred, we don't have to risk this."

Manfred didn't take his eyes off his daughter. "She's standing with her friend," he whispered. "Her mother would be proud."

———

Taluma turned back to the arena. It was as if a dam had broken in her mind. There was no turning back. The roof was off the world and couldn't be replaced. Nor could the past be resurrected. There was only the future which contained the new and strange, but it wasn't all bad. It also held people like Brittony.

The song Brittony's mother sang floated up in her mind.

Beautiful dreamer, Wake unto me.

That's you, Taluma, you're the beautiful dreamer, Brittony cried.

The dream began to form in the air before her. The ghostly wisps generated by her thoughts began to take form.

Starlight and dewdrops are awaiting thee.

A beautiful, gemmed, and white city of towers and delicate bridges took shape. Nateelians and aliens wandered about it calling and greeting each other. Yet there could be no question it was a Nateel city. Her people's spiraling designs and delicate architecture yet scaled for both peoples. It was the future. The vision swelled to fill the arena.

Beautiful dreamer, Queen of my song.

List' while I woo thee, With soft melody.

Taluma could feel the people's approval grow. Hearts unlocked as they gazed into the future she would lead them to. Consensus built in the arena. Sagawa and her supporters pushed back mentally against that welling feeling, but the consensus held. Their opposition faded and was dispelled.

Beautiful dreamer, Awake unto me.

Taluma turned to face the assembly, no longer a princess but a queen, one whose destiny was now clear. She looked up at her giant friend and knew that Brittony felt it too.

There is a future, Taluma sent.

Together, Brittony said, joy in every fiber of her being.

Yes, Taluma said, weary yet filled with hope, *together.*

The End

Also by Edward McKeown

The Maauro Chronicles

My Outcast State

Against That Time

The Lost

All The Difference

When Fighting Monsters

The Shasti and Fenaday Chronicles

Was Once A Hero

Fearful Symmetry

Points of Departure

Hidden Stars

Sha'Daa Series

Tales of the Apocalypse

Toys

Inked

Pawns

Last Call

Facets

The Lair of the Lesbian Love Goddess Files

On the Case

Other Works

Knight in Charlotte

CPSIA information can be obtained
at www.ICGtesting.com
Printed in the USA
BVHW071041210520
580083BV00004B/7/J